THE CITIES OF FORTUNE

the cities of FORTUNE

PAUL H. BOGE

The Cities of Fortune

Printed in Canada
International Standard Book Number: 1-897186-03-7

Published by:
Castle Quay Books
500 Trillium Drive, Kitchener, Ontario, N2G 4Y4
Tel: (800) 265-6397 Fax (519) 748-9835
E-mail: info@castlequaybooks.com
www.castlequaybooks.com

Copy editing by Janet Dimond
Cover Design by John Cowie, *eyetoeye design*
Photo of Paul by Gingersnaps Photography
Printed at Essence Publishing, Belleville, Ontario, Canada

Library and Archives Canada Cataloguing in Publication

Boge, Paul H., 1973-
The cities of fortune / Paul H. Boge.

Sequel to: The Chicago healer.
ISBN 1-897186-03-7

I. Title.

PS8603.O34C48 2006 C813'.6 C2006-900753-5

1

It felt wrong from the beginning.

Lucas Stephens sat in the last row of Flight 912 from Chicago to London doing everything he could to get his mind off the impending danger. He had nothing concrete, nothing definite he could point to—still, he battled a sick feeling in his stomach—a conviction telling him something unforeseen was about to take place. Nothing helped to distract him. Not the pretend chicken lunch the airline served, not the reading, not the baby screaming to his right, or the fat bald man talking on and on about nothing to his left. The air became thicker. It got harder to breathe. He gripped the armrest and tried to clear his mind. But nothing he did made any difference. Ever since they took off it had been haunting him.

Lucas had the unshakeable feeling the plane was about to crash.

He could already see the aftermath. People screaming, begging for help. He shook his head as if doing so could somehow eradicate the paranormal vision into the future. *In through your nose, out through your mouth.*

A slender brunette flight attendant with deep brown eyes walked down the aisle, checking on passengers as she approached. A sudden nervousness came over him—a once powerful pharmaceutical executive now wondering if the beacon in front of him could bring him any peace.

"Excuse me," Lucas said in a tone that was both quiet and desperate.

She stopped and leaned in. Her smile penetrated the bubble of fear around him. She placed her hand on the tray beside him. Perfect nails. Thin long fingers. No ring.

"Can I help you?" she asked.

Can you get us to London any faster? We have to get off this plane. We don't have much time.

"Are there any other seats available?"

She looked into his eyes for only a moment, but for Lucas it felt much longer. It was like they had an instant bond with each other. It made him wish it were Tabitha standing there instead. If this flight attendant could bring him a momentary calm, how much more could Tabitha? Why didn't he take her with him? Or Jake? What about Jake? He had the steadiest nerves out of all of them. Even more so than Edgar, the professor. But Lucas had chosen to go alone to Africa. And if the feelings of dread that were consuming him were any indication, his decision now seemed to be a terrible mistake.

"There's one up ahead," she said, raising her eyebrows in a way that conveyed to Lucas that she understood his irritation in sitting next to an incessant talker.

Lucas pushed his tray back. Maybe this would help. Maybe the change in seating would make the feeling disappear. Maybe some quiet would give him the relief he needed. He stood up and only then did the man beside him realize he was leaving. When he stepped into the aisle the baby stopped screaming, like someone had hit a mute button. All he heard was the drone of the engines. Stillness. The change in atmosphere felt awkward. Like a precursor to what would follow. *Stop it! Stop thinking those thoughts. Get yourself under control.* Lucas glanced back. He saw the baby's mother close her exhausted eyes, lean back in her chair, and kiss the head of her sleeping child.

He followed the flight attendant, taking in the faint smell of her tied-back hair. She stopped a few rows up and showed him an empty aisle seat.

"One less neighbour," she whispered.

Please don't go. Wait. I have an idea. Get the talker back there to move over here so you and I can sit in the back. It's still an hour before we land. We can talk. Or I can just listen to you. I'm a good listener when it comes to interesting people. You're interesting. Tell me anything you want. Just get my mind off this.

"Is there anything you need?"

I need you to spend some time with me. I'll get over this. If you knew what I'd just been through, you'd understand. Five minutes. Can you spare five minutes with me?

"I'm fine," he lied, forcing a smile. "Thank you."

Lucas sat down and breathed in her reassuring fragrance as she walked away. Her presence had set things right for him. But when she left he felt the uneasiness begin to creep in again. He leaned his head back and hoped the dread would not return.

"You think it's going to help?" a voice beside him asked.

Lucas closed his eyes, pretending not to hear.

"Do you?" the voice asked again.

No. No. No!

Were there any more empty seats?

Lucas turned his head to face him. He had enough energy left to tell the person to shut up. He could manage it. One good blast and he would be set free until landing. He looked at the man. Thin. Slicked-back hair. Pale face. Baggy eyes. A lot of dark around them. Thirties, perhaps. He was either exhausted or an addict. And if he were an addict, his clothes indicated he had a healthy means of feeding that habit. He wore a white shirt under a black Armani suit. Lucas admired it. He had two just like it. In his right hand he rubbed a pair of red dice with his bony fingers. He grinded them against each other in a nervous gesture. Faster and faster he twisted them. "You think it'll help our odds?"

As Lucas looked closer, he thought he saw something familiar in the man's eyes. There was an undeniable connection. They both felt it. The man didn't smile. Didn't introduce himself. Didn't even say hello. He just stared at Lucas, giving him the feeling he knew he was going to be here.

"I mean really," the man said as he fidgeted in his seat. He jammed the dice into his pocket and then grabbed the armrests tighter than what would be considered normal. His face screamed anxiety. "It's kind of like, well, you know, changing seats on the Titanic."

It wasn't meant as a joke. Neither of them laughed. The dread came back.

"Meaning what?" Lucas asked, already having the conviction of what the answer might be.

"Meaning what? What kind of question is that?" His voice became more intense. More stern. More desperate. "You know as well as I do."

The flight attendant came back. "How is everything?"

Lucas didn't respond.

She continued by addressing the man to his right. "Sir, you know it's only a little while longer. Maybe for the comfort of other passengers who are sleeping you could...." She pushed her hands palms down a few times to indicate he should stop talking.

"You're right," he said. "Only a little while longer."

She walked down the aisle. Lucas' eyes stayed focused on his.

"What are the odds?" the man asked. "You coming here? Me sitting right next to you? Thousands of flights each day. Hundreds of people on each flight. And yet you and I sit right beside each other. Makes you wonder, doesn't it?"

Lucas felt a rush of ice water go down his spine. They had never met. Never even seen each other. Yet Lucas had the uncanny impression they were not strangers. "Tell me what you know," Lucas said in a quiet voice.

The man didn't move his head. Didn't breathe. Didn't blink. He just stared right into Lucas. "I know the same thing you know."

Lucas swallowed. It felt colder. "I don't know anything."

"You don't?"

"Not for certain."

"But you do."

"I don't."

"You're as convinced as I am," the man said, nodding his head so slightly that it took a few times for Lucas to notice. "The only difference is that I've chosen to accept it, whereas you still pretend this can all be avoided."

"Avoided? Avoid what?"

"What do you think?"

Lucas felt his lips begin to tremble. He couldn't decide if he was shivering from cold or feeling an attack of fear. The only thing for certain was that the man beside him had somehow managed to break into his thoughts. Read his mind. See his fear. It made Lucas want to leave. Get up and go back to the yackity-yack man in the last row. And he would have done just that, had he not been curious to discover if the man was thinking the same thoughts as he was.

"Who are you?" Lucas asked.

"It won't matter. Not in a few minutes."

"It matters now."

The man waited a moment, making Lucas think he might be searching for a phony name.

"My name is Matthias Fisher."

"What do you do, Matthias?"

Another hesitation. This one was definitely going to be a lie.

"I do various things."

Drugs.

"I'm asking you one more time," Lucas said in a slow, angry whisper. It took everything he had to get it out. "What do you know?"

Matthias tried to find the courage to say what was on his mind. This wasn't easy for him. He looked to his right at the woman sleeping next to him. Convinced she could not hear him, he leaned closer to Lucas. Time froze. That chilling stare came back. Lucas waited for his answer. Fear. Calamity. Desperation. He felt the overwhelming weight of Matthias' words sink into him.

"This plane is about to crash."

That was a problem. That was a really, really big problem. Sitting at the back of the plane having delusional thoughts about an aircraft going down was one thing. Finding someone with those same delusional thoughts was a whole different matter.

Lucas saw two options. Either he and the mystery man were both crazy, and it was just plain coincidence that two guys with the same fear happened to be on the same flight sitting next to each other.

Or they had tapped into something that had told them in advance they were all about to take the ride of their lives.

Lucas' fingers hurt from the adrenaline rush. His palms felt as though needles were being jammed into them.

This is crazy. Just relax. Just stay calm. An hour. One hour. You can last an hour.

"You're taking it better than the girl who was sitting there before you," Matthias said. "This gorgeous woman from Las Vegas. I mean, she could melt steel. Reddish-blonde hair. What was her name? Started with an *S*. What was it? Savannah. Right. Her name was Savannah. Almost like that city in Cuba. I told her the plane was going to go down when we stopped in New York. At first she thought I was nuts. But the longer I talked to her, the more I got through to her. She got off the plane. She's going to thank me, you know," he said, and then it occurred to him. "Well, if she could, that is. She won't be able to thank me after this. After I'm gone. After we're all gone." He rotated his neck trying to calm himself down. "I should have made an announcement while we were on the ground. You know—a public address? Stupid, isn't it? The thought never hit me until after the plane took off again."

"You warned someone?"

"Savannah. She wore a bracelet. Silver. With some kind of snake thing on it. Looked expensive."

"You warned her to get off?"

"Yes."

"And yet you yourself stayed on board?"

Matthias seemed stunned. It was as though the error of his ways had just been found out. Lucas looked at him in disbelief, relieved that this had all been a misunderstanding.

Matthias took offence. "You don't believe me."

Lucas breathed in. Less than an hour now. He'd be in London. Maybe take the tube to Hyde Park. Walk around during the stopover before catching the next plane. Everything was alright now.

Though Lucas would not have felt relieved had he known what Matthias was going to say next.

"The floor lights and reading lights are going to flicker," he said. "That's the first sign. Then the plane is going to dip down. And no ordinary turbulence bump either. It'll be a significant drop. That's sign number two. Third, you'll hear this high-pitched whining sound. Like a power saw going off right beside your ear. And then, my friend, the real fun will begin."

Lucas felt nauseated. He clenched his teeth together as if doing so could prevent anything from flying out.

"What are the odds of someone surviving a plane crash?" Matthias asked.

"Stop it."

"And what are the odds of that person being you?"

"Nothing is going to happen."

"What if the plane really does go down and there's only one survivor? You think that'd be fair? As the plane goes down, hundreds will be begging for a miracle—yet only one person gets it. How do you explain that? What if you live and the rest of us die?"

"What if you live and I die?"

Matthias thought a moment and shook his head. "I don't think so. You surviving makes better sense. Don't you agree? Lucas, the healer of thousands. Lays his hands on people with any illness and *poof*—they are healed. I mean, if anyone should live, it's you. You can do more good than the rest of us combined. That must be an awful burden to bear. And to think this would be just the beginning. To think that in retrospect this plane crash will have been the least of your troubles."

Lucas was about to respond when the lights flickered. Anxiety ripped through his body. A few heads looked up. Everything returned to normal. Matthias nodded his head.

"Number one," he said.

"Lights flickering is nothing."

"I agree," he said. He was about to continue when he stopped. He shifted his eyes to the left and then the right. He was waiting for something. "Watch out," he said. Then he became more intense. "Brace yourself." He clutched the armrests even tighter. He felt something. He nodded his head a number of times in a panic. "Here it comes."

The plane jerked down in a sudden and violent motion. People screamed. Passengers who weren't wearing their seatbelts rammed into the seats in front of them. More screams filled the cabin. A drink cart raced down the aisle. It caught the edge of a seat and toppled over, spilling drinks on the floor.

Lucas grabbed his armrest. The captain came over the intercom. Even though he spoke loud enough, Lucas could not hear him. He closed his eyes.

"Do you think prayer will help us now?"

Lucas said nothing.

"Do you think it's fair?"

He opened his eyes. "Fair?"

"Do you think it's fair that you are going to be spared while the rest of us die?" An engine powered up. "I have to know. Just for my own sake."

They heard a grinding noise. It grew louder and turned into a piercing shrill. Lucas turned his head in the direction of the sound. He looked at the wing. One of the engines caught fire. Flames exploded from it, lighting up the cabin. Shouting filled the aircraft.

The plane shuddered, trying to go on.

The brunette hurried down the aisle. Her once comforting look had turned to one of terror and disbelief.

Another drop. This one felt worse than the first. People were suspended in air—as though gravity ceased to exist for that instant. The plane hurtled downward, picking up speed. It rattled and shook, making some passengers wonder if it would break apart.

"There has to be a way to stop this," Lucas said.

Matthias closed his eyes. Even though he had more warning than any of the others on board, it was clear to Lucas he was not ready for the end.

The plane banked heavily to the left. Three people nearby fell out of their seats. An elderly lady crashed against the drink cart, cutting her head open. Bags flew out of overhead compartments. Lucas heard the baby at the back begin to scream.

He wanted to back everything up. Start over again. Return to the airport and pick a different flight. Or no flight at all.

All these people. All these people on board.

He wanted to close his eyes, but couldn't. He wanted to pray, but couldn't find the words. He looked out the window. The sun was setting. The plane burst through the clouds.

The ocean raced into view.

2

Lucas heard a tremendous explosion coming from the back of the plane. His body slammed into the chair in front of him like a crash test dummy in a car commercial. His face smashed against the tray, breaking his nose. His forehead followed with a painful *thud*, creating a gash from his hairline down to his eyebrows. His hands trembled as he tried to brace himself for what would happen next.

The plane jerked up, sending his head back against his seat. Blood ran out of his nose and forehead. Oxygen masks popped down. Some of the passengers tried to put them on. Others were too afraid, deciding instead to keep a firm grip on their armrests, thinking them to be the only sure thing they had left to hold onto.

Lucas tried to concentrate amid the chaos. Tried to block out the screams. Tried to avoid the distressing sound of the dying engines. *We're going down. Good God. We're going down.*

I'm going to die.

He forced himself to change perspective. Maybe the pilot could find a way to get the plane back on course. Weren't pilots trained for this exact situation? Weren't they trained to handle disasters like this? But in spite of his attempt to believe the aircraft could be brought under control, the smoke erupting from the engine and the aircraft's violent shaking made Lucas question his optimism.

Is there a way? Is there a way for us to escape this? Don't let us die. I don't want to die.

And in that instant the plane suddenly became still. The shaking stopped. An unexpected calm. Like they were suddenly on a sea of glass. Cruising along, making everything feel like it had been a strange dream. He and the other passengers waited anxious moments for something else to go wrong. But nothing did. People called out for help, distressed over their injuries and yet relieved things weren't worse.

While others began to cope with what had happened, Lucas only felt his fears grow more intense. Perhaps that gorgeous brunette would come by again and set his world right. The longer he sat there, the more uneasy he became. It wasn't just the fragile condition of the aircraft. It wasn't just the pain. He could feel it. Different. Yes. Quite different. Definitely.

There was an eerie presence on board.

Something walking. Something approaching. He looked down the aisle, waiting for it to materialize. But nothing came. At least nothing he could see. And he didn't need to.

The feeling was enough.

He closed his eyes to block out what was coming. No matter. They had made it through. All of them. He touched his nose. It ached. He pulled his hand away and saw the blood. His stomach heaved. Deep breath in. Deep breath out.

He swallowed some of his blood. More deep breathing. He looked around and saw people exhausted from the ordeal, some calling out for help, others helping those around them. Smoke billowed out of the engine. The plane flew as well as one could expect.

Matthias looked at his right hand. His fingers were twisted in awkward positions from being jammed into the chair during the commotion. He pulled his hand towards his body and turned to Lucas. His eyes were a strange combination of confusion and release.

"I was wrong," he said, leaning his head back and looking up like a suntanner trying to feel the warmth from above. The tone in his voice conveyed his gratitude that what he predicted had not come true. "I was wrong."

He turned to Lucas again. Something ripped through him like a ministroke. He shook for a brief moment. Then the expression in Matthias' eyes changed. Lucas saw a brutal fear in them. Whatever was giving Matthias that awful anxiety found a way to transfer itself inside Lucas. Panic gripped him. Lucas breathed faster.

"What do you see?" Lucas asked.

But Matthias couldn't respond. He wanted to say something. He wanted to warn Lucas. But he stayed frozen. Paralyzed by fear.

Lucas leaned closer. "What do you see?"

And that's when everything went wrong.

One of the engines on the other side of the plane exploded. It erupted into a great ball of blazing fire with such force that windows along that side blew open, creating an unbearable difference in pressure. People screamed as they covered their ears. Air raced through the holes at a deafening pitch. Fire engulfed the wing. The plane dropped. More screaming. It rattled with such power that Lucas' teeth chattered.

Don't let us die. Don't let us die.

The wing exploded at mid-span. Part of it broke off, flipped upwards, and rammed into the plane. It crashed through the fuselage, crushing passengers in five rows. Some were thrown from their seats. Some were decapitated, leaving them as messy globs of headless corpses.

The plane banked left, then right. Those in the front had lost whatever control they once had. Lucas looked out the window. He saw the water hurtling towards them. People struggled to remain upright in their seats, making it impossible for them to do anything but wait for impact.

Oh God.

The nose struck the ocean first. The force of the collision ripped open the windshield. Water burst through and killed the pilots. The plane skidded on the surface. Then it twisted to the side like a car losing control after hitting a patch of ice. The nose veered off to the left, bringing the broad side of the plane forward. The fuselage flipped over, smashing passengers against each other and the seats around them. Skulls cracked together, killing still more as they were thrown from side to side.

Everything went dark. The plane came to a stop. Finally. Half of it was underwater. Passengers hung upside down in their seats. Many pleaded for help. The rest were either dead or well on their way.

Lucas' head pounded. He looked at the water pouring into the cabin. His stomach cramped. He vomited. He looked to his right. Matthias was gone.

So were a dozen other passengers who had been near the hole created by the torn wing.

Waves crashed against the opening, sending in still more water. Blood rushed to Lucas' face and through his nose. He heard people in the distance yelling at each other to unbuckle themselves and swim to safety. Moments later, more frantic shouts echoed in the cabin about water filling the front part of the plane and that the doors could not be opened.

Lucas turned his body to the side as best he could. He snapped the buckle open, fell out of his seat, and crashed into the frigid knee-deep water.

People crammed against each other. Off to one side three men tried to push open the emergency door against the water pounding against the plane. Lucas looked behind him. And what he witnessed made him wish he had stayed facing the other way.

There were two final explosions. The first came from the back of the plane. One moment he was looking at shadows of people in the tail end. The next there was a blinding flash of light. The impact ripped into his chest. He flew backward down the aisle and crashed into the water filling the plane. He grabbed onto a chair and pulled himself up. His body shook with pain and cold. When his eyes adjusted he saw the tail of the plane was gone.

The second explosion came somewhere in the middle of the plane. This blast was even more powerful. A horrible *bang*. A rush of heat. The plane shuddered. People clawed at each other to get to the door that wasn't opening. Water filled the front compartment, pulling the nose down below the surface, drowning people at the front. The plane twisted down at a steeper angle.

Lucas jumped and grabbed onto a seat. Water rushed past him down to the sinking front of the plane. He pulled himself up towards the rising back end. Another wave poured in and pulled at him as he struggled to keep his grip. He reached for the next seat and grabbed onto the bars connecting the chair to the floor. He pulled himself up and reached the back of the plane. It had lifted so far out of the water that the waves no longer touched it. He looked down at the black abyss of screaming people beneath him. A sudden rush of water pounded against those remaining, silencing them. A hand reached up from the water. Lucas heard someone sputtering for air. Then the hand disappeared below.

The plane made an awful moaning sound. The back end lifted even higher. Lucas looked over the edge at the ocean below. It seemed so far away considering they had just crashed into it. The plane jolted. Lucas lost his hold. He crashed against the floor and slid down towards the watery grave. He reached out for a chair and missed, cracking his wrist against the bar. He grabbed onto the next chair. His shivering arms managed to keep hold of it. He heard a woman calling out to him as she crawled up the aisle. He looked down and offered her his arm. She clutched his hand, causing Lucas to think it was a mistake to put himself more at risk. Her hand was frozen cold. She lost her feeble grip and vanished into the water below. He waited for her to come back up, but she didn't.

Lucas pulled himself to what was left of the back of the plane. He stood up on the ripped fuselage and glanced at the water below. He turned back for a final look inside the plane. Through the darkness, all he could see were floating bodies.

Lucas grabbed a seat cushion and clutched it against his chest. He took in a deep breath. Clenched his teeth. And braced himself for the landing.

He jumped into the ocean.

The drop took longer than he thought, making him feel more anxious with every passing moment about the impact that would follow. He felt a horrible, cold shock run through his body as he cut into the water. The force pushed the seat cushion out of his arms. He clawed his way back to the surface and gasped for air. He searched the water for his seat cushion, or anything else that could help him stay afloat. He swam against the waves to get farther from the plane. Amid the rising and falling water he saw two people huddled together, clutching a portion of the wing.

"Get away from the plane!" he shouted.

But they stayed there, too afraid to give up their only means of flotation, and too panicked to consider any other alternative.

"The plane is going to sink and you'll go down with it!" If they heard him they gave no indication. "Move away from the plane!"

But they stayed there. Shivering. Out of Lucas' reach. The back end of the plane lifted again so that it was standing nearly straight up. The two in the middle jumped off the wing. The plane began its descent. The two tried to swim away. But despite their frantic attempts at flailing in the water, the force of the descending plane pulled them down out of sight.

Lucas watched the plane sink. Within seconds, it was gone. Vanished. Beginning its long journey to the ocean floor. He shook in the icy water, carried up and down by the passing waves. He curled up in a ball as best he could, hoping to preserve what little body heat he had left. He kicked his legs to keep from going under. He saw nothing within reach that could be used to help keep him afloat. He saw nothing nearby that could be used to keep warm.

And he saw no ship in the distance.

It was way too early to be her alarm clock. Tabitha opened her eyes in her dark room. She felt disoriented as she turned to her night table. It took her a moment to recognize the sound. Her heart gave a powerful jolt when she saw the time. A reporter's cellphone going off at 1 a.m. meant one of two things. Either someone had a wrong number.

Or there was trouble.

And she would have believed it was the former had it not been for the gripping feeling of fear in her body.

In those few seconds between when she woke up and when she answered her cell, she tried to convince herself nothing was wrong. Time change. Of course. Lucas was on his way to Africa. He was probably in London. That's six hours ahead. He was at Heathrow. Healing thousands. And this was a call from Chester at *The Chicago Observer* telling her to come in and do a story. Maybe it was Lucas calling to tell her about what was happening. Maybe he was missing her and wanted to hear her voice before he caught the next flight. She wanted to believe any of those options. Still, she couldn't deny the deeper reality of the suspicion in her spirit telling her something had gone terribly wrong with Lucas Stephens.

She checked her call display. It was Chester. She hesitated before answering. Panic. Adrenaline. Worry.

"Hello?"

She parked her pristine '67 yellow convertible Mustang and hurried into *The Chicago Observer* building. Normally, Tabitha stopped to talk with the security guard on her way in. Normally, she would come in planning out her day and the stories she wanted to pursue.

But today was not normal.

She took the elevator to the top floor and walked down the hallway. It was Deadsville. Ghost town. Most of the reporters wouldn't be arriving for another five hours.

She quickened her pace. The only sound was her shoes against the floor beating faster and faster, tapping out a worried rhythm as she approached the conference room. She opened the door. There was Chester. Fat Chester. Holding a cup of coffee with something extra in it. Eyes glued to a news anchor on TV. She came in and stood next to him.

"They've lost contact," he said. He looked at her. Gorgeous dark hair. Soft skin. No earrings. Not today. There wasn't time for that. Black turtleneck. Black jeans. Black leather jacket. Anxious look on her face.

She saw the flight number on the screen, 912. She covered her mouth in an instinctive reaction. That was it. That was his plane. The one going to London.

Or at least the one that was *supposed* to go to London.

"Survivors?" she asked.

Chester drank some of his *coffee-extra*—his own special brew from his office. He swallowed a gulp while she waited an eternity for his response.

"The last transmission was 40 minutes ago."

Tabitha felt ill. She lowered her hand to cover her stomach. Her face flushed. Her eyes stung as tears began to form.

"There's a transport ship in the area," he continued. "They expect to be there in 20 minutes."

"Twenty," she replied, wondering if 20 minutes might be too long in ocean water.

"What can I get you?" Chester asked. She couldn't decide. She stayed fixed on the screen as if the news anchor held the authority to make or break her future with Lucas. Chester walked to his office.

Tabitha bit her lip. Maybe Lucas was still alive. Maybe he was out there. And maybe he could hang on for these next few minutes.

Chester came back and gave her a mug of coffee. She held it in her hands, but couldn't bring herself to drink it.

"He can make it. Twenty minutes. Just because they've lost contact doesn't mean the plane is destroyed," she said.

"They've lost contact."

"That could be anything. Bad equipment. An emergency landing. Besides, you can't even communicate with a plane that's on the water. Can you?"

"Tabitha."

"They could all be on board. This is nothing but a stupid waste of time. The ship is going to make it there and get them all off."

"Tabitha."

"They can."

"*Tabitha*," he said with more force. She stopped. Perhaps he could have let her continue, convincing herself of facts that were untrue. But he was Chester and this was news. And there was no room for giving speculation the same weight as the facts.

"The pilots radioed for help. They lost communication when they hit the water."

That cut into her. *Hit the water* didn't have quite the same euphemistic ring to it as *emergency landing in the ocean.*

"Four hundred and thirty on board," he said.

She didn't hear him say that. It just went right by her. Yes, there were many on board. But somehow the figures didn't mean as much when one of those numbers was someone she knew.

Tabitha sat down in a chair. Closed her eyes. Refused the temptation of wishing this wasn't really happening.

Helpless. Hoping. Waiting.

Wondering if Lucas' fate had already been decided.

3

The first hint of sunrise did nothing to help Lucas. The light should have indicated a ship in the distance. A chopper, perhaps, on the horizon. Instead, his situation was just as bleak as before—only now he had lost the anticipation of seeing help when dawn broke. His hair was frosted. His lips blue. His hands and feet numb. He swooshed his legs around in a fading attempt to keep himself afloat. The ring of gold on the horizon pierced him. He rose and fell with the passing waves and forced his chin up as he struggled for air.

A powerful light shone down on him. He tried to turn himself around, but the muscles in his arms and legs would not respond.

"There's one!" a voice shouted. A wave covered him. When it passed he spit out water and coughed. He pushed his waist back and forth trying to keep above the surface. Another wave. This one passed high above him, forcing him to hold his breath. Another wave crashed over him, and he wondered if one more might issue him a ticket to join the rest who had died in the deep water.

This was it. He couldn't move his legs. His arms hung rigid by his sides. What was taking them so long? A tug at his shoulders. A rope around his chest.

"It's alright," a voice with a German accent said. "We got you."

They pulled him onto the deck. The sun broke through. Blinding him. His hair crunched as they put him on a stretcher. He looked up at the morning sky.

All those people.

The next hours were a blur. They brought him to a room. Took off his clothes. Put him in a tub of warm water. Wrapped a towel around his head. Changed his bathwater every ten minutes. Stitched his forehead. Bandaged his nose. People brought blankets. Someone took his temperature. He felt his hands and feet again.

They took him out of the bath. Gave him new clothes. Wrapped him in blankets and put him in a bed. A young man stayed at his side, checking his temperature. Short blonde hair. Blue eyes. Small build.

"Hello," he said, in a way that indicated he was both surprised and relieved that the man from the water was still alive.

Lucas still felt cold. Shivering. As though encased in a thin layer of ice. He managed to make eye contact with the young man.

"Thank you."

The young man smiled and nodded. "That's okay," he said, as though this were routine. "You were lucky."

Luck. Luck. Was that it? If it was, Lucas figured he had a lot of it.

More than the others on board.

"Try to rest. We'll be in London soon," the young man said. Then he became quiet. His smile faded. It seemed as though the weight of what happened was only now beginning to affect him. "All those people." He shook his head. "An entire planeload. And only two of you survived."

Lucas tried to sit up and then stopped halfway. "Two?"

The young man nodded. "There is another."

The phone rang at Chester's desk. He left Tabitha staring at the monitor. Despite holding her third cup of coffee, her hands were still cold. Her feet still numb. Chester went to answer it. When he came back the look on his face told her that one way or the other, she was going to know.

"Lucas and one other made it."

She dropped her cup. It smashed on the ground, spilling coffee in all directions. She closed her eyes and then covered her face with her hands. She pressed her lips together and pulled in a quick breath. She forced herself not to cry. But it didn't work. She exhaled and held her breath. Tears ran down her cheeks.

Moments later the news anchor delivered the news. Two rescued. Four hundred and twenty-eight dead.

The young man left Lucas' side and told him he would return with something to eat. Lucas sat up. He was on the bottom of a metal bunk bed in a small room. A wooden table and mirror to his right. A closet to his left. He dragged his feet out of bed and onto the floor. Blood rushed down into them. He pushed himself off the bed and stood up. His back ached. His forehead hurt. His nose felt like it would explode. He took cautious steps, still amazed he was not in the ocean. Or at the bottom of it.

He opened the door and looked outside. Narrow hallway. Dimly lit. He heard pumps running. Piping overhead. A few feet away he saw another door. Light spilled out from under it into the hallway. A chill went down his back, his body getting used to being warm again. He walked to the door, his leg muscles getting used to being in motion again. He knocked. Hearing no answer, he turned the doorknob.

It was enough to wake up whoever was inside. Just as he opened the door, the person on the bed came out of a deep sleep. Lucas thought it strange that someone would fall asleep with the lights on. He was about to leave, but the glimpse he got of the person inside made him reconsider. He looked closer. A man with black hair and little colour in his face opened his dark eyes. Lucas recognized him.

Matthias Fisher.

"They told me there was another," Matthias said as he sat up in his bed. "Without even checking, I knew it would be you."

"We made it."

"We did. But why not the others?"

"I don't know."

"You think it's chance? Or were we all supposed to die, except you and I got a special pardon? What about the others?"

"Four hundred and twenty-eight."

"Do you think we are any more important than they are?"

"Is that what decides life or death?"

"Being important?"

"Is it?"

"I don't think so. I understand you being rescued. It made sense for you to live. But dear God. Why me?"

"You knew it was going to crash."

"So did you."

"You knew already in New York when the plane made a stop. Savannah got off. But you did not. Why? If you knew the plane was going down, why didn't you get off as well?"

Matthias' pale face became even whiter. He looked down at the ground and then back at Lucas. "Why are you going to Africa?"

Lucas wanted to avoid the question too. He knew why he had left Chicago. Sure, he had all kinds of good reasons that seemed plausible on the outside—to help the poor, perform healing miracles for those who had no access to pharmaceutical drugs. But inside, he wanted to tell Matthias. He wanted to tell the truth and admit to himself why he was doing this.

"I'm running from someone."

Matthias raised his eyebrows. "Aren't we all." Another shiver down Lucas' spine. Matthias studied him. "You feel responsible."

"Responsible?"

"For the plane crash."

"How could I possibly be responsible?"

"Maybe not for the crash, but for not being able to save them once we hit the water."

"Why would I feel guilty for not being able to save them? That makes no sense."

"I agree."

"I don't feel guilty."

"You do. You feel guiltier than I do. What drives you to have so much guilt to make you think you are responsible for not saving them?"

"Come with me to Africa," Lucas said, changing the subject. What he really meant to say was that he was afraid of being there alone. He didn't have Jake, he didn't have Edgar, and he didn't have Tabitha. Granted, Caesar would not be there. That was bonus enough. But that feeling of insecurity, of predicting danger, that he had in the back of the plane hadn't left. And it made him wonder if it had something to do with what was going to happen when he got to Africa.

"No. When I get to London I'm turning around and going to Vegas. Taking a ship this time. Into New York. And then a train to Vegas. No more planes. I'll look up Savannah. Can you take a train to Vegas? How much would it cost? What do you figure? Seeing how the plane crashed, do you think the airline will cover the cost?"

"Why were you going to London in the first place?"

Matthias stalled, like a child trying to decide whether to tell the truth to a parent. They waited in silence. Lucas didn't mind. He'd wait the whole ride to London to hear it.

"Goodbye, Lucas."

"Why were you going to London? What's there for you?"

"Good luck in Africa."

Lucas' body flushed with heat. Like the onset of a vicious flu. He said his verses to himself as he turned to leave. He turned the light off and was about to walk out when Matthias stopped him.

"Leave the light on, will you?"

"On?" Lucas asked, making sure he heard right.

"I can't sleep with the lights off."

Lucas turned it back on. He looked back at Matthias. That pale face. It wasn't just the water. It wasn't the accident. He looked as bad now as he had before the crash.

"You're not well," Lucas said.

"Who among us is?"

Lucas closed the door and returned to his room.

"Of course I should go!" Tabitha said, those earlier feelings of worry and anxiety now ones of determination and conviction.

"What's the angle?" Chester asked.

"He's the most famous Chicagoan and he'll be in Africa healing people. We have the local aspect, the humanitarian aspect. People will eat it up."

A couple of reporters walked past the conference room. One poked his head in and was surprised to see anyone there. He apologized, shut the door, and walked away. Chester motioned for Tabitha to walk with him into his office.

Chester's office. Like hallowed ground. It was the really good or really bad news that was spoken here. And as Tabitha walked in, she felt it would be more the latter.

She closed the door behind them. Chester sat down at his desk.

"Chester, what's going on? This is Lucas Stephens. The miracle man. Why are you hesitating?"

Chester would normally have given her an earful back. Hesitating? Chester? But this time he paused as he formulated his response. Thinking back on it later, Tabitha realized why he was so careful in deciding whether or not to tell her what was on his mind.

Because what he was about to say would change her life.

Lucas' too.

"Lucas is big news, Chester," she said.

"He's big news when he's in America. Not when he's in Africa."

"It's still Lucas Stephens. Chicago adores him."

That didn't come out right. She wanted to take it back. *Chicago is crazy about Lucas* would have been better. The word *adore* felt strange in her mouth, especially considering she used it in conjunction with Lucas. She fixed her eyes on Chester, hoping he wasn't going to read anything more into what she said, and hoping there would be time later when she could sort out for herself if she meant anything more by it.

"Lucas in Chicago is news every day, whereas Lucas in Africa is news for maybe a week. Max. Absolutely max one week. If he heals people on the Magnificent Mile on Tuesday, that's news. And if he heals at Buckingham Fountain or on the South Side on Wednesday, that's news too. But if he heals a kid in Zimbabwe—"

"He's going to Zambia."

"Wherever. It doesn't matter. It's all the same thing happening way out there. You want to go? Go. A week. That's it. Then I need you back here."

He got quiet. It was coming. The important part. Her assignment.

"And? When I come back?" It came out sounding more like *If I come back*.

Chester reached behind him and poured himself more of his special blend of *coffee-extra*. It was his third so far and his normal working day hadn't even begun.

"What do you know about Empirico?"

"Lucas' former pharmaceutical company. Owned by Chicago's Caesar Alexander."

"He's constructing the mother of all casinos in Las Vegas."

"I heard. They unveil the name in a few weeks."

"Right."

"That's news? A casino in Vegas?"

"In and of itself, the biggest casino in the world is news, yes. But there's more to it." He took in a breath and looked behind Tabitha to see if anyone was in the conference room who might overhear what he was about to say. He licked his lips, a sign of nervousness. "A week ago I heard rumours—that's all they were, Tabitha. Just scuttlebutt. You don't repeat this to anybody," he whispered. "Rumours that Caesar couldn't afford to finish his complex. Big, massive Empirico strung out for cash. And yet, only a week later, Empirico claims they can not only can finish it, but they are making it bigger than before—and on a faster schedule."

"That surprises you?"

Chester leaned forward. She had never seen his face so serious. "There is speculation about the pharmaceutical industry, Tabitha. Empirico in particular."

Tabitha swallowed. She remembered what it felt like to be around Caesar. She remembered what it sounded like when those bullets started raining down on Lucas while he healed people outside Wrigley Field. And without anyone being able to prove it, she knew Caesar was behind it. And she wanted to do everything possible to never see him again.

"Meaning?"

"Meaning there is more to Caesar than what we can see on the surface."

Now, more than before, she wanted to go to Africa. And not just for a week. Forever. Whatever it took to get away from Caesar. She wanted to say no. She wanted to get up, slam the door shut, and have nothing to do with Empirico. Not now. Not ever.

"You want me to chase down a far-fetched conspiracy theory?"

"You and I both know Caesar tried to have Lucas killed."

"We don't *know* anything, Chester. Not for certain," she said.

"Three gunmen."

"Three *alleged* gunmen."

"Two dead. The third, Mike, you know him, is in jail. A company capable of killing is likely capable of doing worse things."

"When I come back from Africa you want me to go to Las Vegas because you think Empirico is involved in something illegal?" She wanted it to come out sounding so ridiculous that he would reconsider sending her there.

"No. I want you to go to Las Vegas because it seems *you* think Empirico is involved in something illegal."

"A conspiracy to commit murder?"

"Conspiracy for murder, collusion for price fixing, illegal gambling methods. Just put those out of your head." He put his coffee down. That was serious. Chester without his coffee was a sign that the world had gone wrong. He fidgeted in his chair and leaned forward. "This is how it is. And you will live or die depending on what you do with this information."

She didn't want to hear it. Didn't even want to be here anymore.

"Sources close to Caesar and Empirico say they have a mystery drug. A cure, Tabitha. A cure for a major disease. Something big. Huge. And they're not releasing it."

"Why would they hold back a cure for an illness?"

"That's what you're going to find out."

"What kind of source do you have on this?"

"You track the story and you'll find it to be true."

Tabitha checked behind her to confirm no one was listening. "You can give me your source. Was it Claire?"

"Dig around. See if there's any truth to this. We could be talking thousands, maybe hundreds of thousands of lives at stake here."

"You want me to go after Caesar?"

He nodded in a way that instilled in her a sense that she would soon be on her way to the story of her life. "And best of all, you'll be tracking him down in Las Vegas."

She stood up and had walked to the door when Chester called out to her. "And remember to be careful," he said. Tabitha turned around. "Anything goes in Las Vegas."

But Tabitha didn't need Chester telling her that.

She was going to find that out all on her own.

4

Jake Rubenstein sat on the "L" train reading Tabitha's article about Lucas and the crash of Flight 912. He shook his head. *I should have gone with him. I should have been there.* He felt he had failed him at Wrigley Field. He should have been closer to Lucas to get himself into the line of fire. Protect Lucas. It was his self-appointed job. But he hadn't, and yet Lucas survived. Now here was Lucas again, defying the odds. When they said goodbye at O'Hare, Jake wanted to go with Lucas. He wanted to accompany the man who had helped him get off the streets. But he decided against it. He wanted, needed, to take care of something that happened years ago—an event that ultimately led to his slow and steady destruction from a decent life down to the drugs, alcohol, and crime that filled his existence on the street. He'd been putting this off for years.

It was time to do it. Face to face.

He continued reading the paper, hoping it would distract him long enough so that he wouldn't back out of his mission. He noticed an article below the one on Lucas. It featured a Food and Drug Administration official giving his reaction to the possibility of new patent-breaking legislation for pharmaceutical drugs. It stated that he saw a tension between pharmaceutical companies looking to recoup their high costs in developing new drugs, and the creation of generic drugs to lessen the financial burden on patients needing help. Jake read a few lines, then skipped to a story at the bottom. He read the first few lines about Senator Turtle's $250 a plate dinner happening that evening at an upscale Chicago hotel. He folded the paper and put it down on the seat beside him. Senator Turtle. Rotten, conniving, conspiring Senator Turtle. It infuriated Jake how Turtle and Caesar had colluded together to hold a hearing to put pressure on Lucas, Jake, and Edgar to stop their involvement in the healings. *Senator Turtle. That filthy maggot.*

The train slowed down. Jake looked at the passing buildings. He was getting closer. The long ride here had been easy. It was the getting off part that was going to be tough. And the actual encounter would be the hardest of all. The train stopped. Jake walked to the door. The worst part about it was that he didn't *have* to do this. He could just go right back if he wanted to.

If only he could find a way to ignore the feelings urging him, practically screaming at him, to visit them after all these years and make things right.

Or as right as possible, given the circumstances.

The few clouds in the sky managed to block out the sun, making what was once a bright day seem dreary and dull. Jake stepped off the train and ran his hand through his few strands of hair. He wore faded blue jeans and a dirt-stained T-shirt that barely fit over his bulging stomach. He coughed and felt the effects of his years of smoking. He turned down the street, *their* street, and felt the wind punch him in the face. His knees felt weak. His throat dry. His hands clammy. This was it. This was really it. How many years had it been? Jake tried to remember. But the actual number didn't matter anyway. What did matter was that it felt like a century. It felt like another lifetime ago when he had last seen them. Would they remember him? How could they possibly forget? Maybe they had tried. Maybe seeing him again would only make things worse.

Maybe this wasn't such a good idea.

He didn't need the address written down. He'd tried reaching their house so many times before that he long since had it memorized. He normally made it to about the end of the street before he chickened out. Sometimes he bailed out on the train. Once he even made it all the way to within shouting distance of their house. He had walked up and down the sidewalk on the other side of the street, trying to find the courage to actually knock on the door. But it never came. He thought about phoning. He thought about writing a letter. He thought about a lot of different ways to do this. Would walking right up to their house be too much for them? After all, he'd had years to think this through. For them it would be like jumping in a time machine and going back to an event none of them wished had happened.

There it was. Their house. It used to be red. Bright red. Fire engine red. As red as the ones that came to the accident scene that day. But it had faded over time. And a few years ago they had abandoned the red theme altogether and repainted it a dull blue. It was so bleak it almost looked grey.

He stood on the sidewalk across the street. Why hadn't he done this earlier? Why hadn't he just taken the courage on any of his previous attempts and got it over with? But those previous attempts probably wouldn't have worked out too well. It usually took him a bottle of vodka or rum, his favourites, to get the courage to make it all the way down. And by the time he got off the train or reached their street, he would sober up enough to figure out that a drunk apologizing for destroying their lives would probably not bring the healing touch.

It was a miracle he had made it this far without any booze.

Even in the cool fall breeze sweat formed on his forehead. His throat got even drier. And then he heard it. Maybe it was the sound of the car screeching its brakes down the road. Maybe it was the neighbour shouting for her daughter to come back inside. Whatever it was, something triggered his memory. And he saw it all over again. He saw the car approaching. He felt the impact. He saw her lying....

No. No, he was not going there. This was about meeting them. It wasn't about reliving the past to convince himself not to do this. He wiped his forehead. Where was Lucas? He could help. With him at his side he would find this way easier. Even Edgar. Poor Edgar. He could have been moral support. But as it stood, this was all coming down to the people in that lifeless grey house, Jake, and their past.

He was so nervous that he didn't look as he crossed the street. He made it halfway when he heard a car pound on the brakes to avoid smashing into him. The driver rolled down the window and swore. Under other circumstances Jake would have become acquainted with the driver. Up close and personal. With a bat. Just to set things right.

But he didn't respond. His shaky legs kept walking across the street and onto their property. It was as close as he had ever been. *Don't stop. Don't stop. Not now. This is it. No matter what happens—this is it.*

The stone steps leading up to the porch were cracked. No flowers. No `Welcome` sign. No basketball hoop on the garage. Paint peeled away from the eavestrough. The storm door was half off its hinges, making Jake think that if he had the tools he could fix it for them.

His pulse quickened. He drew a deep breath to calm himself down. Then another. He began to feel light-headed. He closed his right hand into a fist. He brought it up to the door. He paused. It was like information overload. Doorbell or knock? Doorbell or knock? What's better? Isn't knocking reserved for friends?

He stretched out his finger and put it on the doorbell. This was it. He pushed it.

Nothing.

He pushed it again.

Still nothing.

Decision made. Doorbell doesn't work. Knock instead. He curled his fingers into a fist again. He knocked on the door. It was such a feeble knock that even he could barely hear it. But how hard does a person knock when they have this kind of news to deliver?

He knocked again. Harder this time. He listened for any hint of movement. Everything was still. Save for the pounding in his chest.

And then he heard it. Something moved. It scared him. He could run. He could run right now. If he bolted out of here, all this would amount to nothing more than a knock-and-run prank.

But he stayed.

Someone touched the other side of the handle.

Jake held his breath.

The door opened.

A man in his fifties looked at Jake with tired eyes. His hair was greyer than it should be for someone his age. He was short. Six inches shorter than Jake. He stood back as if to hold onto the option of slamming the door shut if the man with the big gut and dirty clothes ended up being a salesman. Or worse.

Jake studied the man. Definitely. It was him. No mistaking. The years had not been kind. And the moment Jake thought that, it occurred to him that since the accident the years had not been kind to him either.

"Mr. Siloa?"

He nodded his head, still wondering about the man on his doorstep. "Can I help you?"

It was such a regular day. The sun was still hidden by those few clouds. Cars were still driving by. A vanload of teenagers pulled up next door wearing Cubs jerseys and caps. For everyone else it was business as usual. But for the two standing there with just a broken storm door between them, it was a day unlike any other in quite some time.

The pause dragged on. Jake wanted to speak but found he couldn't get the words out. He cleared his throat. Five words and then they would both be in the know about what was going on. He swallowed. Now or never.

"My name is Jake Rubenstein."

Nothing. Not a look of shock in the man's eyes. Not a hand to the mouth gesture. Zip. Just a plain face. And that was the worst possible response. Of course he remembered. He was probably reliving that day each and every moment. You can't forget something like that. But you can forget a name. Which is why Siloa stood there trying to figure out why a man named Jake was at his door.

Jake didn't want to have to mention the *k* word. But he was going to have to use it to trigger poor Siloa's memory. He forced himself to look him in the eye. He owed him that. And so much more.

"My name is Jake Rubenstein," he said. "I killed your daughter."

It might have been easier for Siloa had Jake just whipped out a sawed-off shotgun and blasted him in the chest. Siloa started breathing heavier. He blinked as if doing so could erase this moment and he could go back to whatever he was doing. His hands felt weak. He gripped the door tighter. Jake had aged. But there was enough there to pick out a resemblance.

"Just like that?" Siloa asked. Jake swallowed. He didn't know where this was leading. "Just like that, you walk up to my house and tell me you killed my...."

This wasn't working out. Not the way Jake had planned. He expected to be invited in. He expected to talk to them and then leave feeling some closure.

But he had expected too much.

"I never got a chance to apologize."

"Apologize?" The word came out softly. Siloa couldn't find the energy to speak with any force. "Apologize? For what?" He looked like he was on the verge of a nervous breakdown. "For ruining our lives? You can apologize for something like that? Good God, how?"

"I'm sorry for what happened. I'm sorry for what I did."

"And you decided to come here?"

"I needed to see you in person."

"How does your need to come here outweigh our need to forget you? Did you think about us? What is this? Why are you here?"

"I wanted to do what I could to make things better for you."

"And you thought coming here would be a step in that direction?"

"I can't make things right."

"You ruined us."

"I know."

"Jesus God. You know? You know? No. No, you absolutely do not know. How could you possibly? How could you possibly know that by going through that red light you would not only destroy my daughter, but my whole family as well?"

"My life spiralled from the top of a mountain down to the bottom of nothing after the accident. You name it—I've done it. Drugs, crime, prostitution. And as bad as that is, I've known for years that youse people would be doing worse than me. Maybe not on the outside. But on the inside. That's why I'm here."

Siloa squeezed his eyes together. A tear ran down his face.

"Could I come in?" Jake said.

"No."

"Please."

"No. Not with my wife here."

In an unexpected move, Siloa opened the storm door and stepped outside. He sat down on a rickety chair and motioned for Jake to sit beside him on a bench. They looked out at the street at normal people having normal days.

"After the accident my wife went into depression. At first it was mourning. That's understandable. Necessary. But it went on and on. Weeks turned into months. She didn't want to go to the Blackhawk games. Didn't want to see her friends. Didn't want to go to her church. She just stayed indoors. If you press me on it I think she may have made herself sick." He shook his head as if what he just said revealed more than what he wanted Jake to know. "She kept asking God why it happened, over and over and over again. For what reason? Did she really expect God to answer? And now she's on medication. Day and night. My wife is a walking corpse."

He stopped and covered his face with his hands. He waited a moment, regained control, then lowered his hands and continued.

"We had one other child. A daughter. September. We named her after the month she was born. They say a man can conquer anything if he has the right woman by his side. That would be September. She was the strongest of the three of us after the accident. But it was nothing more than a delayed reaction. Neither her mother nor I could be any help to her. September blamed herself. Can you believe that? She blamed herself for the accident. I could never figure that out. It wasn't her fault. And then one day she just left. No plans. Nothing. She still phones once in a while. I don't know where she is. And I think she prefers it that way."

Jake wanted to say something to help but couldn't find any words. One accident. One mistake. And now beside him sat a destroyed man in a destroyed marriage with a destroyed relationship with his only remaining daughter. Siloa was right. Jake had ruined them.

"Who's there?" a frail voice said from inside.

"That's your cue to leave," Siloa said to Jake in a soft voice.

"I'd like to talk to your wife."

"No. She couldn't handle it. You'll send her into a tailspin."

"Who's there?" it came again.

"Goodbye," Siloa whispered.

They stood up. Jake wished Siloa would have used his name. As though hearing Siloa say his name before they parted would have given Jake the sense that his coming here had had some positive effect.

Jake stretched out his hand.

Siloa did not extend his.

"Don't come back," Siloa said. "Not ever. I'm not risking my wife answering the door to you."

"Who is it?" the voice said again, this time with a hint of panic.

"It's nobody," Siloa said, opening the broken storm door and going back into the house. "It's nobody." He disappeared into the house, leaving Jake standing on the porch by himself.

It's nobody.

Jake walked down the steps and took the cracked concrete paving stones to the street. This hadn't worked out. Not even close. And what bothered him most was the convicting feeling that he had only made things worse.

It's nobody echoed in his mind. It was his fault. All of it. If only he hadn't hit them. If only he had been paying more attention. If only. If only. If only.

He reached the end of the street. With separation from the house came some relief. To his left he saw a bar. More relief. *Just one drink,* he told himself. *Just one drink to calm the nerves.*

He crossed the street, looked both ways this time, and walked in. It was dimly lit. A couple sat at a table in the back. Jake sat down on a stool at the bar, trying to keep his mind off what had just happened.

You stupid moron. What were you thinking? You don't just walk up to someone's house like that, especially considering what you did. Only an idiot would do that.

"What can I get you?" a tall woman behind the bar asked.

"Vodka."

She poured him a shot and put it on a black napkin in front of him. He looked at the clear liquid, thinking it looked strangely like water. He grasped the shot glass in his fingers. He lifted it to his mouth and downed it in one gulp. It burned against his throat and calmed him down somewhat. Best of all, it helped to quiet the voices.

For a while.

You only made things worse. You made it worse for them and for you. Why did you do that? Why open up old wounds? What right do you have to barge in there and disrupt the lives of a husband and wife, both of whom had nearly succeeded in forgetting you? You worthless fool. He was right. You are nobody.

He motioned for the bartender to come closer.

One more drink. Just one more. And then that's it. That's all I need to make it through this.

Just one more drink.

5

The ship docked at the Port of Tilbury in London. A powerful horn blew, waking Lucas from his cocoon of blankets. He felt better. Much better. He heard the sounds of muffled shouting outside. The door opened. The young man was there.

"Have you heard?"

Lucas sat up. His nose felt strangely better. And no pain in his forehead. "Heard what?"

"Thousands of people are waiting outside the secured area. Harbour officials say some of them have been waiting here throughout the night. And more are on their way."

It didn't register with Lucas. Not at first. A demonstration, perhaps. Maybe a labour dispute. The young man put a pair of jeans, a T-shirt, a jacket, and Lucas' water-damaged passport on the table.

"Looks like it's time for you to get ready," he said as he closed the door.

Lucas got dressed. He opened the door and followed the young man down the hallway. They walked up a flight of stairs onto the deck.

Lucas didn't want to see the crowd. Not here. Not now. He wanted out. He wanted to avoid it. All of it. And just as he thought that, hope came in the form of a motorcade of three police vehicles and a limo.

"It's like we're predestined to be here," a voice behind him said in a tone as cold as the weather. "Well, me anyways." Lucas turned around to see Matthias leaning against a railing. He wore a jacket that was too short for him and a shirt that was too long.

"You think it was predestined that we survived?" Lucas asked.

"You think it was predestined that they died?"

Lucas turned to face Matthias and waited until he looked back. "I want to know why you didn't get off the plane."

Matthias saw the motorcade approaching. "We don't have much time."

"I have all the time in the world."

"Time? Time, my friend, is something this world is running out of."

"Don't avoid the question. What do you know?"

"Rhoda."

"What?"

Matthias scrunched his eyebrows, searching for the right answer. "Rhodesia?" He shook his head. That wasn't right. He looked like a student during exams who has the answer on the tip of his tongue but can't quite get it out.

"What are you doing?"

"Rhea?"

"Who?"

"This isn't a joke," Matthias said. "She'll help you. Rhoda, Rhea...." Matthias swore. "What's her name?" He shook his head one last time as a sign he was giving up. "Alright. Here they come." They saw two men step out of the limo. "I can't believe I'm here. Good God. I have to get out of this city. Goodbye, Lucas."

"Don't leave."

"Good luck in Africa." Matthias walked to the gangway.

"I won't need luck."

Matthias turned back. "Then I wish you whatever you find in that place between free will and predestination."

He walked past the two men as they came up the gangway to the deck. They saw Lucas. The first one was tall and wore a uniform. His smile was too wide to be genuine. The shorter one beside him wore a raincoat and looked serious.

"Mr. Lucas Stephens," the first one said. "Welcome to London." He produced a badge of sorts. It didn't matter. The motorcade was evidence enough. "A lot of people are waiting for you. We're here to help you."

"Help me?"

"Yes. We've arranged a security transport for you."

"What do you want?"

"Surely you don't want to leave Tilbury and face the crowd, do you?"

"You can take me to Heathrow?"

The taller man hesitated. That should have been a sign to Lucas. "Of course," he said. He nodded to his partner and they led Lucas to the bottom of the gangway.

"A limo is a little much for government, isn't it?" Lucas asked as he got in.

The taller man sat down across from him. "Nothing's too good for you."

"So we're going to Heathrow, right?"

The man looked up. "We'll be there in a moment."

The limo stopped at Heathrow. The driver opened the door. Lucas thanked him as he stepped out. There were three more trench coat types waiting for him. They gave brief hellos. Lucas followed them across the street and through an unmarked door. They walked down a tunnel to a set of security doors. One of the trench coats slipped a card through the card lock and typed in a code. The doors opened. They walked down a hallway and stepped into an elevator.

When they reached the top they walked through another security door. This one had two guards. Both in combat uniforms. Both carried automatic weapons. They reached the end of a hallway and took Lucas to a nearby room. One table. Three chairs. One on one side, two on the other.

"Have a seat," the tall one said, pointing to the single chair.

Lucas sat down. They left. He waited in the plain white room.

Moments later two people walked in. The first was a medium-build woman with a pinstripe suit and amber hair. Early forties. She carried herself well, such that it was nearly impossible to pick out that she was 20 pounds overweight. Dark lipstick. Mysterious gaze in her eyes. Hard to read how much she was hiding. Behind her entered a tall dark-haired man with a short beard, carrying a briefcase.

"Mr. Stephens," she said.

Not good. *Lucas* is fine. *Mr. Stephens* means trouble. Their cold expressions made Lucas uneasy. Lots of ulterior motives behind those eyes.

"My name is Angelica." She added her last name, but the accent was too heavy to pick out. No handshake. No smile. She just sat down. She had something more important than introductions on her mind.

"I'm trying to catch a flight to Zambia," Lucas started.

"I'm Marcus Johnson." The man cleared his throat. It was a bad attempt at pretending to pass off a legitimate cough for an excuse to buy time. He gave a forced smile. "We're with the government."

"What can I do for you?"

"We're interested in having you stay in London for a while."

"Thank you, but I'm on my way to Africa."

"Africa," he said, trying to sound interested but conveying instead that he really didn't care. "A safari?"

"No."

"Vacation?"

"The slums."

"Admirable. You have courage."

"And you have 30 seconds to tell me what I'm doing here or I'm gone. Go."

But Marcus didn't continue. He waited. All of them. In the quiet. Time ticked by. Thirty seconds' worth. And it told Lucas there was more on the table than just his trip to Africa.

"Lucas, I want to make it clear to you that we are serious about having you in London. A week. That's it. And we're prepared to compensate you."

"Compensate me?"

"For your expenses."

"You want to pay me to stay in London?"

"We want to remove any financial burden you might incur."

"And heal the sick here?"

"We would be honoured."

"I don't need your money."

"I agree. You have nine million. Plus or minus. Depending on if you include the yacht in Belmont Harbour or your house in Florida." He had done his homework. Lucas granted him that. Marcus put his briefcase on the table. He opened it. It was stacked with bills. "Nine million. Pounds, that is."

"I'm not following this." That was only partially true.

"We're inviting you here as our guest," Angelica said.

"Not interested." Lucas stood up.

"Please sit down," Angelica said in as kind and firm a voice as she could manage.

Just as they got the impression he was going to co-operate, Lucas opened the door and stormed out. Angelica and Marcus hurried to follow. Lucas ran down the hallway in the opposite direction of the guards. Marcus called out after him.

Up ahead he saw three secretaries. Each had a nameplate on her desk. Marcus shouted to one of the men in combat uniform. Lucas read the name of the one nearest him. Danielle.

He went to the next desk. Esther. He heard Marcus calling his name as he came around the corner with a soldier. He reached the last desk.

Rhonda.

That was it.

Matthias had been close.

"Number for the American Embassy?" he whispered.

She looked at him, confused—then hit a speed dial button on her phone and gave Lucas the receiver just as Angelica and Marcus came into view. "You can't just use my phone," Rhonda pretended. To Marcus: "Who is this? He just walked in here and started ringing a number."

Marcus was just within reach. He stretched out his hand to grab him.

"This is Lucas Stephens. I'm at Heathrow. I want to speak with an American Embassy representative."

Angelica and Marcus stopped.

"Could you hold the line a moment?" Lucas asked. He turned to Marcus. "Are we done?"

Marcus breathed out fire. His nostrils flared. "We welcome you back to London whenever you find the time."

Lucas put the embassy on hold, picked another line and, seeing a phone number on a promotional coffee cup on Rhonda's desk, phoned an airline. He tried to arrange a flight to Zambia, but all planes were booked. He then tried for a flight to Nigeria, but all flights were full. A child sponsorship picture on Rhonda's desk of an orphan in Kenya caught his attention. He enquired about a flight. There was one seat left. Leaving in an hour. Nairobi. Lucas booked it. He then told the American Embassy he had arrived safely in London and was leaving for Nairobi. He hung up the phone.

"Goodbye," he said to Angelica and Marcus. "And this time, leave me alone."

Lucas sat down in the massive waiting area. The gate was announced on an overhead screen 20 minutes prior to the departure time. He walked down the long corridor to his gate and boarded his plane.

He breathed a sigh of relief as it taxied down the runway. Going by plane was the safest way. What were the odds of being on two successive flights that would crash? Zilch. He could relax. He could forget about Caesar. Forget Empirico. Forget the Council. And forget Angelica and Marcus, who had just tried to buy him off. They were all gone. And he was on his way to a world far away from all of that. He assumed it would be smooth sailing from here on in.

But he should have known better.

6

Mike took the pen from the warden and signed his name on the release sheet. One night in jail felt like a thousand. He had managed to avoid any dark corners or shower encounters with other inmates. He hadn't slept. How could he? The big boss had come through. As always. Still, his nerves had been stretched past their limit.

He was about to leave when the tall, bald, strong warden stopped him.

"You and I both know why you're walking out of here."

"Because I've been cleared," Mike said, trying to sound confident but instead coming across as fearful.

"Because you have good lawyers." That was only half true. Really, it was Caesar who had good lawyers and Mike was fortunate to be in Empirico's employ. "Let me give you some advice."

"I don't need it."

"You're going to be back here. And do you know why?"

"Can I go?"

"Because you are no different from the people in here. You have more money. You have a better job. And you have more powerful friends. Other than that, you fit right in." The warden cursed at him.

"If I want to hear your opinion of how the world works, I'll ask for it," Mike replied, swearing right back at him. "May I go?"

He walked away from the warden and followed two lawyers out of the prison. A limo waited outside. The driver held the door open and the three got in. As they drove off, Mike tried to relax. Getting out of prison is normally a cause for celebration. But Mike was getting out of prison and heading to a meeting with Caesar.

Things were not improving.

Mike saw the image of the limo pulling up to Empirico in the baby-blue reflective panels. He was the first to get out. The sooner they started the meeting, the sooner they'd be done. He walked in the front door, said a quick hello to Anne, the Danish bombshell at the front, and went to the security doors. He swiped his card through and walked down a hallway watched by security cameras. When he reached the end, he swiped his card through a second time. Thatcher and Ridley used to stand here. Especially before Council meetings. The last time he had seen them was at Wrigley Field looking down the barrels of their guns at Lucas. In a chaos of confusion, Ridley fell to his death and accidentally fired his rifle at Thatcher. The result: Caesar was down two men. And had Mike pulled the trigger that day like he promised, everything would have turned out differently.

He knocked on the door and, hearing an invitation to enter, opened it.

"Caesar," Mike said as his eyes adjusted to the low light. He closed the door.

"Sit down, Mike."

Only a few days earlier he had been in this office plotting to kill Lucas. And, feeling what he felt now as he sat down in a chair opposite Caesar, he wished he had done it.

Caesar let out a puff of smoke from his cigar. His face was pale grey. His eyes were more puffy and swollen than normal. He ran his fingers over his thinning hair that was combed straight back. He looked terrible. There were rumours. Lots of rumours floating around Empirico that Caesar had a late-stage cancer and that he wasn't long for this world.

And judging by his appearance, Mike deemed those rumours to be true.

"Things didn't quite work out the way we had planned," Caesar said.

Mike had trained responses to all kinds of objections and questions about the products he sold. But he had nothing to combat Caesar. He waited as his boss continued, hoping it would give him time to formulate a reply.

"Either the gun didn't fire, or you went back on your word and chose not to shoot."

"I hear Lucas is on his way to Africa," Mike said, trying to change the subject.

"That's good."

"He could stay there."

"He could."

"He might well decide not to come back."

"But if he does come back to Chicago, or to any of our markets in the West, and continues healing people, our sales will drop. And there's no telling how much damage he can do."

"I think we're speculating," Mike said with a laugh. But it didn't go over.

"I think we're being proactive. And I think we're building a team that follows through on what they promise. What do you think, Mike? Do you think it's important to follow through on promises?"

He should have checked the corners of the room behind him when he walked in. The last time he was here he sat down and only later realized Thatcher and Ridley had been standing in either corner. It made him wonder if Caesar hadn't replaced them with other mercenaries who were now standing behind him. He wanted to turn around to see if anyone was there. He wanted to bolt and run.

"I do," Mike said.

"It's simple," Caesar said. "My instructions are without return. I will not rescind what I gave you to do. Your trial date is set a month from today. If you succeed in your task in eliminating Lucas, or convincing him to stay in nonmarket areas, I'm sure my lawyers will be able to help you. They'll find an angle. You were on the building roof for a better look at Lucas' miracles. The gun was a plant. You picked it up without thinking after the shooting to give to the cops. You were Lucas' best friend, for crying out loud. Garbage like that. They'll get you off." Mike felt a *but* coming. He shifted in his seat, trying to look calm but appearing to be every bit as scared as he was. "But if you don't," Caesar continued, "you'll go to prison."

Those words were like knives in Mike's back. It felt like someone had walked up behind him, those imaginary people standing in the corner perhaps, and stabbed him in the spine. Mike tensed his calf muscles. The room felt smaller. The walls closed in on him. He clenched his teeth. No. Absolutely not. He wasn't going to prison.

"So, Mike? What'll it be? Are you willing to carry out your mission?"

A flight attendant woke Lucas. He opened his eyes. The seats around him were empty.

"Welcome to Kenya," she said, placing a hand on his shoulder. He sat up and felt a brutal kink in his neck. She took her hand away and walked down the aisle. He wished she hadn't left.

Lucas walked off the plane onto the tarmac. He followed the flight attendant into the airport. She directed him up a set of stairs to the customs area where he joined a lineup. Other foreign passengers waited with their passports open to their visa stamps. The line wasn't moving. Lucas looked to the front. No customs officials at the six old wooden desks. No uniformed personnel anywhere. No security cameras. Lucas stepped out of line and walked through a partially open door in the smoked glass wall behind the desks. He walked down a hallway and saw a group of officials coming his way. To his right he saw an exit. One of them looked at him, wondering what he was doing. Just as he was about to say something, Lucas turned in. He saw a set of stairs that led down to the baggage claim area. Dozens of people crowded behind a roped-off area, looking for their loved ones. If anyone was looking for Lucas, it wasn't going to be difficult to spot the lone white man.

He walked down the steps to the security stations at the end. A woman wearing a green uniform nodded that it was his turn.

"No luggage?" she asked.

Lucas shook his head.

"How do you travel without any luggage?"

"I had an unexpected stop," Lucas said, hoping she wasn't going to ask for his passport.

"Your passport?"

He handed it to her. The pages were curled up from sitting inside his chest pocket in the water. She opened it and looked for the stamp from the Kenyan Consulate. His passport was full of stamps from his international travels. She flipped through the pages. She handed it back to him.

"Have a nice stay."

Lucas walked through the crowd and out of the airport. It was dark outside and hard to see the people. They looked like shadows. He could barely make out their eyes, which reflected what little light there was.

"You need a taxi? Hey, you! *Mazungu*! You need a taxi?"

Lucas turned around, trying to pinpoint the voice. He could make out teeth from a wide smile approaching.

"*Habari*!" said a young man wearing a white shirt and a pair of jeans. "You need a taxi? Right this way!" He patted Lucas on the back. "Welcome to Nairobi, my friend. I'm so glad you've come. We have been waiting for you. And we have a taxi just for you!" Lucas followed him to a small white four-door car. There was a man in the passenger seat. Lucas sat in the back.

"My name is Thomas. This is my friend Jonathan."

"Lucas."

"I am so pleased to meet you, Lucas. So pleased! Welcome, my friend! Or as we say in Swahili: *Karibu rafiki yangu*!" He laughed and started the engine.

Thomas drove out of the airport and turned onto a highway. Up ahead Lucas saw a beat-up blue school bus with items hanging off the side. He looked closer. Couldn't be. Impossible. *Are those people hanging on the side of the bus?*

"What is that?"

"What is what?"

"That?" Lucas said, pointing to the bus.

"A *matatu*."

"With people hanging on the side?"

Thomas and Jonathan laughed. "Welcome to Nairobi, my friend," Thomas said. "Where there is always room for one more!"

The taxi pulled up beside the *matatu*. Sure enough. People stood on the side of the bus, hanging onto a ledge at the top as it drove down the highway. On the other side Lucas saw a passenger van. People were packed inside. Some even sat on other people's laps. It could comfortably hold 11. Lucas lost count after 20.

"So, where are you going?" Thomas asked.

Lucas sat back in his seat. *What is it going to be like to heal people in Africa compared to America? What will it be like to be among the world's most destitute? The sick without any money. A pharmaceutical company's dream. The poorest of the poor.*

"I'm going to a slum."

The taxi went quiet.

"Where?" Thomas asked.

"The slum."

Thomas looked at Jonathan, then at Lucas in the rear-view mirror. "My friend. Have you ever been to a slum?"

"Sure. I just came from Chicago."

Thomas let out the kind of laugh that told Lucas he was trying to season his next words to avoid making them come out with too much insult.

"My friend. You are in Nairobi. I have never been to Chicago, but I can tell with absolute certainty that the slums here are much, much worse. You never go to the slums in Nairobi. Least of all not at night. You just don't. I can drive you by there tomorrow, if you like. And when I do you will reconsider. But tonight I will take you to a hotel. There you can talk to people and ask them about the slums. They will only confirm what I say. There is crime there beyond anything you know. The police don't patrol there. They can't."

Lucas nodded his head and tried to ignore the screaming voice inside him to listen to the driver. "Really?" he asked, hoping this wasn't the case.

"Really."

Lucas looked out the window to get a break from the conversation. He felt a sudden shift in what it meant for him to be here. It threatened his optimism.

"So how bad are the slums?"

7

Six hours later (and three times as many drinks) Jake was still sitting on the same stool in the same bar. It was evening. More people had come in. A woman a few seats down from him moved after Jake tried to engage her in conversation. She left a newspaper behind. Jake stood up from his seat, his legs hurting from being in the same position so long, and stumbled as he picked it up.

The tall bartender noticed and leaned forward. She spoke in a firm voice, giving Jake the indication she had done this many times before. He didn't mind. He'd heard it spoken to him numerous times too.

"What do you say? Time to call it a night?"

Jake sat down on his stool and put the newspaper on the counter. He glanced up at her and had to blink twice to get his eyes to focus. She was taller than before. And a whole lot more good-looking.

"Are you married?" Jake asked, flashing his denture smile.

She smiled back, relieved that Jake was not going to be trouble. "I don't think you're my type."

"How can you not be married? I mean, a wonderful woman like you?"

"Have a nice evening."

Jake looked down at the paper. There on the cover was Lucas. And just below him, the story on Senator Turtle and his gala event. Jake's smile faded.

"You're not driving home, are you?"

Senator Turtle. Jake shook his head. Turtle wanted to put them away. Get Lucas off the streets. Stop him from causing Empirico to lose money because of all the healings.

She leaned closer and spoke in a stern voice. Jake looked up. She didn't look so good anymore.

"I think it's time to call it a night."

"Rum?"

"Goodnight," she said.

Jake took the paper and walked out.

He picked up a bottle of vodka at a nearby store and staggered down the sidewalk, talking to no one in particular.

"It's your fault. You're the one who killed her. You put her mother into a depression. You're the reason the other sister ran away. You are a nobody. You are nothing. Nothing."

He took a long swig from his bottle and choked it down. People stepped out of the way to avoid him. Jake was oblivious to them.

He took another drink. Some of it got into his mouth. Some of it ran onto his shirt. He coughed a mouthful onto the brown paper bag as he looked at his newspaper. He pointed with his bottle and shouted at Senator Turtle's picture.

"And you!"

"Get off the street, you bum!" a man walking past him said.

Jake didn't hear him. He continued his conversation with Turtle. "You held a hearing so people would turn against us. And now you're having a fundraising dinner. A fundraising dinner! What if your guests knew what you were really up to? Would they still be supporting you? Would they still think you are such an admirable senator?"

Jake got on the "L" train. He stumbled towards the back. As it jerked forward, he lost his balance and fell to the ground. He dropped his bottle. The contents began spilling out. He cursed and picked it up. It was almost empty. People nearby stood up and walked to the front.

"Thank you," Jake said, smiling as he took one of the vacant seats.

He got off the train and threw his bottle at a garbage bin. He missed and it smashed on the ground.

Jake walked past the Palmer House Hilton to a new hotel farther down the road. He entered through the large double glass doors, read the list of events taking place on a board, and walked up a set of winding stairs to the end of a hall. He heard the muffled sound of Turtle's voice coming from a banquet room. A door opened. A woman walked out. Jake saw Turtle on the podium giving a speech. Stupid, pathetic Turtle.

What are you doing here? Just leave. Just get out.

And he was about to. About to make that obvious connection that being here was a mistake. But then Jake saw a familiar face sitting at a table near the front. It was just a glimpse. But that was enough. Ice water ran down his spine. It was him. Just sitting there. Like he had done nothing wrong. Like he was innocent of the Chicago attack on Lucas. Jake's face flushed.

It was Caesar Alexander.

Part of Jake told him to go. *Just forget this and leave.* But the other part of him, the part that seemed to grow with confidence whenever he was inebriated, told him to take on Caesar. Right now. Right here. *He tried to kill Lucas. Are you going to let that go? Are you going to let him just sit there?*

No. No, Jake was not going to let this opportunity pass.

He opened the door. Before any of the waiters could react, Jake made it past the row of tables at the back. Some of the guests noticed Jake's appearance and realized something was wrong.

Turtle saw him approaching and stopped. In that split second he recognized him from the hearings. Jake pointed his finger at Caesar, who was, up until then, oblivious to his presence. Jake hurled a slew of curses at Caesar. People nearby jolted in fear at Jake's shouting. They turned to see what was going on.

"You think you can just walk away? You think you're untouchable?" Jake screamed between bursts of obscenities. Two men on either side of Caesar stood up. Tall. Built. Suit jackets. Bulges in the inside pockets. Mitchell and Foster. Caesar's new bodyguards.

Hotel security raced in after him. He'd drill him. Just crush him right here in front of everyone. Lay him out. Kill him if he could. He had it coming.

A security guard grabbed Jake from behind. That was a mistake.

He should have waited for the other guard to come. Jake twisted at the hip and drilled his elbow into the young man's head. He snapped back unconscious and crashed against a table. Wine glasses flew up in the air. Nearby guests jumped to their feet. A woman screamed.

Caesar stood up. The others at his table left. Jake got closer, and what he saw confused him. Caesar looked awful. Just plain horrible. *How could people eat with a guy who looked like that?* His puffy eyes were so bulgy it seemed like they were going to fall out and bounce off the table. His skin was grey. Almost white. His body, frail. Where was the intimidating Caesar he had come to know?

A second and third security guard lined up Jake, ready to tackle him.

"I know what you did," Jake said in a slow, even tone, adding a barrage of expletives.

"Take this as a warning," Caesar replied. "Lucas doesn't come back. Not ever. Now get out."

Jake curled his fingers into a fist. He charged Caesar. Mitchell stepped out and clotheslined him, fitting his arm perfectly under Jake's chin. Jake flipped up and crashed to the ground. He tried to stand up but Foster punched him in the face. Jake's head cracked against the floor. He faded to black.

It was mid-morning when Lucas woke. He felt groggy. Like a bad hangover. He assumed at first it was either his 12-hour sleep at the Methodist Guest House or the effect of the time change that was sending his internal clock into confusion. That would account for his uncanny feeling of being on edge. He sat up. Worried. This wasn't right. He'd travelled before. Long distances. This wasn't exhaustion. It felt like he was being watched. Observed. Studied. An invisible person looking at him. That creature from the plane, perhaps.

He got out of bed. His feet touched the cold tile, and for a split second it brought him back to the time he was in the Chinese prison with cold cobblestone floors. He looked out the window, hoping the change in scenery would bring a change in atmosphere. Dark clouds threatened rain. In the distance, past the courtyard, he saw a myriad of trees. One of them was completely purple. Surrounded by green. It seemed strange to Lucas. Such a unique tree, so terribly out of place.

In an instant the room temperature dropped. It was as if he suddenly found himself standing on a frozen lake. He heard what he thought was a breath behind him. A long, drawn-out exhale. He felt a chill go down his back, as though someone's nails were about to dig into him. He whipped his head around, expecting to see some hideous, disfigured being behind him.

He heard the breathing sound again, but saw no one. The room looked darker, like a black mist had crept in around him. It took more effort to breathe.

He walked to the bathroom, and when he grabbed the door handle he winced in pain at the blistering hot metal. He was sure he heard the sound of searing skin. He forced himself to let go. He looked at his palm.

No burn mark. The pain left him.

That chill returned. Colder this time. More mist.

He touched the handle again. No burning sound. No aching pain. He opened the door expecting some alien to snap out its sickening mouth and bite off his head. He looked in. The beige shower curtain was drawn. He saw a shadow of someone, something, behind it. Waiting there. He looked down at the shadow's hand. An object. A club, a knife, perhaps. He looked up the tall, muscular body to the head. He heard more breathing. This time it was unmistakeable. He reached out and grabbed the curtain. He yanked it back.

Nothing.

Another breath on his neck.

He spun around. Frantic. He stepped back into the room. Claustrophobic.

"Who are you?" Lucas whispered.

No response. He backed up to his bed. His eyes shifty. His forehead sweaty. *Get a grip on yourself. Take a deep breath. Start saying some of your verses.* The room got even smaller. The ceiling pressed down on him. He was sure a noxious gas was being pumped into his room.

"Who are you?"

Still no response.

"You're not God, are you?"

He closed his eyes. How did those passages go again? He drew a blank, his mind in a dizzying fog until he remembered them. He sat down on the cold ground and began to recite them. Right from the beginning. Out loud.

He stayed that way for two hours.

Edgar drove with Tabitha beside him in the passenger seat. She checked her watch. One hour until her flight left. Into London and then to Nairobi.

"Any news on Jake?" Edgar asked. It sounded polite enough, but his mind was somewhere else.

"He was still passed out when I stopped in."

"Wasn't he supposed to go too?"

"He told Lucas he'd come to Africa. But if Caesar presses charges, Jake won't see the light of day."

Edgar nodded. He gripped the steering wheel tightly with both hands. His eyes stayed focused on the road. His head didn't move. Tabitha felt his anxiety.

"When's your appointment?" she asked.

He opened his mouth as if to respond and then closed it again. His pause caused Tabitha to regret asking. Was it better to ask or leave it alone?

"Tomorrow," he said, making Tabitha feel better. "Tomorrow afternoon."

"I'll be thinking of you."

He tilted his head in her direction. It was as close as he was going to come to thanking her.

There was silence between them for over a mile.

"Edgar, I don't know why either."

"Tabitha."

"No, I mean it. I'm trying to find something to say that will help. It isn't right. It isn't fair."

"Fair? It doesn't matter if this is fair or not. Is there a court I can complain to?"

"I guess not," she said, searching for something else to say. "Do you think God listens to you? Do you think God hears what you have to say?"

"Which airline are you with?" he asked as he drove into O'Hare.

She gave him the name, for the third time, and looked at her watch. She smiled. "At least you won't be late."

"For what?"

"It's Sunday, Edgar," she said.

"I'm not following you," he replied in a tone that showed how easy it now was for him to get irritated.

"I thought you went to services on Sunday."

"Right," he said, but didn't mean it.

He stopped at her airline. Tabitha got out.

"Need a hand?" Edgar asked.

"I'm okay."

He watched her as she picked up her backpack. She fit so good into those black jeans. She came back to the front. He saw her adventurous spirit ready to travel halfway around the world for a story. Five a.m., no makeup, and yet she looked more beautiful to him now than ever. Lucas was fortunate to have a girl like her. And the longer Edgar looked, the more it began to hit him that a woman like this, or any woman at all, might not be in the cards for him.

"I'll see you when I get back." Edgar picked up a hint of uncertainty in her comment. He nodded. She left.

As she walked into the terminal she thought about her parting words. As a point of fact, no. No, she might not be seeing him again. It all depended on when she returned.

And whether he'd still be alive then.

Reciting his verses chased away whatever was in the room with him. Lucas opened his eyes. Everything looked normal. Everything *felt* normal. He grabbed the phone and dialled the number on the card Thomas the taxi driver had given him.

"Ten minutes," Lucas said. He heard an argument on the other end. "Yes, I'm sure."

He walked down the hallway to the front desk. The attendant smiled when she saw him. Red suit jacket. Hair tied behind her. Extensions. Long extensions that crawled halfway down her back.

"Hello," she said. White earrings. Impeccable teeth.

"Hi," Lucas replied. He asked if she could send an e-mail on his behalf to *The Chicago Observer* letting Tabitha know where he was staying.

"And where are you going today?" she asked.

Those eyes. *Was she wearing contacts? How did she get them so clear?*

"I'm heading out."

"Out?" Her smile widened. "And exactly where is out?"

"I'm going to a slum."

She froze. Her smile faded. "The slum," she said, hoping she had heard wrong.

"I'm not sure which one. I'm told there are many."

"With whom?"

"Myself."

She dropped her smile altogether. Her eyes looked different.

A knock behind him. Lucas turned around. Thomas the taxi driver.

"This is a mistake," she said. "Even Kenyans do not go in alone."

Lucas pretended not to hear as he left. They walked through the security gates to his taxi.

The wind had picked up since the morning.

Jake woke up in a cell. His head hurt. He stank from the dried booze on his shirt and from his putrid body odour. He'd been here before. Waking up in a cell was nothing new. The challenge came in trying to remember how he got here. He was at their house. Right. At their house to talk about the accident. It had not gone well. He went to a bar afterwards. Tall bartender. And then? What happened after that?

His brain throbbed, making him feel his skull would crack open. He wasn't supposed to be here. He was supposed to be on a plane to Africa to support Lucas. He promised him. He promised him he would be there.

"Nice job last night," a young officer said, throwing a copy of *The Chicago Observer* into Jake's cell. He shook his head, and laughed as he walked back to his desk cluttered with burger wrappers and sports magazines.

This time it was Jake's turn to be on the front page. HEALER' S SIDEKICK IN NEED OF A MIRACLE. A security camera image showed Jake walking into the hotel. A photographer's picture showed him being taken away by the police.

"The hotel is not pressing charges," the officer said. "But Caesar? He has his lawyers all over this."

Jake dropped the paper. His face went pale. The blood drained out of his body.

"They're trying for 20 years. How does that sound?"

"Can I go to the bathroom?"

"Twenty years is a long time for a bad night."

"Can I go to the bathroom?"

The officer grunted as he got out of his chair. He unlocked Jake's cell and led him down the hall.

"Just don't get any on the floor. I kid you not. If I come back in here and see any kind of a mess...."

Jake stepped in. He heard the door close behind him. *Oh God.* He looked at the mirror. Bloodshot eyes. Worn-out face. Sweaty, straggly hair. *Bum. Worthless bum.* He shut his eyes and turned away. He butted his head against the wall. Jake wanted to go back to that meeting on the porch. He wanted to turn back the clock, avoid the bar, and just get back on the "L" train. Twelve hours. That was it. Just redo the last twelve hours.

"What were you thinking, God?" Jake asked. "What were you thinking by putting me with a guy like Lucas?"

Jake stood in front of the urinal, wondering how his friend was doing, wondering how disappointed Lucas must be by now, or if in fact he would be disappointed at all. He washed his hands and splashed cold water on his face. He spit into the sink.

"I let you down. I let you down, Lucas." He swore. "Same old, same old with me." He closed his eyes and forced himself not to pretend he could undo this. "I don't know if you can hear me, God. I don't know if what I say reaches you." He looked into the mirror. Jake ran out of words.

He reached for the handle.

When Jake opened the door he felt a tremendous blast of hot air. It burned his lungs to take it in. It was suddenly so bright that he had to squint. When his eyes adjusted he saw a blur of people hurrying past him. Crowds and crowds of black people everywhere. Some were on the sidewalk selling drinks, shirts, shoes, and hundreds of other items. Some rode bicycles. Some ran out to the cars backed up at a light to sell them bananas and soft drinks. A van crammed full of people stopped to take on still more passengers. A young boy ran up to them waving packs of gum, shouting at them to buy from him.

Sweat formed on Jake's forehead. He was sober. That much he knew. Last night he was drunk. Yes. But not today. Not now. He looked behind him and saw a sidewalk. No building. No bathroom. No mirror. No door. Just a sidewalk. He turned around, making a complete circle, and saw street vendors, cars, and streams of people crowding the sidewalk, speaking a language he had never heard.

He stretched out his hand and touched the post of the nearest shop to confirm it was real. He held his breath. He darted his eyes around, looking for something familiar.

Jake had arrived in Nairobi.

8

Lucas looked through the taxi window at the streets of Nairobi. People walking everywhere. Like some massive exodus of displaced refugees. Little kids sat at makeshift tables, helping their parents sell pineapple, drinks and candy. Their clothes were old. Their shoes worn out. Their smiles genuine.

Credence Clearwater Revival's *Fortunate Son* came on the radio. Lucas began to tap out the beat until he recognized the tune.

"Could you turn that off?" It came out sounding more like a command than a question.

"You don't like CCR?" Thomas asked as he negotiated through traffic, nearly hitting vehicles as he alternated between slamming on the brakes and drilling the accelerator.

"Can you turn it off?"

Thomas nodded and changed the station.

They came to a large market area. Small stores made of deteriorated metal cladding filled the streets. They were so shabby it looked like one good gust of wind could bowl the whole lot of them over. People haggled with owners over prices that always seemed to start twice as high as the fair market value. As the blur of cars and stores went by, Lucas saw a white man standing on the sidewalk. A lone white man in the masses—like that purple tree in the middle of green. Lucas looked closer. Just as the man disappeared from view, he thought he recognized him. Jeans. Dirty shirt. Straggly hair. Pot-belly.

Was that him?

"Stop the taxi," Lucas said.

"We are not there."

"Pull over."

Thomas slowed down in the middle lane. Traffic backed up as they came to a stop. Lucas opened the door. He was about to step out when he heard repeated honking. He looked to his right. A *matatu* raced towards him. He slammed the door just as it raced by, nearly scraping the car as it passed. The driver honked at the stupid foreigner who didn't know the simple fact that *matatus* rule the road.

Lucas opened the door against Thomas' advice. He navigated through the honking cars, then made his way through the packed sidewalk. He passed a pushy vendor who grabbed his arm and tried to interest him in a hand-carved chess set. Lucas saw a balding white head in the mix of people. A gap opened in the crowd. He had a clear line to the man. Unbelievable.

"Jake!" Lucas shouted, edging his way closer.

Jake turned around. "Lucas?"

They shook hands, then Jake grabbed Lucas and gave him a hug. He stank something fierce. Lucas breathed through his mouth to avoid coughing. Thomas honked his horn as he pulled over to the side of the road.

"A little different than Chicago," Lucas said, slapping Jake on the shoulder.

"It's different," Jake said, his eyes still wide, his mind still searching for an explanation.

"Your timing is perfect. I'm glad I found you." Lucas' expression became serious.

"What is it?"

"I'm going to the slum, Jake. They say it's dangerous—"

"I'm with you."

They got into the cab. Thomas drove off and introduced himself to Jake.

"You look tired, Jake," Lucas said. "Everything okay? Did you have a good trip over here?"

Jake nodded his head, looking outside to get a better clue of where exactly *here* was. "It was quick."

"Good connections?"

"Very good. Made excellent time coming here. Coming here to...." He stopped. The pause dragged on.

"Nairobi," Lucas said.

"Right. Of course. Nairobi. Exactly. I made good time coming here to Nairobi. Nairobi, right here in...."

"Kenya, Jake. You're in Nairobi, Kenya."

"I know that. Kenya exactly. Chicago to Nairobi, Kenya."

"You alright?"

Jake was about to respond when Thomas told them they were almost there.

The taxi turned off the main road. What was once a scene filled with makeshift shops and poor though self-sustaining people, had now turned to one of dirt and abject poverty. Plastic bags and scraps of paper littered the road. It stank so badly it brought tears to Lucas' eyes. Worse than Jake. Much worse. He covered his nose and mouth to filter what he could, thinking the odour would carry with it some debilitating disease. Children wearing torn, greasy, dark clothes walked barefoot in the ditch. Thomas pulled over to the side. Lucas opened the door.

"Stay right beside the car," Thomas warned. "Do not go any farther."

Lucas and Jake stepped out. They looked out at a sea of dilapidated huts. Thousands spread out as far as they could see, covering the landscape like crowded, brown, dirty umbrellas. They were made of metal siding, cardboard, and in some cases even plastic bags strapped together over wire mesh.

And the people looked worse.

Tired expressions. Dirty faces. Ripped-up clothes. Smoke billowed out from deep in the sea of huts.

On the other side of the street was an approach that dipped down so that Lucas had to take a few steps closer to see below. Children ran barefoot through the mud streets. Women here and there sat at the door of their huts under the hot African sun. A man stopped in front of one of them. They talked a moment. He reached inside his pocket and gave her a coin. She stood up, opened the door, and led him in. Three young girls came out. Then a fourth.

The last one was maybe two years old. One of the older girls took her by the hand and sat down where their mother had been.

To his right Lucas saw a small clearing where two men were squatting down, defecating in full view of anyone who walked by.

The street was a combination of road and sewer. Huge potholes were filled with brown water. A man dumped a pail of refuse onto the street. A group of five boys wearing oily black clothes grouped together outside a hut. They were having an argument with a teenage girl. One of them grabbed her wrist. She yanked it back, yelled something at them, and walked away down the muddy road out of sight.

"How many people live here?" Lucas asked, not taking his eyes off the world beneath him. He'd seen pictures of places like this in magazines. He'd seen those television spots showing the starving children. And if anything, those images in magazines and TV had been too kind. His head hurt. He felt claustrophobic. Panicky. *Get me out of here.* His ankles felt weak. *This isn't reality. People don't really live like this. This is a prop. A set. A movie set. That's it. A movie set. They're about to begin filming and had to create a disaster world for their film. Because people couldn't live in a place like this.*

They just couldn't.

He swallowed.

Jesus. Jesus God. The slum grew right before his eyes. Wider and deeper, much like that endless ocean he found himself in after the crash. It enveloped him. Like some black hole sucking him into their world of horror. He saw a half-naked boy, maybe a year old, walking down the street. The child bent down and stuck his tongue in the sewer water. *Jesus Christ on the cross.* Lucas wanted to look away, but his brain couldn't get the signal to his eyes. He stayed focused on the boy. Unable to shift attention. Waiting for the director to yell "Cut!"

"About a million," Thomas said. "Nobody knows for sure."

"A million?" Lucas felt his throat get drier. He wasn't sure if it was from the dusty air or if his body was reacting physically to what his soul felt emotionally.

A beat-up truck came down the road. Light blue and rusty. It turned onto the approach and made the dip down to the slum below. People moved out of the way. Some of the girls who were playing hurried inside their huts—save the four sisters waiting outside for their mother's shift to end.

The truck door opened. A huge, strong man came out. He towered over everyone else. His head was square. His shoulders broad. Scars on his arms. Sweat glistened on his body. He wore a blue-black tank top and faded black jeans. He walked to the group of boys wearing the oily clothes. People cleared a path for him.

"A drug runner," Thomas said. "They organize the street boys into gangs and arrange for them to transport drugs and commit crimes in Nairobi. Did you see how all the girls ran away when he approached?"

Lucas nodded and watched the strong man as he left the boys and entered a hut.

"They know why he's here," Thomas said. "Recruiting."

Lucas tried to swallow but his throat was so closed up that nothing went down. His fingers trembled. It felt like someone was tying cords around his chest, making it difficult for him to breathe.

"Recruiting?"

Lucas looked back at the four sisters. The door opened. The man came out and walked into the little one, knocking her over. He continued, giving no indication he knew or cared about what he had done. The four girls went back inside. The mother came out and waited for her next customer.

Farther down the road a white diesel Mercedes pulled over to the side. Lucas and Jake saw a black man wearing a white hat and wire-rimmed glasses step out. Early thirties.

"That might be his boss," Thomas said.

"A man driving a car like that is concerned about the money girls in a slum can make for him?"

"No," Thomas said. "He's here to find out which girls look really good. Then he pays their parents and takes them."

"Pays them?"

"He buys the girls from the parents. The good ones will go for a cow."

"What?"

"If they are exceptionally good-looking then perhaps two cows, but that is rare."

"Where does he take them?"

"On a one-way trip."

A young boy came up the approach carrying a bucket. He smiled at Lucas and held out his hand.

"*Habari*," the young boy said.

"He's asking you how you are," Thomas said. "If you're fine you respond by saying *mzuri*."

"*Mzuri*," Lucas replied.

His hair had a whitish-orange look to it. His teeth had deep brown stains. He stretched his hand out even farther and spoke another phrase. Lucas didn't need an interpretation. He reached in his pockets and found nothing.

"I don't have any money with me," Lucas said. He turned to Thomas and asked him for money.

"What? Give him money so that a hundred more can come after me? So that he can use the money to give to his older brothers to buy drugs? You are new to this world, my friend. Giving him money will only hurt him and those around him."

"Where are you going?" Lucas asked the boy. Thomas interpreted Lucas' comments. The boy responded.

"He's going to get water," Thomas said.

Lucas stretched out his hand, offering to take the bucket for him. The boy gave it to him and then reached up to hold Lucas' hand.

"Stop! Don't do this," Thomas said.

The boy tugged for Lucas to follow him. *What are you doing? This is stupid.* Still, Lucas felt a strange desire to follow him. He walked with the boy. Jake followed.

"I'm not waiting here," Thomas said.

The boy led them to the bank of the river at the end of the road. He held up his hands, asking for the bucket. Lucas looked away from the brown river. His stomach felt queasy as a ripped bag of garbage and human waste floated by. He turned away, convinced that if he looked any longer he would throw up. Confident that it had passed, he looked back at the river.

The *river.*

The boy reached his bucket in. Lucas bent down beside him and touched the water as the boy scooped in his family's daily requirements. The water felt cold. He imagined an army of viruses and diseases marching underneath his fingernails, up his arm, and into his body. With pickaxes and knives he felt them trying to rip away at his organs. Millions of them. Breeding exponentially in his system until it was plagued with the death of the river.

The boy stood up. He had no shoes. No shirt. Only a pair of brown shorts that looked like they were probably grey when originally bought. Or stolen. Jake carried the bucket as the three of them walked back to the taxi.

"Lucas," Thomas said. "I understand that for you this is something different and that you want to help. You are a foreigner. All foreigners—foreigners who come here—want to help. But if you want to be of assistance, you need to work through the established organizations. This place is dangerous."

"How dangerous?"

"You've never been in a slum!" His voice grew more intense. More desperate. "These people are animals. They will love you one minute and kill you the next. They don't care. They will put a knife through your throat if only to get your shoes."

"I know this is where I am supposed to be."

"No, my friend. You know this is where you are supposed to die."

Lucas felt a cool breeze on his neck. Then he heard a voice. Quiet. Still. A whisper. It almost sounded like someone, something, had called his name.

"I'm sure of it. This is where I need to be. These people have no pharmaceutical drugs. They have no Medicare. No money. Nothing."

Jake gave Lucas a nervous glance. "Lucas, I'm with you. You know that. But are you sure about this? This isn't the South Side."

"I didn't come here to turn back."

"Lucas, if we go in, there's no way to be sure that we'll come out."

"That's correct," Thomas pleaded. "If you don't listen to me, someone who knows, then listen to your friend!"

"I have the ability to heal. That's my protection. That's my guarantee. Stick close to me and we'll be fine."

"Do you have a plan?"

"I'm working on it."

"Working on it?"

Thomas tried to say something but Lucas shut him off. He took the boy by the hand.

"Lucas? Lucas, you're sure about this?"

They crossed the street and walked to the approach. Lucas stopped. He glanced back at the taxi, at Thomas' I'm-looking-at-a-dead-man expression, and then at the hundreds of people below. His pulse raced. His temperature rose. His mind asked a million questions.

Then he entered the Mathari slum.

9

Some of the youngest children had never seen white men before. They stared from the side of the road, wondering if these were in fact the rumoured *mazungus.*

When Lucas and Jake reached the bottom of the hill they felt a sudden insecurity. Suspicious faces watched them. People stopped what they were doing. Looked at them. Studied them. Evaluated them. Those eyes. Those expressions. Impossible to tell what they were thinking. Or planning.

Plus, it stank. Worse than a sewer. Worse than day-old diapers. Lucas coughed. His eyes started to water. Jake wondered if breathing the air might make him sick.

The boy let go of Lucas' hand. He took the bucket from Jake and walked to a nearby hut. Sheet metal walls. A ripped plastic tarp acted as a roof. No door. Just an opening in the front wall, half covered with a piece of carpet. The boy disappeared inside and re-emerged with some of his siblings. He had a cup in his hand. The children took turns drinking from the bucket.

Jake cursed.

The boy offered them some. Lucas shook his head. He watched as the boys gulped the water. The liquid spilled around their mouths as they guzzled it.

It bothered Lucas so much that he turned around. And when he saw what was behind him, he realized he had made a mistake in letting his guard down.

There were at least ten of them. Men. In their twenties. They formed a semicircle around Lucas and Jake.

The taxi was too far away.

"Hello," Lucas said in a tone much too quiet, and then remembered. "*Habari.*"

The one in the middle yelled in Swahili. Others joined the crowd. Jake stepped closer to Lucas. The middle one spat at them. It caught Lucas in the forehead. Jake clenched his fist. The African men were about to charge when the one at the far left shouted at them. As if by remote control, they stopped. Stood to the side. Made way for a tall muscular figure to pass through. Lucas saw the ominous being. It towered over him. It filled everything he saw.

It was the strong man.

He stepped closer and cast a shadow over Lucas, who came up to his chest. His face was so black it looked like it had been dipped in tar. He looked at Lucas with eyes that were yellow and cold. They didn't look real. Like marbles set in that stone face.

Lucas recited some of the verses he had memorized from the Book of Acts. His lips barely moved. Without any warning, the strong man reached out and clutched Lucas around the neck, creating a terrible slapping sound. He lifted him off the ground and pinned him against the metal shack. Jake put everything he had into a punch aimed at the strong man's jaw, but missed somewhat and caught him partially on the shoulder, deflecting much of the impact. The others rushed to stop him. Jake grabbed one of them by the back of the head. He yanked the man towards him and crushed their skulls together. He head-butted the strong man a second time, and was about to try again when the others wrapped their arms around Jake, who flailed and scratched without remorse.

At the strong man's command, the young boys lifted up a cup of water. He pushed his fingers into Lucas' mouth and pried open his jaw. Lucas felt a pounding in his head, his body's desperate warning signal that oxygen levels were far too low. His vision became blurred. The shouting around him faded. Then it went silent.

The strong man poured water into Lucas' mouth. He released his hold. Lucas choked and fell to the ground, spitting out the water, most of it landing back into the bucket. The strong man picked

Lucas up. This time those eyes weren't so unpredictable. There was a chill in them. Ice. Anger. The fun was over. They were trespassing. Uninvited guests. They had to pay the penalty.

The strong man squeezed harder. Lucas kicked his feet in a frantic attempt to break loose, beating them against the metal shack and making what feeble contact he could with him. He clawed into the strong man's hand. All he heard were the diminishing screams of his friend beside him. All he saw was the strong man's steady, lifeless eyes. And all he felt was his body beginning to shut down.

It was the screams of the boys beside him that served as the only reminder he had not yet left this world. At first he assumed they were shouts to convince the strong man to let go. But these were different shouts. They were shouts of amazement. Shouts of surprise.

Maji! Maji! Maji! they screamed.

The strong man let go. Lucas collapsed to the ground, wheezing. As his vision came back he saw the boys jumping to get his attention. He took short breaths, trying to regulate the thumping in his neck. The others released Jake and came to get a better look. The strong man poured some of the contents of the bucket into the cup. He tasted it and then poured a second cup. Lucas saw the water.

It was crystal clean.

The men pointed at Lucas and shouted. A woman with a bucket of river water came to see what was going on. The young boy took another cup from his hut, filled it with the new water, and offered her a drink. The others pushed to take it from her and in the struggle it fell into her bucket. When she bent down to pick it out she saw that her water had been made clean too. She poured it into the cup and took a drink.

The woman turned to the village and called to the people about what she had found. Dozens came out. Then dozens more. The woman poured some of her water into another bucket of river water and it too turned to normal. Lucas and Jake stood up. The strong man glared at them. He clenched his jaws. Squinted his eyes.

People pressed against them, crowding them to such an extent they could not move. Like a packed elevator that just keeps taking on more people.

More people came. More buckets arrived. News spread.

The crowd shifted past them, somehow forgetting them in the rush of discovering the magical water. And the moment Jake got a chance he yanked Lucas' arm and pulled him to safety. He held on and led him back down the street, refusing to let go, refusing to let Lucas come up with any more ideas.

The strong man looked back and saw them off in the distance. Lucas turned and made eye contact with him. The strong man forced his way through the crowd, struggling to catch up to them. Lucas and Jake hurried down the street, dodging oncoming people who were hurrying to catch up with the maddening crowd. Lucas glanced back and saw the strong man disappear in the throng.

He hoped he would never see him again.

Lucas and Jake crossed to the other side of the slimy street. They saw the approach to the road up ahead and the taxi in the distance. The crowd became quiet behind them.

Lucas stopped at a small hut. The walls were made of worn plywood. The front was partly closed off with a piece of cardboard. Some of it had slid down, allowing Lucas to look in.

"What are you doing?" Jake asked. "He's coming up behind us!"

Lucas stepped closer. A young girl sat crouched by herself in the corner. When she saw Lucas she pushed farther out of sight, hoping that perhaps the man at the entrance had not seen her.

"Are you alright?" Lucas asked. The sun set behind them. It was unlike anything they had encountered in the West. Within seconds it was dark. Black. Pitch black.

She studied them with eyes that became harder to find in the evening sky that had managed to absorb all the light.

"What?" she asked.

"You look hurt."

"What do you want?"

"I want to help you."

She wore a Strawberry Shortcake T-shirt. Her black hair was tied behind her. Maybe 12 years old.

"Go away," she said in a way that revealed to Lucas she was in pain. She brought her knees under her chin and folded her arms around her legs.

"We're leaving. Right now," Jake said. That painful grab in his arms again.

Lucas watched her suffer. He was sure he heard her begin to cry. As they stepped back she blended in with the black night and disappeared.

They walked through an opening in the huts and up to the road. They got in the taxi. Thomas started the engine. He and Jonathan shook their heads as they drove off.

"The two of you should be in Las Vegas," Thomas said. "With surviving odds like that you would do well in the gambling business."

The taxi dropped them off on Methodist Avenue. They waited for the guard to open the gate. They walked down the steps, into the lobby, registered Jake at the front desk, and went down the hall to their bedrooms.

Jake hadn't said anything the whole ride back, astounded they had not died in the slum. But in the safety of the hotel he pushed himself to voice the truth of their stupidity.

"Lucas, this is crazy," he said, rubbing his hands over his face and through his hair. "We can leave now. You can say you've been to Africa."

"I didn't come here to clean water. Those people have illnesses."

Jake shook his head. "Why *are* you here, Lucas?"

Lucas looked at his friend's exhausted face and shared the relief they were even able to have this conversation after what happened that day.

"Tomorrow they'll welcome us with open arms."

"You don't know that."

"Jake. I need to help those people."

"This isn't right," Jake said, walking into his room. "I hope tomorrow never comes."

Lucas stood in the empty hallway. His mind raced through the events of the day and how things could have unfolded. Unable to clear them, he walked out the back and came to a secluded garden.

Jake was right. He was absolutely right. The slums. What was he thinking? He could go back. Back to Chicago. But there would be no guarantee of safety there either.

He had no guarantees regardless.

Lucas looked at the stars. They filled the night canopy like millions of holes poked into a protective glass around the earth. There were far more here than he had ever seen on the clearest night back home in Chicago. *Is this the right choice? Can I run from Caesar forever? Will I have to face him again?* His mind began to swirl, wondering what to do next. And he would have remained locked in that stalemate had someone not broken him out of it.

"What are you wishing for?" an unmistakable voice behind him asked.

His body relaxed in an instant. It was as if the sound of her words injected a calming presence into his bloodstream to dispel all of his anxiety. The slum disappeared. The worrying disappeared. So did the strong man, the poverty, the wondering about the future. It was all gone. Just like that. In an instant. Vanished. How was it possible that a woman's presence could set the world right so easily?

He turned around and saw her. It flooded him with more than he could handle. Hearing her voice on the phone would have been enough. But seeing her in person, standing in front of him, no figment of his imagination, really there, really with him, brought him more than a man could ask for.

It was Tabitha Samos.

Lucas felt a surge within him. He assumed it was the jet lag. Definitely. The jet lag. Plus it had been a long day. Lots of new sights. Different places. Different people. Different language. Nearly getting killed by a mob. The stress of the culture shock. That was it. Seeing all those impoverished people and realizing first-hand how terrifying poverty can be. Any of those reasons would explain why he started tearing up when he saw her.

Perfect black hair that blew gently in the wind. Faded blue jean jacket with a few cool rips in it to show she was both classy and real. Those eyes. Those unchanging brown eyes. They looked at him with such sincerity.

Yeah. Jet lag. Must have been.

"Tabitha," was all he could manage.

"You're looking up at those stars with a lot of intensity, Lucas. Makes me wonder if you're searching for some kind of an answer."

He *had* been searching for an answer. It had arrived. And now it was standing right in front of him.

He walked towards her, not saying anything. Not being able to. They became nervous as he entered that critical one-foot-away zone, and wondered if things would be the same between them here in Africa as they were back home. He held her in his arms and felt the relief a man feels when he's with a woman he can confide in.

Her soft cheek against his. Her breath against his ear. The faint, relaxing smell of perfume. He absorbed her. Her spunk. Her laughter. Her tenaciousness.

Her passion.

They pulled away and held each other around their waists. As she studied his eyes she saw the fear begin to show. She'd seen this before. When they were talking in Chicago. Before the shooting started. Thinking back on it now, she recognized this look.

"What's wrong?"

Nothing. Nothing's wrong. Everything's fine. How could anything be wrong with you being here?

"Nothing."

That hurt the moment it came out of his mouth. *A lie. I just lied. I just finished lying to the woman I—*

"Lucas," she said, looking at him in a way that conveyed she wasn't interested in being protected from whatever was bothering him.

"This isn't Chicago, Tabitha."

"That's a good thing, Lucas. Because it can't be worse for you here than it was there."

"This is different."

"It is?"

He felt the curve of her hips in his hands, and tried hard not to imagine what it would be like to be standing here alone. "How are things back home?"

Tabitha wiped a strand of hair from her face. She moved to stand beside him and looked up at those stars, amazed at how many there were. "Caesar's casino is opening next month."

"How is Caesar?"

"He had a run-in with Jake. Tried to attack him during a gala event. Caused quite a scene."

"Jake never mentioned anything. I'll have to ask him about it tomorrow."

"Jake's here?"

"Took the express."

"Express?"

"From Chicago to Nairobi."

"There's no direct flight."

"There is now."

"He's not here, is he?"

"Get this. Are you ready?"

"Ready."

"Jake comes out of his cell and goes to the bathroom at the end of the hall. When he comes out, he finds himself here in Nairobi."

"Lucas," she said, not amused.

"Ask him yourself."

"I don't have to ask him," she replied, trying hard not to be annoyed. "If you say it, I believe you. It's just that I…I don't believe it. I *can't* believe it." She took a step back from him and wondered if coming here was such a good idea.

"Tabitha, I can't explain what's going on."

"Try."

"I turned dirty water from a river at a slum into crystal clear water."

"Impossible."

"Exactly," he said, reaching out to her. But she pulled away.

"Try harder."

"There's no proof. We didn't get the water tested. But it changed colour. That much we know."

Tabitha walked away from him and stood near a patch of flowers. She ran her hands through her hair. "Lucas. I don't understand this."

"This isn't about understanding."

"Surviving a plane crash?" she said. Now it was her turn to tear up. She recalled what it was like to get that phone call. To feel the panic. She turned back, hoping he didn't notice. But he did. And he waited until the mood changed.

"How's Edgar?" he asked.

"Not good."

"I have to see him."

"Then come back to Chicago. Edgar doesn't know how much time he has," Tabitha said. "Neither does Caesar."

"What?" Lucas asked, stepping closer to her. "Caesar's dying?"

"That's the rumour. It's obvious when you look at him, but he denies it." She turned to face him. "There are other rumours at Empirico too."

"Like what?"

She was afraid of this. She was afraid of testing this subject.

"Lucas, I...." She struggled for the right words. "Between you and me, Empirico may be involved in price collusion—"

"No kidding."

"Or industrial espionage."

"That's a given, Tab."

She became serious. Her eyes steady. Her mind focused. That strand of hair fell back over her face, but it didn't bother her this time. "Or willfully holding back pharmaceutical drugs from the market."

"Willfully holding back?"

"Does Empirico have a cure for a major disease that they are purposefully not releasing?"

They were quiet a moment, each one trying to evaluate what the other was saying.

And implying.

"Empirico is a big company."

"Lucas, they're just rumours."

"Then I'll have to see him again."

"Caesar?"

"Yes."

"He wants you dead."

"But if I don't get to him, he might die with incredible secrets."

"What kind of secrets?"

"Tabitha, I can't get into it."

"Because you don't trust me?"

"Of course I trust you."

"Then what kind of secrets?"

"Tabitha, please."

"Lucas, how can you go back there? How can you leave all these people here who need your help to go back and die at the hands of a power hungry maniac?"

"How do I stay here and not go to Asia, South America or the Middle East? They all need help."

"You think confronting Caesar is worth more than helping thousands of people who have no access to health care?"

"I have to go."

"Why? Why do you have to go?"

"In spite of all the people who need me, I have to know if the rumours are true."

She felt a sudden jolt of panic rush through her body. She glanced back up at the stars. "Then you must be right," she whispered.

"About what?"

"That Caesar has secrets more powerful than we can imagine."

10

When Lucas woke up he felt the remnant of his vivid dream fading away from him. Which was just as well. Those dumb irritating dreams about nothing that linger on, making you wonder what your mind was trying to tell you. All he saw was a rock face. Flat and perfect for climbing. Stretching as high as he could see. Only Lucas had no gear. And there was no one around. Just him and a rock. That's when he woke up.

He knocked on Jake's door at 6 a.m. It took a second knock before it opened. Jake looked horrible. Pale face. Exhausted eyes. Mouth open.

"Jake?" Lucas asked, coming into the room.

"I have a bad feeling about this."

"That's why we're here to pray, Jake. To get rid of those feelings."

"I've been praying all night."

"It should have helped."

"It made it worse."

Lucas sat down on one of the two beds—neither of which had been slept in. Jake sat down across from him. A zombie. Ready to keel over and pass out from exhaustion. Lucas tried to calm himself about Jake's warning. About his supposed premonition.

"I thought this was the right place, but we're wrong," Jake said.

"We're not wrong. How could we be? Look how you got here."

"Then why am I not convinced about this?"

"We have to go out there and heal orphans. That's what we're doing here."

"You're not in the right place. We both know it."

"I am dead centre of where I'm supposed to be."

"I don't know what's worse. Lying to yourself or lying to your friend."

"That's not fair."

"It's the truth."

"Then where?"

Lucas let out a breath, trying his best to remain focused. And optimistic.

"You ever think about going back to Caesar?" Jake asked.

Lucas pursed his lips. He felt a rush of blood rip through him. It surprised him how angry he was getting over the mention of Caesar Alexander.

"There are children dying, and I'm here to help them."

"You can avoid him as long as you want. Stay here. Go any place he's not."

"Forget Caesar," Lucas said.

"You think you can face him?"

Lucas wanted this to go away. He wanted Empirico to go away. But like he had known before, no matter where he went, all roads seems to lead to Caesar. "Knowing that I have the healing gift, I would say that I could."

"What difference would it make if you had it or not?"

"It's leverage."

"Against what?" Jake asked. "It's not leverage. It's a liability."

"I have this gift and I can use it to change him."

Jake exhaled in way that told Lucas he didn't believe him. "Change him? Caesar? You think you can change him?"

"He's attracted to power."

"No, Lucas. Caesar is afraid of power. That's why he craves it."

Lucas rested his elbows on his knees. Was a drink this early in the morning a bad thing? That's what he needed. Just one drink. He stayed quiet a while, hoping the silence would help them change the subject.

They prayed for three hours straight. Sometimes taking turns. Sometimes not saying anything, just kneeling or standing there in the silence. Praying for strength. Praying for direction.

Praying for the power to heal the sick.

They met Tabitha in the lobby. She wore a grey tank top under an unbuttoned brown shirt that hung loose around her, and a pair of beige walking shorts that were short enough to reveal her toned thighs and tanned legs. She picked up her camera bag and searched Lucas' eyes until she found that connected feeling.

They exchanged greetings. Neither commented on the nervousness gripping them. They met Thomas and Jonathan at the taxi. After a brief argument, Lucas convinced them to return to the same spot as yesterday.

They arrived outside the Mathari slum. The children looked more desperate. The huts shabbier. The slum bigger. Perhaps it was just the blistering sun that made things look worse than they were. Or perhaps it was the trio's emotional defences being worn farther down, allowing them to see more of the suffering in the slum. When they opened the doors they were met with a blast of heat, like walking into a sauna. It burned their lungs.

Tabitha looked down at the deplorable conditions below. Teetering shacks. Row after row as far as she could see. Sewage running down the street. Children walking around with only a pair of shorts and some with a shirt. Muddy feet. Dirty hands. Some of them with discoloured hair. *This is a news story,* her subconscious tried to say. *It's not real. Just a story. You're here to capture images. To capture the conditions. An assignment. Get the story. Get the pictures. Get the facts. And then get out. That's all this is.*

It was all she could tell herself to keep from collapsing.

"You alright?" Lucas asked.

"I'm fine. Ready to go?" She put on a safari hat to protect her head from the scorching heat. Lucas wore a cap, Jake a bandana. "So what's the plan?" Tabitha asked.

"We go down there and start."

"Start where?"

Lucas and Jake walked to the approach, ignoring Thomas'

indictment that they were heading to a death sentence. Tabitha grabbed her camera bag and hurried to catch up.

"You just walk in there? Just like this?"

They reached the bottom of the hill. One of the children recognized Lucas from the day before and ran off repeating *maji* as loud as he could. Clouds passed in front of the sun. It went from bright sunshine to heavily overcast in an instant. The wind picked up.

Lucas turned left at a corner and walked down a narrow alley. The huts looked even worse here. Built from combinations of plywood and plastic. It was like they had walked off the slum equivalent of 5th Avenue to the slum equivalent of a ghetto.

"Lucas, where are you going?" Tabitha asked, feeling the claustrophobia of being in a slum. She dodged back and forth, trying to avoid putting her feet in potholes filled with rusty brown water. And the smell. It gave her a headache. Rancid odour. No relief.

Lucas turned another corner. More small children on the muddy narrow road. Some with swollen bellies. Women here and there waited at the doorway of their huts, making their used bodies look as good as they could, trying hard to compete with each other for the male traffic.

Tabitha wanted out. Right now. It was too much. Way too much. Too fast. Too soon. Too intense. Too poor. Too real. She should have taken pictures from the taxi for the day. Get acclimatized to it. Get a feeling for poverty into her blood before being implanted right in the middle of it. Then come back tomorrow and spend an hour max with them. From a safe distance. Gradually increase. But not like this. Not now. She wanted to go back. And she would have.

If she thought she could find her way back through the maze.

Another turn. A baby screamed in one hut. Children screamed in another. The trio heard the smacking sound of hand against skin. A woman shouted. Something crashed against a door. More screaming. Lots of crying.

In the distance they saw a hut with a black shirt hanging on a line.

"That's it," Lucas said, not stopping.

"That's what?" Tabitha asked.

It was impossible to avoid a large puddle of brown guck. Lucas seemed to step through it without noticing. Jake was right behind. Tabitha tried to jump it but didn't make it. It splashed on her legs.

Lucas knocked on the door. There was a pause before he heard a muffled response. Lucas opened it.

"Hello?" Lucas said in a soft voice. His eyes adjusted to the light. He could make out shadows in the room. Smoke filled the hut. Someone was trying to cook. In the corner he saw a woman. Sitting down. Rocking something. He looked closer. A pile of skin and bones. He entered.

He blinked to get the smoke out. The woman watched him with a curious expression on her face, one that had grown accustomed to tragedy and learned to accept, and expect, the worst life had to offer. He knelt down. To his right he saw two children lying on the ground. Shallow breathing. No other movement. Either they were taking a nap.

Or they were dying.

The child in her arms was still breathing. Boy or girl—he wasn't able to tell. He could see each rib. The head seemed strangely oversized for such a pathetic body.

"*Habari*," he said.

The mother stared at Lucas with hollow eyes. Her expression did not change. She made no reply.

"Do you speak English?"

No answer.

"My name is Lucas Stephens and I've come to pray for your family to be healed," he said.

The smoke was brutal. It billowed around the room. Tabitha coughed. Jake had spent enough time in smoked-out places not to care.

"Do you have a husband?"

She shook her head.

"Could I pray for your children? That they could be healed?"

Again, no answer. She assumed that someone who could heal a dying child, or at least thought they could, needed no permission to step in.

Lucas closed his eyes. He placed a hand on the bony child's chest. It breathed in staggered intervals, as though it were suffocating right in front of him. Sticks for limbs. The child screamed in pain. Some vicious disease ripping through its system. That army hard at work, tearing away what little remained of this frail, dying body. He recited his verses to himself. Jake could barely hear. Tabitha took a picture in the haze.

Lucas felt his hand heat up like a stove element. Hotter and hotter until it was nearly too much. He didn't notice the smoke anymore. He rested his hand on the child's chest. The room became quiet.

A cough broke the stillness.

Lucas opened his eyes. The child coughed again. It tried to sit up. The mother came out of her trance-like state. She helped her child. It blinked. It swallowed. It reached out to touch Lucas.

He held out his pointer finger. The child grabbed it. It squeezed.

They made eye contact.

The mother called her other two children. One rolled her head towards Lucas. He knelt closer and got a better look. Twins. Maybe four years old. Their eyes were yellow and surrounded with a white crust. Their hair was rusty brown. Snot ran from their noses. Lucas stretched his hands onto their foreheads. Cold. Freezing cold. Clammy and sweaty. The fire burned through his arms and into his fingers. He prayed and recited his verses. Their foreheads became warm. One of them took a deep breath. They sat up. Their hair was still rusty, the white crusts still there. But their eyes were clear. Crystal clear. They stood up, re-energized, and said something to their mother. She grabbed their arms to check if what she was seeing were true. Smiles came to their faces, entirely different children. They hugged their mother. They hugged Lucas. They hugged their little baby sister. Then they hurried out of the hut and ran down the street, shouting.

The mother clutched her child. She nodded her head at Lucas and raised her eyebrows in acknowledgement of what he had done. No tears, though. Not here. Not in the slum. She had to learn to turn those off years ago. She pointed up.

"God healed your family," Lucas said.

She reached out and held his arm. She grabbed so tight. That feeble hand hung onto him with such force it scared him to think she might snap his arm. She nodded her head.

"You're welcome," Lucas said.

Tabitha wiped sweat from her forehead. Just as she turned around, the plywood door opened. They all looked back.

A young woman. Blonde hair. Grey and maroon striped golf shirt. Early twenties. She held two test tubes in her right hand.

"Lucas Stephens." She was out of breath. "You're Lucas Stephens." They stepped out of the smoky hut. The twins stood at her side. "I can't believe it," she said.

"Believe what?" Lucas asked.

"I have to confirm something. Can you come with me?"

Lucas looked at Tabitha and Jake, then back at the young woman. He nodded and they walked away from the hut. The black shirt hanging on the line fell down and landed in a puddle.

She led them through the slum, turning right and left down pathways with the precision only someone who had been there a long time could have. The trio lost their orientation as to where the main road was. The blonde-haired woman greeted the children with a quick *Habari* as she walked faster and faster. The two children shouted and banged on doors as they went through the slum.

They turned one final corner and came to a metal-sided shack with a yellow door. She opened it and led them in.

She reached up to a cabinet and pulled out a test tube. A child lay on a nearby bed.

"This is impossible," she said. "Impossible."

"Who are you?"

"Brittany Walker," she said, not turning around. "I'm a doctor working here on a relief project." Two other workers, both of them strong black males, came from the back.

The trio introduced themselves.

"Why are we here?" Lucas asked.

"This boy has AIDS," Brittany said, pointing to the child on the bed. "You pray for people, right? I've seen you on TV. You pray for kids to be healed and they miraculously recover." She produced a small test tube with a clear liquid inside. "This is the new instant HIV/AIDS test. Are you familiar with it?"

Lucas knew of it. Tabitha and Jake did not.

"You take a drop of blood." She spoke softly to the boy in Swahili, then stuck a needle in his arm and drew a blood sample. "You put it in this solution." She squeezed out a couple drops. "And you mix it." She placed a stopper in it and shook it back it forth. "Then you wait 15 seconds." She held it up to her face and counted out loud to 15. "If it turns green, your patient has the virus. If it stays clear...." But it didn't. It went green. Dark, mossy green. She brought the test tube down. She looked at Lucas. "I want you to pray for this boy."

"Is this an experiment?"

"Can you pray for him? Yes or no?"

Lucas turned his hands palm up to indicate he was willing. Tabitha took a picture of the green solution. Then she took more pictures as Lucas knelt down and prayed for the boy.

He laid his hands on the boy's neck and said his verses. His hands flared up. Hotter than before. Almost to the point of hurting. The boy took in a shallow breath. He felt no pain so he took in a deeper breath.

Brittany took another blood sample. She placed it in a new tube and shook it while counting out loud again to 15. Jake stepped closer. Tabitha put her camera down. Brittany looked at her watch and the test tube.

Fifteen seconds went by.

The solution stayed clear.

11

The twins ran out of the medical centre, shouting like the young boys did when the dirty water was made clean. Tabitha took pictures of the clear liquid. Brittany stared at the test tube, continuing to count out loud. Thirty seconds went by. She shook her head. Then a minute. Still nothing.

"Do you have any idea what this means?" she said in a whisper. She squinted, then gasped as she tried to understand how this was possible. "Children being healed of AIDS." She looked at him. She was getting an idea.

"We'll set up for you. Right here. You and I. We'll work together. Side by side."

Tabitha took exception.

"Your friends can help," she continued.

Tabitha felt no solace.

"Wait," Lucas said, feeling the pressure of committal.

"We can move you around. To the different slums." She glanced back at the test tube, trying hard to trust her eyes. "Do you have any idea how many we can save?"

Knock at the door. Lucas stood up. Somehow he already knew what was waiting on the other side. He opened it. The others turned to look.

Hundreds crowded the area. Parents bringing their half-naked children. Mothers holding babies. Siblings with their younger brothers and sisters. Lucas saw people packed all the way down the alley.

Desperate faces crammed together for a better look. Some shouted one thing. Some another. They pressed up against him. Mothers pushed their starving, diseased, and dying children at him. A group of small children crouched down on their knees and crawled their way through people's legs to get to the front of the line, where they reached out with their tiny bony fingers for a chance to touch him.

And when Lucas felt those small hands on his legs, begging for him to notice them, he began to cry. He hated losing control like this. *Get a grip. Get a hold of yourself.* But there was no use. Not with those dying hands at his feet. The tears mixed with the dust and stung his eyes such that he had to blink to get them to stop hurting.

That's when things got worse.

His body began to shake. He twitched sporadically.

"Boss?" Jake asked.

"Help me," Lucas pleaded. His eyes took in the sea of desperation in front of him. His brain begged him to turn away.

Brittany shut the door. "He's going into shock."

Lucas sat down on the ground. He lifted his knees under his chin. He pressed the heels of his hands against his temples and held his breath in an attempt to keep whatever was left of him together. His body trembled. He managed to inhale through his nose, trying to calm himself down. But it did nothing to help. *What's happening to me?* He clenched his teeth together. *Christ Almighty. All those people. All those people.*

"It's alright, boss," Jake said, sitting down next to him. Brittany rummaged through the medical cabinets. Whatever she was looking for wasn't there.

Jesus. Those children. Why are they dying?

Tabitha tried to talk to him. But even her unique ability to reach him when no one else could was to no avail. Lucas buried his head in his hands and tried to recite his verses. He was unable to hear anyone. Unable to feel their presence.

Unable to control himself.

An hour later he lifted his head. Tabitha's exhausted eyes showed relief. Brittany placed a fourth towel around his neck—the previous three lay soaking wet in a pile beside him.

"Boss?" Jake asked.

Lucas stood up. His legs felt weak from sitting so long. He went to the window. Hundreds had gathered around the medical shelter. How they managed to jam together so tight Lucas didn't know. It almost seemed like practice for when (if) these people made it out of the slum and had to ride those *matatus*.

"Have them come through one group at a time," Lucas said. "Keep the groups small."

"What?" Tabitha shouted. "You're not well, Lucas. We have to go." She turned to Brittany for support, thinking that perhaps a doctor's opinion might carry more weight in this situation than a friend's. But Brittany said nothing, torn between the welfare of the masses outside and the person able to deliver it.

Jake nodded his head without looking back. He let in the first group—four six-year-old boys. Brittany pulled them up and sat them on the bed.

One of the boys explained that they too had AIDS. One of them also had typhoid. Another malaria.

"I'm here to pray for God to heal you." The crowd continued shouting. "Do you know who God is?"

They nodded their heads and explained that God lived in buildings where the rich people with cars went on Sundays.

Their breathing was heavy—their expressions tired. They looked like they were about to fall over.

Lucas spread his hands over them and touched their chests. He recited his verses and felt a burning power zip through him into the boys. It was as if a defibrillator jolted their little bodies. Tabitha would have dropped her camera had she not had the neck strap on.

The boys were about to jump off the bed when Brittany made them stop. She brought those familiar test tubes, took samples of their blood, and mixed them in.

"They're fine. Just let them go," Tabitha said.

"They have to be tested," Brittany said. "It's part of what I have to do. We have to have a record. We have to...." she caught herself but continued. "We have to be sure."

She waited 30 seconds. No discolouration.

Group after group came to see Lucas, being afflicted with a myriad of illnesses including AIDS, malaria, typhoid, tuberculosis, eye problems and hearing deficiencies. And they were all healed.

In an unexpected move Lucas walked outside to the crowd. Before Jake could stop him Lucas made it into the throng of people. Children wrapped their arms around his legs, clutching him the way a drowning swimmer clutches a life preserver. People clawed over each other to touch him. They grabbed his body and pulled and pushed him in all directions. The crowd pressed against him to such a degree they nearly crushed him.

Lucas leaned his head back and looked up to the sky. Bright blue. Bright sun. He lifted his hands and took in a deep breath amid the confusion. Everything felt warm. As though a massive invisible blanket had enveloped them.

The world went quiet.

It was coming.

A burst of energy shot out from him. A concentric circle, like a ripple forming when a rock is thrown in a lake, pulsed through the crowd. All those within shouting distance of him were instantly healed.

He waited for a second one. Nothing came. Those that were healed made room for the others to come.

News that Lucas Stephens was in Mathari spread throughout the slum. Then it spread throughout Nairobi. A reporter heard of it and aired the story on the radio. A taxi driver heard the news and called his wife who worked the dispatch to tell her he was coming to bring her to the healer to rid her of her infections. She in turn called another driver whose daughter had been diagnosed with a blood disorder.

A businessman skipped a critical coffee bean export meeting to take his daughter out of private school in the hopes of healing her from chronic hair loss. An engineer overseeing a concrete pour left his crew to find his son in the hopes of freeing him from stabbing pains in his neck.

From all over Nairobi, lawyers, doctors, teachers, the rich, the educated, politicians, and the elite raced to their cars and hurried to the packed streets around Mathari, begging for a chance to get into the slum.

A university student about to write an exam heard the news just as she was entering the classroom. She left the campus and hurried to be healed of her migraine headaches.

A bus driver heard while taking passengers on a route. He stopped the bus, got off, left his passengers stranded, and ran down the road to Mathari to finally get a cure for his diabetes.

A mother in a grocery store was about to pay for her items when she heard the radio. She left everything, took her baby born with a rare inability to smile, and ran to her car.

Lucas laid hands on people for hours, curing them of their illnesses. When evening had come, thousands had been healed. They had walked in on death's door and had walked out healed.

At sunset Lucas sat down on a bed in the small medical centre.

"This isn't a safe place for you at night," Brittany said.

"I agree. It's time to go," Tabitha said.

"Can you come back tomorrow?"

"I think so," Lucas said.

"You think so?" Brittany replied, a tone of surprise and anger in her voice. "What's there to be uncertain about?"

"We'll be back."

"You're sure?"

"Yes."

"Tomorrow?"

"I give you my word."

Tabitha put her arm around Lucas and helped him up. "Until tomorrow."

"You can go out the back," Brittany said. "The road is right up ahead. If you stay on it, you'll be safe." She opened a door that led up to the street. "Thank you, Lucas." She put her hand on his arm. "This was incredible."

Lucas stopped. Tabitha let go of him.

"It was a day worth living," he said.

Tabitha and Jake walked outside. Lucas followed.

The cool evening air was a welcome change to the hot day. Lucas was about to follow Tabitha and Jake when a young girl standing by herself behind a hut caught his attention. Lucas looked back at them as they passed over a ridge onto the road.

"*Habari*," he said.

She turned her head. He recognized the Strawberry Shortcake figure on her T-shirt. He took slow steps towards her. As he came closer he saw she had her arms folded in front of her, as though she had the flu or had been punched in the stomach. Her hair was dishevelled. Her cheek was swollen. A dark black spot.

"Are you alright?" Lucas asked.

She tensed her muscles and jerked her head to the side as if bracing herself for a hit.

"I'm not here to hurt you. We met yesterday. In the hut. Do you remember?"

She was upset, but not crying. No tears. Not now. Not ever.

"What can I do to help you?" Lucas asked as he stood next to her. It was here, in somewhat better light, that he recognized she wasn't holding her arms around her stomach. She was holding lower down, as if to protect herself. She bent over slightly, pushed her back against the hut, and slid down to the ground where she sat in obvious pain. Her face got colder. Tougher. She struggled between wanting his help and wanting to be rid of him.

He sat down beside her on the muddy ground, looking out at the garbage on the hill, smelling the stench.

"I didn't see you today," Lucas said.

"She doesn't understand much English, Lucas," came a voice behind him. He turned to see Brittany approaching. A tired yet compassionate look on her face. She sat down on the other side of the girl. The two *mazungus* acted as shields for her. Offering her protection. Offering her a place of refuge.

At least for the time being.

Brittany turned to the girl and translated Lucas' comment. The girl swallowed. Cautious. Then she replied in a quiet voice. Brittany leaned closer to hear her.

"There were too many people," Brittany said.

"I would have taken you had I seen you there."

Brittany translated, waited for the girl to respond, then spoke to Lucas without taking her attention off her. "That wouldn't be fair to the others who got there first, would it?"

"I saw you yesterday at a different hut farther away. But tonight you're all the way over here."

The girl brought her knees closer to her chest. "I move around." She touched her face to see if the swelling was going down. It wasn't. Worse if anything.

"Are you hurt?"

She glanced at him. Her eyes had the chill that comes to people who have learned to shut off their emotions.

"At least they pay," she said, pretending nothing was wrong. "This one did, anyways."

Lucas didn't need the translation. The look in her eyes was enough. Her words thrust into him like a sword. He tensed his shoulders and felt the anguish of wondering if he could handle hearing more of her story.

"Do your parents know where you are?"

She shrugged her shoulders.

"Do you have parents?" Lucas asked. "Do they look after you?"

She shrugged her shoulders again. "Sure. They look after me. They send me to do this. If I bring home money I can sleep in their house." *House.* That word didn't sound right to Lucas given their diametrically opposite interpretations of the words *house* and *hut.* "If I don't bring them money I can't sleep in their house. Then I have to walk the slums at night. Do you know what happens then? Do you know what happens to girls who walk the slums at night?" He didn't want to hear it. Not any part. He avoided eye contact, hoping she wouldn't say anything more, hoping Brittany would stop translating. "It's motivation, you know. When you realize they will close the door on you, forcing you to walk around half-naked—you find ways to make your money."

"Do you make enough each day?"

"It depends."

"On?"

"On how many there are and...."

"And?" Lucas asked, already cringing at the answer.

"And what they want me to do."

Lucas closed his eyes in a desperate attempt to shut out the words he had just heard. He wanted to put his arm around her. He wanted to take her back to the hotel. Give her a room to herself where she could sleep without fear of danger. Let her take a shower—maybe the first shower she'd ever had in her life—and get cleaned up. Take her to a movie with some other kids. Or hang out at the mall. Eat hamburgers and pizza. Watch her giggle as she drank pop through a straw. See her reaction when she comes across a shirt she really wants to have. Let her be a kid again—if she's ever been a kid before. Help her to—

"How old are you?" Lucas asked.

She wiped her nose. Still no tears. She'd been through all of this before. And she'd go through it again. Tears would not help. Without ever hearing it, she knew the message of the song *Tears Are Not Enough.* That was true. Tears were not enough to bring any meaningful change into her life.

Tears were nothing.

"I'm twelve."

Jesus Christ on the cross. Twelve? Did Brittany hear that right? Twelve years old? His arms felt weak. It was as if someone was pumping poison through his veins.

"Twelve?"

"And you?"

Lucas looked at her slender body. Her bruising face. That damaged look in her eyes. Scotty. That's who he needed. Scotty from Star Trek. Two to beam up. Two to beam far, far away from here.

"I'm twenty-five."

"Do you have parents?"

Lucas wanted to avoid the question. *Just lie. Just say anything.* He felt a sudden insecurity, then fought the futility of his worrying. *What difference would it make to have a girl in the slum and a doctor know? How could their knowledge of my parents possibly affect me?* But the longer he thought about it, the more he realized the problem was not in having them know, but in finding the courage to say it.

"Would you believe me if I told you I don't know?"

She studied him and used her twelve long years of experience in determining if someone was lying or not. "If you tell me that is the way it is, I will believe you."

Those eyes. Those unbelievable eyes. What she said hit him right in that part of a man that decides whether or not he will trust a person. Sometimes the most profound things happen in the most unusual places. And for Lucas, it was hearing those words in Mathari. *If you tell me that is the way it is, I will believe you.*

"My name is Lucas," he said. "What's yours?"

She didn't look at him. She just stared ahead at the garbage covered embankment. Her future. She shrugged her shoulders. "My name doesn't matter."

"It matters to me."

"How could it, possibly?"

"Because you are important."

"Important." She shook her head again. He wasn't getting it. "To who, *mazungu*? Who am I important to?" She raised her eyebrows without making eye contact. "To my parents? Am I important to them? How about to the men who give me money? Sure. I must be important to them. For a few minutes. Who, *mazungu*? Who am I important to?"

Her eyes carried inside them a weight too great for any woman, much less a young girl. Those heavy, dark spheres had seen too much in this world. And had felt too little.

"Can I pray for you?" he asked.

"Why?"

"You might be sick. You might have a disease. I want you to be healed."

"Healed?"

"Yes."

"Of AIDS?"

"If that's what you have."

"How would that help?"

"To be healed?"

"Yes."

"You could live without pain."

"Without pain?" she said, trying to ensure she heard right. "Is that what you said? You pray for me and I don't have pain. This is what you're promising?"

"It's what I'm offering."

"Then, *mazungu*, you know nothing." Her face became angry.

As much as he wished she hadn't responded this way, he took comfort in knowing that she still had some ability to express emotion. "You are a foolish stupid man, do you know that? How can you take away pain? How can you possibly do that?"

"I can only offer you what I have."

"Then you have nothing, *mazungu*. Nothing!" She looked back to the embankment and shook her head. "You come here into the slum. You know nothing about life here. You think you do but you don't. The people. You think they like you? You think they love you?"

"I'm not sure."

"Then know this. They will just as soon lift you on their shoulders as take a knife, slit your throat, and hang you upside down so that you can watch as your blood drains out of you onto the street, on your way to death while they dance around and cheer. And for what? For what? Because you didn't heal them fast enough. Because you didn't heal enough people. For any reason. They don't care. They don't care about anything. Not you. Certainly not me. Nothing."

"I can't solve every problem, but I can help you."

"Help? You can help?"

"Yes."

"Do you really think so?"

"Yes."

"Did you notice the younger boys and girls are happy this evening because of what you did, but the older ones do not have the same joy? Did you notice how the twelve year olds, my friends, are not as happy?"

Thinking back on the people who had been healed he realized what she said was right. During the day it didn't register with him why the older ones weren't as enthusiastic. Some of them were even lethargic after being healed. He did wonder about them. Perhaps only subconsciously.

"Why?" he asked. "Why is that?"

"Because those girls at twelve years old realize what the younger ones at six do not."

"Which is?"

"That it's only a matter of time before they get sick again."

The futility of his day's work hung in the balance. Of course the miracles mattered. *Didn't they?* Those kids getting healed and running down the alley. *Wasn't that important? Isn't that why I'm here?* Granted, it might not be life-lasting. That was true. How could it be? Still, he wanted to believe that with those children's healings came a guarantee against future sickness.

"And so you come to our slum to give us health that will fade away," she said. "You may heal me of AIDS tonight, but tomorrow I will need money and in order to get it I will have to find more men, and it will only get me sick again. Just like the way other *mazungus* come for a day or for two days and give food that will get eaten, leaving us hungry again, and making it seem like they were never here. I will go back to work. That is the only certainty. I will get my money—my fee for sleeping in my parents' house. But before I go home each night I will come back here. Right to this spot. I will come here to heal from another day of work, so that I can go home with enough energy to withstand the violence from my alcoholic mother and father."

Lucas looked out at the embankment and had the rare wisdom of knowing his life experience offered him nothing to say in response.

"So, *mazungu*," she said. "Exactly what do you think you are achieving by being here?"

12

Considering it had been such a warm day, it felt strange to Lucas to be sitting behind a hut in a slum sensing the chill of the evening air. The girl beside him touched the bruise on her face, which she did periodically to see if it was getting worse. Night was coming. It was a bad time for her. Second only to day.

Brittany stood up, feeling guilty about not being able to do more to help. "Lucas, you can't stay out here."

And her? Where does she go? Where do they all go? How exactly am I supposed to sleep tonight knowing she'll be out here?

Brittany touched him on the shoulder, turned to say goodbye to the girl, then disappeared into the black night back to her clinic.

"I have to go," Lucas said, knowing that in half an hour he would be back at the hotel and she would be at the mercy of her parents. "I can pray for you if you want."

Lucas wanted to know what was going on inside that mind of hers. Maybe she didn't have the courage to say yes. Maybe being around men was always a nervous situation for her. Maybe she just wanted to be left alone.

He decided to risk it. She'd been through yet another horrible day. Her silence may well have been her request for help.

He moved closer beside her. He put his right arm around her shoulder and touched her forearm. He put his left hand around her knees. It looked like he was trying to shield her. Protect her.

Comfort her. He leaned his head against hers. Her short hair crinkled as he rested his ear against it. She didn't move. Didn't even seem to notice he was there.

He recited verses and prayed for her healing. She felt a burning sensation through her body. At first it felt like nothing more than the sun warming her skin. But then it grew intense and reached inside her, filling every aching bone and muscle.

Lucas finished praying. He continued holding her in his arms. Neither of them said anything. For one evening, or at least for a short while, she would know what it meant to be with a man who wanted nothing from her in return.

"Saada," she said.

Those beautiful African names. Lucas asked her to repeat it. She did. Lucas said it and she nodded her head that he had got it right. She brought her hand to her cheek again. And the way she did triggered in Lucas the truth that Saada's life was a revolving journey from one misery to another. A never-ending cycle where each day was just a horrific repeat.

At that moment he decided he was going to take her off the streets. He'd find a way to get her into a good boarding school. Get her out of Nairobi if he had to. And he would have done just that had those two men not come around the corner and seen him there.

One of them, older and taller, said something. Lucas tried to get to his feet. *Where is Jake?* The young one reached down and grabbed Lucas around the bicep with his powerful hand. He yanked Lucas up and shouted out to the alley. In the distance he heard someone shout back.

A sick smile came over the younger one. "You will like it here with us, *mazungu*."

Lucas pulled back his arm, but the man gripped it even tighter, cutting off his circulation. Lucas screamed for Jake. Saada ran away. Lucas called after her to go up the road to look for the other white man. But she had been here before with drunken men. And she wasn't going to go through anything with them.

Least of all not without getting paid.

She turned a corner. Out of sight.

"I can pray for you to be healed," Lucas said.

The younger one smiled. A waft of piercing alcohol stung Lucas' eyes.

"We will enjoy you, *mazungu*. We will have fun together!"

Lucas ripped a punch at the young man's throat. The man saw it coming and moved such that it caught him on the collarbone. It was enough to send him off balance. Lucas pulled his arm loose. The younger one regained his footing and grabbed Lucas' wrist. Lucas twisted his hips and put everything he could behind his kick aimed at the young man's groin. But his desire for a powerful strike cost him in accuracy. His kick missed the target and landed on the young man's hamstring. Lucas was about to hit him with a third blow when the older one grabbed Lucas around the neck. With incredible strength the man squeezed so hard that Lucas felt his blood pounding in his head. He struggled to take in what little air he could manage. The younger one reached for Lucas' belt and began unbuckling it.

Lucas wriggled his body in a frenzied panic to break loose. The terror of passing out came upon him. He clawed his hands back into the man's face. He dug his finger into his eyes. He managed to push up and back against them in an effort to pluck them out. The man gripped tighter. Lucas couldn't breathe.

"Lucas!"

Jake ran down the embankment. His face was flushed. His eyes intense. He charged at the men who were either too drunk or too engrossed in what they were doing to hear him. Jake clenched his fist and rammed it behind the older man's ear. He went limp and released his hold on Lucas. He fell to his knees and then slammed to the ground, drifting from this world to unconsciousness. The young man, his eyes wild, let go of Lucas. He swung at Jake, missed, and then grabbed him by the throat. Jake grabbed him back. Like wild dogs being fuelled by the thrill of the fight, the two throttled each other as they jostled back and forth. Spit flew from their mouths as Jake ripped out a barrage of expletives at the young man. They pressed their fingers into each other's throats. Jake's eyes bulged with rage. He forced his head back and held the man away from him. Then he pulled him forward and smashed his head into the young man's face. There was a tremendous *crack*.

The young man shut off. He hung there like a dead weight in Jake's hands.

Lucas stood up. Jake started breathing. They looked at the young man.

"Did you kill him?" Lucas asked. That didn't come out right. What he really wanted to say was *Is he dead?*

Jake let go of him. He dropped to the ground. "He's breathing," Jake said. But neither of them was sure.

Jake grabbed Lucas by the shirt and forced him back to the embankment.

"We can't leave him!"

The young man sputtered. Lucas was relieved. Jake didn't care either way.

When they reached the street they signalled for Thomas and Jonathan. A group of people gathered around an open fire saw Lucas and shouted out to those below.

"Where's Tabitha?"

"She left in another taxi," Jake replied, pushing Lucas into the small white car. They heard yelling from below. Lucas looked through the window. All across the street people emerged carrying their sick children. They walked to the car with their arms stretched out, begging Lucas to touch them. Jake locked the doors.

"Start driving!" Thomas shouted at Jonathan.

People pounded on the windows. They pleaded with Lucas to heal them.

Jonathan put the car in gear. His headlights illuminated the crowd gathering on the street. With every passing second it seemed to grow larger. Swelling like a wave. He looked in his rear-view mirror. There were as many behind as in front.

"What are you doing?!" Thomas screamed. "Get going!"

Jonathan honked his horn. He released the clutch and inched forward.

But the crowd didn't move. He leaned on his horn. More people came. Some of the mothers were bringing two and three children.

"Ram them!" Thomas said, his face flushed with horror. "You must go through! You must go through!"

Lucas saw a little girl pressed up against the window. Hollow, sunken eyes. No hair. She stared at Lucas with an expression that conveyed she had no understanding that any other world could exist besides the disease-ridden, poverty-stricken one she called home.

An opening in the crowd. All eyes in the taxi focused on whether there would be still more people waiting in the distance. The lights shone through. There was a chance.

Jonathan took his hand off the horn. He released his foot from the clutch and drilled the accelerator. The car took off.

And that's when everything went horribly wrong.

A child, a boy not more than four years old, became confused in the panic. He straggled a few feet behind his mother. When he saw the car racing towards him, he didn't know whether to take the shorter route to safety on one side of the road or the longer route to his mother on the other side. Instinct won out and he ran in front of the approaching car.

With dozens of screaming people on either side of the road, Jonathan made up his mind to go through, no matter what. Some had sticks. Some were throwing rocks. He gripped the steering wheel and negotiated past the people.

The child slipped. Jonathan saw him fall to his knees. They all felt it in that instant—they knew. There was no time to react. The taxi's headlight crushed the boy's head. Practically ripped it from his body. Blood spattered all over the hood. And then Jonathan made a terrible mistake.

He hit the brakes.

Human nature. Impulse. A trained response. Whatever the reason, it made things worse. The boy was dead. There was nothing that could be done. Not for him. Not for the driver. Jonathan knew he should have just pounded the accelerator and kept going. He knew he should have steadied the course, ignored his nerves, got them out of there, and dealt with the morality of an accidental killing later. But he didn't.

And in that instant the crowd went from frustrated beggars to a violent mob. They swarmed the car. A fist smashed Jake's window. Hands reached in to grab him. Jake swung at the assailants, wishing he had brought a gun. Or at least a bat.

"Ram them!" Thomas yelled.

They broke Lucas' window. A hand reached in and grabbed his hair. Still more hands came in. They pulled at him and tried to drag him out. It wouldn't take much. Not now. Not with his neck exposed. Someone with a knife could reach in and say goodnight without any chance for a defence.

Jonathan hit the accelerator. Guilt over killing a little boy was overshadowed by the guilt of killing possibly more people. Either the four in the taxi were going to die or it would be some of the maniacs in the street.

But the car didn't move. He heard his wheels spinning. They felt the front end of the car lifting up. Lucas looked through the windshield. He saw a huge figure engulfing their view.

It was the strong man.

Massive, hulking muscles. Mouth wide open. Screaming. Smoke rose from the engine. The strong man moved the car to the side. People ran out of the way. He dropped it down.

Before Jonathan had time to switch from the accelerator to the brake, the taxi bolted to the embankment. It raced past the crowd and angled off the road. It flipped over onto the hood, struck a rock, and turned on its side. It landed at the bottom. People cheered.

"Get out!" Jake yelled.

Jake and Thomas opened their doors and climbed out. Lucas and Jonathan followed. They looked around for the best direction to run. The crowd hurried down after them.

"Let's go!" Jake screamed. They ran as fast they could. Away from the crowd.

And into the slum.

For a fat man Jake ran with incredible speed. He and Lucas led the way into an alley. Huts raced by them in a dizzying blur. They heard the crowd gaining on them. Lucas looked behind him. And what he saw terrified him.

The strong man had outrun the entire crowd. He sprinted after them, gripping a wooden club in his right hand that was as long and wide as his forearm, with a rounded piece at the end. He cursed at them in his native language.

Thomas was the slowest of the four. And that would prove to be his undoing. With an incredible show of brute strength the strong man leaped at Thomas. He thrust his club at him in mid-air and caught him on the base of the skull. Thomas' eyes told Lucas everything. In that instant they went from a horrified anxiety to a dull motionless stare. Wherever he was going, he was well on his way.

Thomas was dead before he hit the ground.

They kept running straight, wondering when to veer off. In this disorganized maze too many left or right turns might inadvertently lead them right back in the direction from which they were running. Jonathan was no help. It was his country, his city, but not his slum. He caught up to the other two.

They saw a row of huts at the end of the alley, forcing them to turn either left or right. Lucas turned left and Jake followed. Their feet slammed into potholes as they struggled to keep their balance. They took another turn and realized things had gone quiet. Almost too quiet. They glanced behind them. Jonathan was gone.

Lucas and Jake saw an opening ahead and made another turn. There were so many behind them. So many. Dozens of them could take each of the variations in the paths through the slum to track them down.

Lucas looked all around to see if he could spot the road. Nothing. The slum went on forever. *How many people did Jonathan say lived here? A million? If that were the case, am I heading closer to the boundary or closer to the centre? Were there police in the slum?* He hadn't seen any officers. *No. No, there weren't any.* That would explain the attendant's look at the hotel when he said he was going to a slum. That would explain Jonathan and Thomas' well-placed fear over them coming here.

They ran past women sitting outside their huts. Lucas considered giving them money to hide them. But a club dripping with remains from its last victim would be harder currency than what Lucas could offer.

Plus, white men in a slum looking to blend in was too optimistic.

Lucas turned right. He saw a hill in the distance. He ran faster. Then he noticed the screams behind him had faded off. Maybe they were approaching the boundary of the slum. That awkward feeling came back. He swung his head to the left and then to the right. He felt the sting of panic.

Jake was gone.

"Jake!" Lucas screamed and then realized that shouting was a dead giveaway for his location. "Jake, where are you?" he screamed again. That was it. No more yelling. They could track him that much more easily. He couldn't go back. Good luck finding the place where they parted, much less the direction Jake took after that.

All Lucas heard were his feet pounding against the mud and the thumping of his heart. He passed hut after hut. No one in the entrances. No one in the alley.

Off to the right he saw a small wooden building with three doors. He hurried to it and opened a door at the end. The putrid odour of the latrine filled his nostrils. He closed the door behind him and squatted down. He peered through the crack in the door out at the alley. He heard shouting. A group of men, maybe five of them, difficult to tell with such little room to look, ran past him down another alley.

His heart and lungs showed no sign of slowing down. All he could see in his mind's eye was the strong man killing poor Thomas. All he could feel was the anxiety over whether his best friend was already dead, or if he had somehow managed to find a refuge among the chaos.

And all he could wonder was whether or not there was any chance of making it out alive.

He stayed glued to the door. Something caught his attention. He tried to determine if what he heard was his imagination or if it was really happening. He held his breath and listened. Sure enough. There it was.

Voices in the distance.

And they were getting closer.

13

Matthias Fisher stepped out of a limo onto the jammed street. Black Armani suit. Dark blue silk shirt. Hair slicked back. Leather shoes. No wallet. No cheque book. No credit cards. Just cash. Lots and lots of cash. Stacks of dead presidents in tidy rolls in his suit jacket. He paid the driver with a crisp bill. The driver noticed the denomination and thanked him as he drove off. Matthias looked around and grinned, feeling the connection people feel when they're in a city they love. He straightened his collar and walked through the crowd.

It was time to go to work.

Bright lights flooded the street. People packed the sidewalks—most of them happy, some of them with that shell-shocked look of disbelief. Every walk of life. Every age group. It was evening, but it may as well have been the middle of the day in this town that only seemed to wake up around sunset. This wasn't Nairobi. And it was neither London nor Chicago. This was a city unlike any other on the planet.

This was Las Vegas.

To his left he saw the towering Mirage casino with its gold lining and reflective mirrors. Up ahead he saw Treasure Island. Hundreds gathered on the sidewalk to see the evening show that took place every hour and a half on a life-sized ship. Cannon sound effects went off. Puffs of smoke. The clashing of swords. Huge cheers from the crowd. Up ahead on the right stood the Wynn Hotel, a massive curved structure with sleek black mirrored windows with the owner's trademark signature at the top.

Yet in spite of the grandeur, it occurred to Matthias that in about a month every casino in Vegas would be dwarfed by the one under construction. Up ahead, just past the Frontier, the largest casino-resort ever built in the world was nearing completion. No name had been revealed. No floor plans released. Just a wealth of secrecy about the unbelievable attractions at the newest gaming centre that was about to erupt in the heart of Sin City.

But Matthias wasn't interested in the new casino. Not now. He was interested in the smallest casino on Las Vegas Boulevard. Its official name was The Mystery of the Mayan Civilization. But people referred to it simply as the Mayan—or at least those few regulars who even knew about the place did. It was tucked in at the back, off the Strip, behind the towering new casino.

Matthias walked down an alley between the western cowboy-themed Frontier casino and the new Empirico monstrosity, and entered the Mayan's sparse entranceway. It featured a long walkway lined with large white columns. The walkway turned into a glass tunnel surrounded by water. A school of green and white fish raced by overhead, chased by a larger school of blue and gold.

He reached the end of the tunnel and walked into the gaming area. He took in a deep breath, smelling the waft of excitement and addiction in the air. Matthias was home. He walked past the slot machines. Bells went off. Lights flashed. People sat here and there, yanking on levers, apparently having fun but looking more like zombies.

The carpet was a confusing mishmash of colours and shapes. The ceiling was a dull black with the mechanical piping exposed. The floor was too complicated and irritating to look at, the ceiling too boring to admire, all designed by the casino to force patrons' attention to the slot machines conveniently placed at eye level. Then there were "the eyes in the sky"—those all-seeing, all-powerful cameras, behind which stood a number of employees trained in the art of recognizing known card counters via a computer database, and able to spot people, including operators, involved in illegal gaming. One of them saw Matthias as he came in. The camera took his picture and fed the information through a matching program that tried to compare his face with those who had either been banned from the casino or were on their watch list. Nothing came up. One of the staff watched Matthias as he walked through the slots on his way to the card tables. No. They didn't have him in their system. Not yet.

But they were certainly going to.

Every casino in Las Vegas was going to know all about Matthias Fisher.

No clocks. No windows. Nothing to give any indication of how much time a patron had spent in the casino. A stable consistent environment where only the number of players changed.

He lined up at the cage. When an elderly lady with an infectious smile called him forward, he pulled out one of his wads of $100 bills.

"How much would you like?" she asked.

Ten thousand. That would be a good start. That would be all he'd need. He was about to toss the stack of Benjamin Franklins on the counter when he changed his mind.

"Five thousand," he said, pulling out 50 bills.

He had gone through the statistics. He had done the analysis. It was all laid out. Ten K. That's what he needed. Ten thousand was certainly doable. But with five thousand it would be an even greater challenge. There was something in the air. He could feel it. Things were going to be in his favour.

She gave him 50 purple and yellow chips. He thanked her by nodding. And as he turned to decide which blackjack table to join, he caught a glimpse of a woman walking to his left. His mind screamed at him to stop. Odd, he thought, that in Vegas he would recognize someone. He turned his attention to appease his conscience. And when he saw her, he froze. He was stunned. Paralyzed from going any farther. Captured by her presence.

He wasn't expecting to see her.

Perfect reddish-blonde hair. It couldn't be natural. Impossible. Any woman with natural hair colour like that had to be an anomaly. She had it tied back, with a couple of strands falling on either side of her face. High cheekbones. An even higher black skirt. Low-cut blue blouse that was skin-tight.

And a silver bracelet with a snake coiled on it.

His heart pounded. Her hair. *How in the world did she get it to look that good?* She was relaxed. Almost having fun. Most of the other waitresses he had known were always rushing, practically panicking. But not her. Not the reddish-blonde. The one whose name started with an S. *What was it again?*

This time it was her subconscious speaking to her. It told her someone was looking at her. She tried to ignore it, thinking it to be a customer staring her down. The individual was just to her right. Not that far. Close enough to make serious eye contact. What was the problem with one look? She responded to that voice and turned to see him.

And when she did she nearly dropped her tray of glasses.

There he was. Light brown eyes. Tall. Well, tall-ish. Six feet for sure. Black hair. Her mouth opened. She couldn't believe it. Of all the betting joints in the world she was in the same one as he was.

She was alive because of him. She had avoided a watery grave because of his warning. Because of his premonition. Because of his supposed ability to see into the future.

She walked to him in what felt like hypnotic motion. Smooth as a calm lake. She stopped closer to him than what would be considered normal for a waitress-gambler relationship.

"What are the chances?" she asked in a soft whisper.

"Of you and me?" he replied, realizing that line would be enough to drive most women away. But here, with her, both of them knew it wasn't a line. A casino with dozens of eyes looking down at them made no difference. Besides, those cameras and hawk eyes weren't there anymore. Neither were the slots, the patrons, nor even the casino. Everything around them disappeared.

All that was left were two people.

"I've been thinking of you," she said.

"Good thoughts or bad?" He looked deep into her eyes. They were a combination of green and blue that swirled together like a whirlpool. The longer he looked into them, the more it seemed they were really moving. He'd been wondering about her eye colour ever since he was fished out of the ocean by that freighter.

It surprised him to realize that he could talk to someone for over an hour and then afterwards have no clue what colour their eyes were.

"That makes three in total who survived."

"You ever think about the odds on that?"

"I have," she said. The casino came back. They heard the clanging of slot trays, specifically designed to create as much noise as possible as the coins dropped out. She heard a patron asking for a drink. "Miss. Miss." She cringed. She'd heard lots of names before. Some good. Some bad. But *Miss*? She hated it. Just hated it.

"When can I talk to you?" he asked. "When do you get off?"

"I have another shift right after this." She avoided his eyes as if trying to hide the truth about the kind of *shift* she had. It told him enough. "Where are you staying?" she asked. He told her. "I'll get a hold of you."

Usually that was a surefire way of knowing things were finished. Don't call me—I'll call you. But if the expression in her eyes was any indication, he would be hearing from her.

And soon.

She turned down a row of slots in the direction of the voice. All he saw was her immaculate hair as it trailed off among the players.

Matthias scanned the blackjack tables. He found a Spanish man in his forties dealing the last cards from the shoe. This was it. It was time to begin.

"Can I join?" Matthias asked as he sat down at the table.

Matthias put his stack of 50 chips on the table. Not bad. Not amazing, though. Not compared with moneybags to his right. A woman in her sixties had 30 grand on the table. Purple, green, blue. All kinds of chips. She had a look and feel about her that said she had lots more where this pathetic little pile came from. Matthias placed a chip in a box on the green felt.

And without any delay the dealing started. *Boom*! His heart jumped. *Yes! Yes, this is it!* The rush of adrenaline. The thumping in his neck. *I'm breathing, baby! I am alive and well!* Pound, pound, pound. His heart was doing overtime.

King to her. Eight of hearts to him. Three to the dealer. He gave each of them another card and gave one to himself, face down.

Matthias got the six of diamonds. Not bad. Not great. He waved his hand with a slight sweeping motion to indicate he was standing. Fourteen. That's the rule. Stand on 13 or higher when the dealer shows 3. Madam drew a 3 and then busted with a 9. The dealer drew himself a 10. That made 13. *Dealer must draw to 16 and stand on all 17s.* One more card. A 10. Twenty-three total. Bust.

Matthias won.

The dealer picked out a purple chip from his tray and placed it beside Matthias'. Up a hundred bucks in less than a minute.

With one glance Matthias memorized the cards on the table. Strictly speaking, he didn't have to actually memorize them. Most professional, or obsessed, blackjack players used a card numbering system rather than a memorizing system. But Matthias used both. Face cards and 10 count as -1. Seven, 8, and 9 are neutral and count as 0. Six and under are assigned a value of +1. Count the value of all cards each hand and keep a running total. A negative score means there are more low cards in the shoe—a dealer's advantage. A positive score means there are more high cards left—player's advantage. The higher the positive number, the higher the bet to cash in on it.

Matthias left both chips on the table. The dealer swiped cards out from the shoe. With a dexterity that comes from having done this for years, he flung the cards to land right at their hands.

Matthias drew the 4 of clubs. Not good. The dealer showed 10. Even worse. The dealer threw Matthias a 5 of diamonds. A third card. Seven of spades. Rats. Rats, rats, rats. Sixteen to the dealer's 10. Strategy demanded hitting until 17. The count from the previous hand was 0. Now it was -1. Of the 13 different cards he could be dealt, only 5 of them, ace through 5, would help. The other 8, 6 through king, would bust him.

"Hit me," Matthias said.

He drew an ace. Seventeen. There were worse hands to be had.

The dealer drew a 2. Then an ace. Good thing they came out in that order. The dealer then drew a 3 for a total of 16 against Matthias' 17. The dealer dealt himself 1 more card. Six of diamonds.

Matthias won again.

Within 40 minutes, Matthias turned his 5 large into 14, earning him $9,000 profit. They were nearing the end of the shoe. That's when things became more interesting. Those who used a simplified counting system knew whether there were higher or lower cards remaining. Matthias, however, had an added advantage. Something they didn't teach in those blackjack books. A little extra something he had above the other players, above the dealers and, most importantly, the house. Matthias had a gambling edge.

The kind of edge that tells someone if a plane is about to go down.

They played another six decks. The chips poured in. Matthias looked at his watch. *What is taking them so long? I'm cleaning you guys out. Besides, I haven't got all night. Don't you train these stupid dealers? I would have spotted a guy like me when he walked in.*

And that's when they came. The pit boss had been watching him. The floor manager too. They approached him. He felt their presence behind him.

Showtime.

"Sir, could we have a word with you?"

These guys all seemed to come from the same factory. Stocky. Cheap suit. Facial hair. But their biggest problem was their demeanour. They had to pretend they were upset. No conviction at all in what they were doing. They were at the bottom of their hierarchy. Matthias had run into plenty better.

"I'm fine, thanks," Matthias said, nodding his head to the dealer that he was ready to continue. But the dealer didn't deal. He knew the drill.

"Sir, we'd like to ask you to come with us."

"Is there a problem?"

"If you would, sir. We need you to come with us."

What difference does that make? You cheap fat rent-a-cops can't force me to do anything. I can get up and walk out of here and you two Tweedledees can't stop me. You can't make me come with you. We both know it.

Matthias stuffed his chips in his pocket and followed. People watched as they passed through the casino to the back. The floor manager produced a card from his pocket, swiped it through a door lock, punched in his code, and opened it. They walked up a flight of stairs and came to another door. The floor manager repeated the process and brought them into an office area. Leather couches.

Hardwood floor. A welcome relief from those irritating carpets in the casino.

The floor manager led them into a dimly lit room. One table. A few chairs. He was about to start speaking when Matthias interrupted him.

"Get me Lydda and the Petra Security representative."

The floor manager cocked his head back. Her real name was Lydia. Only those close to her knew her as Lydda. "We're here to expel you from this casino."

"And you're going to get them right now or you're out of a job." The floor manager looked at the pit boss. "The two of you can leave now," Matthias said.

And they did.

Moments later, Lydda Simons entered. Dyed hair. Way too blonde to be natural. Plastic surgery job on her face. She wore three necklaces, a low-cut pink shirt, black leather pants, and black high heels. Her expression was colder than a biting north wind in winter.

"I fail to see what the problem is. You've been asked to leave my casino and you're going to do just that."

Nice try, Lydda.

"My name is Matthias Fisher." He waited for her to introduce herself. She just stared at him, eyes fixed on his. But he saw through the pretend confidence to that panicking person somewhere inside. "And you are Lydda Simons. CEO of the Mayan." That bothered her. He could tell by the way she opened her lips. "The Mystery of the Mayan Civilization, that is," he said.

"You're leaving."

"Not without talking to you and your Petra rep."

"You're not talking to anybody. Goodbye."

"I won some money tonight."

"Congratulations."

"I can give it back to you."

She looked at her watch in a vain attempt to imply she was busy. "What do you want, Mr. Fisher?"

Mr. Fisher. That sounded good.

"How's business?"

"Business is fine," she said, as if delivering a predetermined response.

"That's great. Being near the Frontier and the Stardust. Not to mention Treasure Island and the Mirage. Wynn across the street. I'd think that would be murder for an operation like yours."

"We have a specialized market that we've captured. And we know how to keep our clients coming back."

"Plus, there's a new casino opening right in front of you. The biggest casino in the world."

Lydda's eyes went from cold to downright ice. Freezing.

"Perhaps you've heard of it?" he asked.

Lydda didn't need any reminding. If the competition on either side was crowding her out, the one coming up would certainly drive her into the ground. More hotel rooms than any other complex in the world. More entertainment venues than any casino in Vegas had even thought about. More gaming area than any three casinos combined. Yeah. Lydda had heard all about Caesar's new casino.

So had her creditors.

"I've heard a few things here and there."

"A big casino like that has to have at least some impact on you. Some might even suggest it could have a big impact. Maybe I can help."

"Help? The Mystery of the Mayan Civilization does not need help."

"*Au contraire*," Matthias said, leaning forward in his chair without breaking eye contact. "You and I both know this little dump of yours is about to go into receivership. Even the downtown hotels are beating you. That's embarrassing. A Las Vegas Strip casino being beaten by a downtown joint."

Lydda cursed at him.

"Wrong answer." They locked eyes. If Lydda had had her gun with her she would have been tempted to pull it out and send a bullet between Matthias' clear brown eyes. But instead she sat down, the look on her face being weapon enough. "You're in trouble," Matthias said. "And here's how we're going to help each other." He took the chips out of his pockets and spilled them onto the table. He picked out his original five thousand and set them aside.

"You've had a lucky evening."

"Luck?" Matthias said, raising his eyebrows. "Lydda, luck has nothing to do with it. I walked in here not an hour ago with this 5 grand. And now I have 23 more." He pushed the 5-grand pile in with the other and shoved the lot to her. "My gift to you, Lydda. Twenty-eight thousand total."

That cold expression of hers changed with the introduction of money. "What do you want?"

"Petra Security protects some of the big casinos in Vegas. They also look after yours. Zack Roman owns Petra. I think you know him."

She glared at him, trying to decide if he was about to use extortion or if he had something else in mind.

"I think you and Zack get along pretty well, don't you?"

"Your point, Mr. Fisher?"

Again. That word. *Mister*. Of all the privileges that came with winning at blackjack, being called *Mister* was third only to the money and women.

"Petra is doing the security for the new casino extraordinaire coming up right in front of you. And that's where you come in."

She squinted her eyes as her mind raced to figure out where he was going with this. Something he was implying had caught her attention. "I'm listening."

"The owner's name is Caesar Alexander," he said. "And I want you to help me take his money."

14

The Council had been waiting for an hour. No one said a word. Not to each other. Not to their cellphones. Nothing. Under other circumstances they would be talking—bragging about their recent sales trips. Or they'd be arranging new deals while eating from trays of food lined along the back of the Council chambers. But not today.

Today was not a normal meeting.

They had taken the oath. The vow. No food or drink until Lucas was dead. Too many healings would result in too few profits. So they had drawn lots, and the burden of murder had fallen to Mike. It was his job to go out with Thatcher and Ridley and bring back a dead body. Now, Thatcher and Ridley were dead. Lucas was on the loose. And Mike-the-failure sat in the last row of leather chairs arranged in a semicircle, facing Caesar's lectern. He looked at his watch. Caesar should have been here by now. He reached for his drink of water. It was warm and did little to calm him. He felt so nervous he may as well have been sitting on the stage at the centre of attention while the 40-plus others stared at him. Being at the back did nothing to help. He had let them down. It was his fault Lucas was still alive. All he had to do was pull the trigger. That was it. One simple pull from the rooftop at Clark and Addison. Drop the gun. Down through the building. And then leave with the maddening crowd. It was all laid out. A perfect, easy plan.

If only Mike hadn't had that ill-timed attack of morality.

But with every good deed comes the penalty of explaining to others why the bad deed didn't get done. This was the Council. If they were prepared to kill Lucas—one of their own who was on track to cost them a fortune—how much more would they be ready to kill one of their own who had failed to get rid of that threat?

The door opened. All eyes focused below. Some of the Council members adjusted in their chairs. A man entered. It was Caesar.

At least it *looked* like Caesar.

He was hunched over more than usual. Those puffy eyes looked more pronounced. His face was pale. He walked to the lectern with slow steps that seemed to take careful planning. He put his hands on the glass panel, more for support than for effect. He cleared his throat as they waited for his first words. But instead, he looked each of them in the eye as if doing so could somehow suck out of them any hidden agendas or questionable loyalty. He stopped at Mike. His burning eyes drilled into him. They felt like rotating blades cutting through his corneas, through his eyeballs, and into his brain. Mike swallowed. *Just pass on. Just keep going. Go to the next guy.* But Caesar stayed there, searching Mike with a vicious glare.

"The mission failed," Caesar said. "Two men are dead. We did not achieve our objective."

I'm next. I'm not getting out of here alive. They're going to tape my nose and mouth shut, tie my hands and feet, and throw me into Lake Michigan. Mike's skin itched. His mind raced through the layout of the room. He tried to remember the location of the nearest exit. He closed his eyes and found it strange that even though he had been in this massive room dozens of times before, he had a hard time recalling an emergency route. He wanted to turn around and look behind him to be certain. But that would give the wrong impression. Back and to the left. He was pretty sure that's where it would be. Not far from where he was sitting. He could jump over his seat, race for the door, and hurry down the hallway. But what about the security doors at the end? They would certainly be locked. And oh how embarrassing and fate-sealing it would be if he made a premature dash for freedom and didn't make it.

"And yet on the other hand, it was a success."

Life came back to the room. Mike could breathe again. *Just don't look at me. Please, just don't look at me.*

And he didn't. Caesar gripped the glass lectern tighter. Frail, fragile man. He looked in danger of collapsing. Looked more like a person on the way out than the leader of one of the world's top five pharmaceutical companies.

"Lucas is gone. He's gone to Africa, which from Empirico's perspective is as good as dead."

Mike felt his confidence return. Caesar was right, of course. Perspective. That's all this was. Perspective. Dead or gone. What difference did it make? The attack must have scared Lucas off. It was win-win. Mike avoided becoming a murderer and Lucas stopped posing a threat to Empirico sales.

"Though if Lucas should come back we would need to readdress the issue."

The Council members didn't have to look at Mike. He felt the force of their collective attention.

"Onto other business."

Caesar continued talking, but Mike couldn't hear him. Those words kept running over and over in his mind. *If Lucas should come back.*

Caesar sat down at his desk. He pulled out a cigar, clipped off the end, and threw it in the garbage. It bounced off a copy of *The Chicago Observer*. Lucas and dozens of black children were on the front cover.

He coughed as he took in the first puff. That was unusual. Caesar ignored it and sucked back, bringing the tip to a red glow. He exhaled in the darkness, sending smoke to the ceiling.

A knock at the door. It caught him by surprise. Normally he watched people come down the hallway via the security cameras. He was in fact expecting to see Mike—just not this soon. The cigar was supposed to help him take the news. Calm him down before Mike's words hit his ears. He sat up in his chair and wished he had a bottle of bourbon to help all of this go down—one way or the other. Good or bad, future and present lay on the other side of that door. This was it. A must-make free throw at the end of regulation to send his life into overtime.

"Come in, Mike," Caesar said, his voice a cautious blend of optimism and urgency.

Mike opened the door. He waited for his eyes to adjust to the darkness. He smelled the smoke.

"Yes or no, Mike?"

Mike saw Caesar slumped in his chair, cigar in hand. His mouth was drawn open like it was becoming too difficult to breathe through his nose. And those eyes. Still so piercing. But behind that veil of confidence and the just-give-me-the-facts-and-I-can-handle-it-from-there attitude, Mike thought he saw a hint of desperation.

"They think there's a better than average chance," Mike said. He had rehearsed that line all the way from the research facility to the office. Every time it sounded weak and fearful. But now that he was in front of the big man, it came out just right.

"A better than average chance of what?"

He held the papers. The summary sheet and related printouts from the tests. Five years and millions of dollars of research in his clammy, trembling hands. "They think they will have something ready by the end of the month."

"Something I can try or something that will cure me?"

"They already have the treatments ready."

"The symptom treatments?"

"Yes."

"You think that's what I want? You think hearing news like that makes any difference whatsoever to me?"

"No, Caesar. I just thought...." Mike hadn't practised this far and the new territory was making him feel uncomfortable.

"You thought that by telling me how great it is we have a drug that will help millions suffer less, that somehow might balance out the uncertainty of actually finding a cure?"

Mike ran his hand through his hair. "We should have started research on the cure first," he said. "Long before we knew that you had it."

Caesar nodded. Hindsight. Maybe the powers that be were right in not allowing mankind to go back in time and change things. But at times like this it felt like those powers had made a mistake.

"Sit down, Mike."

He didn't want to. Every second already felt like eternity. But he sat down and forced himself to look at Caesar.

"Mike, we made the right choice. Of course if I had the information back then that I have now, I would have chosen both courses, not just the symptom management...or relief, or whatever we're calling it."

"Growth deceleration."

"Right," Caesar said, his memory verifying that this was correct. He took another puff of his cigar. He held it in his mouth and released it as he spoke. "Mike, I may not live through this."

No. Not dying. Don't talk about dying. Find a euphemism. Find some way of speaking about the issue. But not like this. Not straight out. Why are you telling me this?

"I'm still optimistic that they will finish the research before...." Another puff. "But if they don't, you're in line for a promotion."

He heard wrong. Definitely. The illness was getting to his memory. Maybe he meant something else and the words just came out wrong. Whatever it was, Mike's face screamed confusion, so Caesar continued.

"Pharmaceuticals aren't about recognizing talent or creating new drugs or lobbying politicians. It all comes down to two things, Mike. The entire industry comes down to two key ingredients. You're not going to read this on any website. You certainly won't find it in a textbook. And you're not going to get it from most pharmaceutical companies."

Caesar took another puff of his cigar. This was supposed to be Lucas in front of him. His financial son. His boy by any other means. But that was not the case. Lucas was out. And Mike was in.

"Number one," Caesar said. "The pharmaceutical industry is about recognizing threats. If you forget that, you will disintegrate. All of our research labs? All of our funding for products that may or may not make it onto the market? You can throw those out. Yes, they are necessary. But they are not what fuel this industry. Medical doctors prescribe our drugs, and we make sure we thank them in a proper way. That's just part of the industry. We've sent more doctors to Hawaii than the other top five pharmaceutical companies combined. Now do you think those doctors are going to recommend healthy eating and herbs? No. Do the herbs work? Does cleaning out your digestive system help? Does diet affect health? Of course. But will doctors recommend it? No. Why? Because nature isn't going to offer them a kickback for selling you a five-dollar herb. But get them to prescribe you our drugs and they earn the money. The threat? Vitamins and herbs start working. Organic foods and exercise change people's need for pharmaceuticals. How will you react to that? The future, Mike, is one with few doctors. Lots of lawyers, but few doctors. Few doctors prescribing our drugs. Plus, the government will start legislating food."

Mike's face looked confused again.

"I know. Sounds stupid. But tell Humphrey Bogart during the shooting of Casablanca that the government was going to all but outlaw cigarettes and he would look the way you're looking right now." Caesar took a long puff of his cigar. "Cereal with lots of sugar? Taxed to the hilt. Fat foods from drive-through restaurants? Taxed to the hilt. They did it to the tobacco industry. The government and society may crack down on all this garbage that we eat, but people are still going to shaft themselves with the greatest killer of all. Worry, stress, and anxiety are directly linked to 70 per cent of all illness. So who knows? This may all even out in the end. The point is this: Pharmaceuticals as we know it are on the way out, unless we, you, can cope with that. You have to learn to recognize these threats. Health foods, lifestyle, exercise—simple stuff like this will take out that fragile foundation under the pharmaceutical industry. So how do you get past that? How do you see beyond that? How do you create a need for pharmaceuticals?"

Mike saw there was a lot more behind those eyes. Caesar wasn't giving it all to him. Plots, ideas, maybe even implemented strategies already underway. There was no way Caesar was just talking about this without something in the works to combat it.

"That brings me to number two. The second pillar of the pharmaceutical industry is the ability to have repeat customers."

Mike was expecting more but got nothing. "Repeat customers?" he asked, breaking the silence.

"The purpose of the pharmaceutical industry is not to heal people, but to make them dependent on our drugs. That's why we went the direction we did with this particular drug. That's why we went after the growth deceleration and not the cure."

Mike's face flushed. He had to get out. He needed air. Lots and lots of air. Maybe a bottle of something strong.

"If you didn't have this specific cancer...." Mike forgot the name. It was a type of brain cancer, but his mind stalled, trying to recall what it easily would under less demanding circumstances. Growth deceleration was so much easier to remember than what Caesar had. "If you didn't have this brain cancer...glioblastoma multiforme." It came back to him. Right. He remembered now. "If you didn't have GBM, would we be looking for the cure right now?"

Caesar didn't answer. He just looked at Mike with a cold, unchanging expression.

"If we knew we were on track to cure it, if we knew we could cure GBM, and perhaps cancer in general, then why wouldn't we go after it? Why wouldn't we go full steam ahead and find the cure?"

Caesar leaned forward and put his elbows on the desk. He steepled his fingers while holding the cigar. What was first just a small smirk at the side of his mouth grew into a grin that was more diabolical than content.

"Mike," Caesar said, giving a nod of approval. "Welcome to Empirico."

15

It was time to decide.

Lucas waited in the putrid outhouse. His eyes stung from the relentless smell. The longer he waited, the worse it got. Voices came and went. Figures came closer and then ran off in another direction in search of him. Perhaps by now Tabitha had returned to the hotel, figured out they were missing, and would send help. But waiting any longer did not sit well with him. This was the only outhouse he had seen in this area of the slum. People would be using it throughout the night. Eventually, he would be discovered. This left him the option of opening the door and running for help—an even more daunting task considering he didn't know in which direction help was, if it even existed. And so faced with two undesirable outcomes he made an uncomfortable decision, realizing that either way his friend might already be dead.

Lucas opened the door. Nobody there. If there was a time to make a break for it, this was it. It felt like a game of hide-and-go-seek. Save, of course, for the added challenge of the strong man roaming the slum, waiting to smash his skull in.

A shadow off to his right. He pulled his head back and angled his eye to get a better look. A small girl. By herself. Late at night. Walking the slum.

Don't pick mine. There are 3 toilets. One in 3. My odds are 33 per cent. Those odds are fine in a game of shells. But not so good when life hangs in the balance.

She opened the door beside him. Relief.

I know you can get me out of here, God, Lucas prayed silently. *I know it. I know you can get me out of here.*

Then another person came. Two doors left. Fifty-fifty. Lucas watched as the middle-aged woman approached. He grabbed the handle and debated what to do if she picked his door. No lock on this one. Maybe she knew that.

Maybe that's why she picked the other stall.

If there was a contestant number three who happened to be a tough strong male it would be impossible to run. Lucas opened the door. He decided to make a break for it.

Tabitha stood at the front desk, growing impatient with the attendant's repeated reply that neither Lucas nor Jake had returned. She worried that her haste in leaving had somehow complicated matters. *Why weren't they back? Where had they gone afterwards? They made it out, didn't they? Of course they did.* They were right behind her. *Weren't they?*

Weren't they?

She went outside, got a cab, and headed back to the slum.

Lucas glanced to the right and to the left. Where was Jake? Should he stay and look or run for help? While his heart told him to search every hut to save his friend, his mind told him they were both better off if he went to get the police.

Or an army.

Lucas bolted out of the outhouse.

He raced through the slum. His feet slammed into potholes, making enough noise for anybody nearby to figure out something was wrong. He ran down an alley. All of this looked exactly the same. One long repeat. It was like he was on a treadmill, not making any relative progress. A woman on the corner saw him. So did a young girl sitting on the ground. A baby screamed. A little farther up he heard the sound of a face being slapped. A louder scream.

A man up ahead. Paying no attention. Not until Lucas ran by him. The man shouted at him. His white eyes against the black evening were the only clue Lucas had that he was there.

More shouting. Someone called out after him. Faster. Faster. Left? Right? *Why couldn't there be a straight line?* His original direction had been lost. For all he knew he was going in circles as fast as he could.

A man jumped out in front of him. He grabbed Lucas around the neck in a choke hold. Lucas reached his hands back and clawed at the man's eyes. He dug his thumbs into the man's eyeballs, kicked him in the groin, and continued running.

He came to a clearing. And what he saw in the distance gave him hope. Was that it? Was that the road? Sure enough. There it was.

The embankment.

There were four alleys in front of him, branching out like forks in the road. He tried for the one on the far right. But as he ran towards it he heard a rush of shouting. He changed his mind and went to the next one. Still more screams. Another one. A man with a torch walking and shouting something. The next alley. Two more men. Both with torches. Screaming something. They saw him and ran after him, calling out to the others that they had found him.

Lucas ran back in the direction he had come. A young man approached carrying a torch with three more people behind him. Lucas charged them. He slugged the first one in the face. The one beside him punched Lucas in the chin. Lucas swung wildly at him and caught him in the jaw. One of the others in the crowd hit him in the back of the head, causing him to bend over. He felt a powerful kick in his side. The force was so strong that it lifted Lucas off the ground and knocked the wind out of him.

Then, they all heard a howl coming from the centre of the clearing. Eerie, like the sound of a wolf. The group stopped shouting. Four men grabbed Lucas and dragged him down the alley.

They pulled his half-conscious body to the clearing and sat him down on his knees. He squinted to get the mix of sweat and blood out of his eyes. There, to his right, was a man. Bloodied face. Cuts all over. It was Jake.

At least it looked like Jake.

"Jake?" Lucas asked, spitting out blood.

Jake opened his swelled eyes and felt the welcome relief of a momentary interruption in the beatings. He turned his head in three jerky motions as if making the turn all at once would have been impossible. He looked at Lucas. "Are we getting out of here?"

They brought another man out who screamed and begged them to stop. Lucas recognized Jonathan's voice. His feet were tied with a cord. The group yanked him by the shoulder. Every time he tried to stand up they kicked him in the ribs, sending him back to the ground. They sat him on Lucas' left.

"God, Lucas! Do something!" Jonathan screamed. "Do you know what's happening? Do you know what this is?"

Lucas had an idea.

"Lucas, make this go away!"

The strong man came out of the crowd. In his right hand he held rags and a can of gasoline. Three men brought tires. He looked at Lucas. "You are an evil spirit!"

The crowd screamed with excitement as they formed a ring around them. Sets of eyes crowded all around in the black night, looking like glowing globes amid the torches reflecting off them.

The strong man stepped closer. He spoke with more force. "You don't come to cure the sick. You come to overtake us!"

"No."

"No? You lie!"

The crowd roared in agreement. They began to chant. "*Choma! Choma! Choma!*"

"They want me to burn you. They want me to burn you alive."

"I'm not lying. You saw the people healed today."

"You and the ones in the car killed that little boy. You must die."

"What good does it do to kill us and keep your people sick?"

"*Choma! Choma! Choma!*"

"This healing power. Which of you has it?" he asked, looking to Jake and Lucas.

With words that felt like they would be his last, Lucas looked up at the glistening body of the strong man.

"It's me."

In a strange and supernatural way, the strong man stumbled backward. Those around him fell to the ground. It was as if some powerful gust of wind had pushed them over. He clutched his throat, knelt down, and tried to catch his breath.

"An evil spirit!" he shouted.

Up on the embankment a taxi came to a stop. Tabitha opened the door and stepped out.

"Do something," Jonathan said. "Do something! Save us!"

The strong man turned to the crowd. "*Choma!*"

"*Choma! Choma! Choma!*" they screamed in agreement.

"Why don't you do something?" Jonathan screamed. "We will die! You help everyone else. Now help us. Help yourself! Do something!"

The strong man lifted a tire over Jonathan's head and pushed it down to his waist, pinning his hands inside. He forced him to his feet.

"We are going to die. Do something! I beg you!"

The strong man stuffed oily rags into the tire.

"You fool! You have nothing! You are nothing but a worthless fool!" Jonathan screamed at Lucas. Then he spoke in Swahili to the strong man, begging him to stop.

But the strong man doused him in gasoline.

"Do something!"

Lucas quoted a verse, doing the best he could to remain conscious.

The strong man grabbed a torch from one of those in the crowd. He howled and threw it at Jonathan. It crackled as it flew threw the air, giving off embers when it struck his chest. The torch fell down on the rags and set them on fire. Jonathan twisted back and forth to put the flames out. People cheered. Someone gave a horrible high-pitched scream that almost sounded inhuman. The rubber caught fire. Flames reached up to his head. Black smoke billowed out from the tire. He choked as it filled his lungs. His clothes ignited. His hair burned. He wheezed in and out, sending a combination of spit and blood from his mouth. He fell face down, then rolled over on his back and stopped moving.

The crowd jumped and cheered. The smoke from Jonathan's body gave off a stench that drifted to Lucas and Jake.

The strong man then forced tires over them. Lucas felt the rubber pin his arms against his side. Someone tied their feet. The strong man doused them in gasoline. Lucas mumbled his verses in incoherent stretches, using every last bit of energy to force out the words.

He did the best he could not to concentrate on Jonathan's burned-up body, which looked more like a piece of charred wood than the remains of a human.

The strong man grabbed a torch and shouted to the crowd. They responded in fierce agreement. Some raised their fists. Others made that high-pitched call.

Tabitha walked to the edge. In the distance she saw two white men in the midst of a crowd of angry onlookers. She screamed to the cab driver to call for help. He picked up his radio and called the police.

The strong man pointed at Lucas and gave what appeared to be a pronouncement of guilt. He lifted the torch and cursed at him, spitting in his face. The crowd waited in anticipation. Someone started to chant "*Choma!*" and the rest joined in. Lucas lost the ability to think clearly. Words stumbled out of him like a drunk slurring his speech. The strong man leaned his head back. He looked up at the black sky and howled with excitement.

The strong man then threw the torch at Jake.

16

The torch hit Jake on the shoulder, sending embers into his eyes. He pulled his head back and shook his face, trying to get the burning pieces out. The torch fell onto the rags. He twisted and panicked to shake the torch off. But it didn't matter. Not now.

The rags caught fire.

There was a blinding flash of light. The rags ignited a pocket of gasoline that had collected in the tire. In an instant he was ablaze. A fireball engulfed him in a cocoon of red and yellow. Flames shot out and hit Lucas, setting his rags on fire. He shook himself to get loose, but felt only the unmerciful grasp of rubber around his waist. Smoke filled his nostrils. He kicked his head back and from side to side. His shirt burned. What little chance he had of remembering his verses dissipated when the tire caught fire.

"*Choma! Choma! Choma!*" was all Lucas heard as they screamed with the passion of getting a good night's entertainment. The flames lit up their intense faces. White teeth hidden in a vale of darkness. Some of them clenched their fists as though they had money riding on who would go down first. Some of them cheered with every unsuccessful attempt Lucas or Jake made to free themselves. Some of them taunted and laughed at the burning duo as the flames covered them.

Many of them had been healed by Lucas that same day.

Flames ripped over Lucas' face. He lost his balance and fell to the ground. Some of the crowd cheered. Others were disappointed, wishing the two would not have caught fire so quickly to spread out the event a while longer.

As ironic as last thoughts might be, Lucas expected some great vision—an angel, maybe even God, coming down to see him there. Some great epiphany. Some wild conclusion to wrap all of life's questions into a single answer. But he didn't get that. All he had was a saying he had learned as a child running around in his mind. *Stop, drop and roll. Stop, drop and roll.* That's it. No massive conclusion about life. No answers to the world's most pressing questions. No insights in terms of why he was dying this way. *Stop, drop and roll.*

He tried to roll over but the tire had melted and fused around him, making it impossible to turn. Fire spread over his entire body. He heard the crackling of the flames as a breeze blew past him.

Tabitha watched from the embankment. Her mind was dissociating herself from what she was seeing in a vain attempt to protect her. The police were on their way. But little good that would do them now. And there was no way she could go down there. Much as she wanted to, if she went down to help Lucas, she would find the same fate as he had. Still, there he was. Dying. Burning to death before her eyes in front of a frantic crowd.

And then everything went quiet.

Lucas saw Jake across from him, enveloped by the cluster of flames. His tire burned off. The last of the incredible black smoke rose up to the night sky. He saw Jake get up off his knees and look at him. The strangest expression filled his eyes.

That's when Lucas felt it too.

Nothing hurt. Not his face. Not his body. Not even his hands where the fire had started. No pain. The tire around Lucas burned completely off, allowing him to move his arms. Lucas stood up.

The crowd drew back.

The screaming stopped.

Lucas looked down at his hands. Fire flowed over them like a mysterious wave. He looked through the flames and saw his smooth skin. No char. No burn marks. He turned them over to look at his palms. Flames continued to burn without anything feeding them.

People pointed at them and began screaming, looking at one another for some kind of explanation. Half of the crowd turned and fled in all directions. Running. Shouting. Escaping. The others who remained, either too afraid to leave or too amazed at what they were seeing, moved farther back for fear that the two men on fire would attack them.

Tabitha's ankles felt weak. She trembled, unsure of how to understand what she was seeing. She fell to her knees but did not feel the sting of gravel digging into her skin. She saw the remaining people move farther away, seeking shelter behind pathetic metal and cardboard structures. The black hulk stayed where he was, looking at the two burning men in front of him.

She watched in amazement, trying to make that impossible connection between what her eyes were seeing and what she knew was impossible. The healings. She was getting used to those. Each one was a miracle. No doubt. But seeing men survive fire, to stand there with it swarming around them without any effect, was another category—one that she had no room to accommodate.

Lucas and Jake stepped closer to the strong man. Lucas focused on his eyes. No fear. No hesitation. They stopped in front of him. The fire subsided to a faint blue all around them. Then it died out altogether.

Two against one.

The odds were in their favour.

The strong man had seen horrible events like this before. Kids possessed by spirits lifting cars and throwing them at people. Teenagers jumping five feet in the air, turning sideways and spinning around like a soda can that's sprung a leak. Superhuman running ability so that a possessed adult could catch up to a speeding car. Now, a torching. And he knew how to deal with them as he did all the others who had supernatural abilities. People like this had to be destroyed. People like this had problems only death could solve. He studied them. No indication their shirts or pants had been singed. No burn marks on their faces.

No smell of smoke on their clothes.

On top of the embankment Tabitha received confirmation the police were nearly there. She turned back to the scene and wondered if it was better or worse for Lucas if she yelled to get his attention.

Lucas walked past the strong man. Jake followed.

"You are not leaving," the strong man said. Lucas and Jake continued walking. The strong man shouted in his native language. As if on cue, people came out of the shadows.

"We know how to deal with threats," he said.

The people cut off their escape route up the embankment. Lucas heard sirens in the distance. Then he heard the sound of a pickup truck coming down the narrow alley. He saw the strong man's truck come to a stop. A young boy stepped out. He turned to the strong man for a sign of approval, but got nothing.

A rock flew through the air and hit Lucas on the forehead. Before he could react a second hit him on the base of the skull. Jake grabbed him by the shoulders and charged the crowd. He smashed through the first group, but more than a dozen stood ready behind them. Jake clenched his right hand and drove it into the nearest person's nose. The others grabbed him and forced him down to the ground. An arm strung around Lucas's neck and choked him. A fist pounded him in the face. Two men dragged Lucas to the truck. Another powerful blow to his face. His eyes began to tear up. He drifted in that unstable world between consciousness and passing out. He felt blood drip from his forehead down his face.

Tabitha screamed from the top. She saw flashing lights come towards her. She waved her hands to get their attention.

Sets of hands dug into Lucas' arms and legs and loaded him onto the truck. His back hit corrugated metal. Feet stomped on his torso as people climbed in with him. He forced a trickle of air down his throat. His body shook with pain. The engine started. Lucas felt the truck jerk forward. He tried to say his verses. Tried to clear his mind enough to remember them. Tried to force himself to stay awake. The truck turned down an alley, drove a short distance, and then made another turn. He was sure he could hear Tabitha screaming in the distance as they drove up the embankment and left the slum.

Three green and white police vehicles came to a stop. The flashing lights lit up the night sky. Tabitha ran to them. She pointed to the truck taking off in the distance and then to Jake lying on the ground. Two police vehicles went into the slum after Jake, each driver refusing to go in alone.

The other police vehicle chased after Lucas. Tabitha hurried into the taxi and shouted at the driver to follow.

The truck veered around a corner. The police vehicle made the same turn. As the taxi followed they saw the truck make an unexpected move. Instead of continuing down the road it went back into the slum. The police vehicle stopped. So did the taxi driver.

"What are you doing? Go! Go!"

But he didn't move. He sat there, gripping the steering wheel, both unable and unwilling to continue. Tabitha opened the door and ran to the police vehicle. Inside she saw a young man, maybe 20, with a pale face. The one beside him was no older. "We cannot go into the slum," he said.

"Go help him!" But they stayed there. Paralyzed by fear.

She ran back to the taxi, got into her seat on the left side, and yelled at the driver to take her down there. He refused. She shouted again. Still, he was obstinate. She clenched her fist and drove it in the taxi driver's face. "Go!" she screamed, spit flying out of her mouth as she swore a blue streak at him.

One of the police officers came to the car and tried to calm her down. She pulled her fist back again and drilled the taxi driver in the ear. His head smashed against the window. He opened the door to lean away from her and covered his head. Tabitha pushed him out of the car and got into his seat. The police officer tried to grab her. She shook herself free and put her left hand on the gear shift, trying hard to mentally switch to having the steering wheel on the right side of the vehicle. She put it in gear and then alternated between the clutch and the gas. The car barely moved forward. She hit the clutch again, realized she was in third, and shifted to first. She pinned the accelerator. The taxi took off. It smashed into the back of the police vehicle, sending it into the ditch. She pulled a hard left, crossed over the road and into the slum.

She drove down the hill and shifted to second. The adjoining alleys were too small to accommodate a truck so she continued straight down the main road. She shifted to third. Dilapidated huts raced past her. She barrelled through a clothesline full of laundry. This was madness.

She made it up a hill. The road became narrow. Her car nearly hit the huts. Then it grew wider again. Fourth gear. The huts were nothing but a blur. The car bounced up and down with the pot-holes. She hit a low spot in the road and bottomed out, creating a hollow *thud*. Tabitha hit the clutch and shifted to third to regain the speed she had lost, and struggled to find her way through the muddy and unpredictable surroundings. The road turned right. She took her foot off the gas and yanked on the steering wheel. Up another hill. Every scene looked the same as the one before. *Where is he? Where is the truck?* She gripped the steering wheel tighter and negotiated as best she could through the dark confusion. She reached the top. Roads forked out in all directions. She hit the brakes, clenched her teeth, and tensed every muscle in her stressed body. *Which way? Which way?*

Tabitha put the car in neutral. She pulled the emergency brake and pushed open the door. She ran out and scanned every direction. She made two complete turns, looking out in the distance for any sign of hope. She felt a pain in her chest. A cramp in her stomach. A tightness in her throat. She began to hyperventilate, taking short, staggered breaths as she made another turn. Her face flushed with anger and fear.

The truck was nowhere to be found.

17

The ability to regulate how fast—or slow—time was passing left Lucas. Everything became an ongoing relentless repetition—which would have been fine if he was doing something he wanted to, but as things were he was lying face down in a truck with mercenaries taking him to an unknown and likely unwelcome destination. His swelling and bleeding throat, his freezing cold body, and his pounding headache made every second feel like an hour. Small short breaths. Stabbing pain. Inability to think clearly.

Wondering what was going to happen next.

The men sitting on the makeshift benches pressed their feet against his bloodied body. They pinned his arms, legs, and torso down for fear he might spring up with his demonic powers and breathe burning fire into their faces. One of them, the youngest, sucked back on a cigarette and considered himself fortunate to be promoted to this group.

The truck turned onto an even bumpier road. His body shook with every pothole, forcing him to readjust his head to draw breath. He opened his eyes and saw one of the bare feet pressed against his face. The sun was rising. It was the first time since leaving the slum that he could see anything. He'd been travelling a long time.

And that concerned him.

This wasn't a paved road. It may not even appear on any map. Who knows how long they'd been on this road or how long they'd been on the one before. Or the one before that. If they left the slum at, guessing, 10:30 p.m., and the sun gets up at 5:30 a.m., then Lucas figured they had been travelling for seven hours.

Seven hours away from civilization.

Good luck to anyone who was trying to find him.

The truck came to a stop. The men, or boys (it was so tough to tell their ages), pushed down harder on him, thinking that if he were to attack them this would be the time.

Lucas heard the strong man's voice. The men shuffled to the end of the truck and got off. They grabbed Lucas by the feet and dragged him along the box. As he slid to the end he saw a thin metal rod lying under one of the seats.

Lucas angled his chin down to see if he could get a count. Four for sure. Maybe as many as six, difficult to make out against the blinding tip of the rising golden sun. He reached out for the metal rod. The key was to make lethal contact with the first one. That was critical.

He felt some of his verses coming back to memory. He struggled to concentrate on them. One rod. One pathetic metal rod. What could that do against six assailants plus the strong man? As Lucas spoke the passages to himself he felt a burning sensation in his throat. He coughed and a splatter of blood and spit came up.

They pulled him off the truck. He let the rod go by, and as he did, when he reached that point where he realized it was too far away to change his mind and grab it, he immediately regretted it. He slumped to the ground, landing on his hip first, putting it out of place, and hit his head against the bumper.

The strong man gave instructions. Four of them each took a metal rod and a hammer and began to bang them into the ground. He looked down at Lucas. His black face filled everything Lucas saw. Chiselled cheekbones. Yellow tinge around those eyes. He looked sick. Too many drugs. Too much alcohol. Too malnourished as a child.

He walked behind Lucas, creating a shadow over him. He leaned closer and whispered to Lucas in Swahili. Whatever it was, it made the men next to him cringe. The strong man raised his right leg. He shouted as he slammed his foot down on Lucas' ankle. There was a horrific *crack* as Lucas' heel twisted to the side. A burning flush of heat raced through his body.

The men grabbed four ropes and tied one end to each of Lucas' wrists and feet. He winced in pain as one man tied the rope around his broken ankle. The man yanked back to make a solid knot, then stood up and spit in Lucas' face.

Go limp. Go limp from the pain.

He saw the stakes in the ground. Four of them. Spread out as the corners of a square. His heart raced so fast he thought he was having an attack. And if it were possible to self-inflict one on demand, Lucas might have done it—especially in light of what came next.

They pushed his feeble body to the middle of the stakes. The man closest to him leaned over, getting ready to tie the rope to the stake.

This is it. This is all you have left. You have to get control. You have got to take him out.

With a thrust of strength Lucas grabbed the rope and wrapped it around the man's neck. He pulled back with all his strength. The other men were about to pummel Lucas when the strong man told them to stop. They watched in confusion as Lucas cut off the man's breathing, knowing that should they disobey they would suffer a fate as bad as, or worse than, their comrade.

The strong man clapped and began to chant in a deep throaty voice. Saliva dripped out of the other man's mouth as he tried to claw at Lucas to get free. His eyes rolled back. His arms weakened. His breathing slowed down. Lucas felt the man's strength fading. He turned around to see the others standing and watching in terror.

Inside Lucas raged a battle between two opposing sides. It was as though two invisible people, one on his left and the other on his right, were instructing him on what to do next.

You're going to kill him and then what? Kill the others?

What choice do you have? You have to take him out.

Then what? You're going to take out the strong man? Forget this. Say your verses.

Don't be stupid! The others follow the strong man. Kill the man in your hands and charge the strong man. The rest will run.

Let him go.

Look at the stake in the ground. It's not pounded in all the way. Kill this man and pretend to fall over on your back as you drag him down. Then as the strong man approaches, you rip out the stake and shove it through his mouth and out the back of the head.

Don't do it.

Kill him!

Release him.

Kill him!

If you don't release him, what hope do either of you have?

Do it now! Kill him! Now!

Lucas released his hold on the man. He wheezed and stumbled forward. Lucas pushed him to the side to avoid having him fall on a stake. He crumpled to the ground, grabbing his throat.

The strong man stopped his chant. The passionate look left his face and was replaced with disappointment. His eyes were even more yellow than before. He spoke to the other men in an angry tone. They grabbed the ropes.

The strong man reached down to the ground and picked up a stripped branch about as strong as a broom handle. Then he shouted and the four men heaved on the ropes, pulling Lucas' legs out from under him. His chin hit the dry crusty ground, splitting it open on contact. They hammered down the stakes and tied his arms and legs to them such that he was spread-eagled, face down.

One of them ripped Lucas' shirt off. The strong man told him to continue. The man hesitated but, not wishing to take Lucas' place, obeyed the strong man and took off Lucas' pants and underwear.

The strong man pointed at Lucas and pronounced a sentence.

Lucas tried to quote his verses. They were out of order. Out of synch. He recalled pieces here and there but was unable to produce a coherent string of words among the panic.

The strong man stopped speaking. He stepped beside Lucas and lifted the branch high above him, creating a shadow over Lucas' back.

Everything went still.

Lucas heard a *swoosh* sound as the branch ripped through the air. It smacked down on his back. He felt a blistering sting of heat slice through him as though he had leaned against a hot stove element. He gripped the ropes, hoping to release some of the incredible pain.

The second strike came down in the same spot. He arched his back in a futile attempt to protect that area from future hits. The third strike was dead on again, splitting open the skin and drawing the first spatter of blood. He took fast short breaths, sucking in as much oxygen as he could to combat the pain in his body.

Lucas clenched his teeth and tensed his stomach muscles. He heard the others gather up the courage to shout at him, cheering as the strong man delivered justice.

The fourth and fifth strikes came in quick succession near his shoulder blades. The sixth landed at the base of his spine. The seventh missed somewhat and caught him on the side. He heard a cracking sound.

Lucas' scream changed pitch. This wasn't fear anymore. It wasn't even pain. This was that strange realm on the other side of pain where the body kicks out whatever chemicals it can to trick the brain into not believing what is happening.

By the time the eighth came down he was unable to recall any of his verses. All he could remember was the name God. That was it. No more. He had a son, right? His name? His name was...? He called on God to help him. All he got was another hit. And then another.

And then many more.

By the time he reached 40 cracks pieces of spine stuck through his torn skin. His body twitched. His teeth chattered as though something in his spinal cord had already been severed so that signals in his body were getting crossed. He felt streams of blood drip down his side.

The beating continued.

The strong man lifted the stick and whipped it down on the lower part of Lucas' back. They heard another crack. A definite fracture. A rush of ice water ran through Lucas' body. The last clear conscious thought he had was that he hoped the cracking sound was that of the branch.

I'm numb. That's all it is. I'm numb from the pain. My body is just confused. God of the heavens...Jesus...Jesus God. Oh my God. Oh my God. Why can't I feel my legs?

Lucas tried to wiggle his toes, flex a hamstring muscle. Anything. Anything at all.

But nothing responded.

Dark clouds filled the sky and covered the sun, turning what looked to become a bright day into an abysmal darkness. The wind picked up. A powerful gust blew against them.

His body shut off. One hundred and fifty-three strikes in total. He couldn't feel the stake in his right hand. He couldn't feel the ropes. Couldn't feel the hard, unforgiving ground beneath him. Couldn't feel the pain in his spine from the severed vertebrae and the exposed cord.

Nothing.

Lucas' world went black. The pain concentrated for a moment in his neck and then subsided altogether.

A torrent of rain besieged them. The strong man dropped his bloodied stick. He grabbed Lucas by the hair and lifted his head. He saw a man devoid of expression. But those eyes. There was something different about those eyes. And in that instant, the strong man felt a surge strike out from Lucas' eyes into his body.

He dropped Lucas' head and stepped back, thinking that perhaps he had imagined what had just happened. He passed by the men, trying hard not to show anything but staunch resolve. The men stood still, unable to go with him, trying to absorb what they had just allowed themselves to support. They looked at Lucas' ragged, ripped body and, in an effort to rid themselves of the guilt, tried to convince themselves that Lucas deserved it. What was the reason again? Demonic. Right. He was demonic because he withstood fire. That was it. Forget the miracles. Forget the healings. Forget that he even healed some of them. A man who doesn't burn should die.

They turned and left, leaving his body in the monsoon rain, then hurried to catch up with the strong man as if hoping to find absolution in his presence for their deed.

The strong man started the truck. He saw his reflection in the rear-view mirror. What he saw in his eyes scared him so much he adjusted the mirror away from him to avoid having to look at himself.

It took a number of tries to find first gear. He jammed it in and did what he could to put this out of his mind. They all did. They all wanted to assure themselves that this was the right thing. That they had acted in the best interest of themselves and the people.

But as he drove off in search of the road far in the distance, he realized that regardless of how far he went, he would not be able to leave this behind.

Lucas lay in a pool of blood and water. The rain washed out pieces of flesh to reveal the places where his spine was severed.

Jake. Jake can do it. He can continue the mission. He's better than he thinks he is. He can carry this thing on. So can Edgar. They can find a way. Together. Can they manage to get the gift? Have they been through enough to be able to take it from here?

Lucas felt himself drifting off. He took in one last breath. Then he exhaled. Closed his eyes. Turned off his will to live.

And waited for death.

18

Hours and hours and hours. Blistering sun. Merciless heat. Every tree. Every road. Every stretch of terrain looked identical to the one before it. One long repetitive scene.

Tabitha scanned the horizon from the passenger seat of a police van. She held a map in one hand, pencil in the other, striking out areas as they searched them. So much left to cover. So much uncharted territory. She looked around for anything that might indicate Lucas had been here. She tried to distinguish between the image she wanted to see of him coming out of the bleak horizon and the image of the plain brown landscape before her. She wanted to turn the clock back. She wanted to redo the part about leaving his side. *If you had just stayed right beside him, if you had waited until he was out of the slum, none of this would have happened.*

Jake sat behind her with another police officer, gazing at the unforgiving surroundings, wondering if they were getting any closer. *Is Lucas out there? Is he still alive? How long could a person survive in this?*

After reuniting in the slum, Tabitha and Jake had gone on an all-out attack to make authorities and media aware of the need to find Lucas. The response was nothing short of passionate. Still, despite all the help and attention, they had no leads. No clues.

No hard evidence to support their hope.

The radio crackled. The Kenyan police officer spoke into it in his native Kamba language. Tabitha leaned forward as if doing so could somehow translate what was being said. The officer paused and asked for the last phrase to be repeated. When he heard it a second time, he became quiet and put the radio down.

"What?" Tabitha asked.

"It is not good news," he said. "They have identified the man you described who took Lucas away. The tall muscular man."

"Who is he?"

The officer wiped the sweat from his brow. He looked at her, his eyes filled with fear. "It is not good."

British Prime Minister William Davidson stood with his hands on his hips in his office, looking at Marcus and Angelica seated before him.

"What's our progress?" he asked.

"We have agents in Nairobi looking for him," Angelica said. "Though we believe he has fled the country. Back to Somalia. We have agents in Mogadishu as well. He could be anywhere."

"He's the only one who knows where Lucas is?"

"If Lucas isn't with him, then Lucas is likely dead. There are two alternatives. Either he didn't know Lucas and killed him. Or he does know the healing power of this young man and is harbouring him for a ransom."

"Cut him a deal."

"He's into arms dealing, drug smuggling...."

"No. Find something else. We'll set him up somewhere nice. I need Lucas in London." He paused. "London needs Lucas in London."

"Kenyan police are looking for him," Marcus said. "If they find anything, we'll know."

"That's not enough. We're running out of time."

"We're leaving as well. If he's alive, we will locate him."

"We better."

"Sir. If we do find him and he doesn't come, what do you want us to do?"

Davidson ran a hand through his hair. This wasn't supposed to happen. Money. They had offered him money, for crying out loud.

And he never took it. "Just ask him to come. That's it." He turned to Marcus. "*Encourage* him to come back."

"We will, sir."

Marcus left as Angelica stepped closer to the prime minister. She could sense his worry. His fear. His frustration.

"Seven points," he said. "Two months to the election and we're seven points behind."

"We'll find him."

"One picture of me together with Lucas after he clears out all of the hospitals in London and we could make up that difference."

"We could."

"Two weeks with him in our country and this would become a different campaign. People would forget. They would forget in a quick hurry."

"I'll bring him back to you," Angelica said.

Caesar looked down from his unfinished casino office onto Las Vegas Boulevard. It was a busy night in Vegas. Fight night. Cars packed the Strip. But Caesar didn't care. He had other things on his mind. He had read the papers. He had heard the news—that he had built a monstrosity of a casino for nothing. A pie-in-the-sky white elephant that when finished would sit half-filled at best. But he would prove them wrong. He would prove them all wrong.

He hoped.

Claire sat across from his desk, reading him the latest figures from the construction budget report. She wore a knee-length blue skirt, white blouse and matching blue jacket. She crossed her legs as she turned to the next page to reveal her tanned, toned legs—the result of a disciplined daily treadmill and stepper routine. She finished the summary and put it down on her lap. She cringed as she waited for his response.

"Not quite what we had hoped," he said.

No. No, it wasn't at all what they had hoped. But for a man who was dealing with a potential financial disaster, he seemed to be worried about a great deal more. He coughed and then wiped his forehead as a wave of exhaustion crept over him.

"Pushing the schedule so hard is...." Claire stopped herself. *It's a mistake. Say it. Say it's a mistake.*

"A mistake?" Caesar said, both annoyed at the truth and at her unwillingness to volunteer it.

"Let's go right back to the way things were," Claire said. "We were on budget. We were on schedule—the original schedule. The change in pace is just unreasonable. We're doling out far too much capital for something that can easily wait."

Caesar turned away from the window. The look he gave Claire froze her spine. "Easily wait?" he asked. He stepped forward into the temporary lighting to reveal his pale and tired face.

"Caesar, at this rate the casino will have to make unprecedented profits right from the first night. If it doesn't, we'll have to put up even more equity."

We don't have any more! he wanted to scream at her. But he didn't want to reveal that, even though he was sure she could surmise it. He rubbed his forehead again and turned back to the window. *Two billion. Two billion to put this thing together.*

"There are other alternatives," she said.

He looked at her reflection in the window. "No," he said. "We succeed or we succeed. Those are our options. The schedule stays. We open next month."

"We can pursue the Council's recommendations. The real estate properties in New York. The film business in Hollywood. I understand there's a multipicture deal we can use to set up a production company."

"We're not in the real estate or film business, Claire."

"They are growth opportunities for us."

"We are in the business of pharmaceuticals and gambling."

"Caesar, unless we can develop new drugs—"

"You think they're the same thing?" he asked with a change of tone, catching Claire off guard. He turned to look at her. "Pharmaceuticals and gambling. Do you think they're the same thing?"

"I suppose you take a chance either way. But I'd like to think our pharmaceuticals aren't a gamble."

"Everything is a gamble, Claire."

"Even this casino?"

Caesar thought about her answer. No. The casino was not a gamble. The casino would work. It had to. "Claire, you are an incredible woman. You could have anything in the world. Do you know that?"

She sat up in her chair. "I do."

"That's good. There's nothing worse than a woman with a low perception of herself. You run into women who are full of fear and doubt and feelings of uselessness. That's why I like you, Claire. That's why I picked you."

"Thank you."

"But you have one problem. And once you beat it you will catapult yourself into places you've never dreamed."

Claire wanted to leave. She didn't want to hear this. "That is?"

"You worry, Claire."

"Worry?"

"You shouldn't worry. Not about anything. Not work. Not life. Nothing. People think you need brains to be in business. You don't. All you need is wisdom and courage. That's it. That's all it takes. You have the wisdom. But worry gets in the way of your courage. You worry that things won't work out. They will, Claire. I'm here to see this casino through, and when it does, you'll be there to know how I get things done."

Mike opened the door. That was a break in protocol. Finished building or not, Caesar always demanded a knock.

"I have news," Mike said.

Caesar looked up. Claire turned around. And the moment she saw Mike's expression she felt the conviction that something had gone wrong. She tried to steady her nerves and braced herself for what she was about to hear.

"What is it, Mike?"

Mike didn't know whether to be relieved or distraught. Whether to sit down or stay standing. Whether to blurt it out or go through in step-by-step detail.

"Lucas has been kidnapped in Africa," he said. "Feared dead."

Claire's heart stopped. She wasn't able to breathe. *Feared? He used the word feared. Unconfirmed. How could he have been kidnapped? Wasn't anyone looking after him?* She felt herself struggling not to panic. *Oh my God. Oh my God. Who do I call? Who do I send after him?*

Instead of feeling any emotion, Caesar wondered what this would mean for his company, for his future, for the casino. Was a competitor now finally gone? Would Mike be able to step up and become Empirico's successor? "Go figure," he said, thinking about what it meant to lose his protégé. "I spend all this time wondering about how that kid is going to come back and screw me over—and instead, fate goes ahead and handles it for me." He shook his head. "That stupid kid." He swore. "That stupid, stupid kid." He thanked Mike for coming. "It seems Empirico has been dealt a pair of kings."

What is the matter with you people? Claire bit her lip, hoping it would help her from exploding in a gush of agony. She felt the sting of evil around her. A cool breeze at her back. Her eyes welled up.

Those drastic figures in the report on her lap suddenly felt unimportant.

Lucas had fallen unconscious from the beating. He lay face down in the sand as the temperature in the hot African day exceeded normal highs. His body struggled to keep alive. But he felt none of it. He existed in that strange place between reality and the dream world. It was like he was travelling on a long dark highway with no indication that anything would happen. And then, just like that, he arrived.

He stood at the base of a rock face. The blazing sun beat down on him. He wiped sweat from his forehead and looked up at the towering sheer wall that stretched out forever.

His heart raced in his chest. He felt blood pulse through his neck. He closed his eyes and did what he could to calm his nerves from the terrifying yet inescapable task before him. He took in a deep breath through his nose, held it for a moment, and then exhaled to the count of ten through his mouth.

It was time.

He was as ready as a man gets before taking on a new challenge.

He placed his right hand on the rock. It was cool. He curled his fingers over a jut in the wall. He reached up with his left hand and found another spot. He located a small landing for his left foot.

Down below to the right he saw another footing. He bounced twice on his right leg and then pulled with his arms as he brought his right leg up.

A milestone.

Off the ground.

He led again with his right hand and gripped an opening in the rock. He struggled to make his way as high as a two-storey house off the ground. Sweat dripped down and stung his eye. He blinked to get it out. And that's when he lost his balance.

His right hand went first. It slipped off the rock. He dug in his feet but the ledge offered him no more support. He spun around such that his back was to the rock. He reached behind to grab onto anything, but by then his body had gone too far forward. Lucas fell off the ledge.

He saw the ground below.

It raced towards him at an unforgiving pace.

When Lucas woke he felt horrendous pain in the back of his head. It was as though his brain was about to explode, as if someone was pushing skewers through the soft part under his skull. He had no control over his breathing. No ability to clench his teeth or scream to release some of the tension. He just lay there. His spinal cord split open. His ripped-up muscles and tissue scrambled in a bloody mess, making his back look like a garden that has just been tilled.

He couldn't focus his eyes. Try as he might, all he could make out were shadows and double images. He was consumed by the pain. The horrific pressure in his head. The relentless screaming and pounding.

The prospect of wondering if an animal or death would reach him first.

19

Lucas drifted in and out of consciousness, making it impossible to know if an evening had passed while he was out. He wished for some way to determine how long he had been waiting, or dying, so that whatever life he had left would not become some crazy blur. He thought about stories of prisoners who etched daily marks on their cell walls to keep a record of how long they had been there. They were onto something. Lucas had the same curious human need to know how fast time was progressing. A minute was as good as an hour. And a day was any number of breaths. He lived in the uncertainty of eternity.

He struggled to quote the first few lines of the book he had memorized in prison. *The first account I composed, Theophilus....* The stories of people being whipped for their faith took on new meaning for him, as did the healing story of a man who couldn't walk. All 28 chapters. Two hours each time. Verse by verse. Over and over again. Lucas went from beginning to end and then started again. Anything to get his mind off the pain. Anything to increase his chance for a miracle.

Anything to keep track of time.

Tabitha and Jake had been looking for days. They drove in every direction, handing out pictures, talking to people in rural Kenya, hoping they would receive news that Lucas had been found. That first optimistic day had turned into many. And with every passing hour, their hope faded. The military called off their searches. Angelica and Marcus turned up a blank, much to Davidson's dismay. Foreign journalists covered the story and left. Lucas was but a memory, a shocking disappointment to thousands, millions, waiting for their chance to get close to him. Now, he was gone.

But hope resurrected itself by way of the small boy Lucas had met in the slum—the one whose hand he took when they walked in for the first time. The boy had heard from someone else, who heard from someone else, who in turn heard from someone else, that the man with the white hat and wire-rimmed glasses was back in Nairobi. When Jake and Tabitha returned to the slum, like detectives searching for clues, the little boy ran up to them. He used his hands to form circles around his eyes to imitate the man's circular glasses, and pointed to the ground in an attempt to convey that the man had come back.

Tabitha brought the boy to a vendor down the street to get a translation. The man spoke in broken English and confirmed what the boy said. White hat. Glasses.

"You're sure?" Tabitha asked.

The boy nodded. He was confident of his information. It came from a reliable source.

Or as reliable as could be expected in the slum.

At first Lucas assumed it was just his mind forcing out the result he wanted. That he was imagining what was happening. But the more he quoted his verses, the more he spoke them out loud, the more sure he became that he could feel sand against the thumb of his right hand. Yes. Definitely. Sand.

He rubbed his thumb back and forth. Speaking his verses. Trying not to imagine what the burning sun was doing to his open back.

Why didn't you help me?

Why didn't you stop them?

Lucas forced himself to stretch out his fingers. Then he drew them back and repeated it. He opened and closed his hand in slow movements, concentrating all his efforts to pull against the sand beneath his fingers. He did the same with the other hand. Back and forth until he could repeat it in an even rhythm. It exhausted him. The simple task of moving his hand took all of his energy. What was once nothing more than an automatic response now took careful thought and planning.

He waited, begging his body to respond to his plea to try again. Begging for it to do what he knew it could. He imagined himself stretching his arms out and growing stronger. He pictured himself being able to stand. Being able to walk. Being able to run. Then he stopped. He brought his mind under control and concentrated instead on the verses he had memorized that dealt with healing.

He flattened his palms against the ground. Curving his fingers, he dragged them in as far as they would respond to form a fist.

Come on.

Come on.

He pulled them all the way back so that his fingertips touched his palms. He held the sand in his grip and then opened his hand. Progress. He took in a number of shallow breaths and tried to lift his head off the ground. He struggled, not sure if he was actually raising it or was simply tensing his muscles. He lowered his chin and felt the sand. He angled his head back. Up and down until his muscles were too tired to continue. He rested. Tried again. And counted on the power to come through for him. For three days he remained in that state, quoting his verses, waiting for a breakthrough.

Lucas clawed at the sand. He moved his fingers and clenched his hands to form strong fists. But instead of feeling content with his achievement he knew he was just buying time to avoid tackling the next stage.

He struggled to find courage to go farther, afraid of what might happen if he pushed himself too far. And afraid of what might happen if he went lax and tricked himself into thinking he was progressing as fast as he could.

He took in as deep a breath as he could and lifted his chin off the ground. He waited a moment, battling the urge to lay his head back down and stay content with grabbing handfuls of sand. He turned his head to the side in a slow, uneven movement, testing how far he could make it before pain would stop his progress. He turned the other way, ignoring the threat of snapping some of the fragile healing that had already taken place. He brought his head back to the middle, and then down to the ground, relaxing his neck. Deep breath in.

He lifted his head and turned side to side again. That surprised him. No pain. He managed to make it far enough to look over his shoulder, then gritted his teeth at the unbearable frustration of wanting to stand. He felt sand against his legs. The coarse grains rubbing against the skin on his knees. He twisted his hips and turned from one side to the other. "By stretching out your hand to heal...."

The strong man left Mogadishu at night in his blue truck and began the long trip back. When he heard the news from one of the arms dealers that the man he had killed was in fact *the* Lucas Stephens, he realized that if anyone found his mutilated body, it would serve as proof that he had killed him. For now, there were witnesses who said they saw him and the others load Lucas into his truck and take him away. But his accomplices would swear all they did was take him outside the slum and let him go. They could find other witnesses, or create them if necessary, to convince police they had seen them let Lucas go. What happened to him after that would be a mystery. And it would remain a mystery.

Provided the strong man could bury Lucas' body in the sand before anyone discovered what really happened.

A strange and cool gust of wind came against Lucas. In the distance he heard what sounded like a horse approaching. Getting closer. A rider dismounted. He heard footsteps. It stopped beside him. Someone, something, crouched down. Lucas felt a face beside him breathing on his neck. He saw nothing. He didn't need to.

The feeling was more than enough proof.

You should have killed him when you had the chance. You should have escaped when I told you. Now, look at you. You're finished.

I don't want you here.

But you do. You know that I'm the one who can get you out of this.

I don't need your help.

I can have them find you. I can have them pinpoint exactly where you are.

You can't.

You know that I can. And I can prevent the strong man from coming back to finish you off. You didn't know that, did you? It's true. He's coming. He's coming back right now to bury you in the sand. Bury you alive if he has to. But I can call him off. Just ask for my help and I'll do it. I will heal you. I will help you. I will rescue you.

I'm being healed. My help is on its way.

No. Your help has arrived.

You can help with nothing.

I can help prevent evil things from happening to you.

The first account I composed, Theophilus....

Jake and Tabitha took a taxi from the slum to Moi Avenue in the central business district. They walked into the Hilton and asked the attendants if they knew of a man fitting the description of the strong man's boss. Finding no leads, they searched other hotels as well as restaurants, cafés and stores, looking for the man with the white hat and wire-rimmed glasses. They walked through a promenade area as the sun began to set. A flash of faces pushed past them as people left their jobs for the day. Every person looked like him. Every set of glasses became wire-rimmed. Every hat colour was transformed into white.

Jake opened the door of a two-storey building and let Tabitha go in first. They took a set of stairs up to a dimly lit restaurant. A buffet spread out in front of them. A waitress asked if she could help them. They didn't respond. They gave all their attention to finding the man with the white hat.

And then, there he was.

In the corner. Near the balcony. By himself. Drinking a cup of *chai*.

Jake saw him first. He touched Tabitha's arm and stepped out in front of her. She followed him as they passed a number of empty tables to the man at the back. Jake sat down across from him. Tabitha pulled a chair from the next table. The man looked at Jake, then Tabitha, then back at Jake. Tourists, he figured.

"We're looking for Lucas Stephens."

"Who?" he asked.

It was him. No doubt. Jake felt a surge of hope. The man had crossed his eyebrows too fast and was keeping his guilty eyes too focused on Jake to be genuinely unsure of who they wanted.

"Lucas Stephens," Jake repeated, giving emphasis to each name.

Tabitha noticed a different tone in Jake's voice. She'd never heard this before. Slow. Deep. Cold.

"The healing man? Yes. I heard what happened. Still no luck in finding him?"

"He's a friend of ours. Have you seen him?"

"No."

Liar. "Any idea where we could look for help? We're desperate." Tabitha became scared. Jake's low throaty voice made her think he was about to do something she hadn't seen from him before. "And we're going to do whatever it takes to get him."

The man in the hat coughed. "I'm sorry. You must be under a lot of stress."

"Not compared to Lucas," Jake said, standing up. "Thank you for your time."

Tabitha followed Jake out of the restaurant. "What was that?"

Jake didn't answer. He crossed the promenade and entered a sports store.

"What are you doing, Jake?"

"It's a habit."

"Habit?"

He turned to face her. She didn't recognize the look in his eyes. "Always get a souvenir when visiting a new city. That way you remember it. And, if you're lucky, people there will remember you."

A young girl wearing a Kenyan soccer jersey and a name tag asked if she could help him.

"Can you tell me where I can find the baseball section?"

"I'm sorry, sir," she said with a smile and a British accent. "We don't really have baseball in Kenya. But we do have cricket." She pointed to a section of cricket bats.

Jake walked over, grabbed a bat at random, paid the girl, and left without waiting for the change.

"What are you doing?" Tabitha asked as they went back across the promenade to the restaurant.

"We've tried words, Tabitha. Now we're going to do things the Chicago way."

They walked up the stairs, found the man at the back, and sat down opposite him. This time, the man looked more concerned.

"Hello," Jake said, with an unfriendly smile that revealed his dentures.

"Yes."

"I think you know my friend."

"I don't."

"I think you know what happened to him."

"You're mistaken."

"And you're going to tell me where he went."

"My friend, I am a relief worker in the slum."

Jake pressed his lips together. He leaned forward. "You know what?" he whispered. The man shook his head. "You're not my friend." The man swallowed.

Jake leaned back. "Do you know what this is?" Jake asked. He put his souvenir on the table and kept his hand on it.

"It is a cricket bat."

Jake lifted his index finger and shook it. "No. No, this is not a cricket bat. This, my friend, is a memory bat."

"A memory bat."

"That's right. It helps people recall things. Like where someone was taken after they were kidnapped."

"I think it's time you left."

"You decide how we do this. Either way, I'm getting my answer."

"Get out!" the man shouted, pointing a finger in Jake's face.

As if rehearsed, Jake reached out and grabbed the man's finger. He snapped it back in an unnatural position so it touched the man's forearm. It made a popping sound. The man screamed so loud that Tabitha jolted. People turned around in panic to see the problem.

"Where did they take him?" Jake asked in the same chilled tone. No waver in his voice. The man trembled in pain. He gritted his teeth. Jake let go. The man clutched his hand. His face went pale. "Where did they take him?"

The man began to sweat. He held his breath.

"No answer?" Jake asked as he gripped the memory bat. Before Tabitha could stop him, Jake stood up and swung the bat with all of his might. He smashed it against the man's shoulder, knocking him off his chair to the ground. People nearby stood up and hurried to the front of the restaurant.

Jake kicked the chair out of the way and stepped beside the man. "Where is he?"

The man rolled over on his side. Jake pressed his foot down on the man's shoulder and forced him onto his back.

"I don't know."

Jake lifted the bat over his head. Tabitha brought her hands to her face and pulled her head away. Jake arched his back like he was chopping wood and came down with all his weight on the man's shin. There was a cracking sound like a branch breaking. The man screamed. He tried to roll over but Jake stomped on his arm, preventing him from moving.

Jake bent down and pushed the bat against the man's throat. "Shhhhh," he whispered. Jake grabbed a napkin from the table and stuffed it in the man's mouth. He bit down on it to ease the pain. "I know it hurts," Jake said. "I know because this happened to me. But everything here can be fixed by a doctor. Finger dislocation and broken bones are no problem. But next come the knees and the face. Those the doctors have a harder time fixing. So you decide. Lucas or the doctors?"

A river of sweat poured off the man. He fought to get the words out between desperate sporadic breaths. "I know where they took him."

Lucas began to cry. It was the first time he was able to shed tears since the beating. And what started as a simple stress reaction turned into a deep uncontrollable plea. With his head against the sand, Lucas cried for what seemed like hours.

Where are you?

The rider was gone. Darkness was upon him. As night crept in he continued with his verses. He felt a renewed courage. A renewed hope. Like he had turned a critical corner. He moved his hips from side to side. Later that night he reached out with both hands and touched the stakes.

He felt the first drops of rain hit his spine. Then the drizzle turned into a deluge. Water poured onto his barren back. He quoted the verses louder as rain washed into his back, cleaning out his cuts. He curled his toes and moved them against the sand. He felt the ropes against his ankles. Water filled in around him. Some came up to his face. He dipped his tongue in and brought it to his mouth. It took him the entire night to take in a cup's worth.

The next morning Lucas moved his shoulders. He brought them forward and back to test how far he could go, to test how well the muscles in his back had grown together. Each expansion and contraction of his lungs stretched the connection between what was and what would be.

Meanwhile, the strong man waited on the Somalian border for dusk before he would continue on into Kenya. There was no point risking travel by day. No point in having someone recognize him. He sat in his truck parked on the side of a dirt road off the highway. He bought a soft drink from a vendor in a bright red kiosk and waited in the hot sun.

By evening he would be able to cross the border and finish Lucas off.

Lucas pushed himself up on his elbows. He breathed in, feeling his lungs expand to full capacity. Each breath assured him of how far he had come. He rotated his shoulders, biding time to find the courage to stretch his body. He balanced himself on his wrists and, not feeling confident that this would work, arched his back to check if his muscles and bones had reattached. He pushed still farther. Nothing hurt. The setting sun provided enough light for him to see there was no blood on his side or on his shoulder blades. The rain had done its job. He lay back down on the ground, then pushed back farther than the previous position.

He clenched his fists and reached to pull out the stakes.

Tabitha and Jake followed the directions given by the man in the white hat. His words seemed detailed enough as he lay bleeding on the ground in the restaurant, but they became more vague when they got nearer to the location. As honest as a man becomes when his knees and face hang in the balance, the man could only tell them what he knew, which was proving to be increasingly less than what they needed. He gave them the first highway and the general area of where they were taking Lucas. But in rural Africa, general areas can stretch on for miles.

They hired a van and driver to take them there and spent the day driving around what was becoming a repetitive nightmare. They took various routes and turns and paths, knowing that it would take a hundred vans months to cover all of the trails and places they could have taken him. They asked people for directions, some of them eager to see the *mazungus*, especially the young children, some of whom were seeing white skin for the first time.

The van stopped. Tabitha and Jake stepped out under a dusk sky. They searched the horizon thinking, hoping it would provide them with a clue as to where they might find him. But they both knew the answer. It was just that Tabitha finally had the courage to say it.

"Jake, he's gone."

"He's not gone." But Jake knew better. He had failed at his job. He had let his friend down. And now Lucas was dead.

"I don't know what else to do," Tabitha said, neither of them sure if she was calling off the search for Lucas or just deciding that with the setting sun there was no point in continuing in the dark. She put her arm around Jake, wishing instead he would have done the same for her. They walked to the van, sat down in the back seat, and drove off to Nairobi with much the same uncertainty they had at Wrigley Field after the assassination attempt. Though this time there was no body to resurrect. Jake and Tabitha buried their faces in their hands, feeling the weight of defeat and the bitter sting of wondering what would happen next.

Had they kept their heads up, they would have seen a familiar beat up light blue pickup truck with a strong man behind the wheel, driving past them to a rendezvous farther down the road.

Lucas pulled on the ropes with renewed strength. The stakes were hammered deep in the ground. He felt the one to his right begin to loosen in the sand. He yanked on the rope and the stake came flying out, nearly hitting him in the face as it flew by. He reached over and chewed through the rope attached to his left hand. When it broke loose he pushed himself up on his knees. It was a welcome relief not to be face down any longer. He brought his hands behind his back to touch his skin and worried about what he might find there. There was no exposed bone. No dried patches of blood. No ripped-up flesh. He reached behind and loosened the ropes off his ankles.

Lucas stood up, his shaky frame getting used to being upright again. He lifted his arms, leaned his head back, and exhaled as he looked up at the starry sky. Freedom. The canopy above him seemed like a protective shell, a perfect hemisphere with enough holes poked in to let the light down.

Off to the side he found his jeans, shoes, underwear and torn shirt. He put them on, and was about to gnaw off the rope connected to the stake on his right hand when out of the corner of his eye he saw lights in the distance. A truck approached. He was about to wave his arms when he recognized the vehicle.

And he recognized the driver.

Lucas backed away, then hobbled towards a group of trees, hoping to hide behind them.

The strong man stopped the truck. Lucas raced for the wooded area in unco-ordinated steps as though his legs were in chains. The strong man heard the commotion to his right. He turned his head, thinking it was an animal. Instead he saw a white-skinned man hurrying away from him. He looked at the place where he had caned that evil being and then back at the bush. The figure was gone. The strong man hurried out of his truck. He reached into the back, pulled out an axe and gave chase.

Lucas staggered through the trees, looking for a place of refuge. He heard the powerful strides of the strong man's feet pounding against the ground. Up ahead he saw a clump of bushes and decided to try for them. Each step felt like he was in a dream and couldn't run away. His legs gave out and he crashed to the ground. He crawled to a nearby tree.

Lucas saw the strong man run into the woods. He held his breath and watched as he searched the area for him. Before Lucas had time to turn his body to the other side the strong man spotted him and yelled. Lucas forced himself to his feet. He clutched the stake in his right hand and hid it behind him.

The strong man gripped the axe with both hands. He faded in and out of the shadows as he crept closer to Lucas. When he got within striking range he lifted the axe. The blade shimmered under the full moon. He grunted as he swung for Lucas' head. Just as the blade sliced through the air Lucas dropped to his knees. The axe whizzed over him and stuck into the tree with a tremendous *thud.* Lucas jumped up. His legs screamed in pain. He pulled the stake back and rammed it into the strong man's forehead.

It sunk in.

The strong man stumbled back, stunned that he had been dealt such a vicious blow. The rope between the stake and Lucas' arm tightened, pulling Lucas towards him. The strong man reached for the object in his head and tried to pull it out. With his other hand he pulled on the rope, bringing Lucas closer to him. He wrapped his hand around Lucas' throat and squeezed as hard as he could.

Lucas slammed the heel of his hand against the stake and drove it in farther. The strong man gritted his teeth. His eyes were wild with panic. Lucas smelled the stench of his breath as he struggled for air. He smashed his hand against the stake again, driving it in farther. The strong man's grip faded. Lucas pried his fingers off his throat. He loosened the knot and got his hand free. He pushed away from the strong man and watched as he began to shut down. Whatever existence there was behind those yellow eyes faded out of his body, leaving him a hollow shell. Lucas saw the statue in front of him lean over to the side. The strong man twisted on his way down, falling face first so that when he hit the ground the stake pierced through his brain and came out the base of his skull.

A gust of wind blew through the trees. It made Lucas shiver. He looked down at the once powerful man. Blood ran out of his head and formed a stream down to his feet. He stepped back to avoid it, turned around, then left before the memory of that botched abortion he performed on Tabitha's sister came flooding back too strongly.

When Lucas returned to the truck he saw the headlights fading from a dull glow to nothing. He ripped open the door, climbed in behind the wheel, and turned the ignition. Nothing. He tried again. Still nothing. He took out a shovel from the back, then searched the truck for food and water. Finding none he returned to the strong man. He dug a shallow grave and rolled the strong man into it. He filled it with sand. The strong man's messed-up face was the last part he covered.

Lucas spent the night in the pickup. The next morning he skipped his prayers and opted instead to do them while walking 12 hours down a trail until he came to a road. He stumbled down the middle of it, his feet aching and his body ready to quit, when a *matatu* came up behind him. It honked as it approached. It took a second honk for him to hear it. He turned around. When he saw it he fell to his knees.

People rushed out to help him, bringing water and fruit. He felt the water splash against his parched throat. He saw a myriad of faces talking and staring at him. They carried him into the van, squished together on the other benches so he could lie down on one by himself, and drove to Nairobi. One of the passengers sitting beside him, a medium-build woman about Lucas' height and in her early twenties, gave him whatever he needed from the passengers, who offered everything they had to help this *mazungu*.

When they arrived at the crowded Nairobi bus station people brought trays of food, candy, toys, and drinks to the *matatu* in the hopes of making a sale. Lucas wanted it all to go away. Just stop the flash of colour and noise. No strong man. No people pulling at him. *Make the World go Away* played over in his mind. The young woman led him through the maze of buses, vans and peddlers. It had rained the night before and their feet sloshed in the messy slush of muck. She took him down a sidewalk to a busy intersection. There they turned down a quieter street to her apartment. She helped him up the stairs to her room. She offered him food. He declined but accepted more water. She showed him to the shower and started the water for him. She closed the door.

Alone.

Again.

He felt no pain under the water. Felt no relief either. He stood with the water rushing over his head and down his scarred back. He thought about praying. He thought about reciting his verses. But instead all he thought about was Caesar and wondered how he was doing.

And what his reaction would be when he found out that he was now alive.

He changed into the T-shirt and shorts she gave him. Then she helped him to her small clean room decorated with black and white pictures of her recent Maasai Mara safari. He noticed one in particular of a young girl standing alone on a small bridge, looking out at the fading sunset. She pulled back the red and blue checkered blanket. Lucas collapsed on her bed and fell asleep. She watched him a moment, then closed the door and left.

It was evening when he woke. He saw her laying out new clothes for him. A candle nearby gave off enough light to see her soft dark skin, making it look almost like gold. Her subtle perfume filled his senses, relaxing him, making him think it would be alright to let his guard down. For a while. She wore a pair of blue jeans and a white T-shirt. No socks. Blue toenail polish. When she noticed him looking at her she sat down next to him. She put her hand on his forehead, found that he didn't have a temperature, and gave him a glass of water.

"You're him, aren't you?" she said with a soft British accent. "Lucas. The one everyone thought was dead."

She saw the hesitation in his eyes, the worry that he would be forced to traipse through a hospital, a village or a slum.

She smiled. "You are safe with me. I promise."

Safe. Yes. Safe. He wanted to forget Chicago. He wanted to forget Caesar. He wanted to stay here. Away from all of that.

"I need to go back to Chicago."

Lucas thought he recognized a hint of sadness in her eyes when he said that. She nodded and told him she could take him to the airport.

He debated again about staying in Nairobi. No. No, there was Tabitha. Jake. Edgar too. *Right, Edgar. How was he doing?*

Lucas landed at Gatwick, took a bus to Heathrow, and boarded a plane for Chicago. It backed away and began taxiing to the runway when Angelica came running to the gate. She had received information that Lucas was in London. The passenger manifest of the plane from Nairobi did not show a Lucas Stephens, thanks to the Kenyan woman who knew an official who could keep his identity safe. But his name came up when he went through security at Heathrow, and by the time Angelica heard about it she worried that she wouldn't catch him in time. She called Prime Minister Davidson's office and was transferred to a secure line.

"I need authorization to stop the plane," Angelica said.

"We can't do that," Davidson said, feeling his chances for election slipping away. "The media would find out and that would make us look desperate."

"I can get him for you. I'll go to America. I'll bring him back."

"No," Davidson said. They had been so close. *So close.* Lucas was right in his own country. "He's gone. Let's resolve ourselves to that and make do with what we have here."

Angelica heard the line go dead and felt the sting of failing at her mission. She watched as the plane turned a corner, out of view.

It gathered speed down the runway and took off. Lucas sat in the last row. Again. And he wasn't able to concentrate on the movie, the radio or the food. Again. All he could think about were the brutal events behind him.

And all he could wonder about were the ones yet to come.

20

It rained down on Buckingham Fountain in Chicago with such force that it drowned out the sprays of water shooting up. The dark swelling clouds had been threatening for hours. Then, just when it seemed things might clear up, the skies dumped on the park below. One moment it looked hopeful; the next it was such a torrential downpour that people left in droves, seeking shelter from the relentless deluge. The park became empty—save for one man sitting on a park bench. By himself. Oblivious to the rain.

Oblivious to the world around him.

The rain pelted him and the trees around him. He would have thought it strange that rain could make such a loud noise had he taken the time to think about it. But Edgar wasn't interested in the rain. His mind was elsewhere.

He saw Lake Michigan in the distance past Lake Shore Drive. It was covered by a haze of grey, making it impossible to distinguish between what was lake and what was mist. Edgar stared ahead with a curious expression, a blend of depression and disbelief. He looked like an elderly person in a wheelchair who sits in a nursing home, gazing out a window day after day with an unchanging catatonic expression on their face—and without them saying or doing anything, you get the strangest feeling there might in fact be a whole lot more going on in that mind than what appears on the outside.

Water streamed down his cheeks, making it difficult to determine if he had been crying or if the rain had just done a good job in making it look that way. His jacket and pants were soaked, his shoes in a puddle of water, his hair matted down over his scalp. No blinking. No facial movements. If it wasn't for the slight motion of his chest expanding and contracting, he could have passed for a mannequin.

In his right hand he held a folded envelope. White. Red printed lettering in the upper left corner. His wrist was curled up somewhat as if to protect it from the damaging effect of the water. He could have sat there for hours, and he probably would have, had he not been interrupted.

A man hurried down the walkway, holding a newspaper over his head. He lifted his shoulders to shield his neck from the rain. He alternated turning his head from the left to the right, frustrated that his vision was impaired by the sheets of water. He squinted at something down the path. A set of legs at a park bench. He took a few more steps and saw the shadowy outline of a figure. When he was close enough to confirm that the man was indeed Edgar, he shook his head, feeling both the satisfaction of locating him and the aggravation that this took so long.

The man's name was Glenn Handle. He had previously fired Edgar as a professor at Mt. Carmel University.

"Edgar?" he said.

Edgar didn't hear him. That dull, dreary scene all around had him captivated.

"Edgar?" Handle repeated, shocked to see his friend—at least that's what he still hoped they were—sitting there in some state of shock.

Edgar blinked. The statue was coming to life. Water ran over his eyelids. He turned his head to see Handle and felt the surprise that comes with realizing how fast time goes when things are going well, and how painfully slow it drags on when nothing is working. Edgar didn't have the courage to look at his watch. It could have been hours since he sat down. When was that appointment? Was it today? Was it this morning? Or was it yesterday? He blinked again. It was this morning. Yes. Definitely. This morning. And he had sat down here right afterwards. He couldn't go farther. His legs wouldn't let him.

Getting the news wasn't so bad. He thought he handled it quite well. But by the time he made it out the front door he felt like he was going to collapse. His stomach had felt queasy. His mind disoriented. He had planned to see Handle that afternoon. Here. At the park. He knew one way or the other he had to have someone to share the news with. And so he sat down on the bench long before their meeting, feeling the delayed reaction when the body puts up that initial defence mechanism to help you deal with the pain of a terrible event, and then later, when it thinks you are ready, delivers all of that stored-up emotion in one unbearable dosage, leaving you feeling like those people in old folks' homes who stare out of windows all day.

"Edgar?" Handle said, his tone changing from frustration to concern. Not another soul in sight. Just the two of them in this lonely park that on any other day would be crowded with people. "Edgar, what are you doing?"

Edgar glanced down at the envelope, then back at Handle. It finally occurred to him that it was raining. A hopeless and puzzled expression came to his face as though he were trying to decide why Handle would have to ask. "I'm waiting for you," Edgar said.

"I called you, Edgar. You didn't get my message?" Handle spoke louder to be heard over the rain. "I wanted to meet you in a restaurant or something instead. Not in this."

Edgar leaned his head back and looked up at the sky. He felt the bullets of water firing down on him, hitting him over and over again. Like a million guns up there, aiming at him, giving him zero chance of escape. "I'm sorry," he said, already forgetting what he was apologizing for. "I just came straight here."

"Edgar, let's get out of the rain."

But Edgar wouldn't leave. He clutched his envelope even tighter. Then he pressed his back against the bench as if to convince himself the only sure thing he felt right now in life was still there.

Handle stepped closer. Edgar's face looked so pale. Maybe it was the cold from the rain. Maybe it was more. He bent down and put his hand on Edgar's shoulder. He softened his voice, hoping a whisper might turn his friend around. "Edgar," he said, and then wiped the rain off his face before he continued. "My car's right around the corner. I'll take you home."

Edgar looked out at the drizzle of grey. Jake. Jake would have been really, really good to talk to right now. Straight, honest, and to the point. But best of all, he could listen. Not just to words. He could listen behind the words. How did someone like Jake, who had spent so much time on the streets, develop such an incredible ability to truly hear what someone was saying? And Lucas. Lucas would be good now too. He was coming around. He had learned so much. Life doesn't have easy answers. And maybe in many circumstances there were no answers at all. And Tabitha. Now there was a woman a man could rely on. No, she didn't seem to be sharing or understanding the same passion for miracles that Lucas had, but still, she was real. She was honest. What you see is what you get. He could use that right now. He could use her right now. Any of them. But they were gone. And all Edgar had left to talk to was a man who had fired him.

When he looked back at Handle, it hit him. He felt the frailty of connecting with someone and then realizing how alone a man can get in this world. He saw something unfamiliar in Handle's eyes. And when those tears came they were way more intense than whatever rain was dripping down.

"Is this all there is?" Edgar asked.

"To what?

"To life."

"In what way, Edgar?" Handle asked as he sat down beside him on the wet bench.

Edgar looked back at the bleak grey thinking maybe he'd find something out there he hadn't seen before.

"Is uncertainty the reward for those of us who have followed so closely?"

"Uncertainty about what? About the future?"

"About everything."

Handle wanted this conversation. He wanted to be there for Edgar. He owed him so much. So much. But not here. Not in the pouring rain. Not after what Edgar had just been through.

"Edgar, this is stupid. Look around you. Why are you sitting out here?"

Edgar covered his face with his hands and felt suddenly embarrassed over what he was doing. "I'm sorry," Edgar said. "I'm sorry. I lost track of time. I…I didn't…I'm sorry."

"Edgar, it's alright," Handle said, putting an arm around him to help him up. But Edgar stayed seated. "I'll take you home. You can get cleaned up. And then I'm going to take you out. Whichever restaurant you want."

Edgar nodded his head. He stood up. He agreed to go, though he wasn't hungry.

They sat opposite each other at a table in the Notre Dame Library. Edgar won out—he wasn't interested in a restaurant. This was better anyway. The calm atmosphere and those drop-dead gorgeous brunettes with the leather jackets a few empty tables over beat the drudgery of grey at Buckingham Fountain. Reams and reams of books filled rows in every direction. It was darker in here than Edgar remembered. Maybe it was the weather. The drive from Chicago to Notre Dame was worth it. It gave them a chance to talk through Edgar's random thoughts, making it possible for him to sift through the muddle of confusion to get to what mattered. Still, everything about the way Edgar looked, from his slouched posture to those crossed and mystified eyebrows, told Handle that all was far from well with the man in front of him.

"Because it makes me wonder," Edgar said.

"About?"

"About why we're here." He stopped himself. That wasn't what he meant. "No. No, it makes me wonder about why *I'm* here."

"Why do you think you're here?"

Oh, that was good. That was really, really good. Edgar picked up on the tactic. Don't answer the question. Don't give advice. Just get the person to talk about their issue and sooner or later (hopefully sooner) the solution, or at least the real problem, would present itself.

Edgar took a sip from his water bottle and hung onto it as if doing so could somehow give him reassurance that he was not without help. He rested his forehead against his hand. It seemed to Handle that Edgar had suddenly been struck with a terrible headache. Edgar closed his eyes a moment and then pulled his hand away. His face was full of distress. He forced himself not to lose control. Not here. Not now. He found the courage to look at Handle. "How can a person be certain they know God?"

Handle froze. It was his turn to look like a wax statue. He swallowed. "Of course you know God, Edgar," he said. "Why would you even ask that?"

"Take you, for example. How can you be sure *you* know God?"

"Edgar, the doctor gave you bad news. Horrible news. That you're not getting better. But is this supposed to change your faith?"

A first-year student came to the table and asked if either of them had seen her professor. Handle broke away to give a polite "I'm sorry." She left and Edgar later regretted not acknowledging her presence.

"The first paper I wrote at Notre Dame was a comparison between Cain in Genesis and *East of Eden*. I was so interested in what transpired for Cain to fall out of favour with God. What it meant for God to banish him. To be out there. Alone. Apart from God." Edgar took another sip of his water. "I loved studying in this library. I spent so much time here. Night after night after night." He thought a moment. "I should have spent more time with women." Handle laughed. "I should have partied more with them. Not the bad stuff. You know. Just have fun. Stay out all night. Sit on the hood of the car with some hot blonde and lean against the windshield, looking at the stars with her. Drink some beer."

"You hate beer, Edgar."

"But I could have got used to it. I never gave it a chance."

"You regret that?"

For all that happened, for all he had done, Edgar felt the terrible pain in thinking that perhaps all his efforts since graduation had only taken him backward. "I regret taking things for granted."

"What kinds of things?"

"Everything important."

"Such as?" Handle asked in a way that convinced Edgar he felt in danger of having those same thoughts about *his* life since graduation.

"Faith."

"Faith?"

"How do you describe faith?"

"How would you describe it?"

There it was again. That counselling tactic.

"Somebody once said if you have to ask what jazz is, you ain't never gonna know. I think that's the way it is with faith. Which is why I'm worried."

"Edgar, stop this."

Edgar looked at Handle with a hint of panic in his eyes. Handle recognized it. It scared him, not because of what he saw in Edgar, but because he too had seen that same look in his own eyes reflected in the mirror late at night, asking himself the few questions in life that actually mattered.

"And it has me thinking. It has me thinking more now than ever." He looked at a section of Ph.D. monographs stacked beside him. "I used to think books had answers. I used to think that if I just read more. If I avoided those girls with the tight shirts and short skirts. If I avoided spending too much time at the games. If I stayed here and studied, that I would find the answers. But do they? Do these books contain answers?"

Edgar closed his eyes. He clenched his teeth. He tried to take in a deep breath, but stopped halfway. He brought his hands to his face to prevent himself from crying. "I'm at the end," he whispered. "They're not measuring my time in years anymore. I've been downgraded. Can you believe that? It's in months, now. And you know what's next? Weeks. Then days. I don't have much time."

"Edgar, your faith is stronger than you think."

"You're wrong about that," Edgar said. He'd been thinking about this for a while. Now was the first time he was saying it out loud. "It's weaker."

"It only seems weaker."

"What if it's not perception? What if it's reality? What if what I'm feeling is truth?"

"Edgar, if you base your faith on the confidence you feel on any given day, then you're going to be in and out of faith all the time."

"It's more serious than that."

"How much more serious?"

Edgar leaned forward. That confused looked was gone. It was replaced with desperation. "I'm in trouble," he said. "Do you understand me?"

"No Edgar. I don't," Handle replied with unconvincing eyes. "I'm sorry for this, Edgar."

"For what? For fortune?"

"Do you think your sickness is a result of fate?"

"What more could I have done to avoid it? I follow God. I eat well. I take care of myself. A friend once told me that the good don't always get rewarded and the bad don't always get punished. That's chance. No relation between conduct and result."

Handle mulled that thought over in his mind as he searched for an apt reply. "Albert Einstein once said that God doesn't play dice."

His response should have brought Edgar some comfort. Even if it didn't change the situation, it should have at least changed the way Edgar felt about things. But Edgar shook his head unconvinced. "Albert Einstein was wrong."

Later, Handle excused himself and went to enquire if he could get them tickets for the upcoming game. Edgar watched as Handle walked down the long aisle until he was just a dot at the end of a tunnel of books.

To his left he saw the theology texts. To his right he saw the back of a newspaper with a full-page advertisement. A man standing before a crowd. Dressed in a white suit. Sheridan Corvey. Hundreds healed in Chicago. Below it gave the dates of upcoming crusades. The next one was being held at the grand opening of the world's largest casino complex.

He flipped a few pages, skipped a long section dealing with the potential new drug patent-breaking legislation, until he reached the travel section. He found the number of an agency and dialled on his cellphone. A chipper female voice gave the name of the travel company. "How can I help you?" she asked.

"I'd like to book a flight," Edgar said. "I need to go to Las Vegas."

21

Despite his best efforts to hide his appearance, people recognized Lucas at O'Hare as he walked through the gate. The baseball cap and clothes he had picked up in London did little to hide him. His beard should have been enough to distract attention. But all of those television cameras, newspapers, and magazines that had covered him during the Chicago miracles had etched his face into the minds of millions of people.

A middle-aged woman leaned over to her husband without taking her eyes off Lucas. She whispered that the miracle man was walking right past them. He either didn't hear her or was ignoring her because he didn't even lift his eyes from his book. She stood up and walked towards Lucas. Still, her husband kept reading. Two teenagers recognized him. The cap, the beard, the clothes. He looked different from what they remembered. But the eyes were the same. "Lucas Stephens?" one of them asked, using both his first and last name the way people do when they refer to famous people.

Lucas pretended not to hear, but his quickening pace gave him away. *Not that far to go. Not much farther now to the exit.* He could make it. *Would running make it better or worse?*

The woman followed him. She should have been able to walk faster. A woman her age should well have been able to break into a light jog and catch him in no time. She called out to him. Lucas ignored her.

He entered a wide hallway with a crowded food court on either side of him. People all over picked him out. Strangers spoke to each other, trying to confirm their suspicions. One person shouted out his name. It was obvious now. People stared at him. Many stood up and began walking after him.

Not now. Please, God, not now. Just make them go away. Please, just make them leave.

The woman struggled to keep Lucas within her line of sight. People packed together as they followed after him, some wanting to see the man behind Healermania up close, some shouting for him to heal them. They ran after him, those that could, and surrounded him. Lucas kept walking in spite of the frenzy of people touching him, grabbing him, pulling his arms, pleading with him to stop.

A man hurried beside him. When he recognized Lucas he called back to his daughter to hurry up. Lucas was about to make it through the doors when a swarm of people blocked him off. Two security guards ran in to try and control the situation. Lucas quoted his verses to himself. Hands grabbed his shirt and yanked him in all directions. People reached over each other for a chance to touch him.

The man raised his daughter on his shoulders and told her to crawl on top of the people to get to Lucas. She struggled to find the right places to put her hands and knees. When she was close enough she reached out her hand. It was covered in sores. Blisters ran up her sleeves. "Can you help me?" she asked in a muffled tone. Her face had the same blisters. Lucas assumed they were on her tongue as well, which would explain why she had such a difficult time speaking.

He touched her hand. And the moment he did, electricity ripped through his body into hers. She jolted as though caught in a faulty car battery boosting attempt, and then looked down at her hands. In an instant her blisters shrank, and then disappeared into nothing.

He laid his hands on a few other people and then forced himself through the double doors to the taxi outside. He got in the back and tried to close the door. People pushed past security and reached after him, begging for his help. Just as he was about to get it shut the woman who had seen him first fell to the ground. She pushed her way through and reached into the car. She lifted her hand palm up like begging African children do when they see a white person walk by.

Lucas touched her frozen cold fingers. He let go and closed the door. The taxi drove off, leaving a crowd of disappointed people behind—except those who had been touched, including the woman who, on her next visit to her doctor, discovered she had been completely healed of multiple sclerosis.

The taxi pulled up to Lucas' mansion in Evanston. He thanked the driver by name and walked up the driveway to his home. He punched the security code, opened the door, and felt the relaxation of being in a familiar place.

Stacks of mail flooded his kitchen table. Bills. Fan mail. Loads of fan mail. Requests to be healed. His phone indicated the message storage capacity had maxed out. He picked the receiver off the cradle and sat down on one of his black leather couches. He dialled Tabitha's cell number. It rang three times before her voice mail kicked in.

Lucas paused. Leaving a message wasn't the right way to do this. He hung up and called again without success. He closed his eyes and listened as she gave the message. Her voice. Something about hearing it put him at ease, helped him to really return to Chicago, helped him to realize Africa was behind him. Finally. Even though it was just the standard reply, the tone was classic Tabitha. His Tabitha. Friendly Midwest voice with the perfect inflection to give callers the feeling this was the kind of person you could spend hours with and still have more to talk about.

"Tabitha, it's me." He paused again, trying to figure out what to say. "You're probably wondering what's happened." This was supposed to be easy. This was supposed to be a call where she picked up the phone and went into shock in a good way over finding out he was alive. Maybe it was the long plane trip. Maybe it was finally being in solitude away from the slums, the desert, the crowds of people. But more than anything else, it was feeling as close to her as he had been since they last saw each other on that fateful night in Mathari. He needed her back. Just the two of them. That's it. That's all he wanted. The fame. The money. The gift. It could all disappear.

He would have gladly traded it away to have her by his side, sitting on the beach, up against a rock, late at night, listening to the waves crash on the shore. But here he was. Miraculous healing power. Money to burn. And a mission to confront Caesar.

"I'm back safe and sound, Tab. I'm in Chicago. Can you believe that? I'll try to call you again."

He left a similar message on her home phone.

Lucas sat down in his BMW. The smell of leather filled his senses. He played Tony Bennett's *I've Got the World on a String* as he headed off his property and drove to Empirico.

When Anne, the Danish bombshell at the front desk, saw him come through the front doors, she didn't know whether to feel relieved or shocked. Dead. That's what they all said. That's what they all believed. The powers of Empirico loved it. Lucas the threat was gone. The people, however, were crushed. So was Anne. He walked up to her wearing black jeans, a grey shirt, and a brown leather jacket.

She stood up and just before she revealed how amazed she was to see him, her instinct to protect him kicked in. *What is he doing here?*

"Hello, Anne," he said, looking into her clear blue eyes.

"Lucas."

The entrance was empty. She wasn't supposed to be here. Not this late. Anne stepped out from behind her desk and wrapped her arms around him. He hung onto her longer than he should have. That incredible smell of perfume. The comfort of human touch. Her soft skin brushed past his beard as she pulled back.

"You have to leave. You can't stay here."

"I came to see Caesar. Is he in?"

"No. And even if he were I wouldn't let you near him."

"Anne."

"Lucas. Get out." She spoke in a whisper as though trying to prevent invisible Empirico spies from hearing her. "They still want...." She had a hard time getting the words out. "They still want you dead."

"Where's Caesar?"

He was going to find out sooner or later. One way or the other. Even so, telling him felt like killing him. “In Las Vegas.”

“Mike too?”

“They’re about to open the casino.”

That wasn’t right. Lucas tried to put the pieces together. “The Las Vegas project went ahead? That’s impossible.”

“They fast-tracked the construction schedule. It’s costing him a fortune. But he’s adamant about opening.”

“It’s almost done?”

“Lucas. I’m begging you.”

“Where’s Claire?”

“She leaves tomorrow to join him.” Anne spoke quieter still. “She’s not well. She’s….”

“What?”

“I think it’s better she tell you.” Anne went behind her desk. She wrote down Claire’s cell number and gave it to him. As he took it she reached out with her hand to make contact with him. Slender cool fingers against his wrist. Perfectly manicured fingernails with a glossy clear nail polish. Her skin had just enough of a tan to make it stand out against her blonde hair.

“This isn’t right, Lucas.”

“How much do you really know about this company?”

She didn’t want to reply. Not at first. Rumours were just that. Rumours. Better left unsaid. “How much do you really know?” he asked.

“It depends on what Caesar tells me.”

She breathed in a way that showed her disapproval. “If you want to see him, you’d better hurry. Nobody knows how much time he has left.”

On his way back to his car Lucas left a message for Claire, asking her to meet with him. He hoped she would get the message in time.

And he hoped she would not confirm his suspicions about Empirico.

Lucas drove around Chicago for three hours looking for Jake. He went to the dilapidated complex he used to live in, thinking that maybe he had gone back. No note. No message. Nothing. A Native American man at the rescue mission where Lucas and Jake first met told Lucas he'd seen Jake a number of times, in increasingly degraded forms.

Lucas searched through the drizzling rain, looking in back alleys for his friend. As he listened to the words of U2's *Yahweh* on his CD, he tried hard not to add the images of those starving African children in the slum to the bleak picture of men and a woman drinking and shooting up behind a dumpy hotel. He asked people on the sidewalks, people on the street, homeless people, and prostitutes if they had seen Jake. He got conflicting information and continued driving.

He drove in the middle lane and came to a stoplight. He heard a commotion to his right and saw a man pounding away at a garbage bin. Punching it as though it were a person. The light turned green. Lucas hit a button and the passenger window went down. Cars honked behind him. He looked closer. It might be him. Maybe. Maybe it was Jake. It was so hard to tell without much light. More honking. Cars zoomed by on either side. Changing lanes and parking on the side would be impossible. He hit his hazard button and opened the door.

The woman in the vehicle behind him lowered her window. "Move your car!" she shouted, adding a slew of profanity.

Lucas stepped out. "Go around!" He was about to curse right back at her but caught himself.

He negotiated through the oncoming traffic and made it to the sidewalk. He turned into the alley and saw the man in the mixture of rain and shadows. "Jake?" he asked. "Jake, is that you?"

The man shouted and screamed as he smashed the garbage bin. In his right hand he held a bottle of booze. Sloshes of alcohol spilled on the ground with each passing blow. He leaned his head back and guzzled a load down. He lost his balance, cursed, and fell to the ground.

It *was* Jake.

Lucas ran up to him. He fell down on his knees. "Jake? Jake?" He put an arm around him. "Hey, buddy."

"You get...from me...out of here," he slurred. "I ain't got nothing. You get...you get you away from me." He tried to punch Lucas but his pathetic swing had no effect.

"Jake. Jake, it's me. It's Lucas."

Jake's eyes were bloodshot. His sopping hair was straggled. His tough, scarred face a pale shade of grey. His body reeked of booze and sweat. He reached out his hands and touched Lucas' face. Something registered in Jake's eyes. A moment of calm amid an expression of anger and grief.

"That's impossible," he said. Blood dripped from his knuckles.

"I'm here, Jake. I made it out."

"You are one lucky...." he didn't finish the sentence. Sitting there in the back alley, freezing cold, coming to grips with how far he'd fallen, he began to cry. He clutched his bottle and shook his head. "I let you down, Lucas."

"You didn't let me down."

"I should never...have let you go into that slum."

"It's not your fault."

"I failed you," Jake said, gathering up all the miniscule courage he had left to look back at Lucas.

"I need your help, Jake. And you can't help me like this."

"You don't need my help."

"Why do you think I'm here?"

"Because you feel sorry for me."

"I'm here because I need you."

"For what? To let you down when you're in trouble?"

"No, Jake. Because I know I can count on you."

"Me?"

"You."

"Why? You have everything. I'm nothing."

"You're not nothing, Jake. You're my friend. And I need your help."

"For what?" He coughed and spit on the ground.

"I'm going to take him on."

Jake wiped his mouth. "Caesar?"

"You decide if you want in. I make you no guarantees either way."

Lucas stood up and walked out of the alley. He made it through the lane of traffic and got into his car. He looked back. No Jake. He turned the hazards off. Still no Jake. He put the car in drive and was about leave when he saw Jake stumbling to the sidewalk. He stepped out into the oncoming traffic. A car slammed on its brakes and honked the horn.

Jake paid no attention. He swatted his hand at the car and made it to the BMW. It took him three tries to find the handle. He opened the door and sat down.

"So," Jake said. "Where are we going?"

After a shower and a few bottles of water Jake became more coherent. He sat down opposite Lucas on a couch, his body demanding a drink, his conscience telling him it was time for a break. He talked about his 40-day binge. The blur of his stupor. The self-pity slide down to the bottom.

Lucas listened with the rare ability some have to give their full attention to someone. He would have stayed that way the whole night had Jake not enquired about *his* 40 days in the desert. Lucas tried to avoid the subject, but Jake came back to it. He paused, debated whether to divulge what happened. It was time somebody knew. He thought back to the strong man. Lying there in his makeshift grave. His body decomposing by now. Maybe a lion had found him. Maybe tribal hunters had stumbled on him. Or maybe the strong man didn't die after all. Maybe he had just been unconscious. Found a way to get that hideous stake out of his head. Made it out of that brutal desert.

"I killed a man," Lucas said. His words seemed to echo as they filled the room. He felt strange saying them. Like a criminal sitting at a confession table spilling his guts to a cop.

"Did he deserve it?"

"Should I feel any different either way?"

They heard knocking at the door. It was so loud it made Jake think it was the police. Lucas instinctively thought it was the strong man. Standing there. Stake in hand. Bloody face. Ready to return the favour.

Lucas stood up. More knocking. This time it was more desperate. Offbeat. Panicked. It stopped momentarily and then started again.

"Expecting anyone?" Jake asked.

Lucas shook his head. He'd left the gate open. He remembered now. He went to the door. *Please, not the media. Please, not any sick people. Please.*

"Let me get that for you," Jake said, stepping in front of Lucas.

The knocking started again. This time it was even louder, as though the person at the door had someone after them and this was their final chance for refuge.

"Stay behind me," Jake said. When he reached the door he leaned his head just enough to see through the window, enough so he'd have time to duck out of the way in case he found a shotgun staring at him. "I don't recognize her."

Her? Lucas turned the handle. It wasn't Tabitha. That much he could feel. He opened the door. The woman standing there had a wild look in her clear blue eyes. Mascara running. Dishevelled blondish-brown hair. She wore a pair of blue jeans and black leather shoes with the laces undone. Her black shirt was half tucked in, like she had other things on her mind besides the way she looked when she left. Her grey jacket was unzipped, the collar half turned on one side. She took short breaths, trying hard not to hyperventilate.

"Claire?" Lucas asked, opening the door wider to let her in.

She hurried in, pushing him out of the way somewhat as she did, and looked around from side to side as though expecting to find something. "Is anyone else here? Who's here, Lucas?" She raised her voice. Panic had gripped her. "Who else, Lucas? Who's here?"

"It's just me and Jake, Claire." He stepped towards her to put his arms on her shoulders, but she pulled away wanting instead to keep her distance from him, from danger, from the news she had to deliver.

"They'll see my car." she said, touching her hand to her forehead. "They'll know I came here."

"Who will know, Claire?"

"They'll find me here."

"No one will see your car."

"They will! They will see it there!"

Lucas turned to Jake. He made introductions. Claire knew of Jake from all the media attention. "Can you drive her car around the other side of the garage?" To Claire: "Do you have your keys?"

It was too much for her. She couldn't remember. Did she take them with her or leave them in the car as she normally did when she came to see Lucas? She stuck her hands in her jacket pockets but came up empty. She checked and rechecked them, becoming more and more frustrated that she wasn't finding them. "Where are they?" She swore and breathed even faster.

"Let me help you," Lucas said as he came closer to her.

"No!" she screamed with such intensity it hurt his ears. He stopped. The suspicion in her eyes grew worse. They darted to Jake and then back to Lucas. She jammed her hand in the inside pocket. A jingle sound. Out came her keys. Lucas gave them to Jake who left to move the car.

"Claire?"

She tried to catch her breath and felt the first inklings she might be out of harm's way.

For the time being.

She sat down on the couch, leaned forward to rest her elbows on her knees, and ran her fingers through her soft hair. Some of it fell back down, covering half her face. She turned her head in a quick motion to push it off to the side. Lucas brought her a cup of herbal tea with honey. She held it in her hand and felt the warmth run into her fingers. Jake came in and sat down beside Lucas, across from Claire.

Claire's tired face was beyond the point of exhaustion. Pale, grey, drained. If Lucas didn't know her better, he might have thought she was strung out on drugs. She took a sip of tea; it was too hot, so she held it in her mouth, waiting for it to cool before letting it creep down her throat. Her hands trembled. Lucas watched her eyes for any hint as to what this might be about. She put the tea down and closed her eyes as if to draw strength for what she was about to say.

They waited for Claire to begin.

22

"I've seen things," she said. Her voice was quiet. She chose her words carefully, thinking that, perhaps, she would not have a second chance to relay them.

"What kinds of things?"

Her breathing slowed down. She looked like she was going to keel over from exhaustion. She rubbed her forehead and tried to figure out the best way to say this. "I wasn't supposed to find out about those research development reports." She took another sip of tea. This time it felt better. "Nobody knows that I came into contact with them," she continued. "The research…." Her French accent trailed off. There was so much to convey. So much to think through. Yet so little of it had any real proof. *Just stick to the facts,* she told herself. *Just say exactly what you know.*

"Empirico is working on hundreds of projects. Most of them internal. Some of them funded through universities. A good chunk of them are a crapshoot. Guesses, really. Long shots. Really, really long shots." She softened her voice such that Lucas and Jake had to strain to hear it. "Thing is—sometimes those long shots come in for you."

She felt a piercing pain in her neck. She leaned her head to the side to stretch it out. "There were two streams of research activity. One was aimed at finding a drug that could slow the rate of a type of brain cancer called glioblastoma multiforme. GBM."

"Extend the life of people who have it," Lucas said.

"Precisely. If found successful, this drug would be given to GBM patients to ease their pain and lengthen their lives—perhaps by as much as five years—provided, of course, they would consistently take the drug."

"The other one?"

"The other one...." She took in a deep breath but still couldn't get herself to say it. She touched her thumb and forefinger to the bridge of her nose. This was it. It was time to get it out in the open. "The directive of the other one was to find a way to eradicate that cancer."

Lucas' heart stopped. *Did she say eradicate?* He squinted his eyes and wondered where she was going with this. "Caesar has a cure for cancer?"

"I didn't say that." She caught herself. This wasn't coming out right. All the facts, all the conflicting information, all the secrecy—this wasn't something you could just lay out like a road map. "I'm saying there were two sets of research streams."

"What were the results, Claire?"

She felt sick. *Is it getting hotter?* "They were both shown to be positive."

"What?"

"But development, the actual product tests and government approvals, was only carried out for the drug that lengthened their life span."

"They shelved a drug that may have been able to cure a type of brain cancer?"

"It seems that way."

"That's insane," Jake said. "Why would anyone do that? A person who has a cure for any form of cancer can name their price. They'd be fools not to release it."

"So why all the hush-hush, right?" Claire was finished. She had said what she came to say. She blinked her eyes, trying to focus them, realizing now the desperation she had conveyed. "I'm sorry for barging in on you like this." And then it hit her. She remembered and felt a sudden disappointment in herself for not saying it earlier. "Welcome home, by the way."

Lucas raised his eyebrows to thank her. Surviving the desert was old news compared with what was before them now.

"So what do we do?" she asked. "Do we need proof?"

"Do you think you can find any?"

"Not in Chicago."

"Where then?

"Vegas. That's the rumour. All research to Vegas."

"He's protecting against industrial espionage or a government crackdown. Moving things to a safer place."

"I might be able to get to him in Vegas. I'm being transferred there. As are most of the Council."

She took another sip. Lucas studied her, amazed that she was still awake. *How long had she been going without sleep? Twenty-four hours? More?* "Claire?" She looked up at him. Her eyes were drained. "How convinced are you about this?"

She wrapped both hands around her cup of tea. "Enough to know I wasn't sure whether I'd live to tell you about it."

A surge of challenge and fear cut through Lucas. He could already smell Caesar's cigar. See his beady, puffy eyes. Hear his raspy voice.

Feel his overpowering presence.

"Who do we contact? The FBI?" she asked.

"Do you have any Empirico documents to support this?"

"No."

"Anyone who will verify what you saw?"

She shook her head. "What about the media? We can funnel them anonymous information."

"It's conjecture, Claire. That's all you'll be able to give them."

"So what, then? What do we do?" She finished her tea, set the cup down, and looked at her watch. "I have to go."

The sudden change in her demeanour caught Lucas off guard. "Stay here tonight, Claire."

"No, I've done you enough harm by coming here."

She stood up and walked to the door, that normal French class and confidence of hers exchanged for a feeling of desperation and disorder.

Lucas followed her out of the house to her car, trying unsuccessfully to convince her to stay. He opened the car door for her, thanked her for coming, and watched as she drove off the property, thinking it might be the last time he would see her.

"This is stupid!" Jake said. They stood in the backyard. Under the night sky. Discussing Claire. Discussing their next move.

"We have to. We have to take on Caesar."

"Have to? We don't *have* to do anything," Jake said.

"We can't let him do this."

"Why? Let him hang onto the drug, Lucas. You can heal people without it."

"How many more can get healed with proper medication?"

"You don't even know he has the drug!"

"Claire seems convinced."

"Claire? Claire!" Jake cursed. "You see how messed up that chick looked? She's crazy! You ever consider that Caesar put her up to it? Dream up some dumb theory about a miracle drug and rope you in to bring you down there?" Jake shook his head in frustration. "Why, Lucas? Why do you want to go? Why Caesar? Why not just leave him alone? You do your thing and he does his. I don't understand this!"

"I have unfinished business with him."

"Vendetta?"

Lucas avoided the question. "Jake? Just tell me what's wrong."

Jake looked out at the stars. Not nearly as many as Africa. He wanted a drink. Just to calm the nerves. Just one. Just one drink. He swallowed, shook his head, and turned to Lucas. "I sometimes get the strangest feeling that you and I are going to become enemies."

A sudden momentary rift came between them. It closed as fast as it opened, but they both noticed it. "Enemies?"

"I'm afraid," Jake said. "I'm afraid of what might happen to you if you meet Caesar."

"I can't live by avoiding fear."

"But do you think we're strong enough to battle him?"

It was Lucas' turn to want that drink. He looked back at the stars, felt the chill of the evening air, and hoped Claire was not in danger. "We'll have to find out."

Tabitha stood in line at the Wynn Theatre box office for tickets to Le Rêve. In light of the incredible hype and fantastic reviews she couldn't ignore the strange feeling she had in being there alone, by herself, realizing that after the show there would be nobody with whom she could share the experience. She checked the messages on her cellphone and was relieved that Fat Chester hadn't called. When she heard Lucas' voice she assumed it was an old message. From the archives. One she forgot to delete. But as she listened to what he said she realized it was the first time she had heard it. *I'm back safe and sound, Tab....Can you believe that?*

No. Actually not. Tabitha was not able to believe it. The man, her man, was dead. Gone.

"Next," the box office attendant said.

But Tabitha couldn't move. She replayed the message. This wasn't the real world anymore. The show had already begun. This was a dream. Dead people leaving voice mails. Everything closed in on her.

"Ma'am?" the attendant asked, noticing her distress.

Tabitha didn't respond. She left the line, disoriented, and struggled through the casino, obsessed with a need to get outside for some fresh air. She made it onto Las Vegas Boulevard and sat down on a park bench opposite Empirico's new casino. She waited there, urging herself to come to terms with the news, but finding it impossible to bridge the gap between her reality and the truth she had now encountered.

Lucas had been sitting on the couch for hours thinking about what it would be like to see Caesar again when his cell rang. It was a welcome relief, even at 1 a.m., to get his mind on something else. He picked up his phone and saw her name.

"Tabitha," Lucas said, wondering what it would be like to hear her voice again.

"Lucas?"

"I'm glad you called."

"You're alive?" Tabitha asked while sitting on the same bench, relieved she had finally found the courage to call the living dead. She leaned back and tucked one foot under the knee of the other leg. She saw the massive tarps surrounding the name of Caesar's latest accomplishment. The 5,000-room hotel was already booked. Three more days and the world would know the name. "What happened?" she asked.

The question seemed genuine enough, but something was missing. Lucas recapped the events from the slum to when he left Africa. Tabitha was amazed. Shocked. Surprised. When he was finished they talked about the things people talk about when they try to keep a conversation going, but inside both parties know there's more going on than what they claim to be interested in.

"So you're in Las Vegas?" Lucas asked.

"Covering Caesar's grand opening. Doing interviews. Getting ready for the big unveiling."

"Tabitha?"

The line went quiet. She knew what was coming.

"Yes."

"Tabitha, is something wrong?"

"No," she replied, much too fast to be believable.

"You seem distant."

"Distant."

"I hear your voice on the other end but you feel far away."

"Maybe it's Vegas."

"It's not more than that?"

She paused.

"I'm having trouble with this. With you being alive."

"Can I see you?"

"Sure," she said in a nervous sort of laugh. "Just fly down and say hello."

"Okay. Tomorrow night. But not in Vegas. It'll be too busy."

"Lucas?"

"Hoover Dam. Jake and I get in some time in the early evening. I'll meet you there at ten."

"You're coming to Vegas?"

"Are we on?"

"Why would you be coming to Vegas?" She sat up. This was unexpected. Her reporter's mind continued working and connected the dots. "Caesar?"

"Tomorrow night?"

"You're coming to Vegas to…to what?" Her attention shifted to the casino extraordinaire in front of her. "To take on Caesar?"

"Are we on, or are we on? I have a special treat for us tomorrow night."

"He'll kill you. You know that. Why would you leave a deathtrap in Africa just to come to another one here?"

"The surprise is nothing really out of the ordinary. But I guarantee you've never done it before. In fact, I don't even know why I mention it."

"This isn't a joke."

"Because now that I've told you, you'll think it'll be something great, but really it's just a cool thing to do. That's all."

"I spoke with Claire, Lucas."

The silent night got a whole lot quieter. "So have I."

"Tomorrow night then."

"I'll be there."

"You shouldn't be doing this."

"Until tomorrow."

They hung up. Lucas glanced at the time. He had planned on getting some rest before the trip to Nevada. But as he went upstairs and lay down on his bed all he heard were her words playing over and over again in his mind. Her cryptic comment kept him from sleeping. *You shouldn't be doing this.*

It made him wonder if she knew something he did not.

23

Lucas stood on the walkway, looking over the edge of Hoover Dam. The incredible concrete structure stretched down like a massive skateboard ramp. It was like standing on the 73rd storey of a skyscraper. From either side it caved in towards him, damming the water of the Colorado River on the border between Nevada and Arizona. He watched the water rushing out at the bottom and thought it amazing how people were able to build this project, which harnessed the tremendous energy of nature and converted it to electricity.

During the 45-minute trek to Hoover, Lucas thought about what to say to Tabitha and worked through scenarios of how she might respond. But standing there alone in the night air under a starry sky, the task of communicating with her about their situation seemed about as daunting as planning to construct Hoover Dam.

He heard footsteps coming down the walkway to his left from the direction of the parking lots. He knew it was her. He could feel it. Somehow her presence had a way of stretching out past her and into him. In that moment before he turned to look at her he tried to get a read on what the feeling meant. Was this the sort of nervousness that vanishes once people make contact, or was it a premonition of sorts that things weren't going to work out the way they were supposed to?

She saw him standing there and despite a desire to forget this whole thing and call to cancel their meeting, she kept walking towards him for fear that if she stopped she wouldn't find the courage to continue. There he was. Again. The last time she saw him he was burning alive and carted off in a truck into oblivion. And then, just like that, he was back again. Forty days isn't forever. But it's long enough. Long enough to say goodbye. And now that he was back she wondered what it would be like to start things up again.

He turned and saw a mysterious look in her eyes, making him unsure of how to read her. She wore a pair of skin-tight jeans, blue with a funky green mixed in, that flared out at her ankles, a white T-shirt, and a beat-up black leather jacket that looked classy despite the marks. Her silver earrings were new. She had straightened out her medium-length dark hair. He could have looked at her for hours. It was as if she had managed to drain the stress right out of him. He felt weak. Defenceless. Captivated. He wanted to say something. Anything. *It's good to see you again, Tabitha.* He had this worked out. The beginning was all scripted so they could get off to a good start. Yet whether it was stage fright or just a sheer sense of wonder and amazement, he found himself unable to talk to her.

This was more than just beauty. That brunette flight attendant on that fateful flight to London was a real looker too, but she didn't do this to him. Tabitha redefined beauty for him. Appearance had the least to do with it. And the longer he looked at her, the more he felt the desperation a man feels when he needs a woman.

"Tabitha," Lucas finally said.

She looked afraid. It was as if the sound of his voice managed to break that fragile shelter she had built to insulate herself against being hurt again by the man she cared about. Maybe it was the wind. Maybe it was the emotion of seeing a man she had already counted for dead. Whatever it was, it froze her on the spot while her eyes began to swell. It *was* him. He was really there. And in spite of all her confusion over how this meeting would go, all things being equal, this was exactly what she wanted.

They felt awkward after their long separation, wondering if it was still okay to embrace each other or if things were better left face to face. But Lucas took a chance and stepped closer to her. He placed his arms around her and smelled the relaxing fragrance of her perfume. He felt her soft skin against his cheek. She put her arms around his waist.

This was supposed to be a meeting—to discuss what he was doing here and what they were doing with each other. But instead of trying to sort things out, they let go of their need to explain or understand and chose instead to live in the comfort of realizing there was somebody out there for whom they mattered. They closed their eyes. Tabitha tried hard not to cry. But the more she resisted the more difficult it became. She was not a supporting structure to hold back the emotions of life. And neither was Lucas.

When he opened his eyes he found it strange to be standing at Hoover Dam. He was in Nevada. Of course he was. That was obvious. Yet somehow, in that moment, they had managed to escape to that place people go when nothing else is important but them.

How was it possible that a woman's presence could erase the world?

They turned to look out over the dam. She wiped her eyes and then leaned her arms against the protective wall, folding her hands in front of her. Lucas took it as a good sign. Folded hands were good. Peaceful. Content. That was a whole lot better than where he thought they could be by now. He searched for the right thing to say. *Where to begin?*

"What do you need from me, Tabitha?" he asked.

She saw the trees on either side of the river. She thought it interesting that if she were standing at the bottom looking farther down the river, nothing about what she would see would give her any indication of the dam behind her.

"I need to understand you better," she replied.

"In what way?"

"In every way."

"The miracles?"

"The healings. The mission you're on. The times you escape certain death."

"If I could tell you, I would."

She turned and waited until he looked in her eyes before she continued. "Lucas, you're not a normal person."

He didn't know whether to take that as an observation or a question.

"There's nothing special about me."

Her expression changed from confusion to desperation. She ran her hand through her killer hair. It fell back exactly in place. "When people get shot, they die. When people crash in airplanes, they die. When people get set on fire, they die. When people are butchered in a desert, they die. How do you explain that?"

"Probability."

"Of what?"

"Infinite odds?"

"Doesn't that tell you something?"

"What does it tell you?"

"It tells me this shouldn't be happening. Not to you. Not to anybody."

"Why not?" Lucas asked, hoping she would provide a clue as to why all of this was going on.

She looked back at the trees. A breeze blew past them, wafting her perfume against him.

"Lucas, listen to me. I don't understand you."

"We have that in common, because I don't understand me either." It was supposed to lighten the mood. Instead, it got even deeper at what Tabitha was feeling.

They waited in silence as she formed her response. Time seemed to slow down, making every second feel like forever. She pressed her lips together, getting ready to tell him what was at the core of her confusion. She turned to face him. He was already looking at her. Those eyes. Those incredible eyes of hers. Whoever said the eyes are windows to the soul was absolutely right. Because when Lucas looked at her he saw through the perfect shells of glass right into her.

And what he saw worried him.

"I can't relate to you, Lucas."

That killed him. A shotgun blast exploded into his chest. He felt the horrific impact. He couldn't breathe. *Just give it time. Don't respond right away. When a client objects you're just supposed to nod your head in agreement while you think through a response. Don't get defensive. And don't disagree. That's critical. Whatever else happens, do not disagree. The client is always right. Always. There's a way through this. Just breathe. Breathe, man. You're going to fall over. Breathe.*

He took in a breath as quietly as he could. The initial shock was over. Now came the tough part. How to respond.

"Tabitha, it's just me. It's just Lucas."

"No, Lucas." That confused look came back to her face. "This is about something much bigger than you. You operate...you live in a way that I can't identify with."

"It takes time."

"I've given it time."

"Maybe it takes more."

"Time isn't the issue."

"Then what is it, Tabitha?"

"How do I separate you from your miracles?"

"Do you want to?"

"I need to."

"Why?"

"Because I can't put both of those pieces together."

"Do you have to?"

"How can I take one part of you but not the other?"

The ship was sinking. They'd sustained a devastating hit and were taking on water. Unless they found an ingenious way of patching the wreckage they would disappear under the surface and begin that no-return journey to the bottom.

"Just take everything. Like the way I take everything with you. The good. The not so good. There's not one part of you that I don't accept."

Time to change the subject. It was out in the open now. And more talking wasn't going to solve things. She needed her space. She needed to find a map out of this jungle.

"I don't think you came to Las Vegas just to talk to me."

"It would have been reason enough."

"You know what I mean."

He did know what she meant. The first battle was over—whether they had won or lost he did not know. The second battle was next.

"I'm here to confront Caesar."

"Caesar?"

"Yes."

"Why?"

"Because there are things going on at Empirico that need to be stopped."

"This isn't revenge?"

"No," Lucas said with a hint of uncertainty. Tabitha heard it in his voice.

"Then what is it?"

"I think Caesar may intentionally be keeping back a cure for a type of cancer."

It confirmed Tabitha's suspicions. She recalled the meeting with Fat Chester back at *The Observer*. "Why would he do that? If he has the drug, he's sitting on a gold mine."

"Unless it's not true."

"You've been at the top. You tell me. Is it?"

"I have to stop him, Tabitha."

"You're sure?" That look in her eyes grew cold. Stern. Intense. "Or are you here to call a truce with him? Cut a deal of sorts."

Lucas felt a rush of blood. He'd never been this angry with her before. *Don't say it. Don't say a word. Keep your mouth shut. Fake a smile. Fake a pleasant tone. Do not lose it.*

"A man who controls a cure for cancer has to be stopped. That drug has to be released. I am in Las Vegas to take him down."

She raised her eyebrows, both impressed with his ability to take on huge challenges and worried about how he was going to pull it off. "How will you do it?"

"Set up shop outside his casino. Heal people. Word will spread. The hotels will get booked by people looking to be healed, not looking to gamble. Caesar's new casino will lose money. He'll have to release the drug to make up the difference."

"Do you have any idea how many variables there are in that scheme?"

"Lots. But the premise is good."

"If the hotels are full they jack the rates through the roof and try to make up the difference that way."

"But they don't make nearly as much as they would from the tables and machines. It's gaming and not the rooms that make money for the casino. Plus, thousands of people will make day trips from the surrounding area. It'll work."

"It's bold," she said in a tone of voice that implied *I wish you weren't doing this.*

"It all comes down to what it will take to get him to release it."

"If he even has it."

"Do you think he does?"

"What's your opinion of Claire?" she asked.

"In terms of whether I think she has her facts straight?"

"In terms of whether you trust her."

"I think she's telling the truth as she sees it. But she may not be looking at the right information."

"You think you're the man to do it?"

"I know I am."

"I agree."

"You do?"

"Yes."

"Then you understand why I can't do this alone."

"You have Jake."

"Yes. I need Jake. Edgar too. But Tabitha, I can't take this on without you."

"You can."

"I can't."

They stayed in a stalemate, neither one being sure how to continue.

"My surprise," Lucas said. "This is the perfect time."

He wanted to hold out his hand for her to join him in heading back up to the car, but realized that might be forcing an issue that was better left the way it was.

They walked back to his car in the near empty parking lot. He turned on his CD player, left the door open, and stood out in front of her.

"Here it comes."

"What?"

Tony Bennett came on singing *Close Enough for Love.*

He led her out to the road at the dividing line between two states. He stood in Nevada. She in Arizona.

She realized she had been won over, for the time being, and looked at him in a way that conveyed she accepted his offer. He stepped closer and held her hand. They swayed back and forth under the starry sky, hearing Tony tell them things they hoped would be true in their lives. They didn't say anything. They didn't need to.

When the song ended she whispered "Thank you" into his ear. They waited, wondering how long the moment would last. Both of them felt the uncertainty of knowing a relationship is in that precarious place where, like a level teeter-totter, things can go one way or the other.

"Do you have time for another song? Have you ever heard Tony Bennett sing *Where Do You Start?*

She pulled back from him far enough to consider herself on the border that divided personal space between romance and acquaintance. "Lucas, I don't know where we stand."

"Where do you put us on a scale of one to ten? Ten being the best."

"Lucas."

"I need to know."

"I don't want to assign a value to the chances of things working out."

"Better than 50 per cent?"

She thought for a moment. It caused Lucas' heart to stop. He thought he was being more than generous with 50 per cent. He assumed they were at least at 75 per cent. After all they'd been through they had to be at a place with higher than normal blackjack odds.

"I wouldn't put us any higher than that."

Another shotgun blast. This one worse than the first. *Don't argue. Don't contest it. Not now. Just take the hit and let her know you're confident in your position. That's what will stick with her.*

"I'm sorry to hear that," he said.

"I thought you might be."

"Because I'd put us at a minimum of a hundred."

"Player's odds."

"I'd bet the house on you, Tabitha. Everything. I'd go all in for you."

"I wish I could say the same, Lucas."

He nodded, thinking that on a night like this with Lady Luck against him it was a good thing he had decided not to join Jake at the tables.

She got into her car. He watched her drive off and hoped that time was all it would take to heal old wounds.

With her in his arms he had the confidence of being able to face Caesar. He had that strange, unexplainable *I can do everything* feeling men have when the right woman is on their side. But now that she was gone, all he felt was the impossible task of taking on a man—an entire empire—with nothing more than himself and his friend Jake.

He hoped it would be enough.

24

It felt worse with every passing moment.

Lucas didn't exactly hear Tabitha come right out and say they were on the rocks, but this wasn't about hearing. It was about intuition. And in the game of love feelings speak louder than words. They were on unpredictable ground. Maybe worse. He did the best he could to put the situation behind him, which was about as likely as forgetting the effects of freezing water when you're in the middle of an ocean after a plane crash.

He turned south onto Las Vegas Boulevard and passed the Freemont Street Experience—the dazzling evening light show. On his right he saw the Sin City Oasis. He noticed the name and felt a chill come over him. He took a second look at the small two-storey building, thinking he had been there before. Down the road he saw the Stratosphere, the tallest building in Vegas. When he passed the Sahara up on his left it felt like he had entered a whole new area. There was more space. Bigger buildings. Huge condos being constructed. This was the Strip—the infamous all-American road with the highest concentration of casinos in the world. Farther down people packed the sidewalks. In the crowd he saw a tanned college-aged girl in shorts and a white T-shirt as she jogged through the crowd. Dark hair. Similar build to Tabitha. She looked just like her.

Up ahead Lucas saw Circus Circus and the Stardust to the right and the Wynn to his left. But it was the massive new casino in the distance that caught his attention. His stomach tensed. It was Caesar Alexander's new place. Draped in secrecy with tarps. It towered over all the other casinos, making them look like one collective insignificant wannabe casino by comparison. He looked away thinking that staring at it would get him caught in a merciless tractor beam. He turned onto the approach and drove past the casino, feeling the weight of its shadow on him like the eyes of an unforgiving jury as they prepared to deliver the guilty verdict. Far, far at the end of the massive structure he saw a small casino. The Mayan. The one where Jake said he would be playing. Right behind the new casino Caesar was building.

The one set to open in two days.

"I play the tables. Strictly blackjack. No poker. No roulette. No craps. Blackjack. And I play fair and square. Nothing illegal. Nothing inside. And no help from the dealers," Matthias said.

He sat in a private dimly lit room with Lydda and Zack Roman, owner of Petra Security. Zack was a tall, built, bald man. Scars lined his face. His eyes were light blue, looking almost as if there were pieces of ice lodged inside his sockets.

"I'll play at the $500 a hand tables for 8 hours a night."

"Strictly at Empirico's casino?"

"Right."

"Nowhere else."

"My reasons are my own."

"Vendetta?"

"It's Las Vegas, Zack."

"I prefer Mr. Roman."

"Like I said, it's Las Vegas, Zack," Matthias said, downing a shot of rye. "I'll call you Mister when the money starts rolling in."

"How much are we talking?" Lydda asked in a tone of voice more desperate than confident.

"Let's assume $400 a hand. One hand per minute, depending how many are at the table. Sixty hands an hour. Take off half an hour for breaks. Four hundred and fifty hands a night. My edge will be 65-35."

"That's impossible," Zack said. "Nobody has a 30 per cent advantage in blackjack."

"Four hundred and fifty hands at $400 with a 30 per cent edge."

Zack swore at him. "I'm telling you. It can't be done."

"One hundred and eighty thousand dollars bet each night at 30 per cent profit is $54,000 each night. Half to me and half to you. Well, half to Lydda. You guys decide how to split it up—if you even want to. Twenty-seven large for each of us each night. That's gotta help. Right, Lydda?"

Lydda said nothing.

"Kid, I've been in Vegas longer than I care to remember," Zack said. "We all know that we have to wade through our share of it to get to the top. And plus, 27 large a night? What is that?"

Lydda's face flushed. "Let's play a deck."

"I agree," Matthias said. "I need you and you need me. Make it six decks. How fast can you deal, Zack?"

Lydda reached under the table. She shuffled 6 decks and gave them to Zack. She pulled out 100 chips and gave half to Zack and half to Matthias. Zack dealt. Matthias won the first hand. He doubled his bet on the next hand and won it. He lowered his bet on the third hand and lost. They continued until they finished all 6 decks. Zack's pile of chips was down to 25. Matthias had 75.

"Well, that's a little skewed, mind you. Sometimes I'm up and other times I'm down. Thirty per cent is the average."

"What do you need?" Zack asked.

"Keep me off the registry of known gamblers. I win the money—we split the profits. And Zack? Twenty-seven large a night is just the beginning."

"I can keep you off the list, but I can't guarantee they won't stop you internally."

"That's *my* problem."

"So we're set?"

"I'll need one waitress to help me. She'll be my watchdog for the pit bosses and floor managers. If they get edgy she'll give me a sign and I'll call it a night."

"You have anybody in mind?"

"There's a breathtaking reddish-blonde-haired beauty working here. See if you can't get her a job next door."

Lydda was ready to sign her life away for a deal like this.

Anything to help her fledgling dump. Twenty-seven grand was twenty-seven more than she'd normally have.

"Kid, I'm in. But say what you want. I don't believe that you're in Vegas to simply split money with us."

Lucas searched the tables and machines looking for Jake. He came up empty and sat down at Jack's Bar in the Mayan gaming area thinking he'd stop by sooner or later. He ordered a Caesar from the bartender, drank it faster than he normally would, and ordered a second. He gulped half of it down. He knew this was stupid—drinking this much was insanity. But the sting of Tabitha leaving was just now sinking in. And instead of dealing with it, he chose to dull those nerves until he found time to sort things through.

"First time in Las Vegas?" a female voice asked.

He didn't realize she was talking to him. And perhaps he wished she wasn't, which is why he didn't respond.

"Hey, you in the beard wearing the cap," she said with a laugh in her voice.

She *was* talking to him. He saw her reddish-blonde hair as she sat down on the stool beside him. He noticed a silver bracelet on her right wrist. A snake ran along it with its mouth facing her hand. He nodded to acknowledge her presence and hoped she wouldn't stay long.

"Now you have to help me out. First time in Vegas? No. Wait! Don't tell me." She gave him a playful jab in the shoulder with her elbow and moved her stool closer. She eyed him over. "Veteran. Definitely a veteran."

He looked closer at the bracelet as she continued.

"And you're here because the woman of your dreams is not. Am I right or am I right? But hey, come on. This is Las Vegas. Fortunes are made and fortunes are lost. And, sweetheart, your fortune has just come in."

He studied her eyes. The shell was saying yes but the person behind them was saying no. She didn't want to be here. She didn't want anything to do with him. Out of the corner of his eye he looked at the bracelet again. What were the chances?

"Savannah?"

She felt a sudden insecurity. Had she been with this one before? There were so many. Countless, really. She drew a blank. That exciting look in her eyes disappeared. The part of her that didn't want to be here came through stronger.

"Am I right?" he asked, hoping she wouldn't leave. She had a spunk about her that Tabitha didn't have. The two of them were different women altogether. Savannah didn't have the same strength of character. If Tabitha were a ship, Savannah was a lifeboat seeking to be rescued. Savannah didn't reply. Inside, she was getting ready to go.

"The plane that was headed for London. Matthias warned you about it."

Her mouth opened in amazement. She squinted her eyes as if trying to see clearer who he was. She swore. "You're Lucas Stephens," she whispered.

"You got off the plane. But he did not. Why?"

The bartender asked her what she wanted. She hesitated a moment as if trying to decide if she should stay.

"Strawberry daiquiri," she said and then turned to Lucas. "Let's forget the plane. Let's talk about something else."

Touched a nerve. We'll come back to this. Believe you me, we'll come back to this. "How are things in Las Vegas?" he asked.

"The same as they were yesterday and the same as they're going to be tomorrow. This is the one city on earth that doesn't have a clock."

"Did you always want to be in Las Vegas?"

"Did you always want to be a miracle worker?"

"I wanted to be a medical doctor."

The bartender gave her the drink.

"Now that's a coincidence. I always wanted to be a nurse."

"What kind?"

"ER."

"That's where I wanted to practise."

"Look at that. We're practically the same." She gave him a smile. "What are the odds? If you would have gone to any other city you wouldn't have met me, the most incredible woman on the face of the planet. You see how lucky you are?"

Second most incredible woman on the planet.

She took a drink. "You know how many people wish they could sit right where you are? You have the best seat in Las Vegas." She stirred her drink and smiled again. "Forget Céline Dion. Forget Tony Bennett. Forget fight night. You can even forget Cirque du Soleil. You have a front row seat with me. With me, sweetheart. What more could a man ask for?" She took another sip and put it down on the counter. She raised her eyebrows and looked at Lucas for a response.

"Did your father ever tell you he loved you?" he asked.

She touched her glass and debated again whether she should go. "Did yours?"

Lucas finished his drink. Savannah took another sip from hers. "I don't even know why I order these things," she said. "The more I drink, the thirstier I get."

Lucas ordered her some water. The bartender opened an imported bottle and poured some in a glass. She took a drink.

"Having no father would have been better than my father." She glanced at Lucas to check if he was really listening to her. His expression reassured her that his mind was solely on her. "Yeah, my dad was a real hero. To everyone but us. To everyone else he was the model employee. He was the person who visited the sick in the hospital. He was the one who volunteered for everything. He was the one who had time for anybody else. He was the one who gave Blackhawks tickets to kids in the South Side."

"You're from Chicago?"

She didn't want to divulge that. A little too late now. "Grew up there."

"Why'd you leave?"

That really was more than she was willing to share.

"Things don't always work out the way people want them to," she said. "And yet we're sometimes left with this feeling of wishing we could go back and fix the screw-ups we had."

"Is that what you want?"

"To go back?"

"Do you?"

"Not anymore." She switched back to her strawberry daiquiri. "I can't do that."

"Savannah isn't your real name."

She finished her drink. "Well done, Sherlock."

"Are you in touch with Matthias?"

"I am."

"Is that a good thing or a bad thing?"

"Time will tell."

"Can you put me in contact with him?"

She looked at him and tried to decipher his motive. "I can." She stood up, becoming aware of the time, giving the impression she was late for something.

Or someone.

Lucas paid the bartender. He followed her through the casino to the exit. When they got outside she was going left and he was going right.

"I hope you find what you're looking for in Las Vegas," he said.

She winked at him in an attempt to convince him she really was the cool, confident, Las Vegas-is-my-town kind of girl. But all that came through was a woman in danger of losing what feeble grip she had left on life.

"You too," she said. "Maybe we'll both discover whether this is a town where people find things."

She lifted her hand, gave a short wave goodbye, and walked away. Lucas watched as the Mayan entrance lights reflected off her reddish-blonde hair. He turned and went down the sidewalk. Then he heard her call out to him.

"Hey you," she said, careful not to use his name, respecting his desire to be as anonymous for as long as he could.

Lucas turned around.

"September," she said.

"September?"

She lifted her shoulders and then let them drop. She looked away from him a moment as if embarrassed over what she was about to say. She looked back. "My name. My real first name is September."

He'd heard that name somewhere before. Then he remembered where. "One of my teachers in grade school. She was a September too. Gosh, I haven't heard that name in years."

She stood still under the lights, nodded her head in an admission of despair, and felt the weight of her past creeping in.

"Me neither."

25

Lucas knocked on Jake's door at 5 a.m. When Jake opened it the look on his face told Lucas it had been a rough night. Bloodshot eyes. Straggly hair. Worried expression.

"How were the tables last night?"

He let Lucas in and closed the door behind him. It took Lucas a moment for his eyes to adjust to the darkness. When they did he saw neither bed had been slept in.

"You play all night?"

"No, Lucas," Jake said with a touch of annoyance. "I've been praying all night. You?"

"Couldn't sleep."

Jake sat down on a bed and rubbed his eyes. "This is such a mistake, Lucas. Going to see Caesar."

"Mike first. Then Caesar."

"Both of them. You shouldn't be doing this."

That didn't help Lucas' nerves any. He had walked in hoping he would get some kind of reassurance about facing Mike and Caesar. His horrible night's sleep may just have been the outworkings of his mind playing through the scenarios of Caesar's response to seeing him again. But that coupled with Jake's warning made it impossible for Lucas to cast off his friend's cryptic warning.

"Maybe you're wrong about this."

Jake clenched his teeth, determined to keep himself from losing control. "I wasn't wrong the last time I warned you, was I?"

"I have to take him on."

Jake cursed. "Why do you have to do anything with Caesar?"

"First, because of the cure he's hiding."

"You only *think* he's hiding it."

"And second, I think I can change him."

"You really believe that? Is that what being in the desert did to you? Made you think you can change a guy like Caesar?"

"He's my biggest opponent."

"You're wrong about that."

"If I can convince him that this healing gift is something he should be helping me with instead of fighting me on, then there's no limit to what can happen.

"You don't believe that."

"I do."

Jake stood up and leaned against the bathroom wall. He rubbed his face and felt a wave of exhaustion hit him. "You're afraid he's going to die."

"He can change. I know it."

"Change for what?"

"Caesar doesn't even give media interviews anymore. That was his baby. He loved the media. He loved the attention. But he's delegated all that to Mike. He's gone into hiding these last few weeks. He's close to the end."

"You have to be sure what you're trying to convince him of. You have to have a clear objective with this guy. He'll mess you up, Lucas. He's not like you. You think he is, but he's not. He's one cold, cruel, evil person. Something made him that way. Something turned him into that. And whatever it is, it has death's grip on him. If he has that cure and he *is* holding it back—what does that say about him, Lucas? You think a man like that is within reach of change?"

"He has to be."

A soft breeze came into the room and blew against Lucas' neck.

"You're afraid of him."

"I'm not."

"You're afraid of him tracking you down. You're afraid that this game will go on until you make some kind of resolution with him."

"He's my enemy, Jake."

"You're sure?"

A chill ran down Lucas' spine. He was convinced a third, unseen party was in the room, watching them. Listening to them. He swallowed. Looked at the door. It was closed. There was nobody else there.

Not that he could see.

Lucas drove up to the towering casino. Workers adjusted the last tarp at the top of the building for the grand opening set later that evening. Between those huge veils that surrounded the entire structure Lucas could make out parts of the monstrosity about to be released to the world. The hotel portion had a central circular tube that ran straight up. At regular intervals throughout, sections of hotel rooms veered off at slanted angles from the tube-like branches, making the whole structure look like a gigantic tree. Two massive statues, each as high as ten houses, stood on either side of the entrance. Lucas couldn't get a clear enough look, but it seemed to him they were carrying swords.

He drove to the barricaded parking garage. Two men with bulges in their suit jackets came up to his car.

"Mr. Stephens?"

Thatcher and Ridley's replacements.

"Yes."

"Please come with us. We'll take you in."

Lucas stepped out of his blue Audi coupe. The two men introduced themselves as Mitchell and Foster and led Lucas through the empty parking garage to an elevator. Mitchell, the tallest one with the shaved head, pushed the lobby button. When they reached the floor they led him out to another bank of elevators to his right. Foster, the shorter one at 6'6" with long hair, hit the 70th floor button. The elevator lifted.

"Did either of you know Thatcher or Ridley?"

Neither Mitchell nor Foster answered.

"They worked security for Empirico just like you."

Still no response.

"They died in Chicago trying to kill me."

The elevator slowed down. The doors opened.

"Here you are, Mr. Stephens. We'll see you again."

"I hope not," Lucas said, stepping out of the elevator.

The doors closed.

Lucas stood in a dark hallway. To his left he saw a line of hotel rooms. To his right at the end of the hallway he saw a room with the door open. A faint light shone out from it.

He walked towards it, thinking that at any moment Foster or Mitchell might step out from one of the side rooms, slit his throat, and leave him dying on the floor as his blood soaked into the brand new carpet. He glanced behind him to make sure no one was creeping up from the shadows. He reached the end and opened the door. The smooth carpet was an alternating blend of red and grey in a winding S. Soft white light emanated from pucks in the walls arranged in a similar pattern. Leather couches spaced the area in front of the glass overlooking Las Vegas Boulevard.

"Is this not the best party room in the world?" Lucas saw a figure walking towards him from the far side of the room. Grey suit. Red shirt. Matched the floor. He recognized the voice. "Can you imagine the women who will show up at a place like this?" He stepped into the light.

"You've been a busy man."

"The fun is just beginning, my friend." *My friend.* That didn't sound right. Not anymore. "Tonight is the grand opening. And unlike other pretend grand openings at other casinos where people have already been playing there for weeks, we have a true grand opening. Not one guest has been inside here yet. And we've already sold out—including all 30 of these party suites. Now tell me you're not impressed."

Mike wanted to offer Lucas a handshake but wondered if it would be received. *Exactly how do you shake hands with someone you wanted to kill?*

"I thought you were in jail."

"Out on good behaviour," Mike said with a laugh, though his eyes told a different story.

"Mike, where do we stand?"

Mike took offence but hid it well. He cleared his throat and lost that fake smile. "Lucas, I want you and I to succeed Caesar in running Empirico."

"You want Empirico for yourself just like everyone else on the Council."

"But I'm the only one with a chance. Next to you, of course."

"I'm out."

"So you say. Yet you've come to the flagship Empirico property. Why would someone who wants nothing to do with this company come right to the grand opening? You miss us, Lucas? You miss the real action?"

"I didn't come to join up."

"You'll reconsider. Especially after you see this place."

"I came here to draw the lines. You do your business and I'll do mine."

Mike laughed. "This isn't some sandbox, Lucas. There is no pie to cut up. We're all in each other's backyard here," he said in a way that made it difficult to tell if he was joking or serious.

"I'm not coming back, Mike."

The smile faded. "Empirico doesn't leave you just because you walk out. You know that."

"It did for me." Lucas looked around the room, trying to find a way to change the subject. "Do you have a drink?"

Mike walked to the bar and poured a beer for Lucas and himself. They sat down at a table overlooking the Wynn Hotel.

"Mike, how well do you know the operation?"

"I know it as well as you do."

"I don't know half of it."

Mike leaned back in his chair and pulled out a cigarette, trying too hard to look relaxed. "Empirico is huge, Lucas. Pharmaceuticals worldwide. Casino in Vegas. Rumours about making films in Hollywood. Real estate and other ventures in New York. How could anybody but Caesar know what's going on?"

"This casino is being financed on cash flow, Mike. That's insanity. Empirico needs that money to run the business. They are stretched to the brink. Unless there is some massive infusion of revenue, either from the casino or some other source, this company is in trouble."

Mike took a drag on his cigarette and inhaled. If he was worried about what Lucas said, he was able to hide it well. "Let me give you some good advice. You really want to divvy up that sandbox? Slice the pie so everyone gets their share?" He leaned closer. "Get out of Las Vegas."

"I just got here."

In one violent motion Mike smashed his fist down on the table. Part of his thumb connected with his drink, sending it flying to the ground. It spilled onto the carpet. His face flushed. His nostrils flared. "It is best for you and me if you go to Africa, South America, anywhere—"

"Anywhere they don't sell pharmaceuticals."

"Lucas, don't play games. Not here. The odds are not in your favour. You might win a little here. A little there. But over the long haul, the house always, always wins."

Jake's warning rang in Lucas' ears. The thought of Mitchell and Foster charging into the room and emptying a clip of ammunition into his back played over in his mind.

"Mike, let me return you the favour of being blunt." Lucas leaned his elbows on the table. He was ready to drill Mike in the face if he so much as reached inside his pocket for a cigarette or, perhaps, a gun. "I'm not going. I'm staying right here."

Mike leaned back. His tense face relaxed. He grinned too wide for it to be genuine. "Well, then. This is going to be quite the showdown."

Lucas finished his drink and stood up. "How is Caesar? How much time does he have left?"

"Why don't you ask him yourself?"

"Caesar's here?" Lucas asked, unsure of what Mike was implying.

"Hundredth floor."

"He's not in a hospital?"

"And miss the grand opening?"

Mike stood up and led Lucas out of the room to an elevator. He hit the button. The door opened. Lucas stepped in. He turned back to Mike who stood in the hallway.

"You're not coming?"

"I've said my piece."

"As have I."

The door started to close. Mike's face grew stern. "We're not both making it out of Vegas, Lucas. You think about that." The door shut. Lucas felt the gentle pull of the elevator bringing him up to Caesar.

The door opened to reveal something different from what Lucas expected. He anticipated an office area. Chairs. A secretary. Anne, the Danish bombshell. But instead, what he saw amazed him.

To his left he saw an incredible pool the size of a gym floor. Waterfalls, fountains, and cave-like structures filled the area, creating a maze of tunnels and slides, making it look like some unspoiled exotic island. High walls of aquariums filled with tropical fish with water rushing over them spread out around the island to create the illusion of vertical planes of water suspended in air. A river ran from the pool through a variety of real fruit trees and flowers, and continued to the middle of the room where an incredible fake tree spread up to the balcony above. As Lucas studied the amazing structure with its branches stretched out wider than what he thought possible, his attention was diverted to a man at the top of the stairs leading to the glass mezzanine floor.

"Lucas! You made it back!" Caesar raised his hands in triumph as though his long-lost son had finally come home. He came down the stairs, which spiralled around the tree down to the bottom. He spoke louder and walked faster than what could be expected for a man with terminal cancer. As he drew closer, Lucas saw he didn't have those puffy pink eyes. His skin looked better. He'd lost weight. His face beamed with colour. No grey. No discolouration. His eyes lit up with energy. No slouching. No hobble in his walk. No raspy sound in his voice.

"Welcome to Las Vegas, Lucas!" Caesar said.

Lucas' heart began to race. His throat became drier. His knees felt weak. He wanted to sit down. He *had* to sit down. This wasn't right. This was not at all right. The shock of seeing that man standing in front of him was more than he could take.

Caesar was in perfect health.

26

"Now I thought Chicago was a great city. But Lucas, Vegas is where it's at."

Lucas wanted another drink. Maybe a few. He tried to respond but nothing appropriate came to mind. *Why aren't you dead?* just didn't seem to fit right now.

"We should have come here years ago," Caesar continued. "Let me show you the view."

They walked past the towering tree to a door with a keypad. Caesar punched in three numbers. It released. He pushed it open and they stepped onto a marble balcony overlooking Las Vegas Boulevard. The wind blew against Lucas' back as he walked out to the edge.

"Look at this city," Caesar said. He stretched his arms out like an orchestra conductor ready to begin a concert. "It's the embodiment of adventure!"

"You're in remarkable health."

"Thank you. Coming from you, a man with your abilities, that means a lot."

Lucas glanced down at the dots of people below. He got an itchy feeling in the back of his legs. It wouldn't take much. One good push from Caesar and Lucas would be the first "suicide" in the new casino.

"I've heard rumours," Lucas said, looking down the street in the direction of the Venetian to get rid of the vertigo.

"You're in the wrong town for rumours, Lucas. If you want rumours, you go to Hollywood. If you want outright lies, you come to Vegas." Caesar laughed. It caught Lucas by surprise. It was the first time he had ever heard Caesar do that.

"Some people speculate the pharmaceutical industry is close to finding a cure for cancer."

His laugh died out. All they heard was the wind.

"To think there would be a pill you could take to eradicate cancer? Actually, it's not surprising when you consider it. If we found such a cure, it would be the epitome of the Western world experience. A culture of fat lazy people eat garbage food, live stressful lives, develop cancer, come running to people like you or me for a cure, and pretend they can erase their responsibility for how they got that way in the first place."

"You think we're as close as people say?"

"Pharmaceuticals will never develop a cure. And even if we did, it wouldn't matter. All people will do is find some other way to poison themselves and start the whole cycle over again. We cured polio. Has that helped? We cured TB. Nobody cares about that. Because we have new diseases to take their place. And that will always be the case."

"You think there's a limit to pharmaceuticals?"

"Pharmaceuticals, Lucas, are the biggest sham in the world. Vegas, however, is different. Vegas is honest because people know before they ever even walk into a casino they are being ripped off. Sure, some people win big. But overall, every person walking into that casino knows, or at least they should know, that they are a loser. But not pharmaceuticals."

"Do you think people should be given the best pharmaceuticals available?"

"So people can get healthy? Forget it. You don't need our business for that. Get a decent diet. Exercise. Live within your budget. Find someone you can love. Don't stress yourself. But do people do that? No, they don't. And when things go bad they come begging. And when they do, the pharmaceuticals are there to rape and pillage them up to their dying day."

"I'm surprised to hear you say it that way. It's not like you. It's pessimistic."

"But it is accurate. You want to destroy the pharmaceutical industry? Two ways. One—get a guy like you out there handing out free miracles. Two—get people to clean out their systems and live sensibly. *Whammo*! They'd put us under just like that. But they won't. They won't do it. Why? Because this is a culture of zero responsibility. And this, my friend, this is why Las Vegas exists."

"Las Vegas exists because of zero responsibility?"

"Exactly. You enter this city and you leave all your ties behind. What happens in Vegas stays in Vegas. You can be whoever you want to be. Imagine you're a conservative Republican homemaker back home in your red state. Come to Vegas with your friends and you can be the worst partier this town has ever known. Or be a blue Democrat—come to Vegas and get drunk and act like a lunatic if you want. They come running. You know why? Because we offer anonymity, Lucas. The ultimate escape is not from your situation, but from yourself."

"They say Vegas is a town of greed."

"The Strip might be. The rest of Vegas, though, is like any other city in America. Go for a block in either direction of the Boulevard and you may as well be in Chicago. But the Strip is not just about greed, Lucas. To figure out what makes this town work you need to study the people. Then you find out why this town exists. Then you find out why the hotels get booked. Then you find out why the planes keep bringing 36 million annual visitors here to drop their money in our machines and on our tables and then fly home, only to come back and do it all over again."

"Why do they come?"

"You want a free lesson?" Caesar smiled. It was so new for Lucas. A smile from Caesar. "No way! I wouldn't deprive you of the experience. You need to watch people. You need to listen in on their conversations. Then you'll understand the one basic reason for the existence of Vegas. You take out that one ingredient and this town goes back to the desert it was before the mob built it. There's one ingredient to Vegas just like that one responsibility ingredient to the pharmaceutical industry. Forget lobbyists and governments and laws and social interest groups and studies and religious arguments. One characteristic of human nature. One. That's it. One that is synonymous with Vegas. That's why this town exists. And when you figure it out, you can be the king of Vegas, Lucas. You."

A huge crowd had gathered on the street below. Media trucks pulled up. Camera crews stepped out. Reporters lined the steps.

"Your big grand opening moment," Lucas said.

"And you're here to share it with me." Caesar gave Lucas a punch in the arm. "Come on. Let me show you this place. We only have a few minutes before I give my welcome speech."

They left the balcony, passed the massive tree, and took another set of elevators down 30 floors. They walked down a hallway to the end. Off to the right they saw a crew of construction workers finishing a pour. Lucas watched as the concrete made its way into the forms and covered the steel reinforcing bars.

"In most casinos you have the gaming on one floor and all the rooms up above. This is just so brutally short-sighted. They do that to keep the guests in the hotel and those who want to gamble on the floor. But here at our casino we have special gaming areas set up for people in the hotel on every second floor. Slots. Blackjack. Poker. No high stakes, mind you, except on the highest floors. That way people get to know other people who are in the hotel."

They reached the end of the hallway. They stepped into a glass elevator. "Now for the really fun stuff."

Lucas looked out and saw a gaming area on a glass floor above a tropical fish tank. They passed by an exercise room. "There's one every floor," Caesar said, and then they passed a bar. "Bars are important. Most casinos think that people want to be around crowds and crowds of people when they gamble or drink. Not true. The Internet proves this. People live in solitude. So we create their own little hideaways. People love the privacy and don't want to be interrupted. There are seniors who sit in the same spot at the slots for 12 hours at a time without moving. No joke. Some even wear diapers the whole day so they don't have to give up their machines to go to the bathroom."

"That's unbelievable."

"Not really. Once you figure out that one characteristic I was telling you about everything here will make sense to you. It's the building block for this whole facility. It's how I designed this place."

They passed a floor of nightclubs and restaurants and then a box office with the name VERITAS above it.

"What is that?" Lucas asked.

"I wish I knew. It's our secret theatre production. I told the creator to surprise me. I hear there's a lot of fire and water."

The elevator opened. "Now here, my friend, is something you will love."

My friend. My friend. Those two words felt out of place. Even more so than when Mike used them.

Lucas sniffed a familiar smell but had trouble placing it. He felt a chill in the air. That sound. He knew that sound. They took a few more steps and stopped. When Lucas saw it he nearly fell to his knees. His mouth dropped open. His eyes stayed frozen on the spectacle in front of him. It was perfect. Brand new and perfect. It was even better than the one back home.

There in front of him was the casino's hockey arena.

Purple and yellow padded seats filled the seating area. Luxury boxes formed a ring around the middle. He heard the familiar sound of the Zamboni as it cleaned the ice surface.

"The new NHL home of the Las Vegas Fortune! Seating for 15,561. Plus expansion for the playoffs and sellouts takes us to 20,000. First season is already sold out. Can you believe that?"

"I can," Lucas said, wishing he could see a game.

"This was a tough deal. I had to wrangle with the league to get them to come here. In the end I beat out a smaller market Canadian city for it. Winnipeg. It was close between them and me. The league even got 200,000 signatures from people in that town begging them to come." Caesar laughed. "They only got one signature from Las Vegas." He laughed again. "Mine!"

Caesar patted him on the back. "There's one more thing I have to show you."

More? More than hockey? How much more could this place possibly have?

"Now, the arena doubles as a boxing and concert venue. These 4,000-seat arenas other casinos build for concerts are garbage. Go big or go home. You have a limited event, create demand, and send ticket prices through the roof. Best of all, you're never in a bind with those long-term contracts that always end in dispute if the performer stinks and you want to get rid of them."

They took an escalator to the box seat area. "The future is not just gaming. This is where many casinos fail, whether they be grind joints or luxury properties. Gaming, entertainment, alcohol, food, accommodations, and shopping—that's how money is made, with the future leaning heavily on the entertainment. The combination of it all is what makes it work. And you can't just have one without the other. You have to draw in the nongambler too. This place is the entertainment lovers' place. Why? Because society is shifting its attention from craving money to craving pleasure. We would rather be served than be powerful. We want to feel good again. To be miserable and rich will not be as coveted as being debt-ridden and happy. Plus as an added bonus baby boomers are retiring and have loads of money. So they'll come here. Some will sit in their diapers at the slots or tables filling their drawers all day while others will watch shows and sporting events."

They reached the top. "Entertainment. That's why Sheridan Corvey is coming here tonight. Huge crusade he's putting on. Miracles, Lucas. You know about that." They walked down a wide hallway. On the left he saw the box seats for the hockey arena. On the right he saw another set of boxes.

"Now this is special. First of its kind in the world."

"How do people on the right side watch the hockey game?"

"They can decide what they want to watch. If it's hockey or a concert they go to the hockey side."

"And if it's not hockey or a concert?"

Caesar smiled and motioned for Lucas to look for himself. Lucas stepped into one of the boxes on the right. When he saw what was before him he opened his mouth in amazement. He shook his head in disbelief. Caesar stood beside him, overlooking the new indoor stadium.

"National Football League comes to town."

"Unreal."

"Las Vegas Gamblers. We're going to start a tradition to always go for it on fourth down."

"Seriously?"

"No." Caesar shook his head and laughed. "I'll leave that up to the coach. I just buy the teams. I don't run them," he said with a smile.

"Amazing."

"It is." Caesar nodded his head. His tone became more serious as he looked out over the field. "But this leaves us with a huge challenge to find someone to run the place. No easy task. There are few people who have what it takes. The casino, the pharmaceutical operations. It's tough to find the right man who can put this all together."

Lucas followed Caesar through one of the suites to the private balcony below. They leaned their arms against the guardrail and imagined a game taking place in front of them.

"Rough sport, isn't it?" Caesar asked. "I sometimes have a hard time watching. Especially when way up here you can forecast something bad is about to happen. A wide receiver runs a post pattern. He sees the ball is thrown his way. I mean, it's gotta be going through his mind. That thought of being hit. The corner who has him timed just perfectly. The free safety who makes a good read. Wide receiver has to be a scary job. Always looking over your shoulder. Always worrying. Always knowing that a career-ending injury is just around the corner. What would that be like? Fans love you one minute and you think you can do no wrong. And then *wham*! You drop a critical pass. Or worse, that free safety drills you when you weren't expecting it. And for no reason at all the fans can turn on you. Disown you. Hate you." He turned to Lucas, but Lucas just stared out at the field.

"That's why I like owning the teams," Caesar continued, looking back at the stadium. "From way up here the fans don't even know I exist. I can make decisions that make or break their game and all they can do is blame the poor guy on the field. I'll sit up here and watch the whole thing unfold and be totally protected from the fans, from the opposition, from everything." He turned to Lucas and this time he waited until he looked back. "What do you think, Lucas? Do you think it's better to be a wide receiver or an owner?"

They heard steps approaching from above. Anne called down from the suite. She wore a navy two-piece suit and had a touch of frustration in her voice.

"Caesar," she said, glancing at her watch and then noticing Lucas. It caught her by surprise. She felt awkward about how to respond to him being there with Caesar present. "Lucas."

"Anne, you are right! It is time to party. And time to release the name of my new place!"

They took an elevator down to the third floor and followed Caesar as he led the way to a large terrace overlooking the mass of people. Lucas and Anne stood off to the side. Caesar walked on a red carpet towards a podium to address the thousands who were blocking Las Vegas Boulevard.

When Caesar reached the microphone the crowd cheered. People stretched as far as he could see in both directions on the Strip. Cameras flashed. Video cameras broadcasted him back to new stations around the U.S. and the world. Lucas looked at the throng of people below. He scanned the row of reporters and saw Tabitha shooting pictures. It felt wrong that she was there by herself. It felt wrong that he wasn't with her.

"Ladies and gentlemen…and gamers." The crowd laughed. "It is my pleasure to welcome you to Las Vegas' newest casino!" He wanted to say greatest casino, but this was not the time to put off the other owners. "Your entrance will always be lit up at night to find your way."

Two ten-storey tarps on either side of him fell down. With an incredible blast of heat, flames shot out from huge swords carried by the two statues at the entrance. They were muscular creatures with gold helmets and wings on their backs. Flames burned around the swords, making them look like flaming weapons ready to defend the fortress.

Off to the side dozens of trumpeters blew their instruments. Behind them percussionists gave a drum roll. Camera flashes went ballistic.

"It is my pleasure to welcome you to…."

Caesar lifted his arms. The massive tarps fell down, revealing the casino name in bright gold lights. The crowd screamed. Caesar shouted into his microphone.

"The Garden of Eden!"

The flaming swords gave off another burst of fire, this one more powerful than the first. Streams of red, white, and blue fireworks shot off from the terrace, lighting up the evening sky. Ten sets of doors to the casino entrance opened. Lucas watched as people rushed in. He tried to find Tabitha among the crowd. But instead he saw another familiar face. Tall thin build. Slicked-black hair. Lucas cupped his hands over his mouth and shouted down.

"Matthias!"

He walked right underneath him. The sound of the fireworks coupled with the music drowned Lucas out.

"Matthias!"

But Matthias did not hear him.

He had work to do.

27

Edgar struggled with the crowd to enter Las Vegas' newest and soon to be declared best casino. His face looked tired. His body hurt. Even the slightest jab from people beside him caused pain. His teeth ached. The over-the-counter pills did nothing to help. Every step took careful calculation. He walked slower than the others. It was all he could manage.

Lucas and Anne stood on the terrace above, watching the crowd. If Lucas had looked closer he would have seen Edgar, like the one lame duck in the massive pond. But like so many times when people look at the ordinary, Lucas missed the unique. They left without seeing him.

But Tabitha saw Edgar as he approached the incredible statues and their flaming swords. The fire lit up his pale face. She called out to him. She was sure he was close enough to hear her, but he didn't. She called again and watched as he turned a corner and disappeared in the masses. She took more pictures of the casino and then joined the crowd. When she passed under the swords she felt an uneasy sensation. Like she was breaking the law. Trespassing. Entering a country illegally. She didn't want to go in. Didn't want to be near anything related to Caesar's businesses. She wanted to take pictures of the casino so that she could give readers of *The Chicago Observer* a walking tour of the new megacasino. But she had promised Chester she would get an interview with the acting head of casino operations.

And, as luck would have it, that person was Mike.

Edgar followed the overhead signs in the direction of the arena. He felt uneasy, out of place coming to a casino, this one in particular, for a miracle crusade. First he was running from Caesar. Now he was grovelling at his feet, begging for a healing. He tried to rid himself of the idea that a casino and a miracle crusade both gave people a conditional promise of a benefit, but that they only served to ultimately sucker them out of their money. He shook his head. *No. No. No! No negative thoughts. Don't jinx your miracle with your negativism. It's going to happen tonight. It's going to work. It will. Positive thoughts. Positive results. Tonight's my night. Tonight I'm walking out healed.* The gambling and miracle combination didn't sit well with him. But Edgar's healing clock was ticking, and he decided this was not the time to allow past convictions to spoil his chances for a breakthrough.

Slot machines jingled all around him. An ocean of them spread out as far as he could see. Coins hit the dishes. Lights flashed. People cheered. He walked past row after row of machines, each one occupied by someone with a bucket of coins and a beady set of eyes. In the middle of the gaming area stood a huge tree that reached up five floors. On each of the floors was a table gaming area accessible by escalators. Each floor featured blackjack, craps, baccarat, roulette…everything. The higher the floor the higher the limit, the more expensive the drinks, and the hotter the waitresses. People pushed around, hurrying to tables. The set-up should have been enough to drive even the most casual gambler wild with excitement. But Edgar wasn't interested in gambling.

He was looking to beat the odds with a miracle of a different sort.

He passed the huge tree, the base of which was used for a bar. He felt hoarseness in his throat and reached in his pocket for his wallet. He bought a fruit drink from the bartender and sipped it on his way to the arena entrance.

More people. The place was worse than a mall at Christmas. People jammed through security lines and metal detectors into the future home of the Las Vegas Fortune. When it was Edgar's turn the security officer asked him a question, but Edgar didn't hear it. Now that his life was on the line he had a hard time paying attention to a man in a uniform asking him what he was drinking. The security guard repeated his question.

"It's passion fruit," Edgar said. That wasn't exactly right. He *thought* it was passion fruit. Everything felt like such a daze. Like sleepwalking or a hangover. The security guard asked him to drink from it. Edgar did and walked through.

He found an empty chair at the end of an aisle on the floor. He sat down and checked his watch. Almost there. People crammed into the arena, filling every seat. Beneath his feet was a layer of plywood sheeting covering the recently cleaned ice surface. The massive choir practised on the stage in the centre of the arena. A man walked up and down doing sound checks.

Tabitha found a spot along the lower level near an entrance. She kept a watchful eye out for Edgar, wishing she was sitting beside him, wanting to do whatever she could for him. It felt different for her to be at a healing crusade again knowing that someone she cared about was among the crowd, looking for a miracle.

The lights dimmed. Edgar felt the anticipation of the evening. He closed his eyes and said a prayer, as did thousands of others who had come to be healed. Some were there for the show. Some were there for the inaugural event at the arena. But most were there out of desperation.

A man came on stage and welcomed people. He used clichéd religious expressions that seemed like a prerecorded routine cranked out for all of these evenings. He never used the word *Las Vegas* in his speech. Edgar figured it was probably because after being run so ragged with these shows, these performances, all the events ran together and the city names just got lost in the shuffle. Normally, Edgar would have taken exception to the cookie-cutter spiritual banter. Normally, Edgar would have taken notes and critiqued the event. But these were not normal times. And Edgar was not interested in ruining his miracle evening. The choir came next. Most people stood up. Others stayed in their wheelchairs, trying to believe that they too would be standing by evening's end. Those who knew the words sang them by memory. Others sang off screens. Edgar did neither. The gravity of the moment made it impossible for him to concentrate on his illness and his Maker. He stood there, quiet amid the noise, hoping those two would find a way to resolve themselves tonight.

Hundreds of people packed the top floor of Caesar's party plaza in the Garden. Gorgeous models wearing bikinis swam in pools and doused themselves under the waterfalls. People drank expensive wine and talked with each other while standing in amazement at the trees and streams of water running through the area.

Mike walked up the spiralling stairs to the top of the tree. He took a walkway to the mezzanine area and knocked on the door. It opened automatically. Mike entered and it closed behind him.

Caesar looked at monitors showing the packed-out gaming areas.

"Congratulations, Caesar," Mike said. "You did it."

"Look at this," he said, pointing to the highest gaming area floor. "Even the high stakes are filled right out." Among those players, Matthias sat at one of the tables playing blackjack, betting on average $400 a hand.

"Our first hourly report will be ready in minutes."

"Excellent. I couldn't have imagined a better start."

Mike hesitated. "Any news on Lucas?"

Caesar shook his head. "Let's not talk about Lucas. Tonight we pretend the man doesn't exist. Just pretend he vanished into thin air." Caesar took a drink of his bourbon. He held it in his mouth and swallowed it, feeling it burn against his throat. "Tomorrow is another day."

Lucas pulled out his cellphone on the third floor balcony overlooking Las Vegas Boulevard. He phoned Jake at the motel.

"You're still alive," Jake said, both relieved and surprised.

"I'm at the casino."

"Ready to start the healings?"

"I think so."

"You think so?"

"Something's not right."

"What is it?"

"Can you meet me here?"

"What's wrong?" Jake asked.

Corvey came onstage. White suit. Black shoes. Perfect hair. Hair that seemed it could withstand a hurricane. A single spotlight focused on him. He gave introductory comments. Edgar let them slide. The music swelled. The choir sang. The lights turned a soft glow. That could only mean one thing.

It was time for the offering.

Ushers passed buckets down the aisles. Edgar wasn't prepared for this. *How could I forget?* Before his illness this would have been a no-brainer. Let the bucket pass onto those suckers who wanted to support this masquerade, who wanted to give their money earned from their $6 an hour jobs to pay for Corvey's next $300 pair of shoes. But today, the circumstances were different. Today, that bucket took on a whole new meaning. He reached inside his sweater and pulled out his wallet from his dress shirt pocket. Inside he found about a thousand dollars cash and a credit card. The bucket came closer. *A hundred? That's pretty generous, isn't it? Yeah. That's good.* He took it out. Then he reconsidered. *What if it's not enough? What if I give these hundred bucks and I was really supposed to give a thousand? Didn't he just say something about the generous man being prosperous? What if being stingy prevents me from being healed? If I give more, does that increase my chances of getting healed? It has to. It shows I mean business, right?* The bucket came to him. He saw the meagre offering inside. His mind ping-ponged back and forth between a hundred and a thousand. A hundred and a thousand. He took out all the bills, folded them, and stuck them inside. He passed the bucket to the usher.

Best to have all the bases covered.

Corvey gave a sermon on the story where blind men came to Jesus pleading for mercy. Jesus stopped and asked them what they wanted to receive.

"What do you want God to do for you tonight?" Corvey asked. "Many people pray 'If it be Thy will, please heal me.' I often wonder why they don't just save their breath. There's only one time where someone asked Jesus if He was willing to heal them. And you know what His answer was? It was yes."

That made sense to Edgar. *God is willing to heal.*

"Now granted," Corvey continued, "people take that too far. They ask God for things like big houses, fancy cars—"

And fancy suits like yours? Edgar thought and then forced it out of his mind. *Stop it! Stay positive. Stay focused. Tonight. Tonight.*

"Two blind men came to Jesus. Jesus asked them, 'What do you want Me to do for you?' I mean, go figure. Isn't it obvious? They're blind! But Jesus wants them to be specific. Have you ever told God what you want from Him?" The thousands who had gathered there suddenly disappeared. There were only two people left in the arena. A flamboyant preacher on stage and a struggling, dying theologian amid a sea of empty chairs. "What do you want God to do for you?" Corvey asked. He continued preaching, but Edgar didn't hear the rest of it. He stayed on that line, saying it over and over again.

Corvey asked them all to stand. He gave an altar call. Edgar almost felt like going up. *Keep all the bases covered.* Corvey then prayed for God to heal every person from illness, be it physical, mental, or emotional. The music started. More praying. Then, even more praying.

Then, a miracle.

A woman beside him walked to the front saying "It's a miracle" over and over again. She stepped onto the stage, bending her wrists back and forth, telling Corvey how she had been delivered from carpal tunnel syndrome. Edgar closed his eyes. This was it. It was here. It was working right now. He turned his hands palm up.

More people crowded the stage, saying how they had been healed of everything from a sore muscle to heart problems. A doctor stood at the base of the stairs, confirming as best she could what people were claiming.

Edgar sat down, listened to the music, and waited for his touch. More testimonies. More singing. More words from Corvey. It felt so calm. So peaceful. *Here it is. It's happening.*

Edgar closed his eyes, prayed, and asked God to take away his cancer. He stayed in the stillness, waiting. Expecting. Believing. The world had stopped.

He was in a whole new place.

Somewhere he'd never been before.

Then he felt a touch on his shoulder. "Edgar?"

He didn't reply. The voice seemed so far away, like when you're waking up from anaesthetic.

"Edgar?" the voice said again.

It was closer this time. He left the world he was in and opened his eyes. A sudden fear ran through him. He looked at the front. Then side to side.

The arena was empty.

No Corvey. No choir. No testimonies.

No miracle.

He glanced at the person speaking to him. Tabitha sat down in front of him. She looked at him with eyes that seemed to connect with what he was feeling.

Pain gripped his body. The cancer felt worse now than ever before. Like slimy green creatures running through his body, sucking out his energy and stabbing him all over. He felt a draft against the back of his neck.

She reached out her hand and touched him on the shoulder. He closed his eyes, squeezing tears out. He felt embarrassed being there with her. He tried to decide if this would be easier to take with or without her here.

Tabitha wondered if she was doing more good than harm by staying. "Let's get something to eat, Edgar," she risked. "Everyone's gone. Let's hang out."

Edgar's mind raced into a tailspin. *What's left now? What's left to try? Lucas didn't work. Corvey didn't work. Chemo didn't work. The bullpen is getting thin. Are there any more relief pitchers?*

"I'm not hungry," Edgar said.

She didn't mean it that way. Get something to eat. Get a drink. Take one of those thrill rides here at the casino. Or maybe the Manhattan Express at New York-New York. Go for a walk. Anything. She just wanted to be there for him in whatever way she could.

"Is there anything I can do for you, Edgar?"

He leaned his hands on the chair in front of him and hid his head between them. Tears streamed down. They dripped on the sheeting beneath him and found a way through a crack to the ice below.

"This isn't a good time for me," he said.

Tabitha waited, hoping that some profound thought would strike her that she could share with Edgar to make his pain more bearable. She found nothing but an empty reservoir from which to draw inspiration to help a man who was at the point men get to when there is nothing left to say. She stood up, gripped his shoulder, and left him alone in a brand new arena where some had walked out healed, yet many more walked out in the same condition they had come in and were now, like Edgar, trying to cope with life after being disappointed.

Again.

Jake met Lucas in the packed parking garage of the Garden.

"Outside. Right in front of the casino!" Jake said. "We'll set up shop. We'll make such a splash that people will come to us rather than Caesar's new casino. We'll strangle his operation!"

"Jake."

"Let's stick it to him right now. And then we can get out of this place."

"You don't like Vegas?" Lucas asked. He looked worried. Something was bothering him.

"You have any idea what's going on here, Lucas? You have any idea what they'll do to you? If you think Caesar went nuts over losing money with his pharmaceutical company, what do you think will happen when his most prized possession hits the red? If you want to do this, do it now and let's get out."

Lucas breathed heavier. Even though his eyes stayed focused on Jake his mind was somewhere else. "We're not starting here."

"Starting? You're right. We're not starting here. We're ending here. We put the squeeze on him, force him to release the drug, and then it's goodbye Viva Las Vegas."

"Sixty-eight," Lucas said.

Jake pulled his head back. He studied the expression on his friend's face. Lucas really was someplace else.

"Sixty-eight?"

"Let's go," Lucas said. He pulled a cap out of his car and started walking.

"What? Where? Where are you going? What about the car?"

Jake followed him as they walked out of the parking garage. "Lucas, tell me where you're going," he said, trying to catch up to him.

"I'm not sure," Lucas replied.

He turned off the Strip and walked to the Harrah's/Imperial Palace monorail station.

"Why are we taking the monorail?"

"Sixty-eight. Remember that number."

"What's 68?"

Lucas paid the $3 fare for each of them and sat down in the yellow monorail as it took off. An elderly couple looked at Lucas and whispered something to each other. They rode the line all the way to the end at the Sahara. Lucas got off. Jake followed him.

They started walking.

"Tell me where we're going," Jake said.

But Lucas was in a quasi-trance, repeating that number over and over again. "Sixty-eight. Sixty-eight." They walked past the pink and white Fun City Motel where they were staying. To the left they saw the towering Stratosphere and continued towards North Las Vegas. They passed a number of strip clubs and theatres until they came to a small two-storey white building.

The Sin City Oasis.

A dim light shone above the open security door to reception. Another security gate closed off access to the parking entrance and was left ajar just enough to let people through. The motel had six rooms on each of two levels with a walkway/patio on the second floor.

Lucas knocked. A woman in her mid-thirties, thin, multi-coloured spiked hair that suited her green eyes and fair skin, turned her head from the TV. "Hi there," she said, blinking her eyes as though trying to fight against some bad news she had just received.

"I'm here to see someone in room 68," Lucas said through the bars.

"Sixty-eight?" she repeated and shook her head wishing she could help them. "We don't have a room 68."

"Can we go back to the Garden?" Jake whispered.

"I'm sure it's 68."

"Maybe you have the wrong place."

"I don't."

"Or the wrong number."

"I'm sure of it."

The woman's expression changed to one of curiosity, as if she were making a connection that wasn't there before. She cleared her throat as she stood up. "Though we did have a guy just move from room six to eight."

"Is he still in?"

She squinted her eyes, trying to recall who had gone out and who was already back. "I think so," she said. She tilted her head to the side again as though finding something familiar about Lucas and Jake.

"Mind if I knock on his door?"

She shrugged her shoulders as a sign that she had no problem with that. As they left she tried hard to place Lucas, feeling certain she had seen him before.

Lucas and Jake saw a group of college-aged kids on the main level playing cards at a table in the dry night air. They walked up the stairs to the second floor and knocked on door eight. They heard nothing. Lucas knocked again.

"Hello?" he asked. He tried the door handle. It turned. Jake put his arm out to stop him.

"Let me go first," Jake said.

He opened the door and breathed in a waft of alcohol. He kicked an empty bottle on the ground on his way in. Lucas followed behind into the dark room. He blinked as he tried to get his eyes used to the dark.

They assumed the room was empty until they heard someone panting in the corner. When their eyes adjusted they saw a man. Maybe he was 20; it was hard to tell in this light. He sat on the ground. Knees tucked under his chin. Dishevelled black curly hair. Shivering. Breathing way too fast. Panicked look in his eyes.

Holding a gun in his mouth.

Lucas' spine froze. Jake managed a closer look. Nine millimetre. Beretta. That would easily do the job.

The kid was so strung out on booze and drugs he didn't even notice Lucas and Jake. Not at first. His eyes darted back and forth. His face was pale grey. Sweat dripped off his forehead. He clamped his teeth down on the barrel. Jake looked again. The safety was off.

Lucas knelt down on the ground. He whispered his verses to himself. Jake knelt beside him and put a hand on his shoulder, ready to pull his friend out of the way should the boy panic and start shooting at them.

"Hello," Lucas said, hoping that wasn't the final straw that would cause this kid to pull the trigger.

The young man's face went wild with terror. His eyes crossed as he tried to figure out from where the voices had come. In front of him were two shadows. He opened his eyes wider to help straighten out the blurred image.

He swore at them, his voice muffled somewhat by the metal jammed in his mouth.

"We're here to help," Lucas said. His voice penetrated the room. It seemed to fill the entire space, like a fresh tank of oxygen had been released into a room depleted of any life.

The young man yanked the gun out of his mouth and aimed it in their direction. He found it difficult to pick the right target, in a state of confusion about which of the six people in front of him he should shoot first. He swore again. Loud. It echoed.

Lucas and Jake moved to opposite sides, out of the path of the potential bullet. "I can help you," Lucas said.

The young man let off a slew of curses. He dug his heels into the carpet and kicked himself as far back as he could against the wall.

"You asked for help," Lucas said, as more of a statement than a question.

"Get out of here," he whispered, pleaded.

"You asked God for help. And I'm here. I've come to help."

"That's impossible."

"It's not impossible."

"It don't matter," the young man said. His hand began to tremble. Jake had been in this kind of situation before. Lucas had not, which was why he started trembling too.

"Why?"

The young man swore. "Why did I do this?" He cursed again. Clenched his teeth. Closed his eyes. Wished this were a dream. "Why did I do this?"

"My name is Lucas. This is my best friend Jake."

Best friend. Best friend. Two words Jake wasn't expecting to hear. Not about him. Not ever. He felt a sudden reassurance, odd is it may have been, given the circumstances—an unexpected confidence. Like the way Robin may have felt when Batman asked him to join his mission. An official duo. *Best friend.*

The young man didn't hear Lucas introduce himself. His mind was still doing overtime, trying to get his eyes to focus.

"We can help you," Lucas said.

"You can't." His voice turned to a whimper as he started crying. "Nobody can." Lucas stretched out his hand and touched the young man on his wrist. Immediately his eyes focused and he could see Lucas and Jake. His breathing slowed down. He blinked to get the tears out.

"How did you do that?" he asked. "Who are you?"

"What's your name?"

The young man thought for a moment, trying to decide if it was safe to divulge this or not. "Julius."

"Hi, Julius. You want to tell us what happened?"

"You're not cops?" he asked, sounding more like it was a revelation to himself than a declaration to the other two.

"No."

He bashed the back of his head against the wall. More sweat dripped off his face. He squeezed his eyelids together. His shoulders sank. "Just get out and let me finish this."

"Let's start where things went wrong. When did you get to Las Vegas?"

"Three weeks ago." He bashed his head against the wall again, making a painful *thud*. He covered his face with the heel of one hand and with his gun in the other.

"What brought you to Vegas?"

"What brings anybody to Vegas?"

That one characteristic. That one defining characteristic. Lucas heard Caesar's words replay in his mind.

"You tell me."

"Gambling, you moron!" he said. "What do you think?" He wiped the snot from his nose.

"Did you come to Vegas by yourself?"

He leaned his head against the dent in the drywall and wondered how life could go so terribly wrong in such a short period of time.

"My wife," he said. "My wife and three of her friends were going to drive from Flagstaff to Phoenix for a concert. Which group was it again?" He closed his eyes, trying to remember the name of the band, not realizing that it didn't make any difference either way. "I promised her. I promised her I wouldn't gamble. Nothing. Not even the sports lotteries at the gas bar. Nothing. Just sit in front of the television and watch the games all weekend."

"It didn't work out that way, did it?" Lucas asked.

"I lasted all of ten minutes. I got into our car. Went to the bank. Took out...." He closed his eyes and gritted his teeth, feeling the guilt and embarrassment over what he'd done. "I took out all our savings." That was tough. Taking the money was one thing. Saying it out loud was another matter. Especially considering what had happened. "Seven thousand dollars. Our down payment on a house with enough left over for me to go to night school so I could get a better job to pay for our child that's on the way."

"You gambled it away."

"I was so close! I should have quit after losing the first grand. But I had to go and win it back. Didn't want the casino to get the best of me. Didn't want my wife to find out about it. A string of bad cards. That's all. That's all it was. I've never seen such bad cards before!" He shook his head, wishing he could just turn back the calendar three weeks and try it again. His face went straight white. It looked fake, like he was already dead. "I felt like a zombie walking out of that casino. Shell-shocked. Wondering what happened to me. Like a daze. Living a dream. A nightmare. Some split reality or something. If only...if only I would have just got back in the car and gone home."

More to come, Lucas thought, and wondered how much worse it could get.

"What did you do next?"

"Got plastered. Went back inside to the bar and gave that casino even more of our money."

"Then?"

He bowed his head down and said nothing. He stayed silent so long it seemed to Lucas and Jake that he may have passed out. "Those guys on the sidewalk," he said in a whisper. "The ones that hand out the cards. The cards with pictures of the hookers you can bring to your room?" He looked up to see if they were following. Lucas nodded that he knew. "They gave me a card. I took it. And the next thing I knew this young blonde is leaving my room. I'm thinking to myself, good God, what did I do? What did I just do to my wife? I've been walking the streets for days. I can't find the courage to go home to her. I phoned and told her I got a job on a construction project. She told me that was great and that she was proud of me. I felt so horrible I changed rooms today. Six to eight." He closed his eyes again and swore. The worst was yet to come. "I was so scared I went to the test clinic." He ran his hands over his face, trying hard to escape the reality of dread that had fallen unexpectedly upon him. "I have it. I tested positive. Good God in the heavens. I'm HIV positive."

That surplus of oxygen suddenly left the room, leaving it a cold, heartless, stale environment.

"I can't win you back the money you lost," Lucas said.

"I don't care."

"But I can pray for you to be healed."

Julius stared at them in disbelief. It didn't register. Not at first. His face was full of doubt. But then it clicked. He recognized Lucas. He *thought* he recognized him. His mind reached back to when Lucas introduced himself. *Did he really say his name was Lucas?*

"The healing guy?"

Lucas' eyes said yes.

Julius lowered his gun. What were the odds? "You can do that?"

"I can pray. Can you believe?"

"I can try."

"Trying is not good enough."

"How do you believe?"

"You choose to trust."

"In God?"

"That He wants to heal you."

"I'm screwed," Julius said. "And I can't fix it."

Lucas laid his hands on Julius' neck. He closed his eyes and prayed. A warm feeling ran from his chest through his hands into Julius' neck. His fingers became so hot it felt as though his flesh was about to catch fire.

Julius felt a tingling sensation. He let go of the gun. It banged down onto the floor. Jake picked it up, clicked back the hammer, and slid the safety into place. When Julius opened his eyes he felt a strange calm come over him.

"That's it?"

"That's it."

"I'm better?

The trio stood up. "Are you squared away here?"

"I paid in advance."

"Anything left over?"

Julius shook his head. Lucas pulled out a few bills from his wallet.

"You have a choice, Julius. You can blow this on booze. You can even sell your car and gamble the rest in a casino. Or you can use this for gas money to get back home."

He took the money from Lucas and nodded his head as a "thank you."

"Go back to the clinic before you leave. Have them check you out. Confirm it."

He nodded again. He would go to that clinic. The same one. And they would confirm the unexplained recovery.

As Lucas and Jake left they heard Julius talking on his cellphone. "Hey, sweetheart…I know. I know I'm not at home. But I'm coming back right now…."

Lucas and Jake walked down the steps, past the kids playing cards, and headed south to the Strip.

"Just like old times," Jake said. "A gun. A healing." He laughed, but Lucas didn't join him. His mind was somewhere else. "So what now?" Jake asked. "Do we take on Caesar?" No response. "Lucas?"

"We're going to look back on this thing with Julius and think how lucky we were to have something as simple as this to solve."

"Simple? You think a kid almost ready to kill himself or us is simple?"

"I do."

"Really?" Jake asked. "How so?"

Lucas turned to Jake. It was his turn for his face to go pale. "You think it's going to get any easier for us?"

28

It was Julius who started the chain reaction. A harmless phone call, really. That's all it took. They say a butterfly flapping its wings in China can effect a sequence of events that will eventually lead to an earthquake in California. Maybe that's possible. Maybe not. But when one ecstatic gambling addict in Las Vegas calls his wife to tell her he's been healed of HIV, he creates a ripple effect causing thousands of people to descend upon that city.

His wife's shock of losing all $7000 of the family fortune was offset, for the moment, by her husband being healed by Lucas Stephens. *The* Lucas Stephens. When she hung up she called her best friend. Her best friend logged onto the Net and e-mailed 12 of her friends. Two of those friends posted info on their blogs stating that Healermania was alive and well. This time in Las Vegas.

Within 12 minutes of Julius placing that call to his wife more than 153,000 people worldwide heard the news. Another 12 minutes later the number went up a hundred times. Within an hour, accommodation and flight bookings to Vegas went ballistic. None of the hotels or airlines could explain the near-instant jump in demand. But they would come to understand.

Soon.

Tabitha got a call on her cell while riding the elevator up to see Mike. She checked the caller ID. Chester. Fat Chester. She didn't want to answer it, didn't want to get dragged into some monstrous monologue on her short trip up. She thought about avoiding the call, but then hit a button. He was, after all, paying for her to be in Vegas.

"Hello?" she said in a way that implied she didn't know who was calling.

"Why am I hearing about this on the wire?"

Tabitha searched through the options. Maybe something happened at the Garden. Maybe it was the unprecedented turnout for the grand opening. But judging from the tone of his voice it likely had something to do with the Chicago Healer.

"He's in Vegas," Tabitha said.

"No kidding? He is?" His tone was anything but curious. "I'm in such shock. I'm caught off guard. That, to me, is such an unbelievable coincidence. Do you know why?"

"Why?"

"Because *you're* in Vegas, Tabitha! You! My reporter!"

My sounded so out of place.

"He was at the grand opening. Out of view. He didn't want any part of it."

"That's my point! Isn't *that* a story in and of itself?" Chester stood behind his desk at *The Chicago Observer*, his phone in his right hand, his coffee *à la kick* in his left. He finished the remaining half cup in one gulp, hoping the secret contents inside could calm him down. "Here's what tomorrow's newspaper *should* have read: Miracle worker can't stay away from former boss' spectacular opening." He refilled his cup. "You think that's news?"

"He wanted to be left alone."

That wasn't exactly true. Lucas didn't come to Vegas to be anonymous, and Tabitha knew it. What she really meant was that on matters pertaining to one Lucas Stephens *she* wanted to be left alone.

"Is that what I pay you to do? To let others scoop you—us, the newspaper—because you wanted to respect his privacy?"

"I'm meeting with Mike right now."

"Mike? What for?"

"I can't turn him down now. I scheduled it a week ago, before I knew Lucas would be here."

"Well he's in Vegas now, isn't he? And the competition will be all over this guy, beating us to the punch."

"I can get an exclusive with him whenever I want to. You think any other reporter on earth can do that?" The second she said that she regretted it. She did want to blast Chester right back. Just fill him full of holes from his own malicious gun. But the recoil was more than she bargained for and she knew that she had set herself up for the kill.

"Good!" Chester said between slurps. "Then that's exactly what you'll do."

Tabitha heard the line go dead. She clicked off her cellphone and shook her head. *Why did I take that call? Why couldn't I just have let it go to voice mail and avoid this?*

Why couldn't Lucas just stay away?

Phone lines at every casino on the Strip went crazy. The Bellagio, MGM Grand, Mandalay Bay, Excalibur, New York-New York, The Venetian—within an hour of Julius' phone call they were all booked for the next seven days. Casino internal pricing systems maxed out. As a certain day begins to sell out in advance the price for the remaining rooms goes up. The Mayan, which was the cheapest on Las Vegas Boulevard, normally sold weekday rooms at $50 a night. The last room was booked by an elderly woman with Parkinson's for a mere $900.

A Texan caught a story on Fox News that Lucas was in the gambling hub of the globe. He called his wife over to the TV. She took one look, picked up the phone, and asked directory assistance for a hotel in Vegas. She was connected with Caesars Palace. Her voice trembled. She forced herself to stay calm as she waited for the reply.

All sold out.

She tried Treasure Island. No dice. Sahara. Nothing. Bally's. No go. Tropicana. Zip.

Her husband arranged for his company's private jet to take them there. Then he called their daughter—born with a nervous disorder that got worse with age—to tell her they think they had found him.

The wife called the Mayan. "Money is no option," she said in commanding tone.

"I'm sorry, we've just sold out."

She spoke louder. "I said: Money is no option!"

Sold. One luxury suite for three nights to the trio from Dallas. She breathed a sigh of relief and gave her gold card number over the phone. She didn't hear the total amount. And even if she had she wouldn't have cared.

Thirty-two thousand dollars was money well spent.

Lucas and Jake walked down the sidewalk under the cover of darkness. It felt as though the shadows were coming to life, turning into hideous creatures about to attack them.

"Where are we going?" Jake asked.

"Twenty-eight."

"Twenty-eight? I want to take you to the roulette table. Would your predictions work there?"

"No luck the last time you played? I didn't find you at the Mayan."

Jake became quiet.

"You weren't at the Mayan, were you?"

Quieter still.

"It doesn't matter. Twenty-eight," Lucas said. They saw the Sahara in the distance but turned down St. Louis instead. They made a left at 8th and walked until they saw an old house, painted maroon with off-white trim. Two grey posts held up the ailing porch roof. Trimmed hedges lined the walkway to the front.

"Here?" Jake asked.

Lucas thought it was a miscue as well. "It doesn't feel right, does it?"

Lucas led the way down the path. Jake straggled behind, feeling the uncertainty of walking up to a stranger's home. The last time he was on a porch and knocked on the door things hadn't worked out so well.

Lucas rang the doorbell. It gave off an irritating ring, like the sound prison doors make when the guard releases the electric lock. They heard three locks turn. The door opened. An elderly black woman stood there. She looked at them with suspicious eyes that seemed to mellow the longer she kept looking. Then it registered.

"I'm trying to believe," she said in a whisper that served as evidence of her amazement.

"Believe?"

"I seen what you did on TV. But I never saw you do one like this." She tilted her head to the side to get a different look at them.

"One like what?" Lucas asked.

She opened the door wider. They stepped inside. It felt cold. Colder than it should have. The house was dark. A few tea lights in the room to the left gave off the little illumination they had in the front. Bare walls. No pictures. She turned and took slow steps down the hallway, blending in with the dark surroundings. Her feet made creaking sounds in the boards that were duplicated when Lucas and Jake followed her.

Another set of tea lights in the distance. The faint glow was strong enough for them to make out a bedroom.

"Stay quiet," she said. "As quiet as you can."

Jake kept a careful eye on the doors to either side. All were shut. He listened to see if anyone was coming up behind him. If there was, that person knew exactly where the creaks in the boards were and how to avoid them.

"Here he is," she said in a soft voice. She stopped at the end of the hallway and looked into the room.

Jake didn't want to go in. He'd only been in the house a few short moments, but already he was having enough trouble coming to grips with the bad vibe he was getting from the old woman and her freaky house. Plus, he missed the mesmerizing lights of a casino.

Lucas smelled a stale odour coming from the room. It hurt his nostrils to take it in. For a split second it reminded him of the latrine in the Mathari slum. He walked closer and looked inside, half expecting that old woman to wait until he poked his head inside before she yanked out a butcher's knife and gave him a good whack in the back of the neck.

They saw a wheelchair in the corner beside a made-up bed. No posters on the walls. No sports cards on the dresser. No racing cars on the ground. No pictures of hot bikini models taped to the dresser. Bleak. Dull. Creepy. As they walked closer Jake got the sickening feeling that perhaps this woman was hiding a decaying body in her house. That maybe she had a collection of them that she wanted them to become part of. She walked ahead of them and reached the wheelchair first. Lucas slowed down. He was having the same thoughts as Jake.

"Hi, baby," she said.

That was a good sign. Speaking to the person in the wheelchair was a good indication that he or she must still be alive. Jake looked at her hands. No knives. Nothing sharp with which she could reach out and cut them—except for anything she had stashed in the wheelchair. The room got colder. Lucas waited for the door to mysteriously slam shut, and the woman to turn into some cackling hag and be joined by all those figures from the shadows who had come to descend upon them.

Lucas swallowed. He knelt down beside the woman and looked at the person in the wheelchair.

It was a boy. He was alive. Lucas saw his chest moving.

"This is Philip," she said.

His head lay off to the side in an awkward position. He looked ahead with a vacant stare that Lucas assumed wouldn't change no matter what was in front of him.

"What's wrong?" Lucas asked in a still voice, thinking that if he spoke any louder that little boy might reach out his hand with superhuman power and strangle him.

"Don't be afraid," she said. "They say dogs can sense fear in a person. I think sick people can sense it too. Just relax."

Jake didn't want to relax. He wanted out.

"Is he...." Lucas didn't know how to end it.

"Philip was shot," she said, giving the impression she'd relayed this story a hundred times and had got used to telling it. She spoke in an even tone, as if time had helped create distance from the terrible event, giving an objectivity that wouldn't otherwise be there. "Actually, it's his dad's fault." That came out a little less rehearsed—as though it was an idea she was only now getting used to. "He was into gambling. He got himself into huge debt. All gamblers do. Those that say they make money at it are either lying to themselves or are among the precious few who manage to squeeze through the eye of a needle."

She put her hand on Philip's arm. He gave no response. Just that same blank look, much the same look Edgar had while he sat on that park bench in the pouring rain.

"He had borrowed money from people he shouldn't have. They came to collect." Her shoulders sank. "Collect. That's the wrong word. They came to kill him. They just walked right in. Guns drawn. I was in the kitchen. Philip and his dad sat at the table. I can hear those shots. Bang. Bang. Bang. Bang. Four shots. After it was done one of them just looked at me with this plain expression on his face. It was as if he were about to ask me if he could help me set the table or something." She rubbed her son's arm. "A bullet went right through Philip. And now he's here."

"I'm sorry," Lucas said.

"What are you sorry for?"

That was a good question. Lucas had just said he was sorry because that's what everybody says when something bad has happened in someone's life.

"I'm sorry about evil."

"Evil?"

"I'm sorry it came here."

"Here to my home?"

"To your husband. To the people who shot him. To this city."

"Evil never *came* to Vegas. It was born right alongside this city."

"Maybe I can help your son."

"That's what I'm saying. I'm trying to believe he can be helped." She looked at Philip and then at Lucas. "Can a miracle replace evil? Can it cancel it?"

"It can change the effects."

"Can you solve the problem or can you only treat the symptoms?"

"I can pray for him to be healed."

"Will that be enough to erase evil in his life?"

"I wish it were that simple."

A knock at the door. Then another. Jake glanced at the window. He craned his neck to see the street.

"Unreal."

Lucas didn't look. He placed his hands on the boy's arm. She stopped him.

"Will this make things better or worse?"

"How could it make things worse?"

"Look at him. Evil put him in this state. He may not be living the way you and I are, the way we understand it, but in that world of his, wherever that might be, he doesn't feel it. No men with guns. No alcoholic, gambling, absentee father. No children in schools picking on him 'cause he's not as smart and not as good at sports. Is it better to heal him or to leave him where he is?"

Lucas touched the boy's cheek. There was no response. The boy just looked out at nothing like he was living in an endless, lifeless repeat.

"Which do you think he would prefer?"

The first hint of trouble came from the lowest gaming area—the poor section of the casino. The five-cent slots, the two-dollar blackjack tables, the cheap draft drinks. When the casino opened the floor was packed. But now the crowd was wearing thin. Mike pushed through the beautiful women in swimsuits and other guests on the top floor, trying hard not to look anxious. He smiled at people, giving them less than the greeting they deserved.

He excused himself just as Tabitha came in for her interview. He left her standing in the hallway after giving her a curt "Just give me a moment" response as he passed her. The figures showing the evening revenues from gaming areas one to five should have been rising up to 2 a.m. before dropping off. But instead they took a dramatic downswing at midnight as though the fairy godmother's words had come back to haunt them.

He went up the stairs to see Caesar. He knocked on the door and wondered if Caesar would open it automatically.

"Come in," Caesar said.

Mike entered and closed the door behind him, shutting out the lively atmosphere.

"Something is not right," Mike said and then noticed Caesar at the window.

Normally traffic was evenly distributed between northbound and southbound. But tonight, the majority of cars were headed north. Most people on the sidewalks headed north as well.

"Where are they going?" Mike asked.

Caesar clenched his jaw. He squinted his eyes. CNN was on beside him. A reporter gave a story. She stood on the street. There was a maroon house in the background with two grey posts. He turned up the volume. She reported that Lucas had survived a caning in Africa and was now rumoured to be in Vegas, supposedly in that house behind her. "Perhaps he will be healing people," she said. "Perhaps this is a sign of things to come."

Lucas touched the boy's chest and closed his eyes. He recited his verses. With every passing word the room seemed to feel bigger. Warmer. It was as though thousands of people had found a way to pack themselves into this tomb.

Jake stood up and left the room. He walked to the front door, wanting to be able to warn Lucas in case one of them broke in.

As Lucas continued saying his verses he felt a tingling in his fingers. They became warmer. Then hot. Almost unbearably so. The boy began to breathe deeper. Lucas felt his chest rise and fall with more intensity. He lifted his head. His eyes focused. He turned to look at his mother. She gasped. She remembered what it felt like to look at her son. She remembered what if felt like to see into his soul.

"What was it like where you were?" she said.

Philip studied her face. Life came back to his eyes. "It was different than here," he said.

The boy was back. Back with his mother. Back with the living.

Back with the good and the evil.

Jake's footsteps pounded on the creaking hardwood floor as he ran back to the room. He grabbed onto the door jam to slow himself down. "Lucas," he said.

Lucas turned around.

"It's time."

29

Lucas watched Philip take those courageous first steps out of the wheelchair and wrap his arms around his mother. They stayed there, embracing, in that stinking room. Neither noticed when Lucas stood up.

He followed Jake out to the hallway. They walked over the creaking floor to the front door and looked through the window. And what Lucas saw was a strange combination of what he was hoping for and what he was dreading.

News cameras. Media trucks. Lights. Crowds and crowds of people. They packed the street and spilled over onto the sidewalk, extending as far as he could see. Then, more people. More trucks. More cameras.

A news team came up the steps. A knock at the door. "Lucas Stephens?" Another knock. "Lucas, are you there?"

Lucas closed his eyes in frustration. He ran his fingers through his dark hair.

More knocking. *Go away. Just go away! What is the matter with you people? Who gives you the right to chase after me like this? I don't want you!* He put his hands against the door in an overt gesture to keep them out. He pressed his lips together. "Let's take the night off," he said to Jake. "Forget the whole thing—"

"Stop this, Lucas. You don't believe that. You came here because you want to heal people."

"I didn't come here for this!" he said, pointing at the window to the crowd. "I didn't come here for a barrage. I'm sick and tired of people."

"You don't mean that."

Lucas ran his hand through his hair as if he had a headache. "These people are never going to let me go."

"What is this? Lucas, you know they're desperate for what you have to offer."

In an instant Lucas' face turned from worried to discouraged. From determined to desperate. It was an expression Jake had never seen before. Lucas looked weak. Tired. Exhausted.

"Lucas, what is it?"

Lucas didn't answer.

"Lucas, what's wrong?"

Off to the side, near one of the hedges, Lucas saw Tabitha. Her rugged, cool look with perfect dark hair was unmistakeable. Camera in hand. Leather jacket in the cool evening breeze. His body sent out two signals. The first was the comfort of seeing her again, that feeling of attachment that is not easily broken regardless of what words are said. The second was the understanding that his feelings and reality were not in synch, like some irregular heartbeat. He tried to sift his way through the conflicting messages, tried to sort out the double lives within him. Then he found the answer. He knew why this felt wrong. *Why doesn't she just walk up and come to the door? Why is she standing out there like any other reporter? She has access to me. Anytime. She has anything she wants. Doesn't she want to be the first to interview me? Doesn't she want to see me?*

"Lucas?"

Still nothing. It felt so out of place to see her in the line of reporters and miracle seekers. She was above that. Way, way, way above that. She was his girl. *His* girl. And he was her man.

So why wasn't she acting like it?

"Lucas."

The crowd swelled. More and more people. Every race. Every colour. They packed the street, begging for a chance to be touched by him.

"Lucas," Jake said, putting his hand on Lucas' shoulder and turning him away from the window. They made eye contact. And what Jake saw concerned him. "What is it?"

Lucas fought to find the courage that would enable him to let Jake see the mess inside him.

"It's time to get to work."

"What happened between you and Tabitha?"

"Let's get this over with."

"Did she turn you down?"

"Forget it."

"Forget nothing. A man needs a woman. What happened?"

"I have to face Caesar. I have to crush him. Bankrupt him," he said. "Let's go. It's time to work."

He walked past Jake down the hallway to the back. The reporters at the front door kept banging away. Lucas kept wondering why that couldn't be Tabitha trying to get back into his life. He reached the back door and looked through the curtains. People filed around the tall wooden fence.

"We'll use the backyard," Lucas said, then realized he should have invited Jake in on the decision. "What do you think?"

"I'm with you, boss."

They were about to walk out when they heard a quiet voice behind them. "Is it better?"

Lucas turned around. It was Philip. He looked at Lucas with eyes that showed evidence of having seen much more in this world than most kids his age.

"Is what better?"

"The world out there. Is it better than the world I came from?"

Lucas bent his knees to be at the boy's height. "I think so."

"You're not sure?"

"You'll have to decide that yourself."

"Oh my goodness," Jake said, seeing something out in the distance. He opened the door.

"Jake, wait." But Jake was already out in the yard. "Let in one at a time." Jake didn't hear him. Lucas stood up. "Jake!"

People heard Lucas and started shouting his name.

Jake grabbed a lawn chair and pushed it against the fence. He stood up to get a better look at the crowd. People stretched up to touch him, thinking him to be Lucas. He scanned the crowd. Then, not finding what he was looking for, stepped down from the chair. He felt embarrassed. "I'm sorry," he said as Lucas joined him. "I was sure I saw Edgar."

Lucas remembered what it was like to have Edgar as part of their team and wished he was there with them.

Jake gave instructions to the crowd and just as he was about to let the first person in, Lucas stopped him. "Wait," Lucas said. "Keep it shut." Jake turned around. And what he saw convinced him not to open the door.

From all around the perimeter of the fence, children dropped down to the property. Fathers, mothers, uncles, aunts, guardians, and grandparents managed to push their way to edge. They lifted the children over the fence and lowered them as far as they could. The children clutched their hands as their feet kicked to find the bottom. Some were able to touch the ground. Others had to let go and free fall. Regardless of the method, when they saw Lucas they ran to him with open arms the way children do when they see people they are excited about. They cheered as they clutched his legs.

A heavy-set girl with thick glasses pushed her way through.

"Can you help me?" she asked.

Lucas looked at her and what he saw repulsed him. He squinted his eyes as if doing so could somehow lessen the shock of her appearance. He bit his teeth down, hoping not to give her any indication of what it felt like to have to look at her. But the expression in her eyes told him she had been through this many times before and that his reaction was just one of hundreds she had to endure.

Every exposed area of her body was a glob of blotchy bumps. It looked like a brutal case of incurable acne. The bubbles on her face were so swollen it seemed they were about to explode and release a toxic fluid into his face.

Lucas touched her shoulder and felt the rippled skin underneath.

"What do you want me to do for you?" Lucas asked.

"My skin itches all over," she said, scratching her neck near a spot that had already broken open and had begun to bleed. "The doctors did so much, but they can't help me anymore." She scratched her neck back and forth. It itched so bad that she used both hands to dig her nails in, draw blood, and bring temporary relief to her ailing body.

Lucas laid his hands on her neck and felt the crusted tissue. Those wretched bubbles *were* filled with poison. Had to be. They were going to explode. They were going to burst a green slime all over him. He closed his eyes and quoted his verses. He felt his hands become warmer and felt the patches of skin begin to grow together. His hands sunk farther down as the growths subsided and then disappeared altogether. The girl released the tension in her shoulders. She brought her hands up to her face and touched the smooth skin on her cheeks. Then she touched her forehead. Flat. She pinched the lobes of her ears. They had become so small. So different. So normal. She looked down at her hands and breathed in amazement. She lifted them to her face and turned her wrists. Her mouth dropped open. She shook her head, hoping this wasn't one of the recurring dreams she had each night since the day she heard Lucas had come back to America, where she found herself standing in a stranger's backyard, surrounded by people, and in complete health.

"How did you do that?" she asked, not taking her eyes off her hands. She rubbed them together, looking for any hint of the sickness, but finding none.

"I didn't."

She stopped rubbing. "You did."

"No."

She studied his face with a renewed innocence, one that afforded her the privilege of imagining a new life without illness. "Then how did you do this?"

"Do you believe in God?"

"I believe in luck."

"Why do you believe in luck?"

"Because that's what my father believes. Luck. 'Nothing counts so much as luck,' he always tells me. Is that what this is?" she asked, showing him her new hands. "Is this good luck?"

"No," he said. "This is God."

"So God is like getting your number called three times in a row in roulette?"

"I don't know how I could compare God."

"You think my dad can take God to a casino? Help him win? He's not allowed to take me. Maybe if he won he would have time to spend with me?"

Lucas was about to respond when a throng of kids pressed against him. Parents shouted at their children to touch him, hoping that any attempt to make contact with him might bring them health. The girl thanked him and ran back to her father who was getting ready for a night at the tables.

As more children got healed, Jake walked them back to the respective part of the fence and lifted them back up to the people who brought them. Child after child came to Lucas with every imaginable illness, including AIDS, leukemia, allergies, cleft lips, blindness, heart defects and bowel toxicity.

And they were all healed.

Police arrived and formed a perimeter around the fence. A tall officer with a black moustache helped Jake control the number of people entering. Dozens, hundreds of adults passed through.

A man wearing dress pants and a sweater entered. He walked too slowly for a man his age. Lucas had seen so many people he was about to lay hands on him without even asking the problem. Just as he was about to pray, he looked up.

"Edgar?"

"How are you, Lucas?" Edgar's face was pale. He'd lost weight. His sunken eyes had bags around them. His frail structure looked like it was going to collapse.

"Edgar, have a seat," Lucas said, reaching for a chair, feeling both the connectedness of seeing a friend and the relief of getting a break from the frenzied crowd.

"I prefer to stand."

Jake greeted him and gave a soft hug that made Edgar wince in pain.

"Go figure," Edgar said. He didn't smile. He had no energy for that. Not now. Not anymore. Somehow the will to smile is affected when life's finish line is just down the track. "The three of us. We're all in Vegas. Isn't that something?" He looked like he was about to cry. They were together. The trio. Again. And they felt the same power they had when they were together in Chicago. "Vegas. Of all the places we could meet, we end up here. Is that just the roll of the dice or did God plan it this way?"

"Maybe we all did," Lucas said.

"Or maybe it was just chance?"

"Maybe."

"Do you think illness is like that?" Edgar looked to Lucas and Jake for a response, but they had nothing to say in reply. "Do you think illness is random? Why does one person get healed and another not?"

Lucas raised his eyebrows. "I don't know," he said. It was the only honest reply he could find.

Edgar forced a half smile, but there was no joy in it. "Good answer." He coughed. "Full marks, my friend. I don't know. That may be the key."

People shouted for Lucas to hurry, impatient, afraid that they might get passed over. More police arrived. More media. More people in need of a miracle. More of everything showed up.

Except an answer for Edgar.

"Are we spins on a roulette wheel?" he asked.

"Edgar."

"I'm serious. I have to know if this is all chance. We're in Vegas for a reason. Maybe free will played a part in us being here. Maybe it's like the way we have a choice about where to lay down our marker on the board. But there's predestination in everything—like when that white ball goes around and around and around on the roulette wheel and you get that feeling it knew right from the beginning where it was going to stop." He stared ahead as if in a daze, not focusing on anything in particular. "If only we could ask that little white ball, 'Ball, where do I put my chip so that I can cash in?' I feel like asking God the same question—but it seems I've run out of chips and even if I found more of them I'm not sure playing them would help."

"Why wouldn't that help?" Lucas asked.

"Because you have to lay your marker down before the ball stops rolling. And that little ball knows where the chips are before it decides to plunk itself down. It knows who is going to be a winner and who is going to be a loser long before anybody else does." Edgar closed his eyes. He let out a quick show of emotion, but then pulled himself together with such speed that if Lucas and Jake hadn't known Edgar, they wouldn't have caught what just happened.

"The white ball isn't against you," Lucas said.

"You say that because you think you are supposed to say that. And from your perspective you can still afford to have those kinds of ideas. But when you stand on this side of luck you see things differently. If a player is winning at blackjack, he never suspects the house might be plotting against him. But when he loses over and over again, he either doesn't know how to play the game or assumes the whole thing is just one massive system that's not slanted in his favour."

"I want to pray for you, Edgar," Lucas said, hoping to snap his friend out of this line of thinking.

"I should go. You have people to heal."

"You should stay. You're my friend."

Edgar had long since lost the ability to control his emotions. As if the director shouted "Action!" he squeezed his eyelids together and began to cry. He sobbed so hard that it almost looked like he was choking. Lucas put his hands on his shoulders and closed his eyes. The shouting crowd grew faint. He reached that place.

"God, we need a miracle. I'm asking you personally to come here and do a miracle." Lucas continued with some of his verses. "This is my friend. This is Edgar. God, he's in need. He—"

"That's enough, Lucas," Edgar said. He pushed himself away from Lucas.

"Let's try again."

"It's enough."

"Edgar, we can do this."

"Stop!"

Everything became still. Somebody turned the volume down on the crowd. The three of them stood there, unsure of how to continue. It was silent for so long they wondered if any of them would have the courage to break the fragile calm.

"I'm out of options, Lucas," he said. "Besides, I'm holding up the show."

"Edgar, don't leave. Please. I need you to help me in this."

"I have nothing to offer you."

"You have everything to offer."

Edgar shook his head. "Goodbye."

"Tomorrow. We'll get together. I'll convince you to stay," Lucas said.

Edgar gave him the name of his hotel. He turned, walked out of the gate, and disappeared among the screaming people.

The officer with the moustache spoke with Lucas about the crowd becoming impossible to control. If something went wrong here, there would be no recourse.

"One more," Lucas said. But the officer disagreed and led them through the crowd. Officers held back the shouting throng who reached out for a chance to touch him in the hopes of being healed. Those screams. Those desperate screams. It was too much.

As they got into the car two young Native American boys with torn jeans and no shoes found a way through the crowd and reached Lucas. An officer was about to grab them when Lucas told him to stop.

He looked at the two boys. Long black hair. Tough-looking faces. Maybe eight years old. Maybe they were brothers.

"You can help?" one of the boys asked.

"What's wrong?" Lucas asked, trying to find the problem. They looked normal.

The officer became more forceful with his request for them to leave.

They each pulled back their shirtsleeves on their right arms. Green and blue blisters covered them. Thick stripes criss-crossed the length from their fingers to their elbows.

"How did you get these?"

The boys said nothing. They lowered their eyes. Lucas touched the boys' arms and recited some of his verses. People pushed to get closer. The officer shouted at him to hurry up. There was so much confusion it made it difficult for Lucas to concentrate. When he was finished he looked at their arms. There was no change.

The officer closed the door. The lights flashed and they drove off.

"Those children are being beaten," Lucas said. "Go back."

The officer radioed to the car behind to follow up with the boys and investigate Lucas' claim.

Lucas looked back to get another look at them. But they were gone, blended in with the crowd of people who were angered that they had been left out.

Some pounded on the police cruiser, begging for it to stop so they could get to Lucas. When they left the last of them behind Lucas leaned back against the seat. His face was sweating. He looked disoriented.

"Boss?" Jake asked.

Lucas blinked in an effort to convince himself of what had just happened. "It didn't work," he said.

"Didn't work? Hundreds were healed."

"Those two kids. I prayed, but their arms stayed the same."

"You barely touched them. Besides, be glad we're out of there. We have to organize these things better."

"I didn't feel anything. No heat. No burning. Nothing. It didn't work, Jake."

"Lucas. Please. The glass is more than half full. Think about all those who were healed tonight."

Lucas felt a cool breeze. He was about to close the window to get rid of the draft when he discovered there was no handle. That's when he realized all the windows were closed. He looked at the front. The air conditioner was off.

"You alright, boss?" Jake said.

Lucas made no reply.

And it spoke volumes to Jake.

They arrived at their motel and saw thousands of people packed around the entrance who had gambled on the chance that Lucas would be coming back.

"You have anywhere else you'd like to go?" the moustached officer asked.

There was no hotel Lucas could walk into without being seen, surrounded and crushed. He pulled out his cellphone and called the Mayan.

"Can I speak with…?" He was about to use her real name when he remembered the name she went by. "Savannah."

The line went quiet as he was being transferred to another extension. "Hello?" came a familiar voice.

"It's Lucas." She remembered him. "Do you have a place we can crash for the night?"

September's one-storey red-brick home was in a new development on the border between Henderson and Las Vegas. It served as a far enough getaway from the pace of the Strip, yet it was close enough for her to feel part of the action even when she wasn't working. She stood on the front steps under a starry sky, waiting for them to arrive. She stuck her hands in the back pockets of her faded blue jeans and brought her arms close to her side to protect herself against the cooling evening wind. She wasn't wearing shoes. Instead she went barefoot, revealing her silver nail polish. Her blondish-red hair glowed under the half moon and faded out and back again with the passing breeze. She wore a crisp white tank top that served as the perfect contrast to her tanned skin. Her silver bracelet reflected in the evening light. Down the street she saw a cruiser approaching. It stopped outside her house. She held her breath and wondered what it would be like to see him again.

Lucas and Jake stepped out. Lucas was about to close the door when he heard the moustached officer behind him.

"You want someone to check on you?" he asked.

Lucas thanked him but declined the offer. The fewer people who knew he was here the better. He closed the door and turned to look at the house.

When he saw her a rush of nervous energy ran through him. It disabled him. Surprised him. He stood still for a moment, though for him it felt much longer. He tried to remember if she was this beautiful the last time he saw her. So cool. So calm. So mysterious. Tranquil and waiting to protect him from the world.

She smiled as they walked up to her. She felt his exhaustion. Felt his desire for solitude. Without waiting for a clumsy exchange of greetings she took a step towards Lucas and wrapped her arms around him, touching the side of her head against his. She pulled him close to her. He sensed his body relaxing, as though her embrace could release the tension of a long day. He lifted his hands and placed them on her lower back. In that instant the troubles of his day vanished—he wondered if he was with a woman whose presence could exceed the struggles of life. He took in a deep breath. Her perfume. He'd never smelled this brand before. A gentle, subtle fragrance that convinced Lucas there was no threat here. He felt her hair on his forehead. Her breath on his cheek.

"No more crowds," she whispered.

Which was exactly what Lucas needed to hear.

She pulled back from him, held her arms around his waist, and then let go of him. He felt a sudden chill come over his body and wished they could have stayed like that all night.

"Thanks for calling me," she said.

"Thank you for taking us."

They entered her house. Lucas saw a collection of framed photographs hanging on the walls. All black and white. Bridges, mostly. Brooklyn. Confederation. Golden Gate. Oakland Bay. Lake Shore Drive.

"Did you take these?"

A sudden nervousness came over her. In that split second before she responded Lucas knew he had broached a subject that was better left uncovered. She nodded.

"They're good," Lucas said. "Is photography a hobby of yours?"

She turned away and seemed to be making a mental note to take the pictures down to avoid this same conversation in the future. "I used to be."

Lucas tripped over a pair of shoes. He leaned on September for support.

"You're going right to bed, Mr. Stephens."

"I want to talk to you about the flight to London," he said, indicating he was willing to talk in spite of his exhaustion.

"Tomorrow," she replied, taking him down the hall to a bedroom. She turned to Jake and told him to make himself comfortable in the living room. Lucas tried to stop her, but she put her arm around him and led him to a room.

"I have to know," he said.

"Lucas, you're beyond tired. If I don't get you to bed you're going to fall asleep right here in my arms." She brought him to the end of the hall and opened a door. "You can sleep in my room."

But Lucas didn't go in. "September, I need to talk to you."

That made her feel good. She lifted a finger and placed it over his lips. *I need to talk to you.* She let the words soak in. They sounded so much better than what other men said to her.

"And I need you to listen to me. But not tonight."

"What convinced you that the plane was going down?"

September turned her body to face him. She looked right into him, and in that instant it horrified him to know she had the same ability to connect with him the way Tabitha did. Her eyes. There was so much going on in there.

"Tomorrow," she whispered.

Can you give me another hug? Just enough to feel your breath again. Can I feel what it's like to be in your arms again? I know. I know. It's time to say goodnight. It's just that I'm a little out of sorts here right now. I had this whole Vegas thing planned out. But it's unravelling on me. It's not working out the way I wanted. I just need the reassurance of smelling your hair and knowing that I'm with a woman who cares…or who, at the very least, might be interested in caring at some point in the future.

"Do you need anything else?" she asked.

I wish….

"No," he lied.

Lucas walked into her bedroom. Black comforter on her bed. Three white pillows. Black dresser. White walls. Bathroom off to the side. Large window with the black shades drawn. She closed the door behind him.

Alone.

September walked back to Jake who had already found a chair on the deck.

"Can I get you a drink?" she asked.

"As much beer as you can spare, sweetheart."

September smiled and pulled out two bottles of beer from the fridge. She cracked off the tops and brought them to Jake.

"Be back in a second," she said, and left to respond to an impulse inside her.

She returned to her room and knocked on the door. No response. She opened it and poked her head inside. She saw Lucas asleep in bed with the cover half over him. She walked in and knelt down beside him. She placed her hand on his face and felt the rough touch of his stubble. Tomorrow she would convince him to shave it off. Clean-cut. He would look better that way. She pulled the blanket up to his neck and let her soft reddish-blonde hair fall onto his forehead. She kissed him on the cheek.

"Why don't men like you exist anymore?" she whispered. She smoothed her hand over his hair. She leaned her lips closer to his ear. "What's gone wrong with this world to make it so depleted of men like you? Men who convey everything a woman like me needs with just the look in their eyes." She waited a moment, as if the right words could bypass his subconscious and reach right inside him. "You know exactly what I do here in Vegas. You know what I am." She bit her lip. "So why have you come to my house? Of all the thousands of people out there who would do nothing short of giving their lives for you, why would you come here?" She kissed him on the lips and stayed there, hoping that somehow physical touch would be a way of communicating with him. "I need to know if there is any chance of a girl like me ending up with a man like you."

Saying that out loud, as quiet as it was, caught her by surprise. It was comforting to her that he was asleep, unable to hear those words, as she knelt at his side. The sheer terror of exposing herself like that would have been too much for her. She touched his face, walked out of the room, and left him to recover. But had she stayed she would have seen his foot twitch, a sign that something was wrong in the dream world he was now living in.

Lucas was falling to the bottom of the rock face. He was ten feet up when he lost his balance—a distance high enough to kill yet still within range of being able to walk away unscathed, provided of course he was on the right side of fortune. He bent his knees and rolled on impact. He turned over on his side, came to a stop, and waited for something to hurt. Nothing did—nothing out of the ordinary—just scrapes on his arms and knees. He stood, looked up at the limitless mountain. A flat wall that extended as high as he could see. Forever. That's what he thought. It goes on forever.

All the more reason to start again.

Now.

He grabbed onto the same starting place and lifted himself up. No equipment. The rock felt tougher this time. Less forgiving, if in fact it had been forgiving at all the last time. He climbed up the rock feeling like Spider Man as he alternated his hands and feet. He could make it. He could make it all the way to forever.

The first 10 feet went fine. The next 40 were more difficult. Then, his body began to hurt with every grab. Aching pain. Sweat dripped from his face. He had no water to sustain himself. He glanced up. All he saw was the merciless sun and the endless rock. He climbed farther. His body began to shake. Mind over matter. He could put this away. He could reach the top.

He *had* to.

His right hand stayed frozen in a crevice, refusing to accept his brain's instruction to proceed. His arm felt as unmovable as the rock he was touching. His back seized. His head pounded. He tried lifting his left arm.

And that's when he saw him.

A six-year-old kid. Standing on a cleft in the rock beside him. Grey shirt. Red cap. Looking at Lucas at almost eye level.

"You think you're going to make it?" the boy asked.

"I'll make it."

"All the way up there?"

"I said I'll make it!"

"Look at you. You're nearly finished."

"Don't tell me I'm finished!" Lucas screamed. He took in a number of short breaths to get himself under control. "I have to do this. I have to climb to the top. And I'm going to make it!"

But both his body and the boy knew better.

"You've overexerted your muscles. They are deprived of oxygen, resulting in a buildup of lactic acid. This buildup has exceeded your ability to continue, which is why your muscles are responding by going into cramps," the boy said. "Look down." Lucas did. He saw the ground. "Now look up." He did and saw the eternal rock face with only the sun to mark the finish line. "You're nowhere near the top. You can't rid yourself of the lactic acid. You can't restore your body to normal oxygen levels. You're done."

Lucas gritted his teeth. "I have to reach the top."

"You can't do it."

"I can!"

"You don't have to do this." The boy spoke with a cryptic wisdom as though somehow able to access a wealth of knowledge that otherwise would not be available to a boy his age.

"Then how else do I get to the top?"

The boy didn't answer. He just looked at Lucas with eyes that told him how doomed he was.

Lucas forced himself to reach another level. The talk with the boy gave his body the momentary relief it needed to replenish what little oxygen it could. But by the next grab, he was in worse shape than when he stopped. He looked down. The boy was gone.

He lost his grip.

The signal his brain sent to his hands to grab the rock went unanswered. His arms stayed locked as his body drifted backward. His feet slipped off the ledge. He felt the rush of air around him as he accelerated to the bottom.

All that work. All that climbing.

Gone.

Lucas felt the horrific impact against his head. He felt the ground smash against his back. He heard a tremendous *crack*.

Then everything went silent.

The sun went black.

September grabbed a bottle of water out of the fridge and sat down on a director's chair next to Jake.

"You're going to make me drink alone?" he asked.

"I have my water."

"Water? That's not a drink." He chuckled and toasted her with his beer bottle. "My name is Jake," he said, expecting her to follow by introducing herself as well.

But she hesitated. *September or Savannah? September or Savannah?* She couldn't make up her mind, so she just played along as though Jake already knew her first name.

Or one of them.

"You're from Chicago?"

"Yeah," Jake said. "How 'bout you?"

"Chicago as well. I moved a few years ago."

"What made you come to Las Vegas?"

"I needed a change."

"From Chicago? Who needs a change from Chicago?" He said it with a smile, but the expression on her face told him her reason for leaving was anything but pleasant.

"I left after my sister died in a car accident."

It didn't hit him. Not at first. But in the seconds that followed he felt a painful jolt of fear. It wasn't the alcohol. No way it could have acted that fast. He thought through what she said. Chicago. A few years back. Girl being killed in a car accident.

He knew someone who might fit that description.

"I'm sorry to hear that," Jake said. His heart beat so loud and the blood raced through his system with such speed he thought for certain she would be able to notice something wasn't right with him.

She took a sip of her water. "It's strange how something can happen years ago, yet it continues to happen over and over again, right in front of you, every day for years to come."

Jake wanted a long drink of beer to calm his nerves. *Just suck back on the bottle and drown out whatever you're feeling. Suck it back and swallow it as fast as you can. Just get through the panic for now. Deal with it later. Survive now. Deal later.* And he would have guzzled the whole thing right there had his hands not become numb with panic. That small man he visited before getting drunk in the bar. The one he went to ask forgiveness from for killing his daughter. He mentioned he had another daughter. *What was her name?*

"That's not an easy thing to live with," Jake said, being able to identify with what it means to know time travel exists—only that it exists in the sense that it hangs like an impossible weight around your neck and there is no way of going back in time and undoing things to get the weight off.

His mind raced back to that day when Siloa told him never to come back. He had given his other daughter's name. A strange name. Nice, but different. Didn't he name her after the month she was born in?

"I'm Savannah," she said, with a tilt of her head as if now remembering she hadn't introduced herself.

Inside, Jake breathed a million sighs of relief. Close. Too close. That S sound at the beginning of her name nearly killed him. He managed to guzzle half the bottle down. A victory. Of sorts. *Thank you,* he said to himself. Then he remembered. *It's not September.*

September took another sip, held it in her mouth, and realized she was prolonging the inevitable. "I'm sorry," she said.

"Sorry?"

"Savannah is not my real name."

"It isn't?"

"It is, but…." She took another drink. "It's not my birth name. I just go by Savannah."

Jake felt it coming. *This can't be her. Impossible. There are a million names out there.* All those odds they say about being struck by lightning *and* winning the lottery on the same day? They aren't as far-fetched as they seem.

She looked him in the eye. Her golden-strawberry hair hung down covering part of her eye. She brushed it aside. Jake felt her response before she gave it.

"My real name is September."

Lucas' cellphone rang. He woke and felt the disorientation that comes from a deep night's sleep. He grabbed the phone from his jeans on the floor. It took him a few tries to find the button to take the call.

"Hello?"

"Lucas."

He was awake now. That voice was all it took. "Tabitha."

"Are you alright?" she asked. Tabitha sat cross-legged on her bed at the Bellagio, surrounded by a sea of pillows. She wore black silk pyjamas and drank a cup of herbal tea. Strawberry.

"I'm fine."

"Where are you?"

"I saw you last night. At the healings in the backyard. You were at the hedge."

"You threw quite the party."

"I thought I would get a chance to talk to you."

"Your motel said you never checked in."

"Too many people."

"Where did you go?"

"Tabitha? Did you go the motel to see me or to do a story on me?"

Lucas was hoping she would say *To see you.* But the longer he waited for her reply, the more he downgraded his expectations until he was willing to settle for her to say *Both.*

"To do a story, Lucas."

That hurt. The usually soothing touch of her voice now seemed to have a hint of suspicion in it. Normally, he could relax and not put up any barriers when he was speaking with her. But now that things were indeed on the rocks he put up guards, afraid that vulnerability might lead to damage.

"That's all?"

"Your healings last night raised some people's eyebrows."

"I expected that."

"Lucas, Caesar wants to meet with you."

"I'm not interested."

"I suggest you take it."

"Thanks, Tabitha. I'll turn it down."

"Tonight."

"Tabitha."

"Ten o'clock."

"I'm not going."

"He has agreed to come alone. Just to talk. That's it. He trusted me to pass that onto you. He didn't know how else to track you down."

"Why do you want me to go?"

"He'll meet you at a place called...." she looked down at her notepad.

"Tabitha, why are you calling me?"

The line went quiet. "Lucas...." She didn't want to do this over the phone. Phoning is fine for people climbing the mountain of a relationship. It's brutal for those on the descent. "Lucas, I don't want a repeat of Wrigley Field."

"Is that all you want?"

More silence. "It's what I want right now. I want you safe." She found the name of the location where Caesar wanted to meet him. "You have a pen? I have the place."

No. He didn't have a pen. But one restaurant or building or whatever wouldn't be impossible to remember. "Go ahead."

"The Fortunate Son Café."

Lucas stopped breathing. He hoped he had heard wrong. His fingers turned to ice.

"Lucas?"

He didn't answer. He *couldn't* answer.

"Lucas, do you know where to find it? It's not in Vegas," she said.

"Yeah," he forced out in a faint whisper. It was all he could manage.

Years had gone by since he'd been there last. There was nothing in him that wanted to return there. He had tried to cram that event into the depths of his memory garbage dump in a desperate attempt to find a way to separate who he was from who he would become. Just shove it down there and hope to heaven a time like this never comes, where the past springs out like some wanted criminal hiding in your closet, attacking with a meat cleaver the second the door opens.

He had talked about the Fortunate Son Café with Caesar at some point—exactly when, he couldn't remember. Maybe right near the beginning when they first met. Or maybe while he was drunk at one of Empirico's numerous parties when the two of them would stay up for hours talking about life and money. Whatever the occasion, alcohol must have been involved. He would not have had the strength to discuss it otherwise.

As if in a daze he vaguely heard Tabitha ask him a few more questions, the last being whether he needed directions. He told her he didn't, thanked her, then hung up.

He could make it to the rendezvous. Finding it would be no problem. In a sense, he was already there.

Lucas knew all about the Fortunate Son Café.

30

Lucas drove south on Interstate 15, trying hard to convince himself that Jake was wrong about his decision to meet with Caesar. Yet the farther he went, the more he wondered if he should have listened to his friend back in Vegas. It seemed so right, as things often do in the heat of the moment, while he was arguing with Jake. He told Jake that he had to do this, that he had to meet with Caesar. And now that he was nearly there he wondered why exactly he *had* to do anything.

Especially with Caesar.

But all of his worrying over whether this was right or wrong only served to deflect the real issue. Lucas was going back to the Fortunate Son Café. He was going back for the first time since it happened. And that, more than anything else, was cause for concern.

He had told himself he would never return—never set foot on the property. Never even think about the place. It was a chapter he never wanted reopened. He had made himself promise he would leave this behind. Forever.

If he had turned into a failure, he didn't want to be able to look at that moment years ago when he was there for the first time and realize it was the reason his life had turned out so wrong. But, as it unfolded, his life was both a screaming success and a brutal failure. Med school. Jail. Pharmaceutical giant. Jail in China. Healing gift. He had done alright. And coming back had a different meaning to it. He had succeeded in spite of all the odds against him. Right from the beginning. Now he wanted to know if he could confront this place. He wanted to know if he could look his fears in the eye. Man versus boy. Present versus past.

Lucas versus Caesar.

He looked in his rear-view mirror and couldn't see any hint of Vegas. He was in a world between. So much behind him. So much ahead. He concentrated on his upcoming meeting with Caesar and hoped this event wasn't going to affect him as much as he anticipated. But all of that changed when he saw the approaching road sign.

It was nothing out of the ordinary. Anyone else would have taken one look and kept on driving. But not Lucas. His memory would not allow him to skip over it. He recognized the sign. Nearly twenty years had gone by. Twenty whole years. And that same old sign was exactly as he remembered: JEAN 22.

It brought back a flood of memories. Jean. That was it. That was the name of the town. He hit the brakes and pulled over to the side of the road. His headlights and eyes stayed focused on the name. He gripped the steering wheel as if doing so could somehow anchor him amid the waves that crashed through time. *Why am I doing this?* He felt a magnetic pull from the town, drawing him to return. Maybe it was because of the location. Maybe because of whom he was going to meet. This was both stupid and courageous. Stupid because he knew Caesar had some ulterior motive for choosing this place. Courageous because he was finally coming back to a place he thought had long since disappeared from his life.

Lucas turned back onto the highway without looking. He didn't see the bright headlights in the rear-view mirror. The car behind him swerved to avoid him. He heard the sound of brakes screeching and the *What are you doing, you idiot?* sound of the horn as the car approached. He braced himself for the impact. The horn continued as the car passed by. It stopped just in front of him. Lucas wondered if the driver was going to get out. They stayed there, idling. Then the other car drove off.

Lucas checked behind him this time. Nothing but empty road.

He eased down on the accelerator and drove slower than before. Every tenth of a mile click on his odometer stretched out for hours.

Jean. Fourteen miles. His mind played tricks on him, causing him to think he was seeing the town long before it materialized, like a mirage in the desert. He saw the next sign: EXIT 12 JEAN 1 MILE.

His heart pounded so hard it made it difficult to breathe. To his right he saw the Nevada Landing Casino. All by itself. A beacon of lights. Almost lonely looking compared to the stack of casinos on the Strip. EXIT 12 JEAN 1/2 MILE.

He took Exit 12 and followed the curve around to the right. The road became dark. He saw a Shell station on his right. *That wasn't there before.* And then, out of the blackness, without any warning, he saw it. He slowed to a stop. He looked closer. There it was.

The Fortunate Son Café.

His hands trembled. He felt powerless to move. He wanted to put his car in reverse. Gun the accelerator. Get out of here as fast as possible. But he found himself frozen where he was, unable to contend with the fear of seeing the past in the present.

Was this really today or had he returned to life as a young boy? How was it that twenty years had gone by, yet now that he was back it felt like he had never left? How was it that two decades could somehow have been erased simply with his return?

He drove into the parking lot and got a better look at the café. Boarded-up windows. One storey. Rectangular. Deserted. No lights. It wasn't much of a building. Not then either, at least as far as he could remember. Or maybe that was just the way it looked to his six-year-old eyes. Maybe the building itself was fine back then. It was his life that was ruined here, and his young mind may have projected that onto everything around him, causing him to remember the building to be in worse shape than it was.

It was coming back to him. Gravel approach. No money wasted on niceties. Tin roof that stretched down over the walkway along the building. Wood exterior—it still had the off-white paint with the burgundy trim. It was smaller than he remembered. Then again, there was a time when this dilapidated old structure represented his entire world. There was a reason why his mind remembered it bigger than it was.

There used to be a gas pump in the front. *Was it orange or red?* That's why they had stopped here in the first place. At least that was how it was explained to him. Gas up and then grab something quick to drink in the restaurant. *Just going to stop in for some gas and a pop. You sit down and place your order. I'll be right back. Just wait right here, Lucas. Just wait right here.*

Just wait right here.

Yeah. There used to be a gas pump. But they had since gotten rid of it.

If only they could have done the same with Lucas' memory.

The same Fortunate Son Café sign stood on the roof over the door. Big bright red letters that had faded as if to indicate this was a happy place at one time. Perhaps for some it was. For others it was just a roadside stop—exactly what it was supposed to have been for Lucas. To the left of the name was the six of diamonds. To the right, the eight of hearts.

He parked his car in the empty lot. It felt surreal to be back. Strange. Like he was trespassing. As though he'd entered a time machine and returned to that day. He looked at the boarded-up windows, those pieces of plywood giving the whole place a condemned look. Some of them were left uncovered—the plywood either stolen or removed. But it wasn't the appearance of the building that got his attention.

It was what he saw inside.

He focused his eyes on the figure. Was that him? Couldn't be. Impossible. Absolutely impossible. Yet, there he was. His eyes would not lie.

Through one of the uncovered windows he saw himself sitting alone at a booth.

Six years old. Red cap. Grey shirt. Sucking on a straw from his empty glass. Staring out at the parking lot. Looking for some kind of hope. A waitress came and asked if he wanted more to drink. He didn't hear her. His eyes stayed focused near where Lucas was standing now. The waitress asked again. He looked up at her. White outfit. Tied-back hair. Late forties and not that good-looking, which was why she was working at a café in Jean and not at a casino in Vegas.

"What?" Lucas asked.

"Do you want another drink?"

He looked at his glass and saw that it was empty.

"No," he said, when really what he meant was *yes.*

"There's no charge, kid," she said in a quiet voice, trying to disguise what she was thinking. But he could hear it. He could hear it in her tone. She knew what had happened to him. She had seen this before.

"Okay," Lucas replied, trying to hang onto as much optimism as he could. As she walked away he remembered his manners. "Thank you," he said. He looked back out the window, searching for any sign of hope. He was living in that uncertain place between where things still look like a reasonable explanation can handle all of this, and where it's obvious something has gone about as wrong as it can get. How long had it been? How long had he been sitting here waiting? There are scientists who argue we have a chemical in our bodies that regulates our perception of time. The older we get, the less we have of it and the faster time seems to go, which is why Saturday afternoons lasted forever when we were kids. Yet with every passing decade it seems the days just race by at an ever-increasing speed. And sitting there in that café, waiting on eternity, Lucas had about as much of that chemical as he could have wanted.

He opened the door of his Audi. He felt secure sitting in his car. But the moment his foot hit the gravel all of that changed. Contact. Those other scientists who say time travel isn't possible? They're wrong. Time travel is the most common form of transportation. Lucas Stephens could tell you why. He stepped out of his car and into the past.

It was a calm evening despite the traffic heading into town. Starry sky. Gentle breeze. The rundown café didn't fit in here. Abandoned building and a beautiful evening just didn't go together. How does a piece of junk hold such meaning? The Fortunate Son Café had closed down years ago.

But for Lucas Stephens, it had always stayed open.

He walked to the front door, taking steps that felt heavier the closer he got. It almost seemed like holy ground—like he was treading on property from which he had been banned. He reached out his hand and was about to touch the handle when he heard something approaching behind him.

"Quite the place, isn't it?"

Lucas turned around. He saw Caesar wearing an unbuttoned black suit. White shirt. His healthy appearance still baffled Lucas. No trace of those puffy pink eyes. He almost appeared to have grown younger since the last time they met.

"I'm surprised you remembered," Lucas said, still trying to figure out when it was he had let it slip about this place. He wondered how much Caesar knew.

Caesar walked towards him and lifted both hands palm up, stretching them out to the building. "And to think this is where it all began!" He placed his hand on Lucas' shoulder. "Humble beginnings, my friend. You should be proud. That is always, always the sign of true greatness."

"Is that how you began?"

They looked into each other's eyes and wondered what they would discover. And within moments they found what they were searching for. Definitely. It was still there. They still had a connection.

"It's how we both began, Lucas. The question is: How are we going to end?" Caesar pulled a key from his inside pocket and walked past Lucas to the front door. He placed it in the lock and turned it.

"I bought the place, Lucas," Caesar said, opening the door and motioning for Lucas to enter. "It's mine now."

Lucas recalled the smell of the hamburgers cooking on the grill. The sound of the waitresses taking orders. The hum of people talking. The *ching* of the cash register as patrons paid for their meals. He stepped over the threshold and landed in the café.

Caesar flicked the light switch. One of the 13 overhead lights came on. It flickered and then gave off enough light to illuminate the interior.

"Is it how you remember?" Caesar asked.

Lucas saw the counter with the red fifties-style bar stools where he had first seen the waitress who would eventually be refilling his glass every half hour. Same black and white checkered floor. Same row of booths with red seats stretched along the windows. He noticed one in particular.

"It's still how I tried to forget it," he replied.

Caesar closed the door. "Pick wherever you want to sit. I hear it's not going to be busy tonight."

Lucas had already decided. He walked to the booth where he had sat that afternoon. Third one from the entrance. He sat down facing the door, but stayed near the aisle. Sitting at the window would have felt too surreal. He didn't want to crowd that boy next to him.

Caesar sat down opposite him.

"I'm sorry. I don't have the place up and running yet. Otherwise we could have had a meal together. Maybe we could have had the same one you had the last time you were here. A hamburger and fries, I'm guessing? Was that what you were eating?" He felt it all over again. That split second he sensed the first hint that things weren't working out—that initial moment it entered his mind that something might not be right. He shook his head. No point in reliving it now. He had done so too many times before.

"I didn't have anything to eat."

"Nothing?"

Lucas shook his head.

"Makes sense," Caesar said. "Or as much sense as it can make, given the circumstances. She probably didn't want to stiff the waitress. You, yes. The waitress, no."

"Why did you bring me here?"

Caesar leaned his arms on the table. "To talk about beginnings and endings."

"Yours or mine?"

"Both, Lucas. Because they're the same thing."

"You and I didn't start the same way."

"That's both right and wrong."

"And you assume to know how things are going to end?"

A silence fell over them. Usually when two people aren't talking in a restaurant there's enough ambient noise from the waiters, the guests, and the music to fill the gap. But in this otherwise empty café there was nothing but deadness to fill the void.

"Lucas. You've been blessed with an ability beyond anything this world has ever known."

"Beyond what it has known in recent times."

"Fair enough," Caesar said, neither agreeing nor disagreeing. "You're on top of the world, kid."

"I don't think of it that way."

"There's no other way to view it. You have it all. People. Media. Attention."

"That's not what this is about."

"It doesn't matter what *you* think it's about. It only matters what *people* think it's about. And they see you as the miracle of miracles. The man who can heal. And not just one fluke kid in a wheelchair, mind you. We're talking crowds. The word *multitude* comes to mind."

"You're not prepared to handle the drop in pharmaceutical sales, are you?"

"I'm prepared for much, much more, Lucas." Caesar leaned closer. "The real issue on the table is not me, it's you."

"I'm fine, thanks."

"That's because you can't see down the road."

"And you can?"

"Yes."

"And what do you see?"

"That depends."

"On?"

"On whether you're going to take my advice."

"Which is?"

"You asked me if I'm prepared to handle the shortfall from your miracles. But I turn it back to you. Are you prepared to handle it when God drops you?"

More silence. This time it was deafening. Lucas raced to find an answer. All those sales meetings. All those corners from which he managed to negotiate his way out. But none of his tactics came to mind to deliver a quick response to Caesar.

"I'm prepared to follow this path right to the end."

"Path? Which path is that?"

"The path of healing people."

"Healing them?"

"Yes."

"From what?"

"From diseases, Caesar."

"Oh, diseases. Right. Diseases."

"Yes."

Caesar studied Lucas. "You haven't heard?"

"What?"

"Those kids in the leukemia ward that you cured?"

"What about them?"

"One of them, I can't remember which one, contracted a liver condition." Caesar eased off a little. "I thought you knew that."

"No," Lucas replied, shaking his head, wondering if it might be Angelina.

"So."

"So what?"

"So are you obligated to go back and heal that child? Are you under obligation to heal people who got sick since you healed them?"

"I don't know."

"Isn't every person you touch going to get sick again?"

"I assume so."

"So what's the point of all this? What are you trying to accomplish?"

"I'm here to use this gift."

"Until?"

"Until nothing."

"Then there you have it."

"Have what?"

"You're God's mouse. Running around until God pulls that gift out from under you."

"That's not going to happen."

Caesar leaned back and lifted his hands with his palms facing Lucas as if pleading with him to stop. "I beg you, Lucas. Don't tell me you believe that. You don't. I know you don't. That was just a quick reaction. You're too smart for that."

"God is not going to let me down."

A fire kindled in Caesar's eyes. He clenched his jaw. He lowered his hands and placed them on the table. Without realizing it Lucas backed away from him as if obeying some hidden voice deep inside, warning him of impending danger.

"For as long as I'm alive, Lucas, I want you to etch these words into your soul." The silence echoed in their ears. Lucas recognized that look. Daggers were about to fly from Caesar's pupils and pierce Lucas' eyes, pinning him to the bench. A cool breeze blew against his neck. Lucas swallowed.

But then Caesar's eyes mellowed, as though a spirit of fear came and went in those chameleon eyes of his.

"Lucas." Caesar tilted his head to the side. "When I was like you, young and full of trust, I wish—I can't even begin to tell you how much—I wish someone would have sat me down and told me what I am about to tell you. Because it would have saved me, Lucas."

Saved me? Those words pounded over in Lucas' mind. *Saved me. From what?* He wanted to think more about what Caesar meant by that, but decided to devote everything he had to concentrate on what Caesar would say next.

"When God walks out on you, and God will, I will always be here to take you back."

"That's what you think will happen?"

"It's what I *know* will happen."

"You can't possibly know that."

"My God," Caesar whispered. He leaned back, almost afraid of what was in front of him. He squinted his eyes at Lucas, hoping that what he was seeing wasn't real. "I'm seeing myself."

"Yourself?"

"Déjà vu."

Caesar shook his head and then closed his eyes to rid himself of the mental state he was in.

"Caesar."

But Caesar shook his head again. He then thrust his hand violently to tell Lucas to stop. It scared Lucas so much that for a moment he thought Caesar might jump up, clasp his hands around his throat, and throttle the life out of him—perhaps stick those knives through his eyes.

"I know we don't see things the same way, Lucas. But that look in your eyes. The trust. The certainty. There was a time when I trusted God. But trust can be a risky thing if you don't have a fall-back position. And I see dark times ahead for you. What happens when God walks out? What then?"

"He won't," Lucas said in a tone too quiet, too timid to be effective.

"But what if it happens for you like it happened to me?"

Lucas felt a chill crawl down his back. Something in the way Caesar said it struck him. Was it his expression? Was it the inflection in his voice? The look in his eye? It was so familiar. So recognizable.

"And what if I can help you, Lucas? What if by listening to me you can make different choices? Choices that won't leave you in the same position I was in."

"I'm not going to be in the same position as you."

"You already are. The difference between me and you is that you just can't see it yet. But I'm going to help you see it the right way. We'll do it together."

"We're not on the same team, Caesar."

"We are, Lucas. We are on exactly the same team. Because we're the same person."

"No."

"And we have the same beginning."

"That's not true."

"Six years old. That's a magical number. What is it with that age? Everything you want to know about God is discovered by six. I found that out. So did you. Here at the café. This is your story, Lucas. This is what defines you. Not the prison sentence over the incident with Tabitha. Not China. Not this healing gift. Here. The Fortunate Son Café. This is you," Caesar said. "And it's time for you to turn back before it's too late."

Too late. Too late. Definitely. This really was déjà vu. They'd had this exact discussion before. Not long ago. In Caesar's study. In his home. The day before the assassination attempt.

Lucas placed his hands under the table to prevent Caesar from seeing how much they were shaking. He grabbed his thighs, but it did little to help. The shaking went up his elbows and worked its way into his shoulders, making him feel like a frightened six-year-old kid who wondered what the future might hold. He looked at Caesar and when he recognized the expression on his face he knew he should not have come.

Jake was right.

Those eyes. Those dead eyes. Caesar looked like he was about to explode.

Lucas wished he could disappear, wished Caesar would start counting to ten for him to find his hiding place. Anything to escape his presence.

Caesar reached into his suit jacket pocket. There wasn't a bulge large enough for it to be a gun. A knife. Yes, a knife. Just long enough to fit inside his breast pocket and just long enough to whip out in one swift motion and finish Lucas off.

An envelope instead. White. Thick. Stuffed full of papers. Lucas' name written on it. Block letters. Gold ink.

"Time is moving ahead for you now, Lucas," Caesar said, placing the envelope on the table.

"What is it?" Lucas asked, afraid that if he touched it some unseen force might transfer through the pages, up those trembling arms of his, and into his body. And spirit.

"It's my gift to you."

Caesar pushed the envelope closer.

Lucas felt another magnetic pull. A job offer. Money. A collection of offers from people so that Lucas would leave Vegas—maybe it was from those two people in London, begging him to come and heal the sick in time for the upcoming elections.

"A gift?"

"Surprised?"

"I don't need it."

"You can't say that. You don't even know what it is. Not until you open it."

That look came back. *How did that happen so fast? How did those eyes go from human to something so different in such a short time?*

The trembling grew worse.

"Take it," Caesar whispered.

Lucas stretched out his fingers to the envelope.

"It's yours," Caesar said. "It's yours."

His middle finger touched it first. And when he made contact he felt an eerie calm come over him, like a backdraft in a fire when it recedes, giving the false impression it has died out. Lucas picked it up. It felt heavier than it was. He forced himself to look to the end of the table and then up Caesar's jacket to meet his face. He looked Caesar in the eye and wondered where all this was leading.

"I'm releasing you from the past, Lucas."

Had this been Christmas or his birthday or a year-end bonus from Empirico this would have been no problem. But there was no tree with an angel at the top. No cake with 25 candles. And no fancy suits, gorgeous women, or plates of exotic food.

This was a dumpy downtrodden roadside café. And he was sitting across from a man who was making an offer he knew nothing about. He swallowed and lifted the flap. He felt the pages against his forefinger. His heart beat faster. He took in a breath. Steadied his nerves. Strengthened his resolve to see this through and get away as soon as possible.

He opened the envelope.

31

Lucas pulled the pages out of the envelope and felt a sense of regret wash over him. Maybe it would be better just to leave them unread. But it felt wrong not to look as he sat there in front of his one-time boss with only the envelope between them. Besides, he figured, what good is a gift if it isn't opened?

He glanced at Caesar through his peripheral vision. No evil glare. No fingers in a steeple position or any indication of an I've-got-you-now expression. Poker-faced. There may as well have been a blank wall in front of him.

Lucas pulled out the papers and let the envelope fall to the table. The trembling came back. A chill down his neck. Almost painful. Subconsciously he tried to find—or make up—a reason why there could be a draft with no windows or doors open. He was about to look behind to see what was there, but decided instead to stay focused on the pages for fear of what he might find sneaking up behind him. He looked down.

It was a legal document. Real estate. A title. Lucas saw his name. Caesar's name appeared as the vendor. He read farther down. Purchase price: one dollar. One dollar? He looked farther. Then he saw it. His heart pumped so hard it made it difficult to breathe. He heard the conversation all over again. *I'll be right back. Just wait here.* He saw the waitress beside him. She was still there. Hadn't moved in all these years. Just standing there, offering him yet another refill on his drink. He didn't have to look out the window. What he was hoping to find wasn't there. People coming. People going. Filling up with gas. Walking into the restaurant. Passing him by.

The room went dark. Cold. Empty.

Except for the two of them.

He saw the name of the property.

The Fortunate Son Café.

He felt a battle rage within him as he decided what to do. A tug-of-war pulling him in both directions. What to do.

What to do.

Do I drop the pages? Do I look at Caesar? Is this a buyout? Is this a gesture of good faith? Is Caesar trying to be helpful?

Maybe he understands. Maybe that's why he's brought me here. To show me how to finally win. To help me get over the past.

"I can't believe this, Caesar."

"Lucas, it's yours. To do with as you see fit. I even paid the dollar for you. Just sign it and the Fortunate Son is whatever you want it to be."

"Why did you bring me here?"

The mood changed. Even though Caesar wasn't expecting that response he gave no indication he was upset.

"People do things for one of two reasons, Lucas. They do things for reasons they understand, and they do things for reasons they don't understand. Often we think we know why we do something. But most of the time we do them for reasons we don't even know about or have chosen to run from. Still, they guide us. They control us. They consume us. They are the true self."

"You think we're guided by problems so deep we don't know them?"

"I'm saying *you* are guided by problems like that."

"And you're not?"

"Oh, I am too. We all are. It's just that I know my reasons. Whereas you do not."

"You know what makes me work?"

"It's easy to see from the outside. It's like the man dressed in black in that segment from Cirque du Soleil's *O*. He's set on fire and everyone can see it but him. He's trapped in his blindness."

"I'm not trapped."

"You're not?"

"No."

"Then give me back the deed to the property."

The poker game was not going well. Caesar was calling his bluff. No money at stake, thank goodness. Just a relationship.

And a future.

Lucas held the deed even tighter. "You can have it back," Lucas said.

"You don't mean that. And we both know it. That deed is your key. Your release from the past. Your chance to get connected to that which drives you."

"I know what drives me."

"You don't."

"A love for people."

"People? They aren't consistent enough. A love for people isn't what makes you tick."

"A passion for curing the sick."

"Noble as it may sound on the outside, it's only a surface reaction and a vain attempt to dig that impossible tunnel to get at what really motivates you."

"A search for God," Lucas said, thinking he had finally played his trump card.

"Close. Closer to what drives me, mind you. But not you."

"You're not searching for God."

"Neither are you, Lucas."

"This is pointless."

"You may be 25 on the outside. But Lucas, you are still that 6-year-old boy. You are still sitting there. Right where you are." Caesar leaned forward. He paused as Lucas felt the weight of what he would say next. "You've never left the Fortunate Son Café."

Fear left Lucas. Vanished in an instant. And before peace even had a chance to flood his soul a torrent of rage ripped into him. He felt his blood pound in his veins. He clenched his teeth. Where was that knife? That dagger. He could ram Caesar to the bench. One quick stab in the eyes....

He opened his mouth to let in enough air through his teeth.

Relax. Just calm down. Don't say anything. Don't let him get to you. Don't let him do this to you.

"When I was six, I walked out of here a nobody. I faced every imaginable obstacle to become the highest-ranking member by sales in your organization. I did that. Me. I made it happen."

"This isn't about your success. Your success is the result of what's been pushing you ever since you physically walked out of this place. And I'm here to save you from making this continual mistake. This is about something much deeper."

"This is about finding out that you have a secret drug you're not releasing. But you're going to, Caesar. You will release that drug."

"You're going to discover who you really are."

"I know who I am."

"You're going to find out about the real Lucas."

"I am the real Lucas."

"You're sure?"

"I don't need your interpretation of my life."

"But you do. Because when you see it, your whole life will make sense. It will click and you will agree that everything you do—the business, these healing miracles—it's all an attempt that begins and ends with what defines you. Are you ready?"

Lucas already worried that perhaps there really was some hidden motive in his life, some unseen fear that was ruling him like a ghost at the helm of a ship, steering him in an unknown direction. "Go."

"Your parents."

It was anticlimactic. It felt like a great movie that dies out with a poor ending.

"My parents?"

"Your life, Lucas. This is what drives you."

"No."

"Moulds you."

"No."

"Compels you."

"I haven't even seen them in all these years."

"Your whole life is about your parents," Caesar said. The sudden quiet in the café brought with it a welcome change from the echo of their voices. "This is why you do what you do. This is why you have to be the best. This is why you were at the top in medical school. This is why you tried to perform an abortion to help Tabitha's sister. This is why you succeeded in the pharmaceutical industry," Caesar said, softening his voice. "You did all of this because you are still trying to prove that little six-year-old Lucas is worth being loved. You are still trying to convince the world, and yourself, that you were good enough to be someone's son. That you were good enough to have a mother. That you were good enough to have a father. That you had the ability to make them proud of you. That you could earn their admiration. That you were worthy of being somebody. And yet you were unable to shake that gnawing. And this, my young friend, is why I see myself in you."

Not a word. Not a thought. Nothing but a tear came out of Lucas. His eyes stayed glued on Caesar, unable to combat what he was saying.

"You think I picked you because you were the best? You were a criminal. You think I picked you because you were the smartest? The most talented? No, Lucas. I picked you because you and I are the same. We operate from the same mode of thinking. It's just that I realize it and you do not. Mirrors. That's what we are to each other. For what I see in you is what you see in me."

"I know nothing about you, Caesar."

"But you will, Lucas. Once you understand yourself, you'll know everything about me." He closed his eyes a moment. "You know, I can still smell it," Caesar said.

"Smell what?"

"The outhouse. I prayed there, begged God to keep her safe."

"Keep who safe?"

"Have you ever been in an outhouse, Lucas? You know that smell?"

Lucas recalled the event with the strong man.

"Bandits threatened our property. The outhouse was my hiding place. The place where I prayed to God to keep us safe. But my mother died when I was six. They stabbed her. Butchered her. Pregnant and all. Set the house on fire. Six. When I was older I asked God why that happened. He never answered." He ran a finger through his hair. "No matter. I immigrated to the U.S. and moved to Chicago. Went to school during the day and worked in a drugstore at night. I saw people come in desperate and return a few weeks later healthy. I thought, *This is a great profession. I want to do that. I want mothers to be at peace about their children's health. I want children to know that their mom is going to get better.* So I went into pharmaceuticals. One-hundred-and-ten-hour work weeks, Lucas. Work. Sleep. Work. Sleep. And wouldn't you know it? The land of opportunity came through for me. I was a millionaire by 25. You can relate."

He reached down instinctively for a cup that wasn't there.

"Anyhow. Money and work is no life for a man. And the moment I saw her I knew that. Every man knows where he was and what he was doing when he saw the right one for the first time. When it happens, you know it. A year later we were married with one child. Another year later she developed cancer. So I went back to God. I begged him for her life the way I did for my mother's. But she died. And I was left with my little boy."

From a restaurant to a bar. That's what Lucas decided. He'd change this place from a café to a fully licensed watering hole. If there would be any more conversations like this one in the Fortunate Son, people would need drinks a lot stronger than pop and coffee to help them through.

"My son and I had the best conversations. All hours of the night. But as young as 6 years old he had terrible bouts with intestinal problems. By age 13 he was in serious trouble. When the doctors said there was nothing more I went back to God. And this time I went all out.

"I went to church. It was empty most of the time. But it was always open. Twenty-four hours a day. I walked in and prayed." He gave Lucas the name of the church. Lucas nodded that he knew of it. "First, I gave all my money away. Millions, Lucas. I gave it to orphanages, to relief efforts, everything. I pleaded with God for my son's life. Still he didn't get better. I sold my business. Sold my house. Everything. Gave it to God. Gave it to charity. To prove I was serious. I went into the church and knelt down on the hard floor. Leaned my wrists against a wooden bench. I stayed there, not eating for seven days straight, believing God to finally intervene in my life."

He wiped his forehead as if to draw strength for what he needed to say next.

"I went back one more time after my son died. Not into the church. Just on the steps. It was all I could manage. I couldn't go back in. I couldn't get myself to go through that door. Why was that, Lucas? Why couldn't I go back in? I sat there in the middle of the long row of concrete steps in the pouring rain. No wife. No son. No money. No business. No friends. No family. No God. Nothing, Lucas. Absolutely nothing."

"That was the last time you spoke to God?"

"It was."

"Do you miss that?"

"I didn't have a choice."

"Why not?"

"Because no person can go through life being consistently disappointed by God. Eventually, Lucas, you have to cut your losses."

"Do you blame God?"

"Everyone can point to a critical moment in their life when they needed God and he didn't come through for them. There are times in a man's life when he knows God is against him. And for that there is nothing to blame. It's simply the way things are. Just like you did nothing to deserve having a good life in America and those starving kids in Africa did nothing to deserve their bad life out there."

"But isn't this where faith comes in? To believe when nothing makes sense?"

"I feel sorry for people with faith. They don't know God the way I do."

"Maybe it needed more time," Lucas said, thinking it applied less to Caesar and more to Edgar.

"I'm not sorry I searched as hard as I did for God. But I lost, Lucas. And this is what I'm here to protect you from."

"Protect me?"

"Yes."

"From what?"

"From God."

"Protect me from God?"

"From the God you *think* you know."

"And you know God?"

"Better than you do."

"You walked out on God."

"No, Lucas," Caesar said. "God walked out on me." He leaned closer. "And God will do the same to you."

"You can't predict that."

"I lost my mother, my wife, and my son. Three times God could have come through for me, but didn't. You survive a plane crash, you survive being burned alive, and you survive being caned in an African desert. Three times you should have died, but God came through for you."

"This isn't favouritism."

"You're right, Lucas. It's luck. Throw in your coin. Push the button. Watch it unfold. But don't pretend you have anything to do with the result. Because God is the greatest slot machine in the world."

"I asked for God's help in those situations."

"You can no more influence God than you can influence a game of roulette. Statistics. Odds. Chance. When you win, it's called skill. When you lose, it's called house advantage. It's no different with us. When things work out, we call it God. When they don't, we call it life. But you can't have it both ways, Lucas. This is what I discovered in the pouring rain on those church steps. Sometimes God is just simply not an option. When that happens you have to move on. God decides whether to want you or not. And this is why I am here to warn you that it's only a matter of time before the God you count on will disappear. This is why we are the same."

"The same?" Lucas asked, trying to follow his rationale. "How does any of that imply we're the same?"

"Because time and chance happen to us all. You and I are a mix of horrendous disasters and good fortune. Of bad luck and good luck. Of brutal circumstances and good ones. We have no control over what happens to us. We are children of fate. We are God's cosmic joke on probability," Caesar said. "We are sons of Las Vegas."

"You and I are different. You are withholding a drug that can make people well. I am out there risking my life to see that every person I come into contact with is delivered from illness.

"A minor variance."

"Minor?"

"Minor when you consider you are healing people to earn God's approval, whereas I'm healing them in spite of it."

"You are denying them health."

"You are denying yourself the truth about why you are doing this."

"I know my mission."

Caesar shook his head. "You *think* you know your mission. You'd be wise to critically reflect on it. And soon. You'll be better off for it."

"Release the drug and we'll all be better off."

"I don't have a miracle drug. Not even God does. Not for everyone."

"You're in the wrong place to be talking about God and miracles."

"You think so?" Caesar asked. "Do you think God is against Sin City?"

"Do you think he is against your opposition to miracles being performed here?"

"Opposition? To miracles? You misunderstand me. The problem is not whether or not God performs miracles, it is the unpredictability and randomness with which he delivers them."

Lucas stood up. Even though he looked down at Caesar he felt insignificant in his presence. "This isn't about fate."

Caesar stood as well and looked Lucas in the eye. He didn't blink. Didn't show any of that genuine or near genuine interest he had earlier.

"You are leaving this city and you are never coming back."

Or else. Lucas was waiting for the *or else* at the end. But it never came. And it didn't need to. They both understood it was implied.

"Lucas, there are lots of places in this world you can go."

"Places where pharmaceuticals are not in demand."

"Correct. And that's how you and I can carve up and share the Monopoly board." Caesar put his hand on Lucas' shoulder. "Las Vegas is not your kind of town."

Where was that sharp comeback when he needed one? It would come to him. Travelling down the highway, or some point later, as it does for people when they think back to moments and discover the words they should have said.

"Las Vegas is everyone's town. And I belong right here." Lucas was about to step away when he caught himself. *The deed. What about the deed. Do I keep it or leave it there?*

"The deed is yours," Caesar said. "Unlike God, I don't take things back. Friends or enemies, I want you to know that I did what I could here to help you."

Lucas took the deed and walked out of the café. He let the door slam behind him as he hurried to his car. His heart beat faster, thinking that at any moment a shot would ring out and a bullet would pierce his back, come out his chest, and smash through the window of his car.

He lifted the door handle, slid onto the seat, and started the ignition. He saw Caesar standing outside, watching him as he left. He backed out and drove to the highway, keeping a watchful eye in the rear-view mirror.

Lucas raced down the highway. The unwritten rule that the speed limit increases the closer you get to Vegas held true for him. He was going thirty over and sweating so hard he had to wipe it from his face. It took him three tries to punch in September's number correctly. When she answered he asked for Jake.

"Lucas, what happened?"

"I'm in trouble," he said, forcing his shaky hand to grip the steering wheel tighter to steady his course. "Get the team together. We only have one chance left to get him."

32

Where did Jake say we were going to meet? Bally's, right? Wasn't it Bally's? No. No, it wasn't. Aladdin. Right. It was the Aladdin. No! It wasn't the Aladdin either. Where? Wait. Wasn't I the one who decided where to meet?

Lucas turned off the I-15 onto Las Vegas Boulevard, looking both at the road ahead of him and at the rear-view mirror. He swerved once to avoid side-swiping a car, which he would otherwise have seen had he not been in such a panic to scan in all directions. He searched for anything, anyone, who might be following, chasing him. They would be coming. That much was certain. Mitchell and Foster, most likely. Mike, perhaps. Council members. Someone. Caesar had certainly given the order by now. It was just a matter of time.

He passed Mandalay Bay. Normally the upcoming boxing match advertised on the huge screen would have caused him to turn in and buy tickets. Incredible aquatic centre. Exotic fish from around the world. But he never even saw the advertising. Barely even read the name on the hotel. They weren't meeting at Mandalay Bay. The rest didn't matter.

On his left he saw the drawbridge for Excalibur. Massive white towers were backlit to give it the feel of a medieval castle. Up ahead he saw New York-New York with its replica skyscrapers and the majestic green MGM Grand across the street.

No, no, no! Where is it? He drove farther and turned into the Peppermill Bar and Restaurant. The neon blue and white *Peppermill* sign and the blue neon trim around the building gave it a mysterious relaxed feeling. The lot in the front was packed so he drove to the back of the bar, off the property, and stopped in an empty dim parking area. He switched the lights off and took in a deep breath. He closed his eyes and tried to get the image of Caesar out of his mind. He pulled out his cellphone and was about to dial when he saw a dark BMW in the distance drive onto the far side of the lot. It stopped. He saw the door open.

A woman scrambled out of the vehicle and fell face down on the ground. He looked closer. No. No, this wasn't a woman. A girl. Late teens. Maybe 20. Max 20 years old. Thin. What little light there was in the lot reflected off her skin. No shirt. Just a high cut grey skirt. Blonde hair. Almost white.

A man stepped out. Black hair. Black suit. She tried to get to her feet, but wasn't fast enough. He reached down and grabbed her by the hair. She lifted her hands in a vain attempt to protect herself. He closed his fist and screamed at her.

Lucas put the car in drive. Just as he hit his headlights he saw the man unload a powerful punch to her face. Her head snapped back. She went limp and hung there like a rag doll.

The man dropped her to the ground. He stepped on her face as he panicked to get in the driver's side. Lucas gunned the accelerator. The man closed the door. The BMW took off.

Lucas hit the brakes. He left the door open as he ran to her side.

Blood covered her face. She had suffered much more than one hit tonight. It was difficult to differentiate between what was a bruise and what was makeup, especially around her heavily done-up eyes. She wasn't knocked out. Not completely. She lifted her head, trying hard not to go down for the count. Not here. Not by herself. Not in a dingy dark parking lot. She touched her face and then her lips to see which teeth she may have lost. A stream of blood marked a line from the corner of her mouth down her throat. She moaned in a way that made Lucas wonder if she realized her attacker was gone.

He touched her shoulder. She grunted in pain and in fear, unable to move her broken arm to claw at his eyes with her long nails. She'd dig into them. Try and pluck those pearls out. That would stop him. That would do it. What kind of sick, decrepit, anti-human sloth takes advantage of a beaten-up girl, on her back, lying half-naked and half-dead on the ground?

"I'm here to help."

She trembled. Every part of her. Lucas went back to his car and grabbed his jacket. He put it overtop of her.

"I'm here to help you."

"Get...." She stumbled over her words. She exhaled through her mouth in short, tense breaths. "You the get the...," she swore at him as she dragged her uncovered back against the rough asphalt to move away from him.

Lucas began to recite his verses. She stopped moving. He closed his eyes—that was a mistake—and held his hand against the side of her face. He felt her sticky blood on the palm of his hand. Sweat dripped down his face and fell onto hers. He prayed for her to be healed. And just as he finished he felt that internal warning bell going off, telling him to open his eyes. The sense that told him something had gone wrong.

Somehow she had managed to pull out a switchblade. He saw enough of it in time. She stabbed at his eyes. He jerked to the right to avoid it. It passed right beside his ear, nicking him in the process. She tried again, but Lucas jumped back. She found a renewed vigour and stood to her feet, stumbling as she tried not to succumb to the aching pain in her body.

Now Lucas could really see her. A ray from the street light shone down on her frailty. Her nose was not right. It was bent over to the side. A slobbering mess. Blood everywhere. Her face. Her body. Her hands. Cuts on her shoulder. She couldn't speak properly. It came out in bunches of slurs. She spoke as though high on drugs or alcohol, or both, as she swore at him, cursing for him to leave. She backed up towards a fence near a building.

"I can make you well. Please. Just give me a chance."

"Stay away!" she screamed, firing off an attack of curses in her defence.

Lucas stood up. As if on cue she brought the knife in front of her. She began to cry on reflex and then forced herself to stop, realizing the futility of tears. She backed up some more and then disappeared behind a fence.

He followed after her, finding it difficult to listen to that voice of reason telling him she might be waiting around the corner to greet him. But she was gone. Back to the shadows. Back to the underworld. Back to nowhere.

Lucas returned to his car. He tried to rub the blood off his hands with a tissue from the glove compartment, but ended up smearing it around more than anything.

He thought about that poor girl. Doing whatever she could to get money. Stumbling around out there high and out of her mind, easy prey for the next person. Unless she found a way to safety. Safety.

Safety.

Lucas was about to put the car in drive when it struck him. Panic gripped his body. He looked at his hands. Covered in blood. But it wasn't the blood that scared him. Maybe it was just a fluke. Maybe it was the timing. The place. The type of her illness, condition. Maybe it was a lot of things. But the longer he thought about it, the more it confirmed his suspicions about what was happening to him. He had felt no heat in his hands. He had sensed no peace as he prayed for her. And, most of all, he had seen no change in her condition after he had prayed.

Then a thought triggered. Lucas remembered where they were going to meet.

Caesars. Of course. His memory could be forgiven for blocking that name out.

Caesar walked into his office. Mike, Mitchell, and Foster sat in chairs in front of his desk. No word. No greeting. Not even eye contact. Not until he sat down and faced them. He looked at Mike in particular. It was time to try again. It was time to fulfill those vows.

"Gentlemen, things are not working out with Mr. Stephens. And it's time for us to make amends for our previous shortcomings."

Mike couldn't breathe. *How fast can I get to the door? Are Mitchell and Foster armed? Could I even make it out of the Garden? Elevator or stairs? Don't look nervous. Don't grab the armrests so tightly. Relax. You're just here to talk. To plan. To execute.*

Execute.

Lucas drove past Caesars looking for Jake among the crowd of people on the sidewalk. Jake spotted him as he approached Flamingo Road and waved him over.

"We're meeting at Lady Luck," he said, getting into the car. "We'll have some privacy."

"At a casino?"

"Just trust me."

Lucas parked in a lot on Stewart. It was late. It was dark. Best of all, it was empty. "Are we safe here?"

"We will be."

"The others?"

"Tabitha and Edgar are on their way."

They walked down Third Street, past the reflective windows of Lady Luck, and entered the casino. Jake turned left and led him through the maze of slots. Lucas did what he could not to make eye contact, and the little he saw made him feel this was a whole different crowd compared to the people on the Strip. They reached the back and walked through to the elevator lobby. Jake pushed the button for the east tower.

They got off at the top floor. Jake led him down the hallway. One of the doors opened and for a moment his heart pushed out a hopeful beat that perhaps it was Tabitha welcoming them in. An elderly man stepped out. Pack of smokes in one hand. Bucket of coins in the other.

Jake reached a mechanical room at the end of the hallway. He produced a piece of coat hanger from his pocket, slid it under the lock, and pulled back on it. They heard it release and Jake opened the door.

"Have you been here before?" Lucas asked.

"The ability to disappear is critical in this town."

They walked through a dark aisle and up a set of metal stairs to another door. Jake opened it and stepped onto the roof.

"Downtown Vegas by night," Jake said as they looked out at the buildings. "No cameras. No people. Plus, it's got a great deck! So tough to get a room with a balcony in Vegas these days."

"Too many people jumping to their deaths."

"Too many people getting pushed."

They heard clanging behind them. Lucas turned around. "This is a mistake being up here."

"It's alright. It's either Edgar or Tabitha."

Lucas looked around the roof. This was stupid. No way down. No way to escape.

The door opened.

"Edgar," Lucas said.

Edgar nodded. No greeting. No hello. Just a tired expression on the face of a man struggling in that unpredictable world between confusion and belief. He wore his trademark dress pants and dress sweater. He walked closer and looked at Lucas as if expecting a reason why he had called this meeting. They asked him how he was doing and he replied he was managing, all things considered.

"Edgar, we're taking on Caesar and I need your help."

"Why do you need me?" he said. It came out sounding more like *You don't really need me for this.*

"I'm planning a showdown. Me versus Corvey."

"A showdown?"

"Right."

"Against Corvey?"

"Not against, per se. Just for publicity. I need to set this up and go all out so that Caesar gets the message I'm here to do healings."

"In an attempt to bankrupt his casino?"

"I have to pressure him."

"You're concerned for me, and you think that by including me in your plan you'll make me feel better. You need Tabitha. That I can see. But not me."

"I do need you, Edgar," Lucas said with more force.

The three became quiet, a stalemate. Edgar studied Lucas' eyes. He saw something different in them. Something he wasn't expecting. "What is it, Lucas?"

"We have to put this together by tomorrow night. The next day at the latest."

"You can tell me."

"We have to get as much media attention as possible."

"Something's bothering you."

"That's where Tabitha comes in. She organizes the media."

"Lucas, stop," Edgar said in a feeble voice, revealing how little energy his frail body could put into emphasizing a point.

Lucas felt a wave of fear come over him. He closed his eyes and remembered the two boys with brutal marks on their arms who caught up to him at the police cruiser and begged to be healed, but ended up staying in the same condition as when they came. He lifted his hands, palms up, and stared at them. That teenage girl's blood from the parking lot still clung to him. He felt the trembling of her body and recalled her cuts and bruises and mangled nose. He couldn't help her either. He prayed, but nothing had changed. No juice. No jolt. No fiery sensation. The boys could have been a fluke. But the girl? It was time to accept it. It was time to get his head around what was going on.

"You can tell me, Lucas," Edgar said. "What's wrong?"

Lucas folded his hands as if about to pray. He looked at Jake and then at Edgar with eyes full of doubt and fear. And the longer he looked at Edgar, the more he recognized the same thing in him.

"It's leaving me," Lucas said. "I'm losing the power to heal."

33

Saying it out loud didn't make him feel any better. Worse if anything. The secret was out now. And he worried that perhaps there was a way it might get back to Caesar—that perhaps some eagle had just heard him and was now making its way to the Garden to reveal Lucas' deficiency, taking away his leverage, and reducing him to nothing more than an empty threat.

"Losing the power?" Jake asked. And it occurred to him then that in retrospect Lucas had been shouldering a heavier burden the last few days.

"That's why I have to get Caesar now," Lucas said. "Before it's too late. And when it's all gone I'll need to try and sort this whole business out, which is why I need you, Edgar."

Edgar rubbed his forehead. He walked past them to the edge of the parapet. He looked down at the traffic below and then out in the distance at the direction of the casinos on the Strip.

"Albert Einstein said, 'There are only two ways to live your life. One is as though nothing is a miracle. The other is as though everything is a miracle.' What do you think, Lucas? You think sickness is a miracle?"

"No," Lucas replied, hearing a distinct change in Edgar's tone. There was an eerie feel to his voice. Lucas walked closer to him. Each step he took made him wonder why Edgar had gone so close to the edge in the first place. Just a few more. Just a few more paces and he'd be within reach.

Lucas stopped him at arm's length, trying hard not to make it obvious why he had come out there with him.

"You think getting terminal cancer is a miracle?"

Terminal. That word. Synonymous with giving up. No fight. It made Lucas cringe. He hated it. "I wouldn't use the word *terminal*," Lucas said, and then quickly wished he hadn't. Edgar didn't need any more reasons to jump.

"I can't help you, Lucas," Edgar said. "I feel bad for what's happening to you." His eyes welled up with tears and he started crying. It embarrassed him. He tried to hold it back. "I'm sorry," he said. "It's this cancer. It screws up everything." He covered his eyes and the three of them waited for him to calm down.

"We need your help, Edgar," Jake said.

"You don't understand."

Lucas couldn't be certain, but from his perspective it looked like Edgar was leaning closer to the edge.

"Then help me to understand," Jake replied.

"My sickness is the least of my problems."

Definitely. He was leaning closer. No doubt. Edgar looked down. A tear ran off his face. The wind picked it up and blew it across and down on the dots of people below.

Pull him back, a voice told Lucas. *Pull him back now! Don't you see how screwed up he is? Pull him back! What are you waiting for? Pull him back now!*

Lucas wanted to reach out and grab him. But he wondered how to do it so he wouldn't lose face with his friend, if that wasn't what he was planning.

Who cares if he gets angry with you for thinking that about him! Yank him back!

Lucas put an arm around him. He didn't want to give him a hug. It felt awkward. But it was the least he could do, given the circumstances.

Edgar pulled himself away. "Have either of you ever thought you had something, something you were totally sure of, only to discover it wasn't yours?"

"Meaning?" Jake asked.

"I'm in serious, serious trouble."

"What kind of trouble?" Lucas asked.

"The worse kind there is. Worse than terminal cancer."

That word again.

"How can we help you?" Lucas asked.

"What is faith?"

"You tell me."

"No, you tell me! You tell me! You work miracles. You heal thousands upon thousands. You tell me what it is. You know. Right?"

"I...Edgar, where is this going?"

Edgar turned away from the edge, much to Lucas' relief. "When some people get sick they turn to their faith in God. It's the spare tire when you've got a flat in the pouring rain." That eerie sound in his voice got more intense. Lucas felt a chill as a strange cool breeze came in the hot dry night air. Edgar felt it too. "But what happens when you go to the trunk and realize your spare is missing?"

"Edgar?"

"It hit me when I was sitting on a park bench in the pouring rain at Buckingham Fountain. Looking out over the grey at Lake Shore Drive. Who was I kidding? It's ironic, isn't it? Theologian. I mean, really, that's got to do it, right? Teacher. No. Not teacher. Professor. I was a professor. Granted I wasn't at Notre Dame. But I was a professor, nonetheless. I knew the verses. I *taught* those verses. I gave students grades on their papers, and now I see all of them, most of them, should have got A plus. I wasn't the teacher. I should have been the student. I should have been the one asking *them* questions."

Edgar stared off into nothing as though in a trance. Lucas looked at Jake. They waited for Edgar to continue.

"But I found out. And now sickness is just a minor defect. A small problem by comparison."

"Edgar," Lucas said. "I want you to face me and say exactly what the problem is."

Edgar turned his head. His face was serious. His skin pale. Almost white. His eyes desperate. He swallowed and forced himself to get the words out. "I don't know God."

"We can't kill him," Mike said from his chair opposite Caesar and flanked by Foster and Mitchell. He had to speak up. For his sake and theirs. "At least we can't kill him in any way that makes it look like it was murder."

He stood up and poured himself a drink from the bar in his boss' office. He would have offered Caesar a drink as well, but discussing the fate of his once best friend and, transitively, his own fate as well, made him forget his manners.

"If we kill him," Mike continued, "all fingers will point to Empirico. To you, Caesar. Two of your employees were found dead in Chicago right where the assassination attempt took place. All eyes are on you. If he dies in Vegas by any suspicious means, everyone will accuse you."

"We're getting rid of him, Mike. You of all people understand that."

"It's not about *whether* we get rid of him, but *how* we get rid of him that matters."

Caesar was in his element. This was more like it. He felt such pride in Mike. Such confidence. Plotting a murder. *What more can a boss ask of an employee?* Caesar sat forward in his chair. A sinister smirk came to his face. "I'm listening."

"How can you say you don't know God?" Lucas asked.

"How can anyone say they *do* know God? How can anyone say for sure that God knows them?"

"Just because you get ill doesn't mean you don't have faith."

"This isn't about faith," Edgar whispered. It seemed to Lucas he was trying not to say it too loud for fear that the eagle might take those words and spread them to everyone. "This is about a relationship with God, of which I have none."

Edgar stood there as weak and empty as he had ever known himself to be. There in front of him was a miracle worker he couldn't understand and a recovering drug addict. Had it come to this? Had his existence really come down to standing on a roof in a city he didn't know with people he couldn't relate to? Who knew how much longer he would have with them? Who knew how much longer he'd be here? He wiped a tear from his face and felt the anxiety people feel when the final grains of sand start running through the hourglass and they know they're not ready to go.

"I'm sorry, Edgar," Lucas said. "I'm sorry your illness made you lose your faith."

Edgar saw the Lady Luck sign in big, bold red capital letters on the tower beside them. If there really was a lady luck, she wasn't smiling. At least not on Edgar. "Being sick didn't make me lose my faith," he said. "It just revealed there wasn't any there to begin with."

"There has to be a way."

"I can't find a way to believe."

"We'll find a way, Edgar. Together."

"I wish it were that easy."

"It is that easy."

"For others, possibly. But not for me."

"Edgar, that white ball is going to land on your marker."

"But I'll be long out of the game by the time it does. I've done what I can. I have nothing to offer you. I'm leaving, Lucas."

"Don't do this."

"I can't find God. Can you understand that? Everything else I was coming to terms with. I was coming to terms with cancer. With the end of my life. But God? To realize I don't have what I thought I had? And what's worse is that I know I can't reach God. I can't get there."

"Edgar, I am promising you I will stand with you and you will find God."

"I'm out of options, Lucas. I don't have the time to be chasing miracles. I have a more pressing issue to solve. I'm terrified and I don't know what else to do. What have I done? What have I done to God? Which brother did I kill?"

"God isn't punishing you."

"I can't take that for granted. Not anything. Not now. Not anymore. I feel like I've been banished from God."

"Stay with me, Edgar. We'll find a way."

"I'm sorry, Lucas," he said. He shook his head. His eyes looked so empty. So devoid of purpose. Bewilderment. Fear. Disbelief. "I'm east of Eden."

Edgar walked away and reached the door before either Lucas or Jake could respond.

"You stay here," Jake said. "I'll go after him. Wait for Tabitha."

Jake hurried out to find Edgar. He took the elevator down to the lobby and searched for his dying friend. "Edgar," he said, seeing him head out the main entrance.

When Edgar heard Jake's voice he stopped. He pressed his lips together, being both annoyed at Jake for following him and at himself for not being more direct that he wanted out.

"Edgar, if you want to leave I'm not going to stop you. But if you want to talk, I can take you to the restaurant. My treat. Whatever you want. Besides, I hear the waitresses are really good-looking."

"Have you even been in that restaurant before?"

"No," Jake said, smiling to reveal his dentures.

"Then how do you know they're good-looking?"

"I figured it would help convince you."

Edgar managed a smile. He followed Jake to the restaurant. Just as they sat down a dark-haired reporter with a white shirt, blue jeans, and leather jacket walked in and headed to the elevators.

Tabitha reached the top floor, followed the instructions Jake gave her to the mechanical room door, opened yet another door, and found Lucas on the roof. Waiting for her.

"This is private." She smiled in a way that told Lucas she liked the idea of coming to this clandestine location.

Lucas looked at her and felt intimidated. When they were together he had a palpable confidence that he could do no wrong. But now that they were drifting away, perhaps farther than they knew, he felt the insecurity that came with knowing the woman who could set the world right for him was, at best, one big question mark.

A hug. Can I get a hug? Is it wrong if I tell you I miss you? Is it wrong if I tell you I need you? Am I putting myself too far out on a limb to tell you I can't do this without you?

He explained the plan as best he could and hoped she would buy in.

"Lucas, if you know they're after you, why don't you just leave? Go back to Africa. Go to South America. Go somewhere far away."

"Because I'm on a mission."

"No. Please, Lucas," she said, shaking her head. "I deserve better than that. You deserve better than that." She walked closer to him and for a moment he thought he might be able to touch her. Then she moved past him and stood at the edge of the parapet, looking out at Vegas. "You can tell yourself you're here because you want Caesar to release the drug—the supposed drug—or because you want to heal people. But that's not the real reason."

"It is."

"It is not, Lucas. And I will not let you lie to yourself."

"The drug is there."

"What proof is there of that?"

"I have to release it. I can't get to everyone. That drug will help."

"Perhaps. But that's not why you are here."

"Tabitha."

She turned him. "You are on a vendetta against Caesar." Then she looked more closely at him, as if doing so could draw out of him a hidden rationale for being here. "Or is there something more? I wonder. Is there another reason why the famous Lucas Stephens came to Vegas? To cut a deal? To bargain?"

He did the best he could to search inside and see if she was telling the truth. But his need to defend himself outweighed his need to be open. "There's no deal."

"How else will you ever be rid of him? Or is he not your only danger?"

"Why are you doing this to me?"

"You know that no matter what happens, you will be hunted. Wherever you go. As long as you have this gift you are a target. That must be a terrible burden."

"Stop it, Tab."

"To know that for the rest of your days you will always have to look over your shoulder. Caesar will be your enemy forever. Constantly after you. Constantly seeking to kill you. How would you escape that? How could you be freed? If I were you, why would I come to Vegas? What would I be doing here?"

"I need your help, Tabitha."

That got to her. She felt an incredible pull towards him. *Need.* There was something about hearing that word. *I need your help.* Something about hearing that word come from him.

"For what?" she said, her tone softening.

Lucas looked into her deep brown eyes. He could have stayed there for hours. There was so much going on inside those windows. This would be easier to say if they weren't making eye contact. "I need you to arrange a showdown between me and Sheridan Corvey."

"What?"

"It'll be a huge scoop for you."

"I don't care about the scoop."

I care about you. That was the line Lucas was expecting to hear next. *I care about you.* But it never came. And it served to increase his worries that the ship was getting farther from the pier.

"I need a powerful media event to prove to Caesar that if I stay in town, I'll bankrupt his casino. People are coming to Vegas to get healed, not to gamble. It's already costing him."

"I don't see the need for a big showdown. Plus a promotion like that would take a lot of planning."

"Tomorrow."

"Impossible. It would take weeks."

"I don't have weeks."

"Well then, you're...." She stopped. *I don't have weeks. Is that what he said? I don't have weeks?* "Why don't you have weeks?" Lucas didn't answer. But like a good reporter she didn't let it go. "Lucas. Why can't you wait?"

It should have been easier saying it the second time. But as he looked at her and felt the uncertainty of their relationship he wondered if telling her was the best choice.

"The healing gift is leaving me."

Something changed in her appearance. It was in her eyes. Still the same beautiful brown. But there was something that ignited. A passion. Maybe even for him.

She saw something different in Lucas. She sensed a vulnerability in him that she hadn't known in a long time. Superman had discovered kryptonite. The mighty Lucas was suddenly human. Instead of seeing an icon, she saw a man. Instead of strength, frailty. And as much as she feared what would become of him, she found herself attracted to him—not because of his sudden fall from idealism, but because he was willing to be honest with her about an impending weakness.

"You think it will be gone by tomorrow?"

"No...I don't know. Maybe. No. Not tomorrow. I've still got it. I'm just not hitting 100 per cent. Not anymore. Two brothers didn't get healed. A beat-up girl."

"Do three people constitute a loss of power?"

"It's a trend in the wrong direction."

"Lucas, I don't know that I can be of any help to you."

Just by being here you're more than enough help. Even if you did nothing but stand at my side, I could charge ahead without feeling so much as a hint of failure.

"You can. You can put this stuff—"

"Lucas. I can do the event. That's not the point. I...." She became confused. She had thought about this conversation on the way down. It went so well in the car. All rehearsed. All laid out. In fact by this time she had expected the conversation to be done and that she would have been on her way back. But now that she was standing in front of him, looking into those familiar eyes, her prepared speech was gone. Her confident demeanour vanished. Her goal of doing this without having to dig into her soul was proving to be impossible. And all she had left was the weight of her conscience telling her one thing and the conviction in her heart telling her another.

"Lucas, how do you feel about us?"

Crunch time. This was it. The defendant takes the stand. He felt it. So did she.

"Tabitha, remember when I returned from China? When we got back together? Look what's happened from that moment on. I'm causing financial uncertainty, as they call it in the pharmaceutical industry. Caesar wants me dead. A country tried to bribe, even threaten me to heal their sick and reduce health costs so a politician could get re-elected. I'm in Vegas healing thousands of people right under Caesar's nose and I'm still alive. I'm still doing it. I'm right in the heart of the enemy and I'm thriving."

She could see his passion. She could see his conviction. And she could feel the adventure women feel when they see a man they admire pursuing what they were destined to achieve. But still, something was missing.

"How does any of that affect us?"

He was trying hard to make this clear. Where were the right words? The right thoughts? How could he reach into himself and show her what he believed? But instead of looking inside to sort things out, he looked to Tabitha. Not just at her. Not just at those deep brown eyes. But through them and into her. And when he did he found exactly what he was looking for.

"You give me the feeling I can take on the whole world."

She needed no more than that. Time could stand still now.

"I do?"

"Yes."

"I give you that feeling?"

"Yes."

"That you can take on the whole world?"

"And win."

His words made the tug-of-war within her that much more unbearable. She took in a deep breath, in part to absorb what he had just said and in part to calm herself down.

"Lucas, we're different people."

"We're the same," he said. That scared him. Those words in his mouth felt awful. It horrified him that he had used that phrase. *We're the same.* It was the one Caesar had used on him. And he hoped the virus inside his former boss hadn't found a way into him.

"Lucas, I'm not like you." Her eyes welled up. The perfect evening light gave her both an elegant and mystified look. He too wished for time to stand still. And, judging by the way things appeared to be going, he wished to back everything up and try again. But that option was not available. Not to either of them. And they braced themselves for what lay ahead.

He reached out his hand and touched her shoulder. Connection. "Tabitha, if you can see past this healing gift, you'll see we are identical."

"No, Lucas." She looked out at Vegas as if hoping the answer could be found in those bright lights in the distance. "You survived a fatal plane crash. You were set on fire. You made it through the desert. You sidestepped an assassination attempt. Thousands upon thousands are healed with the touch of your hand."

"I can't explain this, Tabitha."

"I'm not asking you to."

"So why is this a barrier?"

"Because you can identify with this, whereas I can't."

"But you do. You just don't realize it."

"You're not hearing me, Lucas."

"Then what, Tabitha? Don't let the fire and the planes and the bullets and the healings confuse you. That's not me."

"But it is you, Lucas. It defines you. It's who you are."

"I am a man in need of you."

She didn't want to say it. She didn't want it to come out. But her overriding need to be honest crushed her need to be safe.

"I don't believe what you believe, Lucas."

He wanted to respond. He *had* to respond. Still, he found nothing to say.

"At your core you believe in giving up everything you wanted in exchange for being hunted down like a criminal because you heal people. Your reward? Nothing. You have no reward. And this is you, Lucas. A believer in God who makes miracles happen. This is at the deepest part of you. And I can't relate to you there. And because I can't relate to you we have no relationship, even though both of us want it."

She was gone. Still standing there, but they were apart. The connection was lost.

"I'm sorry, Lucas," she said. "We're too far apart."

She walked away from him, leaving him at the edge. She opened the door and went through without looking back. Moments later he looked down and saw her heading out of the hotel towards her car. There was nothing he could do to bring her back. No miracle power he could call on to change her will.

He watched her shoulder-length dark hair enter her car. She closed the door and drove off.

Tabitha was as beautiful as she was cruel.

Jake opened the door, huffing and puffing with those smoke-charred lungs of his as he came onto the rooftop.

"I just saw Tabitha leave. Lucas, what's wrong?" He saw his friend's expression and realized he needed no answer. He shook his head as he stood beside Lucas. "That's not right. What is she thinking? Lucas. Lucas, I'm sorry."

"Can I please not hear that line anymore? I'm getting so tired of it!"

"I'm sorry."

"Jake!"

"I'm sorry. Forget it. I didn't mean anything by it."

Lucas covered his face with his hands in frustration. "Our team has fallen apart," he said. "I am on the verge of taking down Caesar and people are walking on me!" A depressing calm threatened to engulf him. A shadow of defeat crept in. "I'm running out of time."

He closed his eyes, astounded at how horribly this evening had gone. He had taken it for granted they would be together. And now two were gone. And the moment he made that connection he wondered about Jake. He wondered if he too would be gone, leaving him alone on the roof to figure out how to battle it out with Caesar.

Lucas studied Jake's face, looking for any hint of where his decision might lie.

"Well, Jake," Lucas said. "Do you want to go too?"

Jake didn't change his expression. Same worried and frustrated look as before. Same resolve. "Where would I go?" Jake asked. "You're the one who's given me a second chance at life."

Alcohol. Lots of it. Beer maybe. No. Not beer. The hard stuff. Brother Jack. Son of Mr. Daniels. He would do fine. Lots of it. That's what it would take to prevent Jake from breaking apart in front of the only friend he had.

Which of course held true for Lucas as well.

"I'm not walking out on you," Jake said. "We're going to find a way. Media or no media. Miracles or no miracles. Confidence or brutal doubt. We're going to take him on."

Lucas looked out at the empty evening. Tabitha's words echoed in his mind. *We're too far apart.* It was as if she were standing beside him, whispering those words in his ears. Caesar was out there. Somewhere. In that haze of lights.

"I hope you're ready for me," Lucas whispered out into the darkness. "I hope you're ready."

34

The longer Edgar walked, the colder it became. The temperature stayed the same—the problem was with his body struggling to generate enough heat. He headed south on Las Vegas Boulevard to nowhere in particular. It was too early to call it a night and too late to make any plans. He passed the Stratosphere and entered a stretch on the Strip where condos were being built near the Hilton. When he reached the Sahara his mind began to cycle back to the meeting with Jake and Lucas. He tried to avoid it. He tried to avoid realizing they were the last two people on earth who cared what happened to him. He heard the screams of the roller coaster riders on Speed as they rocketed straight up and then hung at the top momentarily before racing backward down the track. He walked along the portion of Las Vegas Boulevard that had become much quieter since Wet 'N Wild left. He saw a man up ahead. Handing out something. Like sports cards. Advertising of some kind. The man tapped the cards in his hand and held out two. Edgar took them. He gave them a passing glance. Forty-four dollars for one girl. Sixty-seven dollars for two. Blondes or brunettes. They offered both. Good-looking. Sultry eyes that seemed to grow duller the longer he looked at them. Edgar dropped the cards on the ground. He did everything he could to resist the urge to go back and pick them up. He forced himself to continue on, thinking that Vegas was not the place for a lonely man.

Up ahead on the other side he saw two college girls laughing as they left Circus Circus with their bleach-blonde hair and short skirts. A couple walked up behind him, talking about how much they were enjoying their honeymoon. Edgar looked at the man as they came up beside him. Roughly his age. He held his arm around his new bride. They passed on ahead as Edgar felt the anguish of knowing that for some people, life works out.

And for others, it does not.

He approached the Stardust intersection. A crowd of people crossing the street pushed around him. Dozens of people packed the sidewalks. He tried his best to fight through the crowd, negotiating his way through small openings between groups of people. But then he stopped. Motionless. People swarmed around him. He heard them talking about the rumours Lucas Stephens was going to be having a massive miracle gathering tomorrow evening. Still more people came. He felt dizzy. Disoriented. Lost. A splash of faces. And as they walked by and new ones took their place it weighed on him that in either days, weeks, or months ahead (whichever it would end up being) he would be gone and nobody here would be any the wiser.

Amid the array of lights and casinos and people and girls he saw a street sign to his left. It looked so out of place that it took him a moment to confirm what he was seeing. Yet the longer he stood there staring in that catatonic way of his, the more it seemed to fit. He looked around him and saw the casinos vying for everyone's attention. And here, off to the left, was a little road that seemed to catch his attention while others passed by. It was as if the street name on the sign was a faint beacon calling out to him in particular.

Cathedral Way.

He turned left and within a few steps everything became still. No crowds. No casinos. No girls. No flashing lights. Just him. His footsteps against the sidewalk. His shadow accompanying him. A cathedral up ahead.

He was amazed to find it here. On the Strip. It captured him. Pulled at him to come closer. Had he had the presence of mind to turn around he may have noticed Foster and Mitchell standing at the intersection. They had been following him and watched as he walked to the cathedral. Then they left.

To his right he saw the towering Wynn Hotel. Up ahead to the left he saw a sign with the mass schedule. Guardian Angel Cathedral. Straight ahead was the building. The front was the shape of a triangle. High above the front doors was a mural of Jesus with his hands stretched down to help three people who had the words *Prayer*, *Peace*, and *Penance* beside them. It reminded Edgar of *Touchdown Jesus*, the mural on the library wall at Notre Dame of Christ, whose lifted hands faced the end zone of the stadium, making it look like a referee was giving the signal that a player had crossed the line. He had prayed there. At the grotto. For help. All to no avail.

Perhaps the change in venue would help.

The closer he got, the more it towered over him. Everything was so calm. So unhurried. So still.

It was as though he had left Las Vegas altogether.

He touched the door handle. It was open.

He went through 2 series of doors and entered the cathedral. He looked past the rows of pews, enough room for at least 500, to the front where he saw another mural, this one more colourful than the first. Images of a man with his arms outstretched. He saw a caretaker off to the right cleaning a room filled with candles.

He walked down the spotless centre aisle on white tiles that were interspersed with small black squares. The shiny floor reflected the images at the front. His steps echoed in the empty seating area. He sat down a few rows from the front.

He closed his eyes, folded his hands, and leaned them on the bench in front of him as he bent forward.

Here he was. Again. Trying either to say something to, or hear something from, God. Not being healed was debilitating. Not hearing from the Almighty was killing him. Maybe this cathedral would help. Maybe praying here would help him convince God of his need for a miracle.

He stayed there for hours. Not saying or hearing anything. The incredible triangular ceiling might as well have been an impenetrable cauldron, preventing any access from those above to the world below and from those below to the world above. He was about to open his eyes when he felt a cool breeze against his neck. He thought at first it was his imagination, but when he felt it again a sudden chill ran down his spine. He hadn't heard the door open, not that he was listening for it, and he was sure he would have heard the caretaker coming up behind him. He opened his eyes and with the slightest turn of his head he glanced over his shoulder.

There was someone there.

Praying.

Or that's the way it looked at first. He turned his head a little more and saw that the person wasn't praying.

He was looking at him.

Edgar's hands felt clammy. Strange, he thought, that in such a large seating area this person had chosen to sit so close to him. He tilted his head and found himself in that precarious position where he could no longer pretend he wasn't trying to find out who it was. He looked behind him. They made eye contact.

The man wore a black suit jacket with a black dress shirt that was unbuttoned at the top. And by his praying posture Edgar surmised Caesar had been accustomed to spending time in the pews.

"Strange place to find God," Caesar said.

"In a church?"

"I've always assumed people find God outside the church and then come into places like this when they lose their faith."

"That can happen."

"So have you?"

"What?"

"Found God."

"In a church?"

"Yes."

"No," Edgar said.

"Does that surprise you?"

"Should it?"

"I don't know. You're the one who believes."

"You don't?"

"Should I?"

"If only faith were that easy."

Caesar raised his eyebrows in a way that conveyed to Edgar he agreed with him. He spoke in a quiet voice, as if the hallowed walls of the cathedral had instilled a sense of awe inside him. "What have you been doing here?"

"I've been begging God for a miracle."

"A miracle."

"Yes."

"And? Did you get it?"

"No."

Caesar nodded his head. He'd been here before too. "Being turned down for a miracle is a difficult thing in life."

"It is."

"To be at God's mercy. To beg for God's help. And then after not getting it you realize you're no better off after asking than you were before. How do you explain that?"

"God?"

"Not getting a miracle."

"I can't."

"Me neither."

Edgar felt a cautious kinship developing between them. Still, he couldn't shake the feeling that as powerful as chance and fate might be, the odds against the two of them being in the same place, a church no doubt, and at the same time was in a realm even probability did not possess.

"You know what it's like?" Edgar asked.

"To ask God for a miracle and not get one?"

"Do you?"

"Yes, Edgar. I know exactly what that's like."

"It isn't right."

"What isn't?"

"Not getting a miracle."

"From whose perspective?"

"From ours, of course."

"Is God under obligation to help us?"

Edgar adjusted himself in his seat. His back hurt from being bent over so long. "No," he said. "No, I suppose not."

"Then why the frustration over miracles?"

"Because God seems to intervene in some cases and at other times does nothing. It leaves me to wonder which category I fall into now that I am in need of help."

"Predictability, Edgar. It's something God does not encourage. What's going to happen? Who will win and who will lose? God keeps those things a mystery. That's why I love Vegas. It asks all of life's real questions. And it gives you the answer with the flip of a card, the roll of a dice, or the pull of a slot machine."

"Is that who God is to you?"

"It's not who God is to me. It's who God is period. You can throw a thousand bucks into a slot machine and get squat. Then some moron steps off a plane, has to ask directions to get to the Strip, gives the machine a spin, and walks out a millionaire. It's no different than what you and I are doing right here."

"How can playing slots be the same as pursuing God?"

"A hotshot multimillionaire kid gets imprisoned in China for drug trafficking. Doesn't care about God, doesn't even care if God exists. And yet God gives him the power to cure the sick, escape certain death time and time again, and do everything but walk on water. You, meanwhile, serve God day and night and sickness is your reward."

"I'm not sure that's a fair comparison," Edgar said in a way that was neither convincing to himself nor to Caesar.

"And therein is the difference."

"Which is?"

"You want God to be fair, whereas I don't want God at all."

"And yet you are in a church."

Caesar nodded. "I wanted a break."

"From?"

"From all the hustle of Las Vegas," he said with a smile. "I admire this church. I really do. It's the one place left in Las Vegas without a slot machine. Think that'll ever change? Think they'll ever put a slot machine next to the holy water at the entrance?"

"No."

"Me neither. People take enough of a gamble when they walk in here."

"You don't think God is a viable option?"

"Nobody ever accused a slot machine of providing false hope. People say gambling addiction is a problem, that it leaves a wake of destruction everywhere it goes. Not by comparison. The boneyard of gambling disasters is nothing compared to the mass of faithless lives running around out there all because God didn't call their number. People like you, for example, who are left to wonder if God is in fact a viable option."

"God is all I have left. The doctors can't do anything for me."

"You've given up hope?"

"I've reached the end," Edgar said out loud for the first time. And when he heard those words trailing out over the cathedral, it felt like the entrance to a tomb had just been shut and his whole world had gone black.

Caesar watched as Edgar crumbled in front of him. He knew that look. That look of desperation. A man willing to do anything to get a second chance at life. He waited for Edgar to look back at him.

"How important is your health to you, Edgar?"

"I need it more than anything."

Caesar unfolded his hands. He leaned forward. Studied him. A sly subtle grin formed. "What if I told you that you could be well again?"

35

Lucas and Jake waited on the roof of Lady Luck for over an hour. Jake sat on a vent. Lucas stood looking out at the Strip, his mind battling between remembering Tabitha's last words and trying to sort out how to continue. Was she gone? Was that a final goodbye or just an *I need some time to think about things*? He could deal with it one way or the other. It was the not knowing and the threat of her really calling it quits that stalled his mind from making a decision.

But enough was enough. Looking at Vegas all night would not make things any easier.

He stepped away from the edge and nodded to Jake.

"Ready?"

Jake stood up and followed Lucas to the exit. "What's your plan?"

"It's complicated."

"Try me."

"I haven't quite finalized it."

"Finalized it?"

"I'm still working on the details."

Jake shook his head. "You don't have a clue, do you?"

Lucas opened the door. "Not yet."

Things did not become any clearer as they left the hotel. Murkier, if anything. They stopped on the street.

"We have to get Edgar back," Jake said. "Tabitha too."

"They're gone."

"Lucas, they're in trouble."

"I can't afford to break this off for their sake."

"For their sake?"

"I can't risk the time to beg them to join us."

"They're our friends."

"Then go find them. Do whatever you think best. I have to continue."

"We'll flip on it, okay?" Jake pulled out a coin. "Heads we go after Tabitha and Edgar. Tails we do whatever you're doing."

"We're not leaving this up to the flip of a coin."

"Why not?"

"Because it's chance."

"We have to do this together." He tossed the coin in the air. Lucas caught it.

"We're not deciding it this way."

"Heads or tails?"

"Neither."

"I'm not leaving you alone. Which is it?"

Lucas looked down at his closed hand. He had the strangest feeling he already knew the result.

"I'm not going back for them. They've made their decision."

"Lucas."

"See if you can talk to Tabitha and Edgar. Don't force them. Just ask."

Lucas pulled back a piece of the barricade fence. He entered the construction zone behind the Stardust. To his right he saw a set of portable washrooms. Up ahead he saw a 28-storey condo, each floor in various stages of completion. He walked past a construction trailer. A light was on. Inside he saw a man in his early thirties, by himself, sitting at a table, poring over engineering drawings.

Lucas reached the building and released a bungee cord that held the makeshift plywood door together. He opened it and walked into blackness.

It took a moment for his eyes to adjust. He took a step and kicked over a pail of nails. He found the elevator bay around the corner. He stepped into one and pressed the eighth floor button.

The doors closed. The elevator lifted. It felt cold all of a sudden. It was as though he were about to fall, like the Tower of Terror ride at MGM Studios in Florida. He had the sense that something wasn't right. He half expected to see someone standing beside him. In the shadows. Waiting for him. The strong man back from the dead, perhaps.

Lucas stepped out of the elevator. He walked down the dusty hallway and saw condos with the interior framing nearing completion. At the end he found a closed door with the number 88 on it. Lucas knocked. He glanced over his shoulder, expecting to see either Mitchell or Foster running at him from out of the darkness with two-by-fours, ready to smash his face in. He swallowed. The air got even cooler. He cleared his throat to break the uneasy silence.

He knocked again.

Still nothing.

He was sure he could feel the *swoosh* of that piece of wood whistling through the air as Mitchell or Foster swung it at his head. In that moment he heard the sound of that branch coming through the African night air and landing on his spine, crushing his vertebrae, and sending his body into the unknown terror of paralysis. A jolt of pain ran down his back. He shivered.

Enough of standing in the hallway.

He tried the door handle. It opened.

"Hello?"

Still nothing. He opened it wider and stepped in.

Black marble floor. A stainless steel kitchen off to the right. A winding wood staircase to the left. In front of him he saw a large open area. Leather couches. A big-screen TV, even bigger than the one he had in his basement. He saw a raised platform with an elegant black table in the back. Candles burned in the middle. Five silver chairs. One at the head.

With a man sitting in it.

Slicked black hair. Dark suit. Off-white shirt. Worried look on his face. He didn't look up. He didn't have to.

"Hello, Lucas," Matthias said. "To think we finally get to see each other again."

Lucas walked on the marble to a hardwood floor and saw that the room expanded out in both directions. He stepped onto the raised area and sat down beside Matthias. His eyes were glazed over. He looked drugged up. Stacks of cards lay piled around him.

"Why did you stay on that plane?" Lucas asked.

"You would have done the same if you were in my situation."

"I need to know."

"You can't know. No one can."

"Matthias, you have a power I know nothing about."

"We have work to do, Lucas. And we both know time is not on our side."

"I want to be clear about something."

"I want to be clear about anything."

"Before you leave Las Vegas, I need you to tell me why you stayed on a plane you knew was going to crash."

A knock at the door.

"And the team begins to assemble."

"Matthias, I have to know."

Matthias looked at Lucas through his glasses, which had a slight tint of blue in them. "Who do you think God is?"

Another knock.

"I'm still learning."

"Do you think God always does good?"

"Could God do evil?"

"You heal people. You make them better. That attracts some people to God. It gives them confidence."

"Isn't that what an encounter with God is supposed to do?"

"Maybe if you have your gift. But not if you have mine."

"Why?"

Those eyes. There was something borderline evil going on behind them.

The door opened. It was Jake.

"Did you find them?" Lucas asked, not taking his eyes off Matthias.

"I can't find Edgar. Tabitha's still unsure."

Lucas introduced the two.

Another knock at the door. It opened. Jake turned around, thinking it to be Tabitha. But the moment he saw who it was a stream of acid chewed through his veins and burned the blood right out of him. His face went pale. He stopped breathing. All he could do was stare and hope the person coming in couldn't see the guilt pounding through his body.

"Hi, everyone," September said. She smiled at Jake. But all he could do in reply was keep eye contact with her and pretend nothing was wrong.

She wore a pair of black jeans and a black leather jacket over her peach tank top. Her soft reddish-blonde hair hung down over her face. She brushed it out of her way as she walked in.

"Alright then," Lucas said, trying hard not to look at her the way he would at Tabitha. "Let's get down to business."

"You think Claire is accurate in her suspicions? That Empirico has a drug that may be able to cure a kind of brain cancer?" Matthias asked. The four of them were seated on the leather couches. Drinks in hand. Trying hard to think critically about things and feeling anything but relaxed. A dim light hung above them, shedding what little illumination it could on their plans.

"It's possible," Lucas said.

"Possible? You worked as an exec. You tell us. Does Empirico have it or not?"

Lucas drank from his bottle of imported beer. "Empirico had a lot of things on the go. Caesar kept us in the dark on purpose about many of the projects in development. Teams would work on seemingly disjointed streams of information. Caesar alone knew all the pieces."

"So Claire is lying."

"She just can't prove what she saw. No evidence of the drug that can cure GBM."

"Is that the same kind Edgar has?" Matthias asked.

Lucas was about to take another swig from his bottle when he stopped. "The same kind Caesar has as well," he said. "Or had. Which could be evidence enough."

"I'm still trying to understand why Caesar would purposefully hold back a drug that he knows could make him a fortune," Matthias said.

"Because he makes more money by not releasing it."

"More money than releasing a cure?" September asked.

Another knock at the door.

"Expecting someone else?" Lucas asked.

"It's for you," Matthias said. His tone was cold. No inflection. No hesitation.

"How can you know that?" Jake asked. "How in the world could you possibly know who is at the door?" He was about to get up, but Lucas was already on his way.

He walked on the hardwood floor to the marble. He swallowed and tried his best not to entertain thoughts of what might be waiting for him. Mitchell and Foster. Shotguns. Sawed off. Kick open the door and shoot him. He could feel those slugs cut into him, sending his blood all over the immaculate floor.

Or maybe it was Edgar. Tricking Lucas to come to the door. To lead him out under false pretenses to someplace where Mike would be waiting.

Lucas turned the door handle. He could already feel the blast of heat. The sound of the shell exploding in the chamber. The screams of the others in the room. The slow-motion dash Jake would make in being too late to rescue him.

Again.

He opened the door. And what he saw gave him the push he needed to believe he could see this mission through.

Tabitha stood before him wearing her perfect dark hair down, a pair of blue jeans and a white shirt, with a look on her face full of the curious combination of doubt and a need for adventure.

"I don't know why I'm here," she said.

The world had just gone right. For even just a moment Lucas had the kind of cards a poker player waits for his whole life. "You don't need a reason."

They sat down with the others. More introductions. They discussed how to find a way to take Caesar down.

"The drug makes no sense. If Caesar has the cure, why doesn't he release it?" September asked. She stood up, took off her jacket, revealing her tanned, toned arms, and poured herself another drink. She put her empty glass down on the counter next to another one. She studied the rack of bottles and picked out a Jamaican rum. She looked back at her glass. She lowered her shoulders in a sign of frustration. She swore. "Which glass was mine?"

Matthias said something to her, but Lucas didn't hear it. He looked at the two identical glasses and watched as she reached for a new one, poured herself a drink, and sat down. Lucas kept staring at the empty glasses, mesmerized by them, as though they were the only two items in the entire room. And for those few moments, for Lucas Stephens, that's all there was.

"Lucas," Tabitha said, trying to snap him out from whatever world he was in. No response. She put her hand on his arm. "Lucas."

"Patent breaking," he whispered.

The room became quiet. Time stopped. All eyes focused on him.

"All of Empirico's drugs are developed under patent protection. It gives them the sole right to sell a drug for the life of the patent. When it expires other companies can develop generic drugs."

"So what?" Tabitha said, unconvinced. "Empirico would more than recoup the cost of the drug under patent laws."

"But that depends on the strength of those laws. What if the news reports are right and there's a decision to relax patent-breaking regulations? What if other copycat, me-too drugs make it to the market? What if Empirico releases the drug and the laws change? Caesar might not want to risk it."

"But he's still better off releasing the drug and having it copied than he is if he just sits on it."

"Not unless he figures he'll make more by keeping it locked up and selling the symptom management drug. Plus, that way he avoids patent-breaking problems."

"You're losing me," Jake whispered.

"A company comes out with a new drug. Another company reverse engineers it and comes up with something close. Something so close that it does the same thing as the other drug, only it's different enough to market under a new patent. The second company can make a lot more money because they don't have the same research and development costs."

"Then why go to all the trouble of manufacturing it and not releasing it?" Tabitha asked.

"They may have started both streams simultaneously, the cure and the symptom treatment drug, thinking if either one proved successful they'd have a winner. In this case they had two. So they could offer both, or just one. Whichever option makes them more money. So they think it through. Patients with GBM might last three years without medication. But if the treatment drug keeps them alive as long as ten years after diagnosis, then Empirico stands to have a long-term client. That's why they'll market the drug as a way to improve the quality of life. They'll show that it prevents rapid growth of the brain tumour."

"But doesn't kill it?" Matthias asked.

"No."

"And it's not supposed to, is it?"

"No." Lucas finished his beer. "Global pharmaceutical sales were more than $550 billion last year. Nearly half of that was in the United States alone. We're talking big money here. Sickness is an industry in this country," he said, wishing he had another drink nearby to make this go down easier. "Empirico makes more money having patients dependent on their drug for the rest of their lives than they do by selling them a cure. It involves a detailed analysis of demographics, statistics, and how much people are willing to pay. In the end it's a simple question of economics. Throw in the potential patent-breaking problem and it's an even easier decision not to release it."

Tabitha leaned forward and ran her hands through her hair. She felt sick. Queasy. She remembered that conversation with Chester about the Empirico rumours. "So if he really has the cure, he'll only release it once he figures he can make more money by healing people than he can by prolonging them?"

"And that will never happen. The modus operandi of Empirico is not about curing an illness. It's about keeping it under control and managing it as a chronic condition."

"That's unbelievable," she whispered.

"This is why we have to pressure him to give up the drug," Lucas said. "Bankrupt him. Starting tomorrow. I'll do miracles right on the Strip. Thousands. Tens of thousands will come to me instead of the Garden of Eden. Forget the showdown. I'll do it alone. Tabitha, can you get the word out to the media?"

"I'll let the networks know. We'll get full national, maybe even global."

She stood up and dialled on her cellphone as she walked to the kitchen for privacy.

Matthias took a drink from his martini. He held it in his mouth a moment and then swallowed it. "Lucas, I think there may be a way for me to make money off Caesar."

"No offence, Matthias. But your few hundred thousand a night at the tables won't make a difference."

"I agree," Matthias said. "But there's been a new development in my gaming."

"Such as?"

Matthias invited them all to spend the night at his place. Lucas left to find a room where he could pray. Matthias took a stack of cards off the table and disappeared down a hallway to practise.

As Matthias and Lucas left, Jake felt the threat of panic knocking at his door when he realized he was going to be alone with September.

"You alright, Jake?" she said.

No. No I'm not alright.

"I'm fine," he lied. "Just been a busy day."

"Need a drink?"

I'll do anything to get my mind on other things.

"Sure," he said on instinct.

Tabitha poured herself a glass of water while finishing a conversation with an exec at NBC in New York. She walked up the stairs and searched each room until she came to the end. She looked through the crack in a door and saw Lucas on his knees, praying. She listened as he quoted his verses. He stopped, and she was sure he could sense her presence. She held her breath. He turned and saw her.

She did not recognize the look in his eyes.

"I'm sorry," she said, both embarrassed and afraid. "How long will you be praying?"

"As long as it takes."

"All night?

"I might have to. I have to do whatever I can to get the power to work."

"The whole night? You plan to pray the whole night because you believe God will answer you?"

"I do."

"Then I was right."

"About what?"

"About you and me," she said. "We are too far apart."

She closed the door, walked down the stairs, and left the building. She returned to the Bellagio and continued making calls.

Jake sat across from September, listening to her talk about life in Vegas. And while he heard her words all he could think about was how much damage he had caused her. Here was this cool, easygoing, fun person who struggled to maintain her life that was ruined with drugs, alcohol and prostitution. What bothered him most was realizing that he was the root cause of it all. He couldn't go on living a lie with her. He couldn't go on not having her know what he had done. He watched as she smiled and realized that was all about to change.

It was time to speak the truth.

36

Sweat dripped off Lucas' face. He took in shallow breaths trying to draw in what little oxygen he could. The air felt cold as he knelt against the bed. He pressed his forehead against his folded hands and tried to recite his verses, tried to kick-start his memory, but found it impossible to concentrate. Reassurance. That's what he needed. He wanted to open his eyes. He wanted to look behind him. But he convinced himself to stay focused on praying for help in the empty bedroom. Besides, looking wouldn't make any difference.

He already knew there was someone behind him.

That cold breeze against his neck. Beside him. Crouched down. Whispering into his ears like some invisible force.

If you force yourself hard enough, you will accomplish it.

Leave me alone. I don't want you here.

Of course you do. Who do you think gets you through all these things?

The first account I composed, Theophilus, about all that Jesus began to do and teach.

I know what's going to happen tomorrow. I know who is going to be there.

You don't know anything. Lucas continued to recite his verses: *Until the day when He was taken up....*

I can make the road straight. I can remove every barrier for you. These people will fall down for you.

I don't want that.

But they do.

It was at least her fifth drink. September and Jake sat on the couches in the otherwise quiet room. She laughed as she told him about an incident earlier that day when a woman went mad with rage over a machine that wasn't paying out.

"This old lady goes crazy! She hits the machine and security comes running. But she grabs it with both arms and starts shaking it, yelling and swearing at it. Now get this. The machine hits the jackpot! It starts spewing out all these coins. But security won't let her have it! I mean, how's that for luck? What are the odds of *that* happening?"

Pretty close to the odds against sitting across from the man who killed your sister.

"Must be a million to one."

She put on a serious face and pointed her drink at Jake. "More. Definitely more. A million to one? Heck, you'd be surprised how easy those odds are to beat."

"September?" Jake asked. She raised and lowered her eyebrows at him. "What is your life like? I mean, what is it like to be you?"

She tilted her head to the side and crossed her legs. "Jake, has anyone ever told you how wonderful you are?"

This wasn't getting any easier. "No," he said. "It's never happened."

"Well, Jake. You are a wonderful man."

"I don't think so."

"Jake, don't sell yourself short. Come on. You are the loyalistist...the loyalerest...the loyal...." She finished a shot of rum in one incredible swig. She closed her eyes and forced it down her throat. She exhaled. "You are loyal."

"September."

She took off her socks and stood on the hardwood floor. She brought her glass to her lips. Realizing it was empty she filled it with a shot of vodka. How many was that now? He was about to tell her in a nice way to cut it off when it occurred to him she would likely be needing all the alcohol she could find to get through what he was about to say.

"I propose a toast." She raised her glass and did the best she could to stand up straight. She wobbled once to the left and then found her balance. "To Jake!" She bit her lip. "Wait. Wait. That was no good. Let me try that again." She cleared her throat. "To our dear, committed Jake. You are the best man on planet Earth." She poured it into her mouth. It burned like gasoline. She held it there, letting the fire dull her nerves, reach into her soul, and coat that part of her that from time to time came up for air. She swallowed it and on instinct turned back to reload.

She did a horrible job filling it up, spilling at least as much on the ground as she got into the glass. "Don't go anywhere," she said. "I'm not done." She leaned her head back and swore in a way that was both comical and sad.

I have to tell her.

"You are the air that I breathe."

No, no, don't say anything. Just hold it in.

"You are the sun on a perfect day." She pointed at him and spoke louder.

Besides, she's drunk. She won't get it.

"You are the dependable person on the other end of the phone!" If Matthias heard her, he chose to do nothing about it. Her behaviour wasn't anything new.

Drunk or not, she'll get it. How long can you go on lying?

"You are committed when everyone else is afraid."

Out with it.

"You are Jake. And you are my hero!" She cheered and gulped her drink. The glass fell out of her hand. It hit the hardwood floor, but didn't shatter. She collapsed on the couch, exhausted from her ordeal. She looked at Jake and threw up her hands. "Well, say something!" She laughed and rolled her eyes. "Okay, I know I didn't throw a routine in there, but I still gave you a pretty good acclamation. I deserve some kind of reply." She smiled and focused her eyes as best she could.

Jake felt the blood drain from his face. Everything felt cold. *Where was that drink? Where was a bottle? A full bottle?*

September laughed again. "Jake, what does the number one man in my world have to say?"

He found it hard to breathe. It was as though someone had clutched their hands around his throat and begun to throttle him. He swallowed and felt the uncertainty that comes before truth is declared. He forced himself to look her in the eye.

"My name is Jake Rubenstein," he said. "I killed your sister."

Lucas lifted his face from the bed. It was sopping wet. His knees ached. His back throbbed. As his eyes adjusted he tried to recall where he was. The world he had just left began to fade. The world he was now in began to consume him. He stood up and felt blood run into his legs.

It was still. Quiet. And that worried him. Where were the others? He walked down the spiral steps, listening for any hint of movement, wondering if, perhaps, the good people at Empirico had finally managed to track him down. When he turned the corner he half expected to see Caesar standing there with a cigar in one hand and a gun in the other. Instead, he saw September. Sitting on the couch. Staring ahead. No expression. A vacant gaze.

A note on the table. Jake's poor penmanship gave it away.

`MATTHIAS AND I ARE OUT. BE BACK SOON.`

"September?" he whispered, trying not to startle her. She didn't move. Her soft hair hung down around her face as though someone had messed it up and managed to make it look like a hairdresser had spent hours on it. Lucas sat down beside her. A sea of glasses on the table.

Jake was gone. That was clue number one. Something he said. Something she said. He watched her suffer in silence. Chicago. Wasn't she from Chicago? Maybe Jake knew her from somewhere. Maybe he knew their family. Maybe something happened.

Maybe something happened.

"There is no escape, is there?" she asked.

There was no life in her eyes. No spark. Even in the midst of pain there should have been some kind of light. But as he looked closer, it became apparent that her eyes were like the windows of a beautiful home that stands empty with a `For Sale` sign in the front yard.

She continued staring as though in a trance, and it made Lucas wonder if she really knew he was there. "Around and around. That's all we have. We think we get out. But we don't. We're on a bus that doesn't stop, Lucas."

That made him feel better. She recognized his presence. She looked at him. "Do you believe in the supernatural?"

"I do."

"Have you found it?"

"Yes."

"I've been looking for such a long time."

"Where have you been looking?"

She glanced up and to the right as she searched for an answer. "You want to go for a ride? I can show you my supernatural world."

Lucas agreed. Though he decided it best if he drove.

Mike stepped out of his Porsche on the top floor of the Bellagio parking area and walked into the hotel. The conservatory gave off the fragrance of flowers, not that Mike noticed. Up ahead he caught a glimpse of the front desk with its team of young international personnel. He turned into the main hallway of the casino where a man played jazz piano at a restaurant. He went through the slots area and then passed the blackjack tables on his right and a poker tournament on the other side. When he reached the end he turned left at the craps tables, went a short distance farther, then turned right and walked down the hall to the Cirque du Soleil *O* theatre. He gave his ticket to the attendant wearing a tuxedo and entered the lobby. The area was crowded with people lining up for drinks. A lady asked him if he wanted a program. But he didn't respond. His entire being stayed focused on how to get rid of one Lucas Stephens. The thought was enveloping him. Consuming him. Possessing him. And he had to find a way to clear his mind. Nothing had worked. Not the women. Not the booze. Not the rides. Perhaps *O* could do it.

Heaven knew his mind needed a break.

He passed through a set of double doors and walked down the stairs taking no notice of the incredible theatre with its light-coloured ceiling. He sat down at the front, Section 103, Row D, Seat 9, arguably one of the best in the house. Beside him sat a young man with an iron ring on his pinky finger. He noticed him studying the names of the synchronized swimmers in the program.

After introductory routines the massive red curtains opened and the show began.

He watched as the hypnotic synchronized swimmers moved together as if one body. Russian divers catapulted themselves off a swinging carriage high into the air and performed a number of flips before slicing into the water. One of them prepared to flip off a stage at roof level. The crowd shook their heads in disbelief. A guy off to Mike's left with a Dutch accent said, "No way. There's no way." Yet the diver jumped, and as he descended all Mike could think about was how he wished that could be Lucas instead, crashing down to a concrete bottom. A character dressed in black reading a newspaper came on stage and was set on fire by Hawaiian firebrand throwers. Even when another character doused him with water the man became irritated, oblivious to the flames that had engulfed him. Mike was captured by it.

And for a moment he was able to forget all about Lucas Stephens.

For a moment.

Lucas called Tabitha from his cellphone as he and September got into his Audi. He started the engine. U2's *City of Blinding Lights* played on his system. He began leaving her a voice mail as he drove out of the lot.

Just as they left, Foster and Mitchell drove in. They stopped and listened to their scanner. They heard Lucas leaving the message. The screen on their laptop showed a yellow dot indicating he was nearby.

Lucas turned off his cellphone and threw it in the back seat. The dot on Mitchell's screen disappeared. Foster looked up at the condo. No lights. No sign of any residents. Up ahead he saw a construction trailer. The light was on.

The highway from Las Vegas to Rachel is repetitive and unassuming—depending on what's going on or, more importantly, what people *think* is going on. Officially it's Nevada State Highway 375 running west of Crystal Springs. But for supernatural enthusiasts it's called The Extraterrestrial Highway.

"You saw an alien?" Lucas asked as they cruised under the starry night sky.

"Absolutely," she said with a grin. "We all did."

"On this highway?"

"Up ahead at Rachel."

"We're near Nellis Airforce Base. It must have been a military plane."

"There," she said, pointing to a restaurant up ahead. "That's where we can stop." Lucas slowed down and turned onto the gravel lot. "Turn your lights off." Lucas did. "Drive around to the back of the restaurant."

Lucas turned around the corner and found a field that stretched out as far as they could see.

"You've been here before?" Lucas asked.

"You'd be surprised how many people from town have getaway spots." She opened the door, and Lucas recalled the safe spot that Jake had on top of the Lady Luck.

As Lucas stepped out he caught a glimpse of her sniffing something off her fingernail. She shook her head and jammed a small container into her pocket. She pulled a half bottle of rum out of her jacket and climbed up on the hood of his car.

Lucas sat down beside her and looked up at the stars.

"It's strange how you have to come all the way out here to be able to see them," he said.

She nodded in agreement as she lifted the bottle and took back a swig. She offered it to Lucas. He hesitated a moment, then reached for it. He touched her hand. Her fingers felt cold and he sensed an automatic reaction to keep his hand there to warm them. But he pulled away, drank half a shot, and gave the bottle back.

"You believe in fate, Lucas? That no matter how much you try, no matter how much you hope, some things are just guaranteed to happen?"

"I don't know how much of life comes down to our decisions. Sometimes it feels like the sun shines on bad people and that it rains on good people. Sometimes it feels like the opposite."

"You ever make a mistake you wish you could take back?"

Where was that bottle?

"I do. I wish there were a lot of things I could do over."

She took a long drink. It made Lucas cringe how much was seeping into her bloodstream. It was a wonder she was still coherent.

"So Jake and I got acquainted tonight." She took another swig. "I couldn't believe it. Hearing his story. That he feels guilty for killing her."

The blood drained from Lucas' face. He felt the chill of the night air. *Killing her. Killing her.*

The combination of whatever she was sniffing and the booze she was inhaling was finally taking its toll. The peculiar tone of her voice and the slurring of her speech made Lucas feel she had entered some world far removed from the one in which he was in.

"I remember him now," she said. "Though back then he went by Jack and not Jake. He's put on weight. Doesn't look at all the way he used to. Looks beat up from the drugs." She shook her head. "Maybe guilt will do the same thing to me. Regardless, it wasn't his fault that he killed her."

"Your sister?" Lucas asked.

She nodded, then fumbled for a better grip on the bottle. She brought it to her lips and poured in a drink. "She had planned out the route she wanted to take after the wedding ceremony was done. From the church to the hotel. Simple and straightforward. A straight line is the quickest route, right?" A puzzled expression crossed her face as she recalled something. "Oh, wait. There was this one guy I was with. He was into physics. He said the shortest path was actually a curved line in space and time. Is that true?"

"I don't know," he said, wishing there was any kind of path, straight or curved, that could take him, and her, back in time and erase those events that had managed to stay with her all these years.

"I changed my sister's mind. I convinced her to take a different route to the hotel. There's this great bridge that overlooks the highway. And being the budding photographer that I was I thought it would make the perfect place to take a picture of them. They were supposed to open the sunroof of the limo and wave as they passed underneath." She paused, tears began to form, then she fought to regain control. "Oh, Jesus," she whispered and covered her mouth. "Jesus, God on the cross, what did I do? What did I do?"

She covered her eyes as if doing so could somehow prevent her from being in that theatre, seeing the movie of her life playing over and over again in her mind. But it was no use. That's the trouble with memories. You can't just get up and walk out when you've had enough.

She took a longer drink, leaned her head back, and swallowed.

"So I waited," she said. "And I waited. And I waited. I'm thinking to myself—they should be here by now. Did they get lost?" She closed her eyes. The skin around them looked grey. Her face was pale. "And it occurred to me something had gone wrong. You ever get that? Ever get that sick feeling?"

Lucas nodded his head. He'd had that before. Most recently on a plane to London.

September finished the contents of the bottle. She pulled her arm back like a pitcher and rifled it into the desert. "I know. I know. Mr. Lucas Stephens. I know." She took out that small container again and tipped out some of the white powder onto her nail. She sniffed it in and froze as though suddenly encased in carbonite like Han Solo in *The Empire Strikes Back.* She unthawed, straightened up, and slipped it back into her pocket. "I know what you're going to say," she said. "That it's not my fault."

Lucas wanted to take her back to the car, drive her to Los Angeles, get her on a plane, and bring her to a tropical beach—someplace far away where she might be able to escape her conscience.

"The guilt started the moment I saw her body at the funeral. *I did that. I did that to her.* And that feeling grew and grew. I know it's stupid to blame myself. But I can't let it go. I know the truth: If I hadn't suggested the picture from the bridge, she would be alive. That's undeniable," she said. "That's my coffin." She lit a cigarette, took a drag, held the smoke in her mouth, and then blew it out. "Her death sent my mother into depression. All her incessant wondering about why it happened. She prayed and begged God to forgive her for whatever she did to cause this. She went on a quest to understand why it happened. Oh yeah. That's a great idea. Try and figure life out. Try and figure God out. Try and figure out why she had to die. *If* she had to die. What we could have done to prevent it. Why God is angry. Why God doesn't intervene. Why God this. Why God that." She took another long puff. "I can't blame her. I was no better."

"Why did you come here?"

"Same reason lots of people come to Las Vegas, Lucas. I came to escape."

"No other plans? No photography? No nursing?"

She exhaled, feeling the disappointment of once-had dreams. "Becoming a nurse isn't in the cards."

"You don't have anything else you want to do?"

"I packed up and left my old life in search of an adventure of a different kind."

"And of all the cities in the world you picked Vegas. You think it's fate?"

"No," she said. "People's hearts are in Las Vegas long before they ever get here."

"You plan on staying?"

"It doesn't matter. Whether I leave this city or not I'll never be able to put Las Vegas behind me."

She inhaled, held the smoke in her lungs for a count of three, and breathed it out. "If you want to be someone other than who you are, this is the place to do it. This town is so fake, it's real. We have fake pyramids. Fake New York. Fake Paris. Fake love from women like me. Fake everything. And that's what attracted me to Vegas. I don't care if it's fake. It's what I want. It's what half the tourists who come here want. The thing is when you've been here as long as me you realize you can't leave. It's part of you. And the part of your life you wanted to forget by coming here? It's there with more force than ever." She sucked on her cigarette. "You know what that's like?"

Lucas wished she hadn't asked that. He recalled the panic when he and Tabitha tried unsuccessfully to perform an abortion on her sister, killing both her and the child in the process. He felt the anxiety of sitting and waiting all those hours as a six year old in the Fortunate Son Café. Then he felt those screams from his mother. Those first screams that, in retrospect, started everything. *It wasn't my fault. It wasn't my fault. I didn't mean it. I didn't mean for that to happen to him. I didn't mean for my brother....*

No! he shouted inside his head.

September finished her cigarette and flung it to the ground. "So what do you say?" she asked, looking at Lucas with eyes that were a heartbreaking blend of emptiness and pain. "You got a miracle that can wipe out somebody's past?"

"I'm still looking," he said.

"Well, you be sure to let me know if you find it."

It was an hour later when Tabitha arrived. September had since passed out. Lucas had placed her in the back seat. He stood out in the field a football throw away from the car. It was dark. He had been praying and hoped that by now he would have had some reassurance over what to do tomorrow.

"You're worried," she said when she came up beside him.

As she leaned up against him he wondered if it was safe to let down his guard and fall for her again, a woman with whom he had a maybe-yes, maybe-no relationship. He felt the soft touch of her hair. That cool black leather jacket against his arm. He breathed in the soft scent of her perfume and felt the comfort a man feels when he's in the presence of a woman who can put him at ease and make the world go away.

If only for a short while.

37

The unforgiving sun pointed down at Lucas like a judge delivering a guilty verdict. He lay on his back after his fall off the rock face with his hands outstretched, unable to feel or think. He twitched his fingers. Then his toes. He blinked. For hours he stayed there. Maybe days. Maybe longer. Time didn't exist. He lived in a state of endless pain—and with no motion of the sun it was impossible to tell how long this eternity of horror might last.

He heard a deep rumbling. He felt a tremor in the ground. The vibrations rippled through his body, shaking every part of him. With each wave he felt a surge of strength pulse into him. A burning heat passed through him. The pain dissipated.

Lucas stood up.

In the distance he saw a ridge. He had begun to walk towards it when his attention was diverted to the ground. Part of the sand near him began to move. He bent down to get a closer look. More sand began to swirl. The sun vanished behind a canopy of black clouds. Everything in his body told him to get up and run. His hands shook. He saw the face of a person, of sorts, emerge from the sand.

His throat closed up. He pulled his head back as he looked at it. The face had cut marks all over it. White worms crawled around what was left of the mangled flesh. The face opened its mouth. The eyes opened. No pupils. Suddenly, two hands burst out of the sand and grabbed Lucas around the neck. The creature tried to pull him down.

It was the strong man.

Lucas smashed his fist into the mess of blood and slithering critters. He jerked his body back and broke free from the strong man's clutches. He stumbled backward. The strong man stepped out of his grave. Lucas searched the ground and found a rock. He picked it up, took aim, and hurled it at his assailant. The rock ripped through the air and struck the strong man in the forehead with such force it sank into his skull.

The strong man wobbled from the impact and then regained his balance. He stared at Lucas with those lifeless eyes, then reached into the scabbard behind his back and pulled out a machete. He screamed a horrible yell and ran after him.

Lucas tripped and fell to the ground. The strong man raised his machete over his head. Lucas watched as the steel blade sliced down towards his neck.

He heard a whistling sound in the air. Much too high-pitched to be the machete. An arrow pierced through the strong man's hand. A second and third arrow followed, striking him above and below the first arrow. He dropped his weapon. A fourth arrow smashed through his wrist and tore his hand clear off his body.

A series of arrows flooded his chest cavity. An arrow pierced through the back of his head and exploded out his mouth. The strong man closed his eyes and dropped to his knees. Lucas scrambled out of the way as the body pounded into the ground beside him. Dozens of black crows descended on his body and consumed what remained of his flesh.

The sand opened and swallowed him.

Behind him Lucas heard the rumbling sound approaching. He crawled towards the cliff. Lay down on his chest. Peered over the edge.

And saw what was causing the roaring, marching sound.

Lucas woke from his bed on the ground in the desert. It was still black outside. He turned over and leaned on his knees and elbows, praying for God to somehow release him from this unbearable anxiety. He stayed that way for an hour until his cellphone rang.

"Hello?"

"Lucas, it's Edgar."

"Edgar?" he said, wanting to shut this thing off for fear that someone, i.e., Mitchell, Foster and Co., might be tracking him. "I can't talk. Can we meet somewhere?"

"You have to hear this and then I'm gone," Edgar said from a pay phone outside a T-shirt store across from the Garden of Eden.

"Gone?"

"No matter what happens. No matter what I tell you, you can't come near me. Not for any reason."

"Edgar, what's going on?"

"It's all true, Lucas. Everything. Everything Claire told you is true."

The line went dead. A rush of fear swept over him. Lucas returned to the car and saw September sacked out in the back. Tabitha was fast asleep in the front. He wished he could feel the same connection with her as he had with Jake and Edgar. He wished he could hold her hand and feel the confidence a man feels when he is united in purpose with the right woman. But the longer he looked at her the more apparent it became. He believed. And she did not.

She was right.

They were too far apart.

Edgar stood under a dark sky on Cathedral Way looking at the Guardian Angel Cathedral. He'd been there an hour. Standing. Watching. Waiting. Hoping. The faint lights did a perfect job in welcoming people through its doors. But for a man dying of cancer, unsure of who he was or what he had spent his life believing, lights would not be enough to overcome the walls in his soul.

He heard footsteps behind him. His normal reaction would have been to turn around, especially this late in the evening. But somehow he didn't need to. He knew who it was. He could *feel* who it was.

"It's hard to go in, isn't it?" Caesar said. He wore a black leather trench coat, black suit, blue shirt, and had his hair slicked back.

"I'm no longer sure what the point is."

"Of life?"

"Of going to church."

"You're not getting the answers you need?"

"I'm not sure I deserve them."

"That's the problem," Caesar said. "We don't get what we need and then we wonder if we're condemned to make life work on our own." He noticed Edgar shiver in the cold. He took off his coat to put around his shoulders.

"No, thank you," Edgar said. But Caesar didn't listen.

"It's okay, Edgar."

"I don't want it."

"But you need it, Edgar. It's my gift to you. Regardless."

Regardless. That world felt like a hundred coats on Edgar's back. He put his arms into the sleeves.

"Thank you," Edgar said, and braced himself for what would follow.

"The world isn't a fair place, is it?"

"Was it meant to be?"

"That's good," Caesar smiled. "You theologians and your insights. Was it meant to be?" Caesar thought a moment and nodded his head. "Yes, Edgar. I would say at some point it was meant to be fair. But those days are long since gone. And perhaps God with it."

"Do you think God is still involved in the world?"

"I don't know, Edgar. I'm no longer able to distinguish between God and chance."

"Because of your life?"

"No, Edgar. Because of yours. Well, mine too. But I've long since put to bed trying to understand the God-probability relationship in my life." He looked at the mural on the church. "Though it does sometimes give you that desire again."

"A desire to communicate with God?"

"A desire to want an explanation. That's where I went wrong."

"Do you blame God?"

"Would it help?"

Edgar felt the impossible distance between him and God. Straight line or curved, there was no shortest route. "I've lost communication with God and I don't know how to get it back."

"Would you want to?"

"I do."

"Edgar, we have a more pressing matter at hand." He turned to face him. "You have an ailment and I have an enemy who is trying to destroy me. I think we can help each other."

"You propose to trade the drug for Lucas?"

"Imagine that you hold the key to releasing a cure for your disease."

"Why wouldn't you put it on the market regardless?"

"You don't understand my business. But you do understand Lucas. So I suggest you get those theologian brains of yours to invite Lucas to a quiet, out-of-the-way place. Then I will put the drug on the open market."

"This isn't fair," Edgar said.

"Of course it isn't," Caesar replied. "It's Las Vegas."

Matthias and Jake hurried through the Mayan parking garage. They looked over their shoulders, hoping not to find any laser beams attached to firearms searching the area to take them down. Lydda's voice on the phone sounded more than panicked. She was downright horrified.

Jake knocked on an unmarked door. A tall man opened it and pointed them down a hallway. They reached the end and found another door. He knocked again and the stocky security guard Matthias had seen before opened the door.

Matthias and Jake walked into a dimly lit room. Matthias could make out Lydda with Zack Roman beside her. "Alright. Let's have it."

"I can't say it any plainer than this," Zack said. Matthias held his breath. This was not good. It was Lydda's place. *Why wasn't she speaking?* "Caesar is onto me. He's probably onto you as well. So all bets are off. We split the money we've made down the middle like we agreed."

Matthias swore. "We're just getting started!"

"We're finished, kid."

"Don't release my name."

"I have to."

"Give me time."

"You're on your own."

"Do I have your word that you won't release my name?" He was about to call him Mr. Roman. Anything to get this last request out. "Do I?"

"No! You're not going back to Vegas!" Tabitha said as she took the keys out of the ignition. "I'm taking you out of here!"

"You can't."

"Lucas. Leave. Leave this city. Please."

"I've called the police. They're giving me an escort into Las Vegas."

"Do you remember what happened the last time you had a police escort into a city?"

"We'll pick up Jake on the way in," Lucas said. "It's time to decide, Tabitha. Are you with me?"

Lucas took a moment to steady his nerves. He had prayed as much as he could about the healings and about Caesar. He had thought it through as much as possible. This was it. It was do or die.

But preferably do.

"He'll be here in ten minutes," Mike said, entering a private office in one of their nightclubs. "The Strip. Knowing Lucas he'll pick a spot right in front of us." His face was flushed. His hair messy. He'd been up all night thinking of a way to get rid of Lucas. And the longer he thought about it, the more he wished he had pulled the trigger when he had the chance.

Caesar looked through the one-way mirror down to the massive dance floor. Hundreds of scantily clad women and still more drunk men strobed in and out of view. Dance music reverberated through the floor beneath them. "Lucas," Caesar whispered to himself. "Why are you coming back?"

"We have to take him out."

Caesar stepped away from the glass. "This isn't going how I had planned."

People shouted as the police escort drove Lucas and Jake down Las Vegas Boulevard. Thousands packed the sidewalks and spilled out onto the street as they passed. Lucas glanced out the window at the masses. He wished Tabitha was with him. Wished she hadn't gone with September to pick up Matthias. She promised she would catch up with him. Meet him on the Strip. He wondered about her sudden strange decision not to join him in the cruiser. Perhaps she knew something, felt something, that warned her against it.

Jake sat beside him feeling every bit as nervous as the last time they had done this. People banged on the cruiser, begging him to stop. His stomach felt weak. His mind refused to settle down. *Caesar knows I'm coming here. He's got a shooter in the crowd. A Lee Harvey Oswald type. Waiting for me.*

The cruiser stopped in front of the Garden of Eden. A police officer opened the door for him. The crowd went crazy. People screamed and pressed against the row of police officers, begging for a chance to be touched by Lucas. Jake stepped out first. Those who didn't know better thought he was the miracle man and shouted to get his attention.

Then Lucas stepped out. The bright sunlight blinded him like a flash grenade going off right in front of him. When his eyes adjusted he saw a figure crouched on the roof of the T-shirt store across the street. Then another one on the building beside. They drew their rifles. In front of him he saw the Oswald-type walk through the crowd. He made it to the police line and no farther, but that was close enough. *Here he comes. Somebody stop him. Someone.* But no one reacted. At least not in time. The man pulled out a small six-shooter. It wasn't fancy but it was enough to do the job. He aimed his gun at Lucas and fired. Bang. Bang. Bang. The riflemen began their assault and rained ammunition on Lucas. There would be no mistake this time. Bullets ripped into his torso, jerking him left and right. Lucas stopped hearing the shots after the seventh bullet struck him in the eye.

"Boss?" Jake asked.

"I'm alright," Lucas said, his eyes adjusting to the sun. No one on the rooftops. Oswald-type wasn't anywhere to be seen in the crowd.

"No, you're not. You're doing this for an hour and then you're finished."

Finished. Finished, Lucas thought.

If only he could be so lucky.

Caesar met Mayor Gibbs in a sectioned-off area of the parking garage under the Garden. He did what he could to maintain his composure. What he wanted to do was reach out and throttle Gibbs. Kill him right there in his own building.

"Whose side are you on?" Caesar asked.

"Side? You really *are* new." Gibbs was taller than Caesar, had a pockmarked face, and never smiled.

Caesar swore at him. "And don't give me that. It's simple. Every casino in this city is losing money."

"People vote me in, Caesar. Not casinos. Besides, even though the houses are hurting, you're the one wanting to stop him. To kill him. I've had zero complaints from them."

"Who said anything about killing Lucas?"

"Don't pretend."

"Do I have your commitment or don't I?"

"I can't give you Lucas Stephens."

"What kind of town do you run here?"

"I don't want you in Las Vegas."

"I don't care."

Gibbs got into his silver Mercedes and drove off. Caesar spit and walked into the building. At his office he dialled his old pal Senator Turtle. Perhaps the good senator had had a change of mind seeing how it was time for re-election and Lucas, the poster boy, was nowhere near Chicago.

Person after person came to Lucas. Children. Seniors. Married. Single. Educated. Dropouts. Rich. Poor. They came to him with every kind of sickness and went away healed.

Next came a little girl with a club foot. She was so marred by the beatings from her alcoholic mother that it made it difficult for Lucas to look at her face. She hobbled up the makeshift stage to him and tripped as she approached. Cameras caught her every move.

Lucas laid his hands on her. He prayed and waited for the rush of heat to flood his body. He felt nothing. So he continued praying. The first few seconds came and went. No power. No impulse. No reassurance. He prayed again. The crowd became restless. Thirty seconds. Nothing. He said his verses louder. His pulse quickened. A minute. An entire minute. Still nothing. Reporters commented. Cameras zoomed in closer. Two minutes. People waited. Anxiously. Five whole minutes. Eternity. Still nothing.

"Boss?" Jake asked.

He bent down and touched her feet. Still nothing. His hands felt dead. Cold as ice in the warm Vegas afternoon. He felt his body drain as though someone had siphoned the blood right out of him.

Kneeling there at her feet he suddenly became aware of who he had become. He recognized this person. He recognized this feeling. Like how he felt before he was in prison. Like how he felt before he left for China.

Like how he felt before he had the gift.

"I'm sorry," he said to the little girl. She looked at him, feeling the embarrassment of putting everything on the line and getting nothing in return.

Jake led her down the stairs in the same condition as when she went up.

Then came a man in his thirties wheeled in by his aging mother. He had lost a significant amount of weight. His hands were bent in. Saliva dripped out one side of his mouth.

He pushed himself out of the wheelchair and forced himself up onto the first step.

"Wait," Lucas said, getting off the platform and walking down the stairs to him. He met the man at the bottom and did his best to control his fear. He laid his hands on the man's greasy, sweaty head and prayed for him. But the verses felt hollow in his mouth. Like a foreign language. He may as well have been repeating some childhood rhyme. He finished and looked at the man.

No change.

Reporters fired questions at him. "Is something wrong? Why isn't he better?" This was news. It went global in an instant. Every major news station had him. Lucas the miracle worker who could heal thousands, Mr. Healermania himself, made headlines around the world.

"Can't you help me?" the man whispered.

"I don't care how you do it! You get him. You find a way to take him out!" Caesar screamed into the phone.

Turtle leaned forward on his desk at his home in Chicago. It was getting close to re-election. The coffers were dwindling. The competition rising. A 60-year-old mother of 10 and committed wife, who just happened to be an all-star crown prosecutor, had won the unlikely opposition party race and was competing against him. Advertising. That's what Turtle needed. And that was going to cost money. Lots of money.

Caesar's kind of money.

"He's in Vegas!"

"So?"

"So how does a senator from Illinois do anything about an icon in Vegas?"

"Talk to the guys here in town. Find something!"

"I can't," Turtle said. "I'm sorry."

Re-election or not, his wife's cryptic warning about harming Lucas never left him. He wasn't prepared to go against her advice. Not for the sake of his position. Not for the sake of helping Caesar.

And certainly not for the sake of harming Lucas.

Caesar stormed down the hallway. He was about to smash open the doors to the Council chambers when Mike called to him from his office.

"You have to see this."

Caesar noticed the shock on Mike's face. He turned into his office. A television showed a blonde reporter speaking while Lucas prayed for the sick in the background. "They say all good things must come to an end," the reporter began. "But tragic for millions, if indeed that's the case for Lucas Stephens."

Caesar's bad day had just become a whole lot brighter.

"Get me out of here," Lucas said. Jake led him to a police cruiser. Tabitha tried to follow, as did September and Matthias. But the cruiser drove off through the crowd as reporters raced after him to get a comment.

Lucas hyperventilated.

"Where are we going, sir?" the driver asked.

"Just go!" Lucas screamed. All those people. Standing. Waiting. Expecting him to come through for them. Lucas buried his face in his hands.

"Boss?" Jake said. "What happened?"

Lucas couldn't reply.

He was having enough trouble dealing with it himself.

38

The first plan was to go to September's house, but like most plans this one was subject to change. Lucas wanted, needed, someplace different. Someplace far removed from what he had already experienced. So when they got off the Strip Lucas and Jake stepped out of the police cruiser and into Tabitha's car. They drove for an hour until the highway became quiet. Until it felt like Vegas was truly behind him. The road looked dead on either side.

"Drop me off here," Lucas said.

Tabitha looked in the rear-view mirror and then turned around to see him.

"Stop the car!" he shouted, and then regretted raising his voice at her.

She nodded her head, giving a soft "Okay" as she put on her blinker, trying hard not to show how much his words had cut into her.

The car hadn't come to a complete stop when Lucas opened the door and stepped out. Just before he slammed it shut he told them not to come after him. He walked across the ditch into the desert. The setting sun made him into a perfect silhouette, the lone figure walking into nothingness.

He covered his face and felt himself begin to crumble under the pressure. *Why is this happening? It's just for a moment. It'll come back.* But he felt more than exhausted.

He felt vacated.

He dropped to his knees and pulled his hands away from his face. They felt dead to him. No fire. No electricity.

No power.

"I'm not leaving him out there," Tabitha said.

"He needs his space," Jake replied.

He needs me.

Tabitha opened the door.

"Don't go, Tabitha."

But she left the car and walked out to him.

Lucas heard footsteps coming up behind him. If it was Jake, he'd ream him out for not realizing he needed his space. If it was Tabitha, he'd wonder how she would react to his state.

She stopped behind him and worried that her next move might push them even farther apart. She searched for the right words to say, the right way to say them. She knelt down beside him. She felt his fear. His unrest. His struggle to find direction.

"I need your help," he said. "I need you to find a hospital. Not in Vegas. Someplace out of the way. I need to find a group of sick children to pray for."

"Lucas, we've just been through this."

He placed his hands together and brought them to his nose. "Right now the media knows it failed. But they don't know it's gone. Not for sure." He closed his eyes. "But I have to know. And I have to know in private."

They waited in silence. Then she went back to the car, feeling the uncertainty of realizing that as soon as she had drawn close to him, he had sent her away.

The location of the hospital was perfect. Away from Las Vegas. Away from the lights. Away from the media.

A security guard met them at the door. Tall. Black. Dark blue uniform. He looked at Lucas for a moment and then showed them in. "Follow me." He led them down a corridor and turned left into a room. Six children. Lying on beds. No hair. Still. "The nurse comes back on her rotation in five minutes. If you want this a secret, be gone by then."

Lucas entered. Jake followed him. Tabitha watched from the doorway.

"This doesn't feel right," Lucas whispered.

"Since when does feeling have anything to do with it?"

Lucas breathed in the chill air. He swallowed and tried to find the courage that once came so easily to him.

"Are you the man on TV?" a faint voice asked.

He turned his head in the direction of the voice. He saw a young boy. Maybe ten. Hard to tell without any hair.

"My name is Lucas."

The boy smiled. Relieved. His eyes grew wide. He took off his covers. Lucas placed his hands on the boy's bald head. He recited his verses and waited, counting on God to come through.

Lucas reached the fifth verse. That was a problem. It never took that long. Next, he could hear people around him. That was the second indication. Normally the world around him disappeared. Here, he heard the children. Heard them talking. Heard them wondering. Heard them worrying.

He heard the boy's thoughts and felt his anticipation turn to anxiety.

Lucas opened his eyes. No hair growth. No stubble. Nothing. No burning sensation in his hands. No assurance that power had gone out from him.

"Am I better?" the boy asked.

The door opened. It was Tabitha. "Wrap it up, Lucas. The nurse is coming."

The other children climbed out of bed and crowded around him. They knew the dream had come true for them. It was now within their reach.

Or at least it should have been.

Lucas laid his hands on another boy. He felt nothing but ice. He quoted his verses. They felt heavy, like having to listen to a song played too often on the radio that was once a great hit, but has now become irritating and annoying.

"Now, Lucas!" Tabitha said. Jake tugged on his arm.

"It has to work!" Lucas prayed for another boy. Zip. A girl. Still nothing.

"Lucas! The nurse is coming. If she sees you, she will contact the media."

Jake grabbed Lucas and forced him to leave. Lucas saw the painful expression in the first boy's eyes. So hollow. So disappointed. And it made Lucas sick.

They left the room and hurried down the hallway. The children ran out to bring him back. The nurse heard the commotion and called out to them.

Lucas broke into a jog. The children chased after him, shouting out his name, begging for help to get off their one-way train headed for a dead end.

The trio ran out of the hospital and hurried into Tabitha's car. The children burst through the doors, screaming for him to stop. He gritted his teeth and waited those anxious moments for the car to move. The young boy caught up to him. He put his hand on the window, wishing that touch would be enough to get him healed. Lucas watched him as the car drove off, leaving him barefoot in the cold parking lot, his bald head unmistakable in the night sky, with an expression that conveyed he neither understood his illness nor why his only hope was now driving away from him.

Lucas closed his eyes. All he heard the entire ride back was that terrible sound of the children pleading for his help. All he saw was that boy's painful eyes. And all he felt was the weight of despair—that everything he had given his life for had fallen down around him.

Lucas and Jake stood at the fence in September's yard looking out at the unpredictable evening. They hadn't said anything in such a long time that it seemed they might just wait for the sunrise to break their silence.

"So what does this mean?" Jake asked. "Is it finished? Are we done?"

"No, we're not done!" Lucas said with so much force he regretted it as soon as the words came out. "I'm sorry."

"We'll figure this out," Jake replied, giving his friend a pat on the back. He turned to go, having that rare wisdom friends have when they know it's time to leave.

"There's nothing to figure out," Lucas said to himself. "The power is gone."

It was only a few minutes later when the panic attack hit him. What started as the inklings of a headache turned into a sudden unbearable pressure. At first it seemed like he was losing his balance. Like everything around him was moving. Then it became difficult to concentrate. All he saw was Caesar's face glaring at him. He closed his eyes to get rid of the image, but it did nothing to help.

Matthias came out with two bottles of beer. He held one out to Lucas who didn't respond. "Lucas?"

He turned to Matthias and took the drink. The world stopped spinning. "It feels different," Lucas said, trying to get his mind on other things. "I don't know how to get Caesar. I don't know how to pin him down." He took a drink of his beer. "I'm tired of thinking."

Lucas saw Matthias rubbing a pair of red dice in his hands. Faster and faster he twisted them back and forth. It mesmerized him, drawing him in as though there was some secret code in the rotation of numbers.

"I thought you were strictly cards," Lucas said.

"I am. But cards bend too easy in your fingers when you're nervous." He looked at Lucas with the same cold pale expression he had when they met on Flight 912 to London. "Do you feel it? You feel the same weight of premonition about what's going to happen? You feel the disaster that's on the horizon, don't you? What do you think? Do we make it out this time? Maybe just one of us? Maybe neither? Tell me, Lucas. Can you feel it?"

Lucas heard the grinding sound of the dice against each other. "You want my theory on why you didn't get off the plane?" he asked. Matthias stopped twisting them. "The plane took off from Chicago. It stopped in New York on its way to London. I only had the feeling it was going down after we left the Big Apple. But you had it before. That's why September got off. But you stayed on. And now I know why."

"Don't play this game, Lucas."

"Why does a man stay on a plane that he knows is going to crash?"

"I'm warning you."

"Why wouldn't you get off?"

"Don't do this."

"It's because you wanted to die."

Hearing those words coming from someplace other than his own mind brought Matthias a welcome peace. There was something freeing about not having to shoulder that secret anymore.

"You wanted it to be over," Lucas said. "You have some kind of mission you're avoiding in London. What is it, Matthias? What's in London?"

Matthias didn't answer. He looked out over the fence. He started rubbing the dice again.

"Then you play cards. You memorize them, really. You play cards all the time. When you aren't gambling, you're practising. And when you're not practising, you sleep. With the lights on. That's your life. Sleep and gambling. But it's not about the gambling, is it, Matthias? The gambling has nothing to do with it. It's just an attempt to get your mind off what you're supposed to be doing."

Matthias stopped twisting the dice. "Empirico put me on an experimental drug called Fi-li. Trouble was it had brutal side effects. Screwed up my brain. Left me petrified of the dark."

"Fi-li. I know that test drug. It was supposed to help people who have hallucinations or hear voices," Lucas said, piecing this together. "You tried it for the same reason you memorize cards. To clear your mind. That's why you memorize cards and gamble, isn't it? To get your mind off whatever it was that was taking you to London."

In a violent show of emotion, Matthias turned to Lucas and cursed so hard at him that Lucas felt the blast of air.

"And you've come to use your blackjack skills to make a whack of money off Caesar, not only as a vendetta, but more so that you can set yourself up in some fancy condo and stay far away from London. Tell me, Matthias. What's in London?"

"You have a gift."

"I *had* a gift."

"Healing helps people. It takes sick people and makes them well. When people came to you they were guaranteed good news."

Lucas studied Matthias' eyes. There was something frightening in them. Matthias leaned closer. "What if you had a different gift? A different calling? What if on your shoulders was placed the burden not to heal people but to...."

"To what?"

Matthias gave Lucas his dice. "Keep these."

"They're yours."

"Keep them as a reminder."

"Of what?"

Matthias finished his bottle and threw it over the fence into the ditch. He turned to leave and looked at Lucas. "Of the way the world used to be."

Lucas heard steps approaching behind him. "It's bad news, isn't it?" he asked.

"The children from the hospital," Tabitha said. "It's all over the media. The world knows your power is gone."

Lucas closed his eyes. "I have to find a way to take Caesar out."

"Do you feel called to take on Caesar or to heal people?"

"It doesn't matter. Without the healing gift I can't help people and I have no collateral against Caesar."

"How do you know?"

He lifted his hands palm up to her. "Because these are as good as dead."

The Empirico entertainment suite on the 99th floor of the Garden of Eden was awash with women and expensive suits. The news of Lucas' demise was only two hours old, but that was enough time for Caesar to organize an all-out bash. He walked through the crowd, clanging glasses and kissing dancers. Claire tried her best to look happy, feeling that she was the single person in the crowd of Council members who wished Lucas was still able to heal.

Mike caught up with Caesar on his way up the stairs. "That's fate for you!" Caesar said. "Most days it is totally against you. But other days it surprises you and comes through."

"The hospital confirms he was there."

"Of course he was there. And he failed. He fell right flat on his face." They walked into Caesar's office. "But his loss is your gain. And now we hunt him down and root him out once and for all."

"We have to decide how we're going to take him on," Lucas said. Tabitha and Jake sat on a couch, Matthias in a chair, September leaned against a table.

"Don't do this," Tabitha warned. "You don't have anything to fight him with."

"That's what I have to ensure."

"You already have it confirmed," she said, rising to her feet. "If you go, he could pull you back into Empirico. Is that what you want?"

"Tabitha."

"Why are you pretending to be able to take him on with nothing?"

"I know that I have to go."

"This is stupid. You're going because inside you hope he will take you back and give you your old life."

Lucas looked over the group. Tabitha became anxious. "I'm going," he said. "Who's with me?"

39

Lucas turned off Las Vegas Boulevard and drove into the Garden of Eden parking garage. He found a spot on Level E, Row 7 and let the engine idle, hoping for a sudden rush of courage to help him combat Caesar. Jake sat still beside him, looking out ahead, wanting to say something, but unsure if this was the right moment.

"I'm afraid," Jake admitted.

Lucas took in a breath. This wasn't helping. "What are you afraid of?"

Jake turned to face him. "I'm afraid of losing you. I'm afraid that someday you might join Caesar and take over his empire. That someday you and I will become enemies."

"You're not going to lose me, Jake."

"You think he'll just let you go knowing there's a possibility the gift may return?"

"I have to face him, Jake. I have to know if God has called it quits on me."

"What happened at the Fortunate Son Café?"

A sting of adrenaline ran through Lucas' body. He felt a pain in his fingers. He gripped the steering wheel for support, closed his eyes, and let out a deep breath to calm himself.

"I met with Caesar."

"No. The first time you were there. Caesar wouldn't have suggested a place like that without a reason."

Lucas reached down to the console and picked up the dice Matthias had given him. "My mother took me there."

"Where was your father?"

"He left."

"Left?"

"After my brother died."

"How did your brother die?"

Lucas clutched the steering wheel with such intensity his fingers turned white. The dice dug into his palm, but he did not feel it.

"It wasn't my fault," Lucas said.

"Nobody's saying it was."

"It wasn't my…." Lucas let out a gasp. But like a good soldier, or a man who has learned not to deal with the past, he clenched his teeth and forced himself to stay under control.

"Was he older or younger?"

"Younger," came Lucas' faint reply. His hands began to shake. The trembling worked its way through his wrists and into his arms.

"How did he die?"

Lucas shook his head. That wasn't coming out. The truth would not be revealed. Not again. Not to anyone.

Least of all not to himself.

"Why did your mother bring you to the Fortunate Son Café?"

"To get gas and something to drink." A tear fell from his eye. Then another. "I wanted to stay and help her. I can do that for you, Mom. I can hold the nozzle. I'm big enough. But she took me to the restaurant and told me to sit down while she gassed up. I watched her at the pump. The waitress came to take my order. When I looked back, the car was gone."

"She never came back."

"No."

"Why didn't she come back?"

Lucas shook his head.

"Lucas, why didn't your mother come back?"

"Because I wasn't good enough," he said.

"That's not true."

"I should never have…."

"It's okay, Lucas."

"I should never have...."

"You don't have to try to undo what's happened."

"It's my fault."

"This isn't about fault."

Lucas closed his eyes. "My brother. Tabitha's sister and child. Losing the healing gift. All my fault."

Lucas struggled to regain control. Jake waited, wishing there was some way he could hit a button and eject those memories from Lucas' mind. Wishing there was a delete key that would erase all the damage the past had done. Wishing there was some override command that could set everything right—if not for himself, then at least for his friend.

They waited in silence. When Jake thought the moment was right he responded.

"I used to try so hard to fix all those things I had done wrong in my life. Tried to patch up all the holes. But it didn't work. My guess is that even if I could pay back ten times, a thousand times, what I screwed up, it still wouldn't make it better."

Lucas let go of the steering wheel and wiped the tears from his eyes. He turned to Jake. "So how do I get out?"

A black suburban slammed on the brakes behind them. Doors opened. Mitchell and Foster hurried out. Mike came up behind them. Foster opened Lucas' door.

"Caesar wanted me to welcome you personally," Mike said.

"That's great. I haven't been through the gaming area since it opened." Lucas stepped out of the car. He walked beside Mike, flanked on either side by Mitchell and Foster. Jake got out and followed them.

"We won't be going through the gaming area," Mike said. "There's a private elevator that will take you to Caesar."

The doors opened at the top floor. Lucas followed Mike. He heard waterfalls and the rushing sound of the river. He saw the massive tree amid the sea of chairs and tables. No people.

They walked up the stairs to Caesar's office. Mike opened the door and Lucas took a step forward. Jake was about to follow, but Mike stopped him.

"No one else."

Lucas entered and Mike closed the door behind him.

Caesar sat at his desk. His eyes had a hint of grey around them, tired from his victory party. "That's the thing about this town," Caesar said. "Your luck can change in an instant."

"You told me you knew the key to Las Vegas. That it was built on one characteristic of human nature."

"You're a good listener."

"Which characteristic?"

"Give away my secret?" Caesar smiled. "Let me offer you a drink."

He poured them each a glass of bourbon from his bar. Lucas took a drink and held it in his mouth, letting it burn against his gums before swallowing it.

"Now that you've had a chance to feel Vegas out, what's your impression of it?"

"A city of extremes," Lucas said. "Some people enjoy Vegas for what it is. They control the city, so to speak. Others are controlled by it."

"And it's that second category that keeps this Strip humming. Those are the big spenders. And they share a common trait, Lucas. Most of them don't even know it. This city is so good at appearance that some people are oblivious to why they really come here."

"So what attracts them?"

Caesar finished his drink in one gulp. He put the glass on the counter and looked down at the Strip beneath him. "This town is built on misery," he said. "That's why Vegas will never die."

"Misery? I would have thought adventure."

Caesar shook his head. "It's escapism at its best. What happens in Vegas stays in Vegas. This town is entombed in a fog of secrets. The lonely housewives who don't get any attention from their husbands? Two or three of them get together and say they're going to Phoenix or L.A. Except they come down here instead and get a taste of what they're missing. Then they keep coming back. Not even because they want to. They think they want to. But that's not what's happening. They're just looking for a way to get rid of the loneliness. They've tasted the fruit of Vegas. It gets in their blood. Who cares about the cost? Who cares if it's real or not? People want to believe their lives can be different. And Vegas is their place. An eternal bond between city and person. That's why the lights are so bright on the Strip."

"I'm not following you."

"The lights prevent you from seeing what's really here. It makes me wonder what would happen to people if someone shut off the power. I wonder what people would think? Maybe their emptiness would suddenly become apparent."

"Has your emptiness become apparent?"

"This isn't about me."

"You kill me, Caesar. You think you can see through this city? Misery and lights and emptiness? You're the one who has built this massive fortress of a casino because you're scared people will see through *you.* You're in Vegas because you're running from your conscience. Chicago wouldn't hide it for you. And you think Vegas will. But you're wrong."

"This isn't about right and wrong either. It's about your future."

"You are going to release that drug."

"Based on what? Your impotent healing abilities? Your threat against Empirico is over. Just like I told you it would happen. You're finished. It's time to move on. It's time to move up."

Lucas pulled out his dice. "I'm not joining you."

"Open your eyes. This is all for you, Lucas. The empire is for you. Not Mike. Not Claire. No one but you."

"If I'm ever standing where you are, I will consider my life a waste."

Caesar's face turned to anger. He did his best to hide it, to control himself. "Get out," he said. He had a gun in the top drawer. He could get there before Lucas could leave.

"I've come to warn you."

"Warn me? Warn me? You come into my casino! Into my office! You have nothing and you're going to warn me?"

What do I do?

"You warn me?"

This is it. Do or die.

"Doesn't that just sound stupid in your own ears, Lucas?"

Do or die.

"It's beyond pathetic, Lucas. Embarrassing."

Lucas pulled out the red dice and rolled them down the counter. They hit Caesar's empty glass and turned up with a two and a one.

"Dice? You are attacking me with dice?"

"Release the drug."

"I don't have it."

"I'm not here for games."

"Goodbye, Lucas."

Caesar's eyes were cold and steady. Yet the longer Lucas looked at them he thought he could make out a hint of uncertainty.

"You're going to wish you hadn't turned this down."

"You are not in a position to argue."

"Remember those words, Caesar."

Lucas walked out of the room. Jake followed him as they went down the stairs and into the elevator. Jake hit the button. They waited those anxious moments for the doors to close.

Caesar picked up Lucas' dice. He held them in his hand and squeezed them as hard as he could. His fist began to shake. His face flushed. He hurled the dice against the wall. They smacked against the glass blocks. Then, in a strange bounce, they came right back and stopped in front of him. He looked down at the count.

A two and a one.

The doors closed and the elevator began its descent.

"What's going on?" Jake asked.

"This, my friend, is where the fun begins."

40

When they reached the bottom floor Jake stepped out first, hoping to protect Lucas should someone be waiting for them. He clenched his hands into fists and turned right towards the parking garage.

"Not that way," Lucas said. Jake turned around. "Through the casino."

Colour came back to Jake's face. "Right. A crowded place."

Lucas walked to a sea of slot machines. No empty chairs. People of all types faithfully pushed away at the buttons. Elderly, young, thin, fat, men, women, rich, poor, healthy, sick, good-looking, haggard. A young man with a loosened tie, exhausted eyes, his jacket hanging on the side of the machine, looking like he'd been there for hours, studied the shapes as they spun in front of him, oblivious to the two teens in short skirts beside him laughing as they lost money, trying to figure out how the game worked.

Lucas slowed down as he passed them. Jake nearly bumped into him as he felt the pressure of those eyes in the sky watching their every move. No doubt the people operating the cameras had spotted them and were directing Mitchell and Foster to the entrance from which they would be leaving.

"Let's go," Jake said, his tone sounding panicked and angry.

"You ever get the feeling your luck is about to change?" Lucas asked.

Suddenly, the young man's machine went crazy. The lights on top turned on and flashed like a police cruiser. A siren went off. Blaring and loud. The teens cheered. The one nearest put her arm around him. Coins poured out. The first few dozen clanged into the tray, then the steady stream grew into a mountain and began to overflow. The young man grabbed a container. The teen bent over and cupped her hands around the dish to help filter the money towards him. A casino employee came with two more buckets to scoop up the ones that had spilled onto the floor.

The crowd grew bigger around the machine, as though the pull of good fortune had a way of insinuating that those nearby could tap into it as well.

Lucas stepped to the side, hoping to go before the crowd realized who he was. But just as he was leaving the next machine went off. This one even louder than the first. The teens screamed. They covered their mouths and looked with amazement as the coins spilled out of the machine. Still more people crowded around. Another casino attendant arrived.

One of the plainclothes security officers spoke into his microphone. Two machines side by side going off with the jackpot? No way. There was absolutely no way that was on the level.

Which is why he knew something had gone terribly wrong when the entire row of slots lit up.

Lucas walked to the end, and with every step the machines on either side of him showed three sevens or three bananas or three of whatever it took to make the slot sing. Lucas turned down the aisle. As he passed each row, every slot machine went crazy. It sounded like a brigade of fire engines screaming into the casino. People covered their ears at the shrill sound, yet when their own machines lit up they found the resolve to grab onto buckets and cash in.

Pandemonium broke loose. People screamed with excitement. More security personnel shouted into their microphones. Every step Lucas took set off a row of machines and the *pang*, *pang*, *pang* of the coins against the metal dishes.

He pushed through the crowd and walked to the card tables. Every person playing blackjack began to win. The house busted on each hand.

Matthias heard the commotion on the fifth level. He looked down and saw Lucas passing by slots on his right and tables on his left. Like a wave of fortune, every step he took made those around him win.

And, best of all, he was headed Matthias' way.

Matthias grabbed his chips and dumped them as best he could into a bucket. He had been playing well at blackjack and was up a hundred grand on his starting point of 13. He hurried into the baccarat area, spilling chips on his way over.

Caesar was working at his desk when he received the phone call. The floor manager was frantic on the other end, begging his permission to shut the whole thing down.

"Shut what down?" Caesar asked.

"The casino! Shut everything down! Every machine is paying out the max. Every table is losing. You have to shut it down!"

Caesar cursed and gave the order to halt all gaming operations. Every second was costing him hundreds of thousands. "Get everybody out. I want the casino cleared!"

Matthias hurried past the last of the blackjack tables to a gold roped-off area. A small well-built Chinese man wearing a tuxedo stood in front of a black curtain. He looked like the villain in *Goldfinger*—same suspicious smile, but no attack hat. The Chinese man glanced at Matthias as if using X-ray vision to see if he was for real. Matthias' stack of chips satisfied him that he had more than the minimum $1000 a hand to play, so he moved a stanchion and held the curtain back for Matthias to enter.

Matthias placed his chips on the counter. "A hundred thousand," he said. "All on one bet."

The dealer swallowed. He was an elderly balding man with a kink in his neck. He wore a vest and seemed to fit more with the bellhop crowd than the gambling side of the operation. He'd seen this sort of thing before. But he never got used to the reality that people had more to gamble with in five minutes than what he had to live on in two years. He nodded in a polite way and counted the chips. The young trying-to-look-confident baccarat manager entered. The dealer repeated the amount to him and he nodded.

Matthias sat in the 14th seat. To his right was the last seat at 15. To his left was the seat marked 12. He was technically sitting in 13, but, like the floors in some buildings and hotels, the 13th seat in baccarat was called 14 to avoid superstition. His mind raced to recall how to play. Only a few more seconds before the casino would shut down. He had one chance to win at this single hand opportunity. The rules came back to him. Bet on either the *banker* hand or the *player* hand. The dealer plays both hands. Lay your bet down on either corresponding row and watch. Gambling at its simplest. Just pick. One or the other. Dealer deals two or three cards depending on the combination to the player box and to the banker box. The combination closest to nine wins. If there are two digits in the two-card total, the first digit is simply dropped. Banker usually takes it, but it also charges a commission. Satisfied with his ability to remember, Matthias placed his bet on player. That was a mistake. He knew it as soon as he did it. He sacrificed speed for accuracy. Matthias held his breath.

The dealer dealt the cards. Banker got an eight of hearts and six of diamonds. Fourteen. Less the ten makes a total of four. Player had a four of hearts and a four of spades. Total of eight.

Natural eight. Player wins.

He exhaled, and only then did he realize how much oxygen he needed.

Just then the Chinese man came in and, having heard the announcement through his earpiece, told the dealer to shut down. Matthias watched as the dealer matched his chips. Then he followed the Chinese security guard who motioned for him to come out of the curtain area.

"I'm sorry. We are closing the casino," he said.

Matthias had no problem with that.

Better it happen now than a minute ago.

He cashed in his chips along with the hundreds waiting to exchange their winnings. He joined Lucas and Jake on the way out of the jammed casino. People pressed against each other, begging for a chance to get into the Garden.

The trio reached the parking area and got into Lucas' car. "I'm up a hundred grand!" Matthias exclaimed as he turned to Lucas. His hands were full of money. "Everything is paying out. How did you do that?"

Which was exactly what Caesar was wondering.

The casino was empty. A ghost town. As though some plague had hit it and it was now condemned by city officials. Drinks all over the floor. Broken glass. It should be teeming with people. Packed to the roof. Gorgeous waitresses. Happy gamblers.

Now all that was going on was finger pointing and guessing as to what could possibly have gone so wrong.

Caesar stood by himself on that confusing carpet, looking at the vacant machines and unmanned tables. He walked through the slots area to the craps tables, hoping that by retracing where Lucas had been he could somehow make sense of what happened.

He picked out the two red dice from his jacket and leaned against a table. He should have been hearing the cheers of gamblers as the casino raked in their money. He should have been hearing crowds of people unwinding after a good show, watching with anticipation the results from the dice.

But instead, all he heard was the silence broken only by his thoughts as he wondered how all of this came to be.

He chucked the dice against the far end of the table and watched as they came to a stop in front of him. All this money. All these people. Gone. When he looked back at the dice he felt a sudden chill in his body. He looked closer.

A two and a one.

Mike came up behind him. "We've checked all the machines. Nothing. We found nothing wrong."

Caesar didn't answer. He stared at the dice.

"Caesar?"

He picked up the dice and rolled them again. He watched at they bounced off the back and came to a stop. Same result. A torrent of rage filled his veins.

"What do we do? Do we open?"

"No, we don't open!" Caesar screamed. It echoed in the massive yet now dull casino.

Mike clenched his jaw and regained his composure. "Caesar, we can't afford this. Every lost hour is pushing us to the brink with this place. You know that." Mike went to the bar and poured himself a drink. He downed it in one gulp, hoping to find the resolve he needed to face the situation.

"We have a day. Absolute maximum. Then we have to—"

"What? Open the casino? And lose how many untold millions more?"

"We can't stay closed."

"We can't afford to open!"

Another drink. "We can draw on the pharmaceutical cash flow."

"How long, Mike? How long do you think we can do that? How long can we keep the casino floor empty?"

"We built this thing too fast. Too much, too soon," Mike said, loud enough for Caesar to hear it.

"Call Tabitha. Ask her to get in touch with Lucas. Tell her I want to meet with him."

It was 3 a.m. when Lucas walked past the security guards and the chained-off casino area of the Garden of Eden. The lights were turned down. No music. No life. No other people.

Except for Caesar sitting by himself at the craps table.

Lucas walked down the multicoloured carpet and stood beside him.

"We analyzed the slot machines. All of them. We even took some apart and put them back together. And all they do is continue to come up winners. I've been rolling these dice for I don't know how long, and all I get is a two and a one. Sometimes, though, I get a one and a two. So there is variance, mind you. But no real change." He looked at Lucas. "You have any idea on the probability of that? Staggering." He stretched out his hands and pointed to his entire gaming area. "You are witnessing the unexplainable."

"Release the drug and you get your casino back."

"It's such a strange thing." He stood up and exuded the curious calm successful people maintain even when their world is crashing down around them. "Want a drink?" he asked, reaching for a bottle on the nearby bar counter.

Yes. Two shots of rum. And a cold beer. Import.

"No thanks."

"Astounding, really." He poured himself a bourbon. "No. No, that's not right. It's cruel. But not in the way you think." Caesar's face grew sombre. He swirled the contents in his glass and looked out over his vacant empire. "Isn't it interesting that God can make dice turn up the same way over and over and over again…?" He was lost in some train of thought, travelling down a track he had long since wanted to abandon, but was forced to remain an unwilling passenger. "And yet God can neither save my mother, nor my wife, nor my son." He closed his eyes and wished to escape. Only for Caesar, there was no escape. All he had was a pair of dice that weren't doing what they were supposed to.

"Let's start over," Lucas said.

"I agree. Call off God and come work for me. I have to hand this over to somebody. I want it to be you. Run it the way you want. Tell me this doesn't interest you, Lucas. You want this. You know you do."

Lucas looked at the casino. Out in the distance he saw a purple slot machine that seemed out of place compared to all of the others around it. *Is he giving this all to me? Plus freedom from being hunted down?* "This isn't about what I want," Lucas said in a tone that seemed to indicate otherwise.

"Then here's the deal. You convince God to be reasonable and take his hand out of the slots and dice. In return, I offer you the drug."

"It exists? The drug really exists? You have a drug that can—"

Caesar cursed at him. "Do we have a deal?"

"What stage is the drug in?"

"Ready for approval."

"Then we're done," Lucas said as he stood up. "Goodbye, Caesar."

"Take your dice with you. I'm sick of looking at them." He tossed them to Lucas. "And do us both a favour and get out of this city."

As Caesar watched Lucas walk away he felt the sting of losing. "One bullet," he muttered to himself. He wanted to chase after Lucas and smash his face into a slot machine. Drag his body up the stairs. Dump him over the railing onto a blackjack table. Watch him die.

Instead he dropped a coin in a slot machine and pressed the

button. He waited as the spinning objects came to a stop. No triple sevens. No triple cherries. No triple anything. All he got was a gold bar and two bottles of perfume—one dark coloured, the other light.

He smiled.

Caesar was back in business.

Tabitha drove Lucas and Jake to the hospital. The words of the desk clerk at Edgar's hotel churned in her mind. She had gone to invite him out to a show, cheer him up, do what she could to help. But when she didn't find him waiting for her she went to the front desk. The attendant told her that Edgar had collapsed in the lobby, that he had been taken away by ambulance.

Collapsed. Exactly how bad did *collapse* mean?

When they arrived at Emergency the triage nurse told them where they could find him. They entered his room and saw that he was half awake. His face was pale. An IV line ran into his hand. It was the first time any of them had seen him in anything but his precious dress sweater and dress pants.

Lucas stood at his side. "Edgar?" He opened his eyes and recognized them. "Edgar, we're here." He nodded his head. "The hospital tells us you collapsed."

Another nod. He spoke with slow, deliberate words. "Apparently it's worse than we thought."

"Help is coming, Edgar," Lucas said. "Caesar's going to release it."

Edgar wanted to feel optimism, to feel that his ship threatening to go under in the storm could still make it back to the harbour.

"I need your help, Lucas," Edgar said. His eyes were full of doubt. He reached out and grabbed Lucas' wrist in a way that told Lucas he was desperate for an answer.

Jake and Tabitha closed the curtain. They left the room.

"I'm in no position to help you, Edgar."

"You have to be." Edgar coughed and then battled to clear his throat. He gripped Lucas even tighter and whispered, as if to hide what he was about to say from unsuspecting ears around him. "Is there no room for suffering in God's plan of healing?"

"Edgar, I don't know why this has happened to you."

"Is it all so airtight that every sickness is a curse, every ailment a judgement?" He shook his head, feeling the frustration of getting off course. "Remember the story of the man born blind? Jesus' followers asked him whose fault it was that this man couldn't see. They wondered who sinned to make God angry and punish him with this illness. Was it the man's fault? Was it his parents' fault?" He coughed again, then gripped Lucas so tight it cut off his circulation. "Remember what happened then?" Lucas couldn't recall. "Jesus said it wasn't about God being angry. He healed him because he says that's the kind of person God is. That He is our healer. So why…?" He closed his eyes a moment as he struggled to absorb a sudden pain in his head. "Why am I not being healed?"

"I'm getting you the drug," Lucas said. "I can take away your cancer."

Edgar felt no peace. He felt no relief. He looked at Lucas with desperate eyes, hoping to clear his doubts. "But can you make me better?"

Edgar began to fade in and out and then fell asleep under the exhaustion.

Lucas left the room and joined the others. "When we get the drug we'll give it to Edgar, and then anybody who wants to can join me in getting out of this town."

The Garden of Eden opened the next morning. Thousands lined Las Vegas Boulevard anxious for a chance to cash in on good fortune. Reporters covered the "re-grand opening," speculating that perhaps Caesar had done the stunt on purpose as an advertising blitz gone wrong. People crammed through the doors and ran to *their* slot machines and to *their* tables—as though being reunited with a long-lost relative.

Caesar stood in the security area looking down as people jammed into his fortress. Every table, every slot machine—packed. Nothing was left vacant. The lineup at the cage was over a hundred deep. Scantily clad waitresses pushed their way through the crowd trying to deliver drinks. Dealers handed out cards. People placed their bets. Hundreds of thousands of dollars pouring in while he watched.

Caesar hated being forced into this trade-off for his drug. Hated having to concede. Hated what Lucas had done to him. His hands had been tied—he had been boxed in. He had been pressured to release it, to relinquish control of his wonder cure. It was his. All his. But now he had to give it up. He had to hand it over.

And he would have done just that.

But when Caesar saw that his casino was full—and that he was making money again—he changed his mind and decided not to release the drug.

41

Not good. Not good at all. Claire calling was in and of itself fine. But Claire calling now, especially when Caesar was supposed to have released the drug, put Lucas on edge. Tabitha answered her cellphone and handed it to him.

"He's not releasing it," Claire said from her posh office in the Garden of Eden.

She continued, but Lucas didn't hear her. *He's not releasing it.* That was all that he got. That was all that he needed.

His first reaction was anger at himself. *I should have forced him to put it in my hand right there. I should have forced him to give it to me.*

Then came anger at Caesar for his conniving lies.

"You can't go after him," Tabitha said as Lucas and Jake walked out of September's home to his car. "You think he'll let you in after what happened?"

Matthias caught up to Lucas. "We're going back for one last round."

"I wouldn't do that."

"I offer you the same advice. Besides, one more evening and I'm done."

"And then you'll have enough so you can drown out the voice you've being trying to avoid? What? Get a stack of money to insulate yourself from what you've been called to do? You ever think about using your ability for something other than your own gain?"

Matthias studied Lucas a moment, as if contemplating whether to reconsider his next move. "Look after yourself, old boy. Maybe our paths will cross again." He and September left to take their chances with Caesar. They drove off without saying another word. And from that moment on, Lucas felt the regret of angry farewells.

"Don't go back," Tabitha said in a final attempt to change his mind.

"And leave Edgar lying dead in the hospital?"

"Lucas, there are two inescapable facts. Even if you go in with a boatload of media attention he will invent a way for you not to get in. He's afraid of you, Lucas. Second, you've lost your healing gift. You can't help Edgar."

That cut into Lucas. Into all of them. She waited for his reaction, wondering if she had convinced him of the facts.

"Jake?" Lucas said, without breaking eye contact with her.

"I'm with you, boss." Jake replied. Tabitha closed her eyes a moment, realizing that defeat of her motion was now inevitable.

Lucas stretched out his hand to her. "I want you to join us."

"What?"

"Step out on the water."

"I don't understand how you think you can win."

"This is not about understanding, Tabitha. It's about doing. Your head says it can't be done, but what does your conscience say? Do you feel it?"

"No," she said.

"Do you want to?"

"Believe?"

"Do you?"

Tabitha saw his hand. She saw his eyes. She sensed the resolve in his spirit—that part of him that was so terribly far away, yet in this instant felt closer than anything she had experienced with him before.

She debated going with him.

"Set up four separate security entrance tunnels. Wide enough for exactly one person," Caesar said from his desk to Mike, Mitchell and

Foster. "Checkpoints at each one. If you see him approaching, you call *Action!* into your radio and we shut the casino down before he gets in."

"But he could cripple us indefinitely! Every time he walks up we have to shut down—it's the same as being closed," Mike said, hoping all of this didn't once again come down to him needing to pull the trigger to end it.

"This is where Tabitha and Jake come in," Caesar said. "As do Matthias and Savannah."

Lucas waited with his hand outstretched, hoping Tabitha would take it, hoping she would choose to bridge the gap as much as was her responsibility.

"I don't know that I believe, Lucas."

"The believing comes after you choose to follow."

"I don't know if this is going to work."

"Neither do I."

"Then why do it?"

"Because I can't allow Caesar to withhold the drug. I have to take him on and I have to do it now."

"I don't want to pretend that by taking your hand something magical will happen to make my doubts disappear."

"They won't disappear. They'll just be eclipsed by the new confidence you'll find."

"I don't know what I'm saying yes to."

"Then perhaps it's time you found out."

"Perhaps?"

"I can introduce you to the way life is supposed to be lived."

There were two of her in that instant. One wanted to run away and forget she knew him. The other one was convinced this was the opportunity of a lifetime. She struggled in-between those people, trying to determine which one would yield the best outcome.

And then, unable to decide and unwilling to wait any longer, she reached out her hand and held his. It didn't feel any different. No magical *whoosh.* No rush of power. Just a commitment to ride this thing out. To see where it went.

To see if she had made the right choice.

42

They parked at MGM Grand and took the monorail to Harrah's/Imperial Palace. They passed Treasure Island—a crowd gathered on the wooden gangway to see the outdoor show. Then they passed the Frontier—electric bull riding and bikini mud wrestling advertised on their large sign. Up ahead they saw the flaming swords hallmarking the Garden of Eden.

They got off and walked to the new security tunnels that cluttered the front entrance. People were backed up to the street. The lineup moved with all the urgency of security at an airport.

"There's Mitchell," Jake said, seeing the tall Empirico enforcer just ahead at the turnstile. "We should have gone in different rows."

"What do we do?" Tabitha asked, her pulse quickening now that the first test was at hand.

They moved closer.

"We trust."

"In God?"

"Next," Mitchell said.

Lucas stepped forward. He saw the bulge in Mitchell's suit jacket. Shoot to kill. No doubt those were the orders. And the moment they made eye contact Lucas felt the futility of what they were doing.

"Move forward," Mitchell said. They came to the turnstile. Mitchell looked right at Lucas. Expressionless. It seemed to Lucas that Mitchell wasn't focusing properly, like the way people who need a heavy prescription feel when they take off their glasses and are unable to see anything clearly.

One foot away. That's all he was. Practically face to face were it not for the difference in height. Mitchell called out to people behind them. A young Asian couple. Tabitha turned around and watched as the couple walked up to them. She tried to step out of the way and realized they were walking too fast and were about to bump into her. She braced herself for the impact.

But instead, oblivious to her presence, they made no attempt to avoid her. They walked right at her.

And then *through* her.

Tabitha froze. *That didn't happen. That did not happen.* She looked to Lucas for an explanation.

Mitchell motioned for an elderly woman to approach. The walkway was narrow. Too narrow. There was no way she was going to make it around.

And she didn't.

She walked right through them as though they were nothing more than holographic images.

Lucas grabbed Tabitha by the hand and led her through the turnstile. They passed through without turning it.

Tabitha squeezed Lucas' hand, desperate for the reassurance of some form of reality. She tried hard not to hyperventilate. Tried hard not to faint. Tried hard to balance that world between what she knew and what she was experiencing. "Lucas?" she asked.

"Tell me you're glad you took a chance in doing this," Lucas said, as he tried to come to terms with what was happening. He took her through the crowd, through person after person as though they were ghosts.

"Lucas, what is going on?" Panic was setting in. The inability to understand. The horror of walking in a world unimagined. Unexpected. Unexplainable.

"Tell me you're not bored."

They walked through a group of college kids high on life and low on cash. Right through a middle-aged married couple in the reverse situation. Right through a woman Tabitha's age who was unaware of their presence.

"I'm not bored," she whispered.

They walked through slot machines, through more people, through security guards, through the elevator door. It closed. The elevator lifted.

"I don't get it," Jake said, relaxed. "We walked through an elevator door but we're standing on the elevator floor. How does that work?"

Tabitha leaned against the wall, on the verge of losing the battle to get her breathing under control. "How can you just ask a question like that? What's the matter with the two of you?" She swallowed, then grabbed the railing, trembling, trying to assure herself something was still for certain. "Aren't you wondering what's going on here?"

Lucas touched her shoulder. He felt her fear. It ran up his hand and dissipated into his arm.

"This is our world, Tabitha. We don't explain things here."

That didn't help. She needed an answer. She needed more. "Because you don't want to?"

Lucas shook his head. He looked into her eyes, trying to find some way to transport his confidence into her uneasiness.

"Because we don't have to."

The elevator reached the 100th floor. The door opened. They stepped into the luxurious garden. Normally, Tabitha would have focused on the magnificent space. Normally, she would have wanted to walk through the area, taking in how it was made.

But these were not normal times. And she didn't even notice her surroundings.

Lucas led them up the stairs to Caesar's office. They passed through the closed door.

Caesar was on the phone, his back to the three of them, standing while speaking on the phone with Mike. His face was full of anger. Spit flew out of his mouth as he screamed. "You do whatever it takes to kill them! I don't care where! I don't care how! And I don't care who sees what!" Caesar ripped out a rampage of curses. "Whoever sees them next, kills them! That's final!"

Caesar slammed the receiver down and blasted out another curse. Where was that drink? He found it on his desk, grabbed it, and gulped it down. He felt a momentary calm, then fired it at the far wall, shattering it on impact. He turned to the window and looked down on Las Vegas Boulevard at the cars and hotels below. He tried to clear his mind and pretend he could fast-forward to the time when he would finally be rid of Lucas.

Once his own.

Now his nemesis.

But the longer he looked, the stranger things seemed. Something wasn't right. It felt eerie. Like being at home by yourself late at night, yet having the distinct feeling someone is watching you through a crack in the door in the other room. Perhaps his subconscious recognized it first. Or maybe his mind just refused to admit reality. But whatever it was, when he recognized their reflections in the window, a pulse raced through his body with such force it nearly caused him to scream.

No warning from Mike, Mitchell, or Foster that they had broken through the gate.

No secretary telling him they were on their way to his office.

No door opening.

They were just there.

Top right-hand drawer. *How many bullets did it have? Was it that old six-shooter? No. No, there was an upgrade. Never did check the number of bullets it could hold in the clip.*

It was worth a try.

He tilted his head slightly as if to get a better look at the south end of the Strip, when really he was trying to confirm through his peripheral vision that the window wasn't lying to him. Yes. It was true.

They were there.

He ripped open the drawer and pulled out his gun. None of them had time to react. He fired the first bullet.

It was a terrible shot. Far off from any target. Right between Lucas and Tabitha. It smashed through the wall into the open area. Tabitha screamed. Jake grabbed both of them and threw them to the ground.

The second bullet went into Jake's chest. It travelled through and came out the other end.

Caesar stepped out from beside his desk and fired the third and fourth bullets at Tabitha. They raced through her skull, into her brain, out the back and through the wall.

She felt nothing.

Caesar saw Lucas on the ground and emptied the clip into his body. The banging sound was horrific. Smoke rose around Caesar's face. The gun recoiled as the bullets flew into Lucas' head and chest and into the floor.

When he had spent his ammunition, Caesar took a step back. The smoke cleared. Lucas stood up. *I need better guns.*

Tabitha's hands shook. Jake put his arm around her and led her out of the room.

Caesar dropped his useless weapon, frustrated at realizing Lucas could be dead right now if only the laws of physics had just worked the way Isaac Newton said they would.

"I want you to release the drug. Now," Lucas said.

"Get out," Caesar replied, his eyes reverting back to that familiar cold, beady, puffy look. "And stay away from me."

"Give me the drug."

"I'm not giving you anything!" He stumbled back in his chair. "Get away from me. Get away from me!"

"You will stay true to your earlier promise," Lucas said. "You give me the drug or you will reap more of your miserable reward."

"Get out," he whispered.

"There are two paths, Caesar. Two roads. One wide. One narrow. I'm going to cram you through the eye of the needle. I'm going to get that drug."

"You get nothing. Now leave."

Lucas walked down the stairs and joined the others. Tabitha looked horrible. The worst he had ever seen. They took the elevator down and walked the casino floor. Lucas stopped at the aisle between a row of slots and a blackjack table.

"What are you doing?" Tabitha asked.

The players placed their bets. The dealer handed out cards. She dealt herself a 21 and beat the other 5 players. The next hand she dealt herself the same result. One of the players cursed the bad luck.

"When do the slot machine lights go off?" Tabitha asked.

"Should have happened by now."

But the slot machine area was dead silent. No clanging bells. No coins hitting the trays. The dealer dealt herself yet another 21. Then it happened a fourth time. The players had a hard time believing it. Then, a fifth and sixth time.

"This is fixed!" one of the men at the table said, adding a choice rhythm of expletives.

The next blackjack table experienced the same thing. Lucas walked closer. The players were dealt high hands, 18 to 20, yet the dealer had 21. Five times in a row. Players shook their heads. An elderly drunk woman stood up and left. Then, all the blackjack tables in the casino delivered the same result. Every player lost. Every dealer won.

Every single time.

People threw their cards down. Some began shouting.

Similar complaints happened at the roulette wheels. The ball always landed on the number where the least bets were placed. All across the casino a wave of bitterness swept through people. Shooters consistently threw snake eyes at the craps table.

Upstairs where Matthias was playing things were no better. He played at the high-stakes blackjack table and went from $200,000 down to $32,000 in a matter of minutes. *Never show frustration. That's rule number one. Just relax. Take a deep breath.*

Which is hard to do when you've lost that much.

Sweat formed on his forehead. *The card count is +12. Plus 12! How is this possible?*

September gave the predetermined signal for him to leave. He stood up and walked out, frustrated, baffled, consumed in that haze gambling addicts experience when they leave a table and try to comprehend who that guy was who had lost all their money.

"What was that?" Matthias asked.

"You should have left the game sooner. You knew it was going bad."

"On a +12 count?!"

He went to the balcony to get some fresh air and some distance from his place of defeat. But when he saw Lucas walking through the floor he understood what was happening.

People at the slots plugged their money in and got nothing in return. Some shook their heads. Others cursed.

Blackjack players hurled insults at dealers who were on perfect streaks. One of the players, overloaded on drugs and alcohol, screamed at the dealer. Security guards moved in, grabbed him firmly by the arms, and took him away.

As soon as they had done that another spat between a player and dealer broke out. This player lost 13 straight hands, as had all the others at the table. He jumped off his stool, grabbed the dealer, and punched him in the face. One of the players tried to stop him, but in doing so messed up the chips on the table and set the other players off.

Two more fights broke out in the roulette area. One in the craps area.

Then things got worse.

Fights broke out all over the floor. People stole chips from each other. Even those not prone to anger were suddenly filled with rage. Throwing drinks. Punching strangers. Shouting. A wave of madness gripped the casino.

Lucas, Tabitha, and Jake hurried out of the casino and right though Mitchell as he ran inside.

They boarded a monorail that said LAS VEGAS: CITY OF I DO and sat near the back.

"This is crazy," Tabitha said, her hands refusing to stop shaking, her eyes shifty.

Seeing Tabitha react this way reminded Lucas of the first miracles he saw. The tall guard. The boy in the wheelchair. Right. That's how it felt. That strange need to explain. To understand. To be able to make sense of it.

"Caesar sees us but the rest can't. We can walk through people, but we can stand on floors?" She shook her head.

Lucas sat closer to her. She bit her lip, feeling the intensity of having to grasp something that can't be contained. Her shaking grew worse. Her body colder. Her fear greater.

And the longer Lucas looked at her, the more he regretted asking her to take the step into the place he now called normal.

Caesar shut his casino down. Again. Mike came into the office. He noticed the bullet holes in the floor and wall. No body. No blood. He ran his hand through his hair and then covered his mouth. It was all he could do after seeing the latest financial figures.

"Just say it, Mike!" Caesar shouted. "Haven't I taught you anything? Just give me the news!"

"We are screwed!" Mike screamed back and then stopped himself. It was the first time he had ever shouted at Caesar. It was the first time anyone at Empirico had raised their voice at him. "Do you understand that? The casino is on the verge of bankruptcy. Bankruptcy! We have to reopen right now."

"With what, Mike? With gamblers? Gamblers are people who expect some reasonable chance of winning. And from what I'm told, the floor is cursed with losing."

Mike covered his eyes, as if afraid to look at something. "And the hockey game."

"How bad?"

"Eleven-zip."

"That's not the end of the world," Caesar said, lowering his voice. "I saw a game finish 12-2 once."

Mike clenched his jaw. Then he formed his hands into fists in a futile attempt to control his anger. His face burned. Then he exploded. "The first period isn't even over yet!"

He leaned his head back. One bullet. All it would have taken was the courage to pull the trigger when he had the chance. He wished he could go back and make things right.

"It's time to rethink this."

"Rethink nothing," Mike said, feeling the courage to play at Caesar's level. "Find some way to appease Lucas or the casino is finished. Do it now. Right now."

"No!"

"Caesar, we'll be forced to use the cash flow from the pharmaceutical company to float this place. Look around you. The casino is empty. People have cancelled reservations in the hotel. Every other hotel is at full occupancy. But we're dry as a bone. Why is that? The food in our restaurants that was brought in today has already spoiled. The Fortune play the Patriots tomorrow and we just found out that our quarterback, two wide receivers, and three offensive linemen have sustained unexplained injuries."

"I will not negotiate with Lucas."

"Then we are finished," Mike said.

"We're not finished," Caesar replied, as a renewed confidence came back to him. He stepped back to the window. It was coming to him. Yes. There it was. There was the solution. "If Lucas Stephens is looking for a fight, we'll give it to him. He doesn't hold all the cards," Caesar said. "And it's time he found that out."

43

Lucas and Jake knelt in the vacant grounds in front of the Hilton. The lights were off. The people gone. The only indication of an outside world was the faint hum of the monorail passing by in the distance. Strange place. Strange for Vegas, to have a spot near the Strip that was so quiet, so devoid of anything seeking to draw attention. They stayed there. Listening. For direction. For conviction. For God. They'd already been there three hours—still, they had no reassurance about what to do. They had Caesar pinned. But, as it now seemed, that didn't really matter. Especially not after Caesar called Tabitha requesting a meeting with Lucas.

Tabitha watched them from a distance. From her car. Then while walking around the calm Avenue of the Hiltons. Then while leaning up against the monorail support. She saw Jake stand up and come over to her. "How long will he stay there?" she asked.

"As long as it takes."

As Tabitha walked out to Lucas she wondered if he would hear her steps and turn around to see her.

"Lucas?" She received no response. "Lucas?"

He opened his eyes.

"Lucas?"

"I'm going to face him."

She was afraid of that. "Will this never end?"

"I have to go. And I want you to come with me."

Her dark eyes conveyed her compassion and fear. "I can't do this. I can't do any of this. Lucas, I'm not like you."

"This is not about me. It's about you discovering what you were designed for."

She was supposed to feel an adventurous spark, like when a man wants to wrap a woman up in some brand new world. But she didn't feel that. What he was saying felt worlds away.

"I don't know how we can go on."

Lucas felt her struggle. He felt her uncertainty. He felt his own. He stood up. "We will make it," he said.

"I don't know how you can be so sure about us."

He reached out and touched her arms. He studied her eyes and waited until he found that place that defined her for who she was. "Tabitha," he said. "I will do whatever it takes to convince you that I am the man for you."

She felt his passion. His conviction. Still, she saw two Lucases. One was the confident determined man with the courage to challenge a pharmaceutical giant. The other was the man who could call upon unseen powers and heal crowds, survive being burned, and walk through people.

And for all her trying, she wasn't able to put those two people together.

"I don't doubt whether you're the man for me," she said. "I doubt whether I'm the woman for you."

"Come with me to see Caesar."

"Lucas."

"Let's take him on. You and me."

"I can't."

"You can. Just say yes."

But she didn't. She stayed on that relational bridge between them, not wanting to make the mistake of going forward or retreating.

Lucas touched her hand. She wished he hadn't done that. Saying goodbye would have been easier had he not added the powerful effect of touching her skin.

"We make a good team, you and me," he said. "You have a taste of the world I live in. You belong here. You just need to switch from understanding to believing."

"I'm supposed to ignore rational thought?"

"You need to understand its limitations."

"I understand that Caesar will kill you."

"And I believe that I've been called to confront him this one last time."

"I'm going to lose you," Tabitha said. Then she took in a breath as if wanting to retract those words and to prevent them from becoming some self-fulfilled prophecy.

"If you don't see life the way I do, then you've lost me already."

She wanted to have what he had. She wanted to believe what he believed. But the distance from her to him was so much greater than from him to her. She shook her head and wished she had it within her to nod.

"Then I have to go."

Lucas walked away, leaving her by herself. Standing there. Thinking. Trying to discover that path into the realm beyond to find a better vantage to see the world. To see Lucas. To see herself.

"You need to look after her," Lucas said when he reached Jake.

"You can forget that. I'll let her look after herself before I'll watch you go there alone."

"If this fails, Caesar will kill both of us. I can't have that."

"And I can't do this without you," Jake said, angry that Tabitha was now the reason he was being asked to abandon his post.

"You might have to, Jake."

"Don't say that."

"Jake." Neither of them wanted to hear what he had to say next. "You need to resolve yourself to that option. Whatever happens, do not come after me." He grabbed his shoulder and looked into his trusted eyes. "Goodbye, my friend."

As Lucas walked away Jake called out after him.

"I think I have it figured out."

Lucas turned around. It felt good to hear Jake's voice. He had already begun to wonder if he would ever hear it again.

"Have what figured out?"

"All the bad things that have happened to you." The monorail passed by as Jake took a step closer. "Why? Why did you have to go through them? I couldn't get my head around it. What was the point of all of it? The plane crash. The attacks in Africa. The beatings."

Lucas hadn't spent much time reflecting on why certain events in his life had unfolded the way they had. In part, it was because he was afraid of the answer. In part, because he was afraid there was none.

"Why do you think they happened?" Lucas asked.

"It was one big test, Lucas. All of it. To see where your loyalty lies. To see if you would turn against God. To get you ready for this moment. To face Caesar and not give in when he throws the world at your feet. How many people could withstand something like that?"

"I don't know."

"Not many, Lucas. Maybe only one. I wish I was more like you."

"You are like me, Jake. You're better than me."

Jake's eyes began to sting. He tried to avoid it. This was no time to break down. This was the time for courage. This was the eve of battle.

"I'll take good care of your woman for you."

Lucas was about to nod when he stopped himself. "I'm not sure if she's mine."

"We'll see you soon."

They turned away from each other to go their separate ways. They did their best not to dwell on the goodbye. Did their best not to think about what they might lose.

There was a more pressing issue at hand.

Lucas walked down the hospital hallway to room 20. He breathed in short bursts as if subconsciously wanting to avoid catching the germs that were keeping these people in their beds. He knocked on the door and opened it. As he entered Edgar's room he worried he might find an empty bed.

His face was paler than before. His body looked somehow smaller. Thinner. Older. Lucas stood next to him, and though there was a chair nearby, he chose not to sit down so that Edgar would have an easier time looking at him.

"I don't have it yet, Edgar."

Edgar spoke in slow, methodical phrases as evidence of his inability to organize his thoughts as clearly as he once could.

"What do you want me to do?"

"Edgar?"

"What do you want me to do…for you?" he repeated.

"Nothing. Nothing. I'm fine, Edgar."

Edgar shook his head and cleared his throat. "That story. You know the one?"

"Which story?"

"The blind men. They came to Jesus and asked for help. He says: 'What do you want me to do for you?'" He swallowed in a way that looked like he was gagging down knives. "Can you imagine? Asking blind men what they want?"

"You're wondering why the blind men were healed and why you're still sick?"

He shook his head and swallowed again. More knives. Sharper this time. Lucas wished for the healing power to come back. One more time. Right here, for Edgar.

"The last part. Do you remember the last part?" Lucas did not. "After they got healed it says they followed Jesus." He took in two heavy breaths. His eyes began to water. "What does that mean?" He pulled his frail hand out from under the covers. He grabbed Lucas by the wrist. Those eyes. Inside Edgar's eyes was something Lucas had never seen. This wasn't panic. It wasn't fear. It was much, much worse. "What does it mean to follow Jesus?"

Lucas met Mitchell and Foster at the casino entrance. No words. No greetings. What for? They led him through the empty gaming area, past the normal bay of elevators, and down to the end of a hall. Mitchell slipped a card through a card lock. The elevator door opened. They entered. Lucas looked at the panel. The lights for the floors did not show numbers. Instead they showed letters. A through H. Mitchell hit the H. The elevator descended.

When the doors opened Lucas saw darkness.

"Get out," Mitchell said.

Lucas stepped into the abyss. The doors closed. He heard the elevator leave.

To his left he saw nothing but emptiness. He looked right, and as his eyes adjusted he saw a faint glimmer of light coming from a doorway far at the end. He walked towards it, feeling the unnerving sensation that someone was gaining behind him, getting ready to plunge a blade into his spine and sever it like the caning did in Africa. He wanted to turn around. Wanted to confirm his mind was right. He felt a chill against his neck. Regardless of what his eyes might tell him, there was someone there.

He listened for the footsteps of the man with the knife. Hearing none he continued and saw a large double black door with gold handles. Both sides had two horses, each of a different colour, with riders in armour. He reached down to the handle.

He opened the door.

Tabitha drove Jake to the hospital where Edgar was staying. Where he was dying. They found his room. Tabitha sat closest to him. Jake and Edgar made eye contact and conveyed the relief friends feel when all it takes is the look in each other's eyes to know how much the other means to them.

Edgar tilted his head in slow jerks, like a robot that has lost fluid motion. "Do you believe?" he asked. His tone was direct. His voice intense—as though dying had given him a sense of urgency he otherwise would not have had.

"I'm trying," Tabitha said. "But I don't know how it's going to turn out. I need to be sure before I begin."

"The only guarantee is the person you are believing in. The rest is a mystery."

"Then what do I believe in?" she asked. "What does Lucas believe in that gives him those powers?"

Lucas saw a large black dining table. There were seven candles in gold stands placed at even intervals down the middle, eleven tall black chairs on either side, and one at either end. A waterway flowed around it like a moat, wide enough that a person could not jump across. A wood bridge connected over to the island. More candles lit up the walkway.

"Do you know the common factor involved in most school shootings?" Caesar sat off to the right behind a series of burners and covered metal dishes.

Lucas turned to see him. A fire started. It lit up his face. "No."

"No? That in and of itself should convince you of the influence the media and the powers-that-be have." Caesar stretched out his hand and motioned for him to join him as he crossed the bridge. It relieved Lucas that it was only Caesar in the room.

At least as far as he could tell.

Caesar pointed to the chair at one end of the table. He sat down at the other. A fruit salad appetizer lay before them. Mangos, cherries, kiwi, passion fruit, apples stacked together in the shape of an S and decorated with an array of mint leaves.

"What is the common factor?"

"Turns out, and a study shows, that the majority of students involved in school shootings were prescribed antidepressants to control their behaviour." Caesar raised his hands. "Can you believe it? Antidepressants are linked, directly linked, to school shootings. You think it's coincidence?"

"These kids may have had a host of problems. Antidepressants might have been used to help solve some of them."

"Optimism. You still have that belief that the world works the way people say it does. That's to be admired. Let me know when you change your mind. There's more going on than what you can see."

"You blame pharmaceuticals?"

Caesar took a bite of his salad and held it in his mouth. "How's your salad?"

Lucas shook his head. Eating was the farthest thing from his mind. "I'm not hungry."

"That's too bad," Caesar said, taking in another mouthful. "Think about it this way. A kid has behavioural problems. What is the solution? Drugs. Drugs. Drugs. And then? More drugs. Does Dad choose to take Johnny to a baseball game? Does he choose to take him to the backyard and play a game of catch? Does he have time to take him fishing? No. Because Dad is off with another woman thinking that his happiness is the ultimate goal, or he's pretending that life is too tough and that he has to move on, or he's at the office until midnight trying to prove that he's a man, or whatever. And what about Mom? Well, Mom's either off at work or stuck raising the kids, and either way is exhausted and can't cope, so she's in no position to deal with Johnny. What's the result? What do we have, Lucas? We have a problem. And what do we do when we have a problem? We go to the problem solvers. The problem solvers, Lucas! And who are they? Who are the problem solvers?"

"You tell me."

"The problem solvers are those who can make the situation go away. Enter you, the miracle man—or the at-one-time miracle man. And enter me. The drug man. The world comes to us, begging on their knees. They say: 'We are horrible parents. But we want to make believe that we are good people, so we want to project all of our problems onto a medical condition. We know, oh pharmaceutical giant, we know that this medical condition does not exist....' Well, actually Lucas, we do know that it exists. The condition is called lack of love. You know all about that. But back to our parents. They go on to say: 'We know the condition doesn't exist, so just make it up for us. Just invent something out of thin air that absolves us of our responsibility to discipline and love our kids. We can then blame this godforsaken illness and claim that we are doing all we can by buying some useless drug that will only make Johnny worse. But, oh giant, I need this drug, I need medical verification that this condition exists, because that's the only way I can ignore my screaming conscience telling me to buy the baseball ticket, stay in the marriage, or come home from the office.'"

"You don't think those drugs help kids?"

"You see, Lucas, you're catching on. The drug is not for the kids. That's the great joke. That's what's so ironic. The drug isn't for the kids. It's for the parents. It's for the teachers. It's for society. We don't want to love. We want to inject. We don't want inconvenience through sacrifice. We want to make the problem go away. We don't want to address the concern, the root cause. We don't want responsibility. We just want everything bad to disappear. And this is why the pharmaceutical industry exists."

"You know what the worst part about you is?"

"Actually no, Lucas. I'm discovering there are layers of evil within me, and I'm sure I haven't found them all. Enlighten me."

"There are people who are swept away by madness. And there are those who create and thrive on it. The worst part about you is that you are pushing drugs you know won't work and then withholding a drug you know will. You do nothing to stop the problem."

"Stop? Please, Lucas. Stop what? Stop the shrinks from thinking they know best with their degrees and their lists of drugs? Stop the parents from being irresponsible and then pleading for solutions? Stop the government from drugging up kids to turn them into lifeless zombies so they behave in class in their comatose state? Stop people from living their nonactive lives and eating terrible food? Stop that?"

"The blame has to start somewhere."

"Blame! Of course! How could I forget? The kid is screwy; blame the doctors. The job sucks; blame the boss. Life is unfair; blame God. Not enough money; blame the bank. That is the chief aim of people. To pretend that the problem is their work, their family, their boss, their God…anything but them. There are those who come to Vegas and find out that here, everything works—except the addicted gamblers, but so be it. Everything here is fun. Everything here is ideal, unless getting a disease from a cheap prostitute isn't your version of ideal. We seek to reinforce the belief that the problem must be with everyone else. Some people come for fun. Others come as slaves to this place. They have to escape. This is their identity. It's their home. It's their alter ego. Their necessity. And that's why Las Vegas Boulevard exists."

"But you still have a casino that is draining the life out of you."

"And you still have a friend who is dying of cancer."

"Give me your drug."

"Release your curse."

"It's not mine."

"Whose, then?" Caesar raised his eyebrows. He laughed in amazement. "God? Please tell me! Is God back in the curse business? I mean this is too much. First, God makes you heal. Then he makes you useless. Then he brings you to rain down curses on people."

"Just you."

"Lucas, the deal is this: you walk out and promise never to return. I, in turn, release the drug."

"This is your last chance."

"My money will outlast Edgar. Tell me, Lucas. Are you willing to wait?"

Lucas wanted to pick up the knife beside him and hurl it at Caesar.

"That's good," Caesar said. "I admire your anger. Your rage. You want me dead."

"Release it."

"You call God off. Or we're not going to talk."

"No deal."

"How much longer does Edgar have?"

"Release it!"

"Ask God to take the curse off this casino and we'll talk."

"And lose my negotiating position?"

"Keep it and lose your friend."

Within an hour the Garden of Eden reopened, albeit this time to smaller crowds. The former prospect of winning it big on machines and tables that had a supernatural generosity to them was an easy ticket—but the opposite, the threat of having money sucked away by a casino conspiracy, was not as inviting.

To offset the nervous patrons Mike initiated a temporary three-to-one payback on blackjack, cheaper drinks, and higher payouts on slots. News spread and people let go of their bad experiences. The crowds came back. The people poured in.

And among them was a tall man with a black Armani suit jacket, slicked back hair, $32,000 in his pocket, and less than three hours to make as much money as he could before his picture would be released as one of the known card counters.

"Thank you," Caesar said, pouring Lucas a glass of red wine. "Now that the Garden is up and running, you and I can talk business."

"There's nothing to discuss."

"Here's my offer. I give Edgar the drug, and that's it. You leave, and we part ways."

"You said you would release the drug."

"To Edgar."

Lucas felt the anger of being forced into a corner. He looked at Caesar whose face was half hidden in the shadow created by the candlelight. "I've had enough, Caesar."

"But you haven't even eaten yet. I have a killer salmon recipe."

"You're going to do things my way."

"You don't hold the cards. And besides, from what I gather, you're no longer bulletproof." That dark glow in his eyes returned. "You're going to do things my way."

Caesar resumed his meal. He was confident he had steered himself out of this mess. He took in a taste of wine, held it in his mouth a moment, swallowed it, and felt himself begin to relax.

He looked at Lucas and searched his eyes. He should have seen defeat. He should have seen a beat-down opponent. But he didn't. He saw the same look poker players see when they know their opponent isn't bluffing. Caesar shook his head to clear his mind. *Lucas is bluffing.*

Definitely.

Lucas is bluffing.

44

The trouble with sitting face to face with Caesar was that no matter how terrible things got for him he always appeared to have the upper edge. He had lost millions, but he was prepared to lose more. Lucas was on the verge of losing Edgar and he was not prepared to let him go. He didn't have the same *let it ride* option that Caesar did.

Which is why he lost his negotiating power.

"I have you, Lucas. You know that I can kill you or I can release you. Your fate is in my hands."

Lucas folded his hands on the table. He straightened his back and leaned his head forward. "Caesar, what is it going to take for you to make that drug public?"

"I don't answer hypothetical questions. And this, my friend, is not a bargaining table."

Lucas refused the temptation to panic. *I can do this. I can get him to release the drug. I can save Edgar. I can destroy Caesar. I can do it.*

Matthias exchanged his 32 large at the cage and headed up the escalators to the 5th floor blackjack area. September was already there. Short leather skirt. Low-cut blouse. Tinted glasses. She stood near a table with a seven count. Good, but not great. Still, seven was as lucky as any number. She ran her hand through her hair to confirm the number. Matthias sat down. He placed five $100 chips on the table.

And waited for fate to deal him his destiny.

Tabitha got into her car, slammed the door shut, and covered her face with her hands. "Lucas is going to die."

"Don't say that," Jake said as he sat down.

"He's going to die and it's my fault." She leaned her head forward. Jake said something to her, but all she could hear were her own thoughts. *Why didn't I believe? Why did I let him go? I have to help him. I have to do something.* But then she heard something else. Something different. Something strange. Even though the windows were shut and the air conditioning was off she felt a cool breeze against the back of her neck. Painful. As though someone had sliced a butcher knife against her....

You can't help him. Not now. Not anymore.

Yes, I can. I have to. We have to.

With what? How do you help him? You don't even know his power. And besides, it won't come to you. You're not like him. Look at your life. Look what you've done. You can't possibly expect to receive it.

Lucas did.

Lucas is different. It is his battle.

Stop it.

You are not in this league. You don't belong.

I can help him.

You can't.

Stop it!

She opened her eyes and wondered where she had been. All she could think about was Lucas dying at the hands of Caesar Alexander. "We're going to help him." She blinked to get her eyes to focus. She saw the clock on the dash—9:12—and turned to Jake. "I need a crash course," Tabitha said. "What does it take to get the same power Lucas has?"

"I want to know the bottom line," Lucas said. Sweat showed on his forehead. That was bad. Elementary rule of negotiating. Never, never, never show them how desperate you are in making the deal.

"To release the drug?" Caesar asked.

Negotiating was finished. This was plea bargaining.

"Name your price."

Caesar didn't hesitate. He knew the answer. So did Lucas. He sensed it in Caesar in that split second before he responded. "My price is you."

"Me."

"Yes, Lucas. You die—I release the drug."

A flush of panic rushed through him. *Die? Is that what he said?*

"I've done the math," Caesar continued. "No more curses on this casino. No more potential healings of the masses. You die and I can afford to give out the drug to the world. Edgar lives."

But Lucas couldn't process the argument. He was still hearing *die* echo in his mind.

"Think it through, Lucas. We both know we can't go on like this."

Impossible. The table *was* cursed. Cursed! Bad, bad, bad luck. Matthias glanced around the table. No one else seemed to be as plagued. He started with $32,000, but before the dealer reached the bottom of the shoe Matthias lost $22,000. Insanity. The count was in his favour. He had memorized every card played so far in the six deck pack. This wasn't going the way it was supposed to.

Against his better judgement, and the numerous warning signs September gave him to leave the table, Matthias continued on, driven by that curious and hideous impulse that pushes gamblers to turn off their reasoning and follow the path of destruction.

And 21 hands later Matthias was down to $300.

Those chips felt worse than pennies on the table. The dealer didn't speak to him. Neither did the other players. What was there to say? A gambler down on his luck represented all their fears.

Matthias took his three chips off the table and walked away. He was in a daze. As if waking up while sleepwalking. He felt September come up behind him. He felt his anger rising. He felt like screaming on his way down the escalator. His money, gone. His deal with Lydda, gone. And now he was reduced to a suit, a girl, and a net worth of three Las Vegas dollars.

"Tabitha, this isn't just about miracles," Jake said, as she drove down Paradise Road to avoid the traffic on the Strip. "There's more to it."

"Get to the point, Jake," she said, going through a red light. "I can learn as I go." She gunned the accelerator. "What does it take to rescue Lucas?"

"You have to get out of Las Vegas," Matthias said, stopping outside the casino, relieved that he could at least for the moment force himself out of that place. "This life is garbage for you."

"And do what?"

"Whatever you want. Become the nurse you always talked about."

"I'm 73 grand in debt. You tell me how I pay for that?"

"I can't," he said. "All I know is that I have to go back to that casino."

"Stop running!" She started crying, feeling the emptiness of knowing the man she cared for was drifting away. "Who are you trying to escape? You are so full of panic…and…fear."

"I have to win my money back."

"Where? In a casino that in five minutes will know exactly who you are? And with what? Three hundred lousy dollars?"

"I'm no good for you, September."

"We're going to make it through this."

"We're finished." That killed her. He saw the change in her expression, the sense of loss in her, the kind that destroys women who have sunk all their emotional hope in a man who is not able to contain it. "You go your way. I'll go mine. We're done."

"Don't go out there. Please."

But Matthias left. To fire away his last chips and discover like countless others what it meant to be a zero in Vegas.

"This is your last chance," Lucas said.

"You're wrong. It's yours."

"Give me the drug and I'll go quietly."

"I gave you the ultimatum." Caesar said. "Now you choose."

"Time is running out for you."

"I don't want things to end this way."

"They won't."

Caesar felt a chill in the air. He adjusted in his seat and then felt it again. A touch of fear knocked at his door.

Lucas saw it in his eyes.

Matthias sat down with his three chips at the same table. The players tried not to notice, hoping that by ignoring him they would let him die in peace and avoid any more humiliation.

"Are we playing?"

The dealer nodded and dealt him a card. A cool breeze blew around them. The women with sleeveless dresses rubbed their arms. They felt the cold go down their backs. Some of them looked up to see if they were standing underneath a vent. Matthias felt nothing. A man dependent on winning never does.

He won the first five hands and managed to climb to three large. The chill became unbearable for those around him. But Matthias didn't care. The cards were turning up the right way. Another five hands and he was up to six grand.

Players on all the levels complained about the drastic drop in temperature. Some left. Those on the main floor were shocked that they could see their breath in the cool air. More people left, complaining to security on their way out.

Tabitha and Jake parked their car at the Mayan and hurried to the Garden. They saw hundreds of people filing out of the security tunnels, shivering, commenting to each other about the brutal cold.

"This is it, Tabitha," Jake said. "You walk through those doors and all bets are off. There are no guarantees in our world."

Tabitha nodded her head. That didn't bother her.

She already had that part figured out.

Matthias had every card memorized. He had the count bang on. He was up to $60,000. Those stares from the people beside him vanished. Some even moved closer, those who had enough clothing to stand the frigid air, as if doing so could get some of his good fortune to rub off on them. He brought his hand to his forehead to hide his face, and wished time could stand still to avoid the eyes in the sky from picking him up.

Tabitha followed Jake as he pushed through the exiting crowd. People's lips were blue. Their eyebrows had frost on them. Tabitha felt the air get colder as they forced their way up the security tunnel.

Matthias checked his watch and felt much the way Cinderella did when she heard the clock strike midnight. His three hours were nearly up. He looked at his stack of chips. *Know when to quit.* He was doing so well. *Know when to quit.* One hundred and forty-four grand. *Just one more hand. One more hand.*

Zack Roman sat at his computer. He stared at a picture of Matthias. Actually, he stared at seven pictures of Matthias. All kinds of different looks. He held his finger over the enter button and waited for the second hand to pass by the 12.

Three hours were up. He pressed the button.

It blipped on a security screen at the Garden of Eden. The photos automatically fed into the database, which was linked to the security cameras watching every person on the casino floor. Height, weight, eye colour, hair colour. It searched for matches. Thermal imaging was still coming to the Garden. For now the computers and the people watching the screens would have to make matches.

And it was a young kid, new on the job, who spotted a suspicious-looking lanky man at the high-stakes table who seemed to match the description that just came up.

"Well, that's about it for me," Matthias said. He shoved his chips into a bag and stood up, feeling a cold blast of air. To his right he saw a security guard speaking into a radio and heading in his direction. Matthias hurried to the escalator and went down as fast as he could without drawing attention to himself. When he reached the bottom he passed September who whispered to him.

"Third stall on your right."

He didn't have time to thank her. He just gave her the chips and went into the bathroom. Inside the third stall he found a bag. He opened it and found a uniform like those worn by staff at the hotel. He put it on—it didn't fit—and left.

He passed two security guards who pushed their way to the bathroom. September handed him the bag of money from the chips she cashed in and looked over her shoulder to see how fast security was coming from the other direction. "Hurry," she whispered. When they reached the doors she ran to the rented convertible. Matthias, however, walked slower. Relaxed. Almost indifferent. Almost wanting them to catch him. September shouted at him. Security reached the door and then stopped and watched. Matthias got in. She drilled the accelerator. He sat back and grinned.

It's not every day a bellhop walks out of a Las Vegas casino with $153,000.

"Time's up, Lucas," Caesar said. "I suggest you leave and never come back. In return I give you enough of the drug for Edgar. Take it, Lucas. It's the better option. This is the best for both of us."

"But it's not the best for the rest of the world."

"You and I aren't responsible for the rest of the world."

"We are if we're in a position to help."

"Which you are not."

A painful rush of cold air swept into the room. The water in Caesar's glass turned to ice. He swore in amazement. The intercom crackled. It was Mike.

"We have a problem," Mike said.

Caesar glared at Lucas with an expression that was as close to worry as Lucas had ever seen. "You're going nowhere." He left the room, locked the door, and took the frigid elevator up to the main floor. He shivered and rubbed his arms to keep from freezing.

When the door opened he saw a near-empty casino.

But that was the least of his worries.

Every slot machine, every table, every bar was covered in a film of ice. His lungs hurt as he breathed in the frigid air. Farther to the back it looked like a freak snowstorm had blown in. People packed the exits, hanging onto each other for balance. An elderly man with a tank of oxygen beside him pulled on a slot machine handle. It didn't move. He pulled harder without success. Shivering, he pushed every button. Still nothing. He swore and hit the machine. The lights flickered and then died altogether, as did the lights on all the slot machines. He cursed again, then left, dragging his cart, muttering to himself, taking careful steps on what had become a skating rink, and walked out with the last of the patrons.

"My God," Caesar said, looking out at his ice palace. He returned to the elevator and hit the H.

Mike walked in with him just as the doors closed. The elevator didn't move. Caesar pushed the button again. The door crept shut and the elevator jerked its way down. "Get the Council together," Caesar said. "Fly them in from wherever they are. We meet tonight."

When they reached the bottom the doors didn't open. He and Mike pried their fingers inside and pulled them apart.

And when they did, Caesar turned left.

"Where are you going?" Mike asked.

Caesar crossed his arms in front of his chest to keep warm as he stepped on snow to the end of the hall. Mike followed after him, concerned, then worried about what was happening. They reached a door with a glowing blue panel. Caesar placed his palm on a screen.

"Caesar Alexander. Empirico."

The door opened. Caesar entered.

The room was the size of a high school classroom. Black marble floor. Black tile ceiling. Tables and lab equipment in the middle. White walls lined with large stainless steel cabinets. Caesar opened the nearest one. It was filled with metallic silver cylinders about the size of a coffee travel mug. He pulled out two and closed the door.

"What's in these cabinets?" Mike asked.

But Caesar didn't respond.

"Caesar, what is all of this?"

He pushed Mike out of the way. The door closed behind them as they walked down the hallway to the other end. He unlocked the door with the two horses on either side and stormed back in. He sat down at the head of the table and glared at Lucas.

"Call your God off."

"Give me the drug."

"Call God off!"

"Give me the drug."

Caesar flung the first cylinder down the table as though it were a game of shuffleboard.

"For your friend. I hope there's still time."

"No more games. The other one as well."

Caesar hesitated a moment, then threw it down as well. He leaned forward. His eyes bulged out. "Take your drugs and leave. And don't ever come near me again. Because the next time I see your face, I promise you, I will kill you."

Lucas pushed his seat back. He saw Caesar's breath in the chilled air like a violent horse about to charge. He felt Caesar's eyes on him as he left the room.

And as he did those bulging eyes focused on Mike. All he could think about were Caesar's words from days ago about what would happen if he did not succeed in killing Lucas: *You'll go to prison.*

He felt that tall, built, bald warden standing beside him again, grinning and gloating about being right, that Mike did in fact come back.

"Do you have any idea what you've done?" Mike asked.

"Don't argue with me!"

"When the public finds out that we've been withholding a cure for brain cancer?" Mike cursed at him. "What happens then?!"

Tabitha and Jake ran into the empty casino. They took in a cold breath and felt the sting against their lungs. The entire gaming area looked like it had been sprayed with foam. Jake led them to an elevator bay and pushed the button. No response. Tabitha opened the stairwell door and was about to run up when she saw a waterfall of ice blocking her path. To her left, down below, she saw the stairs descending.

Lucas pushed the button for the elevator. The light went on, he heard the ding, but the doors only partially retracted. He pulled them apart but found no elevator. He looked up. It was waiting a number of floors above. He glanced down and saw the bottom about a storey beneath him.

Just as he turned around he felt a pain in his spine, a warning about what was waiting.

It was Mike. He smashed his fist into Lucas' face, catching him in the cheekbone and sending him flying back. Lucas grabbed the elevator door. He felt himself drifting perilously close to the point of not being able to make it back.

"Mike!" Lucas shouted. He lost his grip. The two of them waited those anxious moments for gravity to do its work. Isaac Newton was back.

Lucas reached out for Mike.

"Goodbye, Lucas."

He lost sight of Mike. Lucas' heels slipped off the ledge. He felt a rush of air pass by him. He saw the elevator getting farther away. He hit the concrete, head first, and crumpled on the ground.

45

Lucas looked over the edge. He felt the rumbling pulsate through the ground, shaking his body. There, beneath him, marched a massive army. They wore sleek steel helmets and silver body armour that reflected in the sun. Some carried swords. Others on the flanks carried bows and arrows. They passed him with such speed that Lucas had a difficult time concentrating on an individual member. They looked like a river, flowing in unison, until they were gone, out of sight.

Lucas stretched over the edge, hoping to see where they were going. The unstable rock gave way. He reached back too late and slid down the embankment, feeling a huge lump in his throat as he anticipated the impact.

Lucas crashed onto the rocky ground. He waited a moment, then stood up, unhurt, and looked out at the mile-wide path cut by the army. It seemed he was in a large dried-out riverbed. In the distance he saw what looked like a house. He walked towards it.

He heard a loud crack of thunder. He glanced behind him and saw that the sky was engulfed in black heavy clouds. Lightning flashed in erratic bursts. A bolt came down on the ledge where he had watched the army. It split the rock, causing it to fall down the side.

Lucas ran to the shelter. His feet ached against the blistering sand. Up ahead he saw an 1800s homestead. Wraparound porch. Grey sagging roof. No horses. No troughs. No water.

He opened the door. Inside he saw people drinking and laughing. Someone played the piano. A jig of sorts. A short bartender with a handlebar moustache poured beer from behind the counter. "What can I get you?"

"There's a terrible storm coming," Lucas said. The music stopped. The talking stopped. The beer stopped. People turned around.

"Storm?" the bartender asked.

"Huge clouds."

"Clouds?"

"Rain clouds. We have to leave. Right now. We're going to be wiped out."

The room exploded with laughter. A drunken woman spilled her drink. The piano started up again. The bartender poured more. "Wiped out? How?" he asked.

"The water!" he shouted back, trying hard to be heard over the laughter. "We're in a riverbed."

"There is no so-called rain here," the bartender said.

People cheered with their glasses.

Lucas saw a young boy off to his right. Red cap. Grey T-shirt. Running shoes. Sitting at a table. By himself. Staring out the window. He turned. They made eye contact. The boy walked towards Lucas. He was the one colour photograph amid a wash of black and white.

"Is that really going to happen?"

"We don't have time. Are you with me?"

The boy nodded. Lucas took him by the hand and led him out of the saloon. A rush of water streamed by them.

"Where do we go?"

Lucas stepped into the water and felt it flow around his ankles. Far off to his left he saw the impossible tower. The sheer rock face that stretched up into the sky that he had been trying to climb. To his right he saw water rushing towards them.

They ran downstream. Their feet splashed through the puddles. Behind them they heard people coming out of the saloon, laughing at them. Then the patrons marvelled at the lightning and the water.

Lucas and the boy ran faster. Within seconds the water was up to their calves, making it difficult to move. Some of the people stopped laughing. Seconds later it was up to their knees. The people clutched the railing as the water rose. Lucas grabbed the boy and put him on his shoulders.

"What do we do?" the drunken woman screamed. Suddenly, the water came with such force that it knocked Lucas over. He and the boy fell under the surface and clawed their way back to the top. Lucas grabbed him around the waist. The boy lost his cap and watched as it floated down the river.

People at the saloon shouted for help. The water level rose to the height of a ten-storey building. It covered them like a massive tidal wave. They flailed in the water, screaming at anyone who would listen. But the water rose still higher and pulled some of them under to their graves. A final wave engulfed the rest and drowned them, dragging their bodies to the bottom.

The water pushed Lucas and the boy to the rock face. The riverbed filled to overflowing. The water lifted them up to the top. Lucas grabbed onto the ledge and helped the boy up. Then he climbed out of the water.

A table. Two chairs. A glass of water on one side and strawberry ice cream on the other. It was an island the size of a picnic blanket. Water surrounded them as far as they could see. The clouds vanished. The sun shone down.

"Which one do you want?" Lucas asked.

"Ice cream," the boy replied.

The boy sat down. Beside him, another baseball cap. Red. He put it on and smiled as he ate a scoop of ice cream. Lucas took a sip from his glass. The water receded somewhat. To his right he saw a narrow causeway.

At the end, four horses

Tabitha and Jake saw Mike emerge from a door at the far end of the gaming area. He wiped the frozen sweat off his forehead, hit a button on his cellphone, and disappeared through another door.

When Lucas woke he heard a terrible moaning sound, like the sound ships make when they are about to break apart. The ground was cold; his body shivered. He looked up and saw the elevator hanging above him, coated in snow. He grabbed the elevator guide rail and climbed up.

The elevator began to descend. He reached the ledge and let go of the rail. He heard the elevator screeching towards him. He pulled with all his might and made it up to his waist. He clawed at the ground for more leverage and thought how sick it was going to feel when the elevator cut him in half. He pulled his waist up, leaving only his knees exposed. He anticipated his legs crunching, the disgusting sound of bones snapping.

He lifted himself out just as the elevator came to a stop. The door opened. Tabitha and Jake.

She came to his side, touching the back of his head where he had hit the ground. She helped him up. "Mike's gone."

"He's going to get Caesar. To prove that I'm dead."

They took the elevator back to A level and walked past the slots to the exit hallway. That's when they felt it. They stopped. There it was again. A tremor beneath them. Tabitha grabbed Lucas' arm. Jake grabbed a slot machine.

Another tremor. This one worse than the others. The ground shifted with such force that it knocked them to the ground.

To their far right, off in the distance, they saw Mike, Foster and Mitchell. Foster and Mitchell drew their guns.

Lucas got to his feet. The gaming area shuddered. An earthquake shook the casino. There was a terrible cracking sound. A crevice divided the floor in two. The sides fell down as a large section of the floor caved in. Slot machines and card tables fell into the abyss. The frozen structural steel in the balconies cracked, bringing sections of the vacated floors crashing down.

The first bullet zipped by Tabitha's head. She heard it smash into the slot machine beside her. The trio looked back and saw Mike, Mitchell, and Foster climbing over debris, headed in their direction.

"What do we do?" she screamed.

The ground shifted beneath them as though they were standing on Jell-O. Another bullet. This one grazed Lucas' cheek, creating a small cut, and crashed into a pillar beside him. Another section of the floor swung down, narrowly missing them.

Lucas looked out at the massive opening. It was like a bomb had exploded in front of them, forming a massive crater. He looked down at the sheer wall beneath him. Behind him and to his left he saw the chunks of fallen concrete and steel.

"Tabitha?" he said.

She looked at him with eyes that begged for a solution. "Lucas?"

"This is it. You wanted to know."

"Are we finished?"

He looked over the edge and gave the impression he was about to fall in.

"Lucas!" she shouted.

He turned back to her. "It's time to believe."

Then he stepped over the edge.

46

"Lucas!" Tabitha screamed.

But her fears were unwarranted. His step landed on what appeared to be an invisible floor—invisible to Tabitha, invisible to Jake, invisible to the approaching evils. She watched in amazement, her eyes confused, her mind perplexed, her spirit sensing something she'd never felt before. She saw him standing in the middle of the air.

"Who's coming with me?" Lucas asked.

Jake stepped past Tabitha and, without flinching, walked off the shaking ledge onto nothingness. The two men stood on air.

"This is what it takes, Tabitha," Lucas said. "You wanted to know what it was like. This is it."

"I can't do this!"

A bullet shot over her head. Lucas stretched out his hand to her. "You must believe."

Tabitha looked at the trio in the distance and then back at Lucas. She reached out and took his hand. There was something in his eyes that burned into her. Something real that she envied. Something different that she wanted. She gritted her teeth, held her breath, and felt the anxiety that comes when it's time to step from one world into another.

And then she let go of his hand.

"I can't do this, Lucas."

"Tabitha."

"Go."

"Tabitha."

"I've made my decision."

Lucas turned slowly, then left with Jake.

Mitchell fired at Lucas. The bullet grazed the bridge of Tabitha's nose, causing a burn mark when the force of air pushed against it. She turned to face him. Another bullet veered off course. It raced past her ear.

Tabitha looked down at the hole beneath her. She swallowed. *Now or never.*

Now or never.

Lucas stopped. He turned around.

Tabitha raised her foot and kept her eyes locked on Lucas. She stepped out, shifted her weight, and passed the point of being able to return to the ledge. She brought her foot down and landed on solid ground. A fierce shock ran through her. More bullets. She looked at her feet and saw a gold and red checkered floor made of a marble-like material. It stretched out across the entire casino like an incredible chessboard.

She took her other foot off the ledge and stepped on the new floor. Then she ran out to meet Lucas in the middle. He took her hand and the three of them ran to the other side. Lucas glanced back as Mitchell and Foster stopped on the edge. They took a step and found the solid invisible ground. They shot at them and gave chase. Mike was about to step off the ledge when he saw a massive section of concrete on the second floor break loose and swing down at Mitchell like a gigantic pendulum. Mike screamed at Mitchell. He tried to duck, but the warning came too late. Exposed rebar stuck out of the broken concrete like a series of lances. Two of them smashed through Mitchell's eyeballs and exploded out the back of his head. The force ripped his body in half. His legs and waist stood there a moment like an unfinished mannequin and then crumpled over. His torso flung off the rebar and hit Foster, knocking him to the ground.

Foster grabbed the bleeding half corpse and tried to push what was left of Mitchell off of him. He looked up and saw a chunk of concrete begin to crack. Just as he pushed Mitchell away the concrete broke loose. It crashed down on Foster's head with such force that it flattened it. His body fired out one last nervous twitch, as though doctors were trying a final attempt with the defibrillators. Then he lay there, blood running out of his severed neck into oblivion below.

Mike watched as Lucas, Tabitha, and Jake raced out of the casino.

"Meet us at the Fortunate Son," Lucas said to Tabitha.

"Where are you going?"

"To Edgar."

"I'm coming with you!"

"No." He saw that passionate look in her eyes, and in that split second he felt a surge of confidence. "Please, Tabitha. Take your car. I'll pick you up. Don't answer your cellphone. Just leave. You have to get out of this city."

Lucas got in the car with Jake and drove off to the hospital.

September stood at a pay phone on the Strip down the road from the Garden. "I'm right here in Vegas. I can come for an interview," she said, fiddling with the snake bracelet on her arm. "How does right now sound?" She squinted her eyes as if hoping to hear good news. She took her bracelet off and turned it over in her hand in a nervous gesture. "I'll be right there." She was about to hang up when she remembered. "About how much does it cost?" She took off her bracelet and without realizing placed it beside the phone. "$20,000 a year? So $80,000 for the 4-year nursing program?"

She hung up the phone and walked back to the car, expecting to find Matthias there. She didn't. All she found when she opened the door and sat down in the driver's seat was a note from him wishing her all the best.

And the bag with $153,000 cash in the seat behind her.

Nearby, a man stood up from a bench and, seeing that September was off the phone, went to make his call. He noticed her silver bracelet.

September put the car in drive and headed off to the university.

"Hey lady!" the man shouted after her. "You forgot your bracelet!"

But September did not hear him.

Matthias walked into McCarran and headed to a ticket counter. He passed by people, oblivious to their presence, a dazed and distressed expression on his pale face as though he were some Manchurian candidate sent on a mission. The airport was crowded, yet all he saw was the available flight agent. The place was loud with people talking and steady intercom announcements. All he heard was his heart beating louder and louder until he stood in front of her.

"May I help you?" she asked.

He hesitated. This was it. This was finally it. She waited for his response and, not getting one, repeated the question thinking him to be either strung out on drugs and alcohol or suffering the delusional shock gamblers feel when they've lost a fortune. Matthias drew in a breath and forced himself to get out the words. "I need a ticket to London."

And the moment he said that, a terrible dread came over him.

When Lucas and Jake opened the door to the hospital room, they discovered an empty bed. A surge of adrenaline rushed through them. Lucas confirmed the number on the door. They had the right room. Much to their dismay.

A nurse came down the hallway. Lucas watched her eyes for any hint of direction as to whether his fears would be confirmed or denied.

"You're looking for Edgar?" she said, in a tone much too quiet to be reassuring.

Lucas nodded.

"He's not here," she said as she fumbled for words. She looked awful. Her skin was so pale it was green. She kept her mouth open, as if unable to breathe through her nose. She clutched a chart with both arms, much too tight to be considered normal, and seemed to be bent over as if she were about to get sick.

"Where is he? What happened to him?"

She took in a breath and shook her head, trying to find what little grip she could on life. "You're Lucas Stephens, right? The healer?"

Has-been healer. Lucas nodded again.

"He's been taken to Los Angeles. When you see him there, someone might be able to explain what happened to him. Because nobody here can."

"Is he better?"

She looked to her right down the hall, hoping nobody was seeing her talking with them. "He had cancer. You know that." She paused as if to decide whether saying this would result in being fired. "We saw him getting progressively worse. That was expected. But then we saw him go to a state none of us have seen before." She covered her mouth, realizing she had spoken words the hospital director had told none of them to relay. But she had gone this far, and the burden on her was too much to bear. "They did tests," she whispered. She pinched her lips together in a vain attempt to keep from spilling the truth. Her eyes began to moisten. Her hands began to tremble.

"What happened to him?" Lucas asked. Demanded.

She drew in a breath through her teeth and held it in, determined not to let it out.

"What happened to him?"

She blinked and released a stream of tears. She spoke so softly they had to strain to hear her. "The tests," she whispered. "They showed that he not only has cancer, but that he's contracted HIV, Huntington's, MS, a blood disorder. The list goes on. We couldn't do anything for him. He…He doesn't…He doesn't even look human." She backed away, shaking her head, pushing her hand out towards them, begging them not to ask her any more questions.

Caesar looked at the destruction. All five levels of the gaming area lay crushed in a concrete aftermath. The chill in the air was gone. The building was empty. Save for the Council waiting in the back room for Caesar's instructions.

He walked away from the ledge, forcing himself to hang onto some form of control, hoping to pass off the horror of the moment for the sake of getting through the event. But inside he felt the gripping certainty that it was only a matter of time before he would lose the struggle of pretending that reality did not affect him.

Emergency personnel entered the building. The invisible floor was gone. Pieces of Mitchell and Foster lay in the carnage.

Caesar walked down a hallway and then down a long corridor to the room. He opened the door. The 40 members of the Council said nothing. Not even Mike.

He stood at the front in silence. The men and women before him sat motionless, unable to understand what had just happened, unwilling to consider whether it was warranted. Caesar looked up and searched through the rows, making eye contact with each one of them. They felt his ominous stare pierce them as he looked past their veils of confidence, seeing the true nature of what was driving them.

"Whoever kills Lucas Stephens becomes the new CEO of Empirico."

He waited for their reaction. Waited for the first indication of a flare in their spirits and a courageous resolve to carry out his offer. His order. They felt that familiar and awful feeling of the burden of murder upon them. Many had the conviction in their eyes that indicated they would do it. But a select few had the burning desire to take off right now after Lucas to repay him for what he had done.

And none so much as Mike.

Lucas and Jake raced down the I-15, zigzagging around cars until they found a clear stretch of highway. He phoned Tabitha to relay the news about Edgar. Then he turned to Jake.

"They'll be coming after us," he said.

"You have a plan?"

"It's not finalized yet."

"How close are you to getting it finalized?"

"A few more odds and ends to work out."

Jake nodded. "That close?"

Lucas took Exit 12. He drove past the gas station and turned in to the Fortunate Son Café.

"Jake," Lucas said as they hit the gravel and slowed down. "I have no guarantees. I don't have a clue what's coming. I've put an impossible responsibility on you." They came to a stop. Lucas looked at Jake. "What I'm saying is that I don't expect you to go any farther with me."

"Then you should learn to expect more," Jake said, watching as Tabitha came to the car. "Especially considering that you and I may have to train a whole new teammate in how this world of ours works."

Tabitha opened the door, out of breath and out of patience. She slammed it shut and did what she could to calm herself down. Lucas drove back onto the I-15 and headed for L.A.

"Was that floor real?" Tabitha asked in-between breaths of air.

"Define real," Lucas said.

"I don't know!" she shouted, rubbing her forehead and trying to make sense of what had just happened. "Not anymore."

"Do you want to know what reality is?"

"That depends."

"On?"

"On what's going to happen next," she said.

Lucas checked his rear-view mirror. He punched the accelerator. That curious rush of confusion and adventure filled the car.

"I think we're about to find out."